DOT. EXE

JANEEN LEESE-TAYLOR

*Dedicated to all the writers and artists
Who chased the fox out of the henhouse
You know who you are*

<u>Content Warnings</u>
*15+
Tobacco Use
Strong Language
Mentions of conversion therapy
Mentions of religious trauma
Mentions of domestic violence
Implied non/con
Amputation/dismemberment of an Android*

Homophobia and infrequent use of slurs
Depictions of grief and PTSD
Mild sexual content

PROLOG(UE)
Gateway

CROSSROADS BIOS v.122.3.1
BIOS Date: 12/04/2079 04:43:29 Ver 2.1.1
Copyright © 2056–2080, Crossroads IE, Inc.
ACM 899772 Runner Droid: 01113 Revision: Beta
BIOS Extension: v.2.1.1 Applied
Memory Test: 125,371,044Kbs OK

Initialising… Done
C:\...

The text scrolled up before Runner Droid 01113's eyes, as red as a Christmas ribbon, and illuminated from within by his own internal systems. Line after line appeared across its HUD in a pattern of numbers and letters, the digits moving at a slow, methodical pace as its systems booted for the first time that day.

It blinked as its processes came to life, systems whirring softly as it began all of its usual boot-up protocols. Fingers twitched at its side as energy flooded from one part of its artificial body to the other and before it the door to its containment block began to slowly rise. Each section of the corrugated steel folded in on itself like an intricate origami design, creating dull music from the resounding *clanks*. Warm, electrical light began to pour in through the gaps the mechanism was creating, lighting up the Runner Droid's small world.

There was a part of 01113, a small and secretive part that it couldn't quite yet understand, that longed to know what the real sun must have felt like up there on the surface of the world, what it would be like to experience it first hand on its outer shell. Smiling to itself, it tilted its arm first to one side and then to the other, watching the dust catching in the filtered light, dancing and twirling as it fell.

The warm glow cascaded over its Chrome chassis, the skin-like shell designed to make it appear Human, and 01113 imagined its false exterior reacting just as a living person's might – the tingle of heat, the hair rising, and freckles spreading over each pale inch like stars appearing in the sky at dusk.

A new objective appeared in the bottom-left corner of the Android's sight line, and it stepped out of its container obediently, grabbing its pack from the usual spot at its feet. It made its way through the warehouse, each barefooted step quiet and precise, calculated by a hundred automatic processes buzzing through its head. Rows and rows of white containers lined each side of the dimly lit warehouse, their inhabitants in a state of half-wakened suspension. Tubes linked each of their bodies to a series of metal fastenings, a dark liquid pumping in and out of each of the floating figures in turn. The smell of their coolant was pungent, and the ground glistened with artificial rainbows as 01113 walked through the wide, concrete space. The Android listened to the familiar song of machinery as it passed by the repair line, glancing upwards as the large, white cranes hoisted its brothers and sisters into the air, ripping apart their components as if they were nothing more than children's toys.

Alert('error')

An error message flashed up on the corner of the Android 01113's HUD and it quickly dismissed it, pushing down the unsettling sensation that accompanied it. Whatever this particular feeling was, it was not one that 01113 was meant to experience.
The dark-haired Runner Droid directed its vision towards the floor and kept following the path it had been set on, focusing on the cold touch of the cement of its bare feet. The sensation was intriguing, sharp and vivid as it coiled within its processors, as if it were experiencing it all in the highest definition. 01113 much preferred this feeling to the one before. *Cold* was a measured scale, a constant, knowable variable, but *fear* was harsher, more complex.
The Android halted when it came to a square container lined inside with clothes. Each of the gold and blue uniforms inside were hanging in neat, ordered rows, organized by a mechanical hand. 01113 raised its hand to the screen next to the opening and it flashed blue for a moment as the machine inside compiled the required data. A slot in the container door sprang open and 01113 reached inside to grab the uniform it had been assigned with both hands. It dressed without effort, pulling the singular piece of fabric across its tall, slender frame. As it pulled the zip from the centre of its body to its throat, the metal collar on its neck began to glow, the word 'ANDROID' appearing in solid, blue letters. The illuminated digits perfectly matched the shade of its unnatural eyes.
The Runner Droid tilted its head and frowned at its reflection in the steel container before turning towards the wide tunnel that was slowly opening to its left. It could already feel the cold air from the darkness within rippling at its uniform, like the tiny hands of a dozen children beckoning the Android inside.
It stepped in through the entranceway, glowing eyes peering through the endless shade and down into the runes of Old Dublin City. 01113 pulled its pack tighter onto its shoulders, securing the distribution of weight evenly.
This was the part that it liked the most.
01113 offered the lost world a smile it shouldn't have been capable of.
Cf
And then the Runner Droid started to run.

CHAPTER 1
End User

The video games and movies of the early 2000s painted the picture of a future that was bright and garishly neon, with tall glowing buildings and advertisements beckoning from every street corner. The stories spoke of corporate greed and the fall of mankind, all pencilled over with abrasive shades of yellow and magenta that were impossible to ignore.

But in reality, the world's pallet had not changed much in the decades that followed the end of the world.

The concrete was still black and hot as Hell, sticky underfoot from the latest out-of-season heatwave. Although the majority of vehicles had since been made electric, the air remained hazy from the smog of cheap businesses and even cheaper morals. Ireland's beautiful greenery had long since succumbed to the pressures of a changing environment, and in its place grime and rotten slick clung to both the buildings and their inhabitants in equal measure. It was a dog-eat-dog world and any dog that barked or growled in New Dublin was quickly put to sleep.

Augustus Jackson stood in the very centre of it all, head raised as he breathed in the warm, autumnal breeze that caressed the long, red tresses of his hair. It was rare that he had a moment to himself like this. Lately it had felt as if the 41-year-old had been suspended in time, his life consisting of little more than walks to and from the office, and late-night dinners collapsed in front of crappy reality TV. He had had more than one mid-life crisis since hitting the big milestone just the year before.

August brought his phone up to scroll through the feeds as he meandered slowly towards the direction of his office. Unlike most of the people that were ten years younger than him, he didn't go in for all those Chrome implants. A part of him, the no doubt outdated part, still preferred the old-fashioned touch of a physical device. Plus, he despised the annoying buzz of notifications in his ear on a constant loop throughout the day. The pop-ups on his visor alone already drove him to distraction.

He flitted through the news stories on the small screen with lazy swipes of his thumb as he walked, not really taking much interest in the heavily edited faces or the general goings-on in the world. The false saccharine sweetness of the news flow was almost enough to make him tune-out altogether. Not much was said there that he actually believed anymore. Not since the main stations had been bought out. Horrific stories about political rivals were the norm, but rarely turned out to be anything substantiated.

August glanced up occasionally, trying to keep a vague awareness about himself as he crossed the busy roads. The bright lights overhead changed from red to green, signalling that he could walk, and he could hear the familiar song coming from the overhead speakers as he stepped up onto the curb at the other side.

Penny Lane is in my ears and in my eyes…

Looming above him and blocking out much of the remaining sunlight, the Crossroads building was a titan of white marble, deep red accents drawing his eyes across the sign and up towards the spire at the top. The windows that faced the north side glistened in the sunlight and, if he squinted, he thought that he might be able to make out some movement on the floors above his own. He wasn't able to see the very top floor from ground level, the point of the tower peeking out through the city's bubble and into the space beyond.

The glass dome that covered New Dublin was faintly translucent, lined with a billion tiny screens whose pixels hid the devastation beyond from the view of the residents. In the years following the Climate Emergency sanctions in 2031, global warming had only increased in its overwhelming furiosity. The time to save the world had long since passed, so the United Governments had come together to do the only thing they could, erecting huge shelters over the remaining cities, and sheltering the last remnants of Humanity inside.

There were still some scientific minds out there that believed another planet would be their salvation, though August sincerely doubted it. As far as he could see, it was just another flag-waving, dick-measuring contest, but this time *in space*. Looking up at the hulking sphere of glass and metal on his usual morning commute, he sometimes felt like an ant under a child's enormous spyglass. He wondered what, if anything at all, could be peering down on them from way up there.

A large clock, suspended on the side of the dome, counting at a leisurely pace, and reading a time of 08:42am in bold, crimson digits. Underneath was listed the conditions that had been planned for the day. At least six more hours of mild, sunny weather with rain scheduled for the mid-afternoon to push away some of the heat. *Nice to not get completely bloody soaked for a change*, August huffed to himself. He raised his right hand to the tall front doors with a yawn as he approached, the scanner in the camera making quick work of reading the biometric ID chip through the soft skin of his palm. The doors made a soft buzzing sound before they pulled apart and August pocketed his phone as he entered.

Bill Franklyn was stationed at the front desk as usual, his feet perched up on the countertop in front of him as he reviewed the Morning Herald. He eyed the red-head sleepily as he walked past, lifting a wordless hand in greeting as August called out, "Mornin' Bill!"

Bill grumbled as he turned over to the next page of the newspaper. Ever the conversationalist. August smiled to himself, exhaling an amused puff of air. At least he wasn't the only non-morning person in the building. He'd have to drop him down a coffee later, see if he could rouse a few more words out of the man.

He took the stairs up one at a time, immediately feeling his heart rate beginning to climb. *I really have to start running again*, he mused, gripping the handrail for support as he covered up his heavy breathing with the sound of a cough. It was embarrassing to note the sweat that had already formed on his palm from only half a flight. He knew the younger version of himself was scowling somewhere right now.

The doors to the next level slid open for him with a pneumatic *ffsh*, and he stepped out into the wide, white floorspace, immediately veering right in the direction of the breakroom. He reached into his shoulder bag, as if on autopilot, and pulled out the package inside. Yanking open the fridge and scowling when the old mechanism didn't immediately give in to him, he added his lunch to the growing pile assembled there. He noted Susan's ever-present dry salad and wrinkled his nose in distaste, as if the very appearance of it offended him.

If she turns out to be serial killer one day, I don't think anyone would be surprised, he thought.

He jumped, swearing to himself as a familiar face appeared behind the now closed door. Jared Matthews was stocky, dark-eyed, and foul-mouthed in a way that would make even the hardiest of sailors blush at times. He grinned, leaning one thick bicep against the makeshift counter as he ran a hand over his shaved head,

"Mornin' Augustus," he greeted, his tone teasing, "Lose your hairbrush again today, did ya big lad? You look like a fuckin' yeti."

"Ah, fuck off, ya prick," replied August with a toothy grin, running a hand through his thick mane of greying ginger hair, "You're lucky I show up at all, givin' the state'a this place."

Jared let out a barking laugh, patting the marble counter beside him in amusement, "Ya wound me, Gus!" he rebuked playfully, his other hand moving to clutch at his chest, "After all I've done for ya!"

"What? Like paying me a decent livin' wage, ya mean?" August countered, quirking a single dark eyebrow as the ancient coffee machine behind his companion gave out one last hiss of steam.

Reaching into the billowing cloud, Jared pulled out his topped-up mug, a chipped thing with a picture of a cat on it and something about *Mondays*, and turned to head out of the breakroom again, "Don't push your luck, Jackson," he called back over one shoulder, "You know I only keep you around 'cause you're pretty."

"Yeah, pretty much the only person who can put up with your crap, you mean," August droned, turning his own attention to the coffee machine. It was made with cheap, recycled plastic, an antique from the early 2030s, and filled the room with steam each time one of the valves at the back opened. A floor full of tech support, and not even one person knew how to fix the damn thing. August doubted that they would ever replace it either, likely half the people on the floor felt a kind of kinship with the thing, watching an old machine chugging on way past its prime. It spoke volumes about the kinds of people he worked with on a daily basis.

Extending a hand out towards it, he flipped the top open, pulling out the used tray and unceremoniously dumping the remnants of Jared's brew into the bin. He was careful not to nip his fingers as he slipped a new pod into its place and closed up the lid again. It beeped at him twice as it set to work, and August let out a low grumble, not unlike a sigh, as he settled back against the counter and checked his watch. 08:57am. He was cutting it a little fine with the office chit-chat, but he didn't much care. As much as Jared liked to talk a big game, his boss was never going to find anyone that could do what he did. Machine Learning Technicians weren't exactly hanging about on every street corner looking for work these days. He could thank 10 years of academics for that lucky little skill set.

He glared at the black plastic casing as it rotated the disk inside to show its progress. It was slowly ticking past 9am but he knew there was no way he was going to get anything done without a buttload of caffeine in his system. Gone were his rock-star days when he could survive on 30 minutes of sleep and a wet dream. Now he ached and yawned his way through a full 10 hours and needed at least 4 coffees to get him through his initial meetings.

When did I get so bloody old? he thought, watching steam bursting from the top of the machine like a volcano preparing to erupt. He took a small step back out of habit before he decided to reach for the seal, springing it open and dumping the used pod before he grabbed for his own coffee mug. Though half of the image had been worn away from overuse, and a too-high temperature in the dishwasher, the words *'this is my thinking face'* were still just about visible on the curve of the ceramic. He turned to leave the room, following the colourful shapes on the carpeted floor as they guided him towards his usual desk in the far corner. All the desks on this particular floor were made from identical sheets of solid, white plastic and glass. Designed to be seamless and elegant, August could hardly even make out the details on the keys without his glasses. Their leather-backed chairs bore the company's logo surrounded by black and yellow honeycomb-like patterns, and at least one had been placed at each workstation. Although August liked to complain about a lot of things, he had developed a strange fondness for his own chair, the soft cushion divoting in just the right way to support his shape.

The screens that extended outwards from the tables were paper-thin, light shining through the translucent glass surface. Privacy protectors built into the frame stopped the text from being visible from the rest of the office, or so he had been told. It wasn't a theory he had ever had to test before.

August waved a hand in front of his own screen as he took a seat, the system booting up and greeting him based on his registered ID; Augustus Jackson, Technical Team, EU, 3rd Floor, New Dublin branch.

The sprawling tabletop lit up before him, exposing the letters and numbers that formed the in-built keyboard. Sometimes, August missed the simplicity of paper and pen, but it was hard to argue with the clean look of a desk like this one. He touched the screen with the very tips of his fingers, opening the files that he had been analysing the day prior, and set to continuing the task.

He leaned on one hand, absent-mindedly bringing his own mug to his lips and taking a sip. He gasped as he slammed it back down again, swallowing the too-hot liquid with a rush of tears in his eyes. With more than a few swears and sharp breaths, he reached for the drawer and ripped out a bottle of water, downing several mouthfuls as another figure took their place in the seat next to his.

Geoff was in his late 30s, skinny as a pencil, with a puff of dark brown hair that formed a perfect orb around his head. Geoff was a brilliant mind, raised around machines and able to speak their language with a fluency any linguaphile would have been envious of. He had heard that both his mother and his father worked on the upper floors, though August never saw them talk at work. He had showed a high aptitude for engineering and brought with him an energetic passion that could be infectious if pointed in the right direction.

August knew for a fact that he had a good head on his shoulders, in the rare cases that he felt like using it.

The man flopped down into his chair with an exaggerated sigh, spinning it towards him with a smile that was way too illuminous for pre-10am chatter, "What's up, Gus?" he asked cheerfully, kicking out with both feet like an excited primary school kid, "Please, please, *please* tell me you got assigned to Project Hare this week too? I'm only 15 minutes into my shift and I'm already losing my damn mind with these figures."

August snorted, daring to take another sip of his coffee, "And I'm betting you haven't even seen what Ericka sent over yet, have you?"

Geoff's dark skin seemed to pale before August's very eyes, "No," he responded, already looking horrified, "Do I dare ask what?"

August nodded his head towards the far wall of the office where glass dividers separated them from the managerial team, "They rushed through the order and tried to double the output," he said, "Fuses were *blown*."

Geoff groaned loudly, burying his face down between his legs as if to hide his misery. August noticed more than a few other heads in the office turning to look into their direction.

"But it was *working*, Gus!" he whined, shaking his head and fingering his tight curls in frustration, "Why can't people just leave it be when it's *working*?"

August swallowed another warm gulp of his drink, leaning back in his chair, "Apparently the higher-ups wanted it to go faster."

The other man gave him an incredulous look, "It's a *Runner Droid*, August. It already goes over 50 kilometres per hour! If they want it to go faster, they should've given it bloody *wheels*!"

August chuckled low in his throat, shrugging as he replied, "You know how the marketing guys think; bigger, better, *faster*. The new adjustments caused a total system shutdown. The report says one of the Android Units is still completely offline, poor sod."

Geoff frowned thoughtfully, resting his head in his arms on the desk next to his, "You ever see one in person? A Runner Droid, I mean?"

"Not sure I would know the model if I saw one," August answered, swiping at something on his screen and adding a few more numbers to the column there, "We never had Androids around when I was growing up. There's one that works on the reception desk upstairs though. Seems like a nice girl."

The dark-skinned man shot him a weird look, "*Girl*?" he repeated questioningly, "It's not a *girl*, Gus. Not really."

August continued typing, adding further information to the program before him. It was monotonous work, the kind that made the clock run in the wrong direction, and without his coffee he was certain he would have lost concentration already.

"She looked like one to me," he said.

Geoff sat back in his seat and waved a hand to control the info on his own screen, "That's the point, Gus. They're *meant* to look like people," he noted, "Supposed to make us less *uneasy*, I guess. My parents had a Social Droid for a while when I was growing up. Bella, I think they called it. It mostly helped Dad in the study and picked us up from school sometimes if they were both running late."

August peered across at his work mate curiously, "And after all that time…you still thought of her as a machine?"

Geoff scrolled up and clicked to open a new tab without glancing over, "I never really thought about Bella as a '*her*', more of an '*it*'," he said thoughtfully, "Hard not to when we work with their code all day."

"I suppose that makes sense," August replied, draining the final dregs from his mug and placing it down again.

The next few hours passed like any other day. Reams and reams of code trailed past his eyes, white and black and white and black, in an endless array of stationary progress. Meetings cropped up every hour or so and August tuned out, as he always did, whenever Ericka began ranting about company targets and personal failings.

After his fourth coffee, August rose from his chair with a groan, stumbling tiredly towards the break room and its blinking florescent lights. He squinted towards his phone screen in search of the time, greeting a few familiar faces as he tried to locate his lunch in the fridge again. Two of the women from accounting smiled as they passed him by and he slid into their vacated seats at a round, white table with his food.

His phone vibrated where it still rested in his palm and a familiar envelope symbol appeared to move across the screen. He tapped it absent-mindedly and his work emails sprang open as he pulled off the Tupperware lid and revealed the meagre contents of his sad excuse for a lunch. As he shovelled the first forkful of cold noodles and chicken into his mouth, he noted the new message waiting for him at the very top of the inbox. A red exclamation mark set it apart from all of the other messages waiting for his attention. He didn't recognise the sender, the name a series of numbers rather than an email address. He raised his head to look about the kitchen space before selecting to open it, praying he wasn't about to give his old Samsung model phone the electronic equivalent STD.

Shuffling forward in the chair, August pulled the glass of his visor down over one eye, resting the small frame again his nose like one might wear a modern day monocle. The image before him became magnified as if the contents of the phone were being held closer to his face.

The body of the email itself was made up of a series or 0s and 1s with the letters S and O repeating throughout. He scanned over it again and then clicked on the sender's name, bringing up the contact information. It was marked with the 'internal memo' tab he had come to recognise, but it wasn't in any format that he had come across before. His thumb hovered over the bin icon in the top corner for a moment but something in his chest made him hesitate.

Something doesn't feel right about this, he thought.

Curiousity piqued, he scrolled on down to the bottom of the email, noting the little icon of the paper clip was turned on its side.

There's an attachment here.

With another click, the download started on a second tab. The document was headed with the label *'My Soul'* and was followed up by pieces of code and seemingly randomized numbers.

No, he thought, *not randomized. This is code from a Runner Droid.*

His heart began to pound in his chest as he abruptly stood, pushing his boxed leftovers to one side and hurrying back towards his desk. Brushing the empty mugs he found there aside, he selected to open up a new document, typing in the code before his backside even had a chance to meet his seat. He allowed his fingers to dance across the various keys, following the path generated by the information in the attachment like a campfire about to set a national park ablaze.

Geoff glanced over at him with a curious smile, "Wow, what's got you all fired up?" he teased.

August frowned, tracing the lines of numbers and letters into the system before him, "You ever hear your parents chatting about a program called *Soul*?" he asked.

Geoff's smile fell by a few molars, "What are you reading there, August?" he questioned warily.

August couldn't tear his dark eyes from the screen before him, "It came through in an attachment," he explained, "It's from an internal email. Somewhere upstairs, I think."

"Wait, did you say *upstairs*?" Geoff repeated, "August, my dude, you need to report that. Like…right now." He shook his head, uncrossing his legs and then crossing them again anxiously, "We're not supposed to have access to that stuff."

"Something isn't right here," August muttered quietly, studying the moving patterns in the text as he ran a hand through his long, bright-coloured hair, "It's listing components, parts of a Runner Droid I've never even heard of before."

Geoff reared back, as if the information had physically burned him, "Maybe because we aren't *meant* to hear it, August!" he cried out, reaching up to cover both of his ears, "You need to call Ericka. Something's gone wrong. You shouldn't be able to-"

He froze, staring open-mouthed as August's screen began to fill with text. Bright-coloured words repeated over and over again before their eyes with a kind of urgency. August yanking his hands away as a video popped up on the screen, expanding to fill every pixel. A man was talking to the camera, eyes glowing with a soft, blue light. His voice was muted, the file type showing it was video only.

"Is that…an *Android*?" the younger techie asked, coming to stand at August's shoulder and bending forward to see within the privacy frame.

"Yeah," August breathed, "And it looks fuckin' terrified."

Chapter 2
Violation Detected

'It... it's doing the Turing Test,' August said softly, recognising the images from the testing room plastered along the wall behind the Android. He had seen the room only once before, when he had first been hired as one of their technicians nearly 8 years prior. It was hard to forget those fluorescent tube lights and the too-bright white tiles lining the walls.

The Turing Test was the final phase for each and every Android unit that passed through their doors, a series of complex problems that were meant to determine whether the being was considered '*sentient'* or not. It was considered standard procedure for any company dealing in Artificial Intelligence.

The Android on the screen looked towards them and raised a hand to shield its eyes from the glare, its pupils tracking someone moving behind the camera. The collar around its neck glowed blue where its arm cast a shadow over it, the same shade as its eyes. The word 'ANDROID' was stretched across it in block letters. The Android itself had tanned-coloured skin and hair in a light shade of brown that cascaded down over the side of its face, framing its high cheekbone there. It had a mole just under its left eye and another down near its small lips. It was distinctly male in appearance and if it hadn't had been wearing such an obvious identifier around its neck, August never would have thought that the man was actually a machine.

The Android recoiled from something unseen, his eyebrows jumping upwards as he jerked backwards in his chair. Though August couldn't see the man's hands in the recording, it was clear by the rocking of the chair that he had been restrained somehow. The stranger's neck tensed as he battled against his holdings, his eyes narrowing into slits as he shouted towards the camera and likely the man behind it as well. There was a look of desperation on his face, his skin paling in a very human way as he frantically began to shake his head.

Another figure stepped out into the frame and August and Geoff watched as he placed something over the Android's head, pressing down the fittings on either side to seal it tight.

"August…what is this?" Geoff questioned aloud, his voice quivering slightly, "What are they doing to it?"

August could feel his hands beginning to shake where he was gripping the table, "Jesus Christ," he muttered.

Vibrant blue eyes looked once more towards the screen, the edges of the man's iris's igniting from within as if he were trying to convey a wordless message to his audience. August felt his throat tighten as he held their stare, watching as his lips began to move, forming slow, precise words that felt directed only at him.

Please, he begged, *save us.*

August jerked back in alarm as light burst from out of the Android's mouth, his body spasming as electricity rushed down from the instrument on his head. Black liquid erupted from his lips, dribbling down his chin as he fell suddenly still, his head slumping forward and to one side. His Chrome corpse was steaming in the chair, sparks flickering from the dark holes where only moments ago his eyes had been. August's stomach churned violently, and he cupped his mouth with both hands, trying to keep himself from vomiting. Saliva filled his mouth, the taste of copper on his tongue from where he had bitten his own cheek to keep from shouting.

To his right, Geoff had flopped back into his own chair, his eyes wide as his lips moved wordlessly around his frantic thoughts. He tilted his head to regard him, swallowing past the lump that had formed in his throat, "Gus…that was…"

"It passed the test," August finished for him, reaching the same conclusion, "So they destroyed it."

He felt something in his chest tightening slowly, like a hand wrapped firmly around his lungs. It was like he couldn't quite take a full breath.

He clambered to his feet, the sound of scattering papers enough to rouse his colleague from his stupor. Right now, Geoff looked exactly how he felt; like a deer caught in the headlights of some oncoming car.

"What are you doing?" he asked, watching his friend's movements with a frown.

"I...I don't know," August answered honestly, holding onto the too-white desk as he surveyed the room, "But I need to do *something*."

Geoff followed him to his feet, quickly taking a hold of the other man's sleeve, "We have to tell Ericka," he implored him, "We have to-"

He froze, turning to stare open-mouthed at something over August's shoulder. The red-haired man slowly turned to follow his line of sight, feeling the hairs on the back of his neck prick up. A stranger had just walked through the door at the end of the room and was looking over each of their heads curiously. He was dressed in a pristine blue suit, one that would not have looked out of place on Wall Street or the back rooms of a brothel, and his hair was gelled back so tightly against his head it appeared as if it had been drawn on with a Sharpie. Falling in on either side of him were the forms of two, tall Androids, who walked in perfect tandem one pace behind him. The man raised his head to peer over the rim of his amber-coloured glasses, "Where is Augustus Jackson?"

His voice was monotone, colourless, and he glared down at the man seated directly in front of him with piercing dark eyes. When he bent forward to slam a hand into the poor technician's desk, the worker visibly recoiled.

"S-sir?" he squeaked.

"Do not make me repeat myself," the suit-wearing man rasped.

"Who is that?" August hissed across to Geoff, making sure to keep his voice down low. He could already feel his hands growing wet with perspiration.

"Big leagues," Geoff answered nervously, "He's from one of the top floors. He must have seen the video, August. There's no other reason for him to come down here like this. He shouldn't even know our names."

August growled low in his throat, clenching his teeth as he turned to face the other side of the room. There was an emergency fire escape there that led straight down to the old city. If only he could...

He sucked on his teeth thoughtfully, a plan forming in the back of his mind, "I'm gonna need you to cover for me here, kiddo."

His companion's eyes darted towards the emergency exit and then back again, "Are you insane?"

"Just show him some figures of something, I dunno," August grumbled, "All I need is enough time to get that door open."

He took a deep breath in and held it, moving himself in that direction and keeping his pace as even as he could so as not to draw attention to himself. He felt the moment the stranger's eyes fell on him, the searing burn of them on the back of his head as he brought his hand down to rest of the door's metal release.
"Mr Jackson," a deep voice called out to him as its owner raised a hand into the air, "May we have a word? It won't take long."
"Sorry," August called back without turning, his grip on the lever tightening fractionally, "Just on lunch right now. Maybe catch you in an hour?"
The clattering of chairs behind him made adrenaline rush into his legs and he turned to meet the glowing blue eyes of the two Android's the man had brought down with him. It was like seeing a pair of tigers emerging from the undergrowth.
"I'm afraid this cannot wait, Mr. Jackson," the manager continued, his voice a deep purr in the back of his throat. He narrowed his eyes, glancing towards the point where August's hand was still resting on the door, "Please accompany us upstairs."
Upstairs.
Upstairs was never good.
August's mouth was bone dry, his tongue like sandpaper as he traced it over the line of his bottom lip. He steeled himself as he turned his head back to face the door again.
Well, shit.
The door opened before him and he took off at a sprint, the sounds of the office echoing around him as his name bounced back from every wall. His joints rebelled loudly as he bounded downwards, using his grip on the black plastic-coated banister to swing himself around each approaching corner. Already his heart felt like a rabbit in a cage, throbbing wildly against the wall of his breastbone. He knew his stamina wouldn't last long but he had to put as much distance between himself and those machines as he could.
He had been there the day they had first released their advertising for the black and yellow security droids. *Hornets*, they called them. They served as everything from bodyguard to trained assassin, their speeds almost matching those of a Runner Droid. Their built-in weaponry made them by far one of the most dangerous machines the company had access to.
Though he had never seen them in action before, it didn't take a lot of imagination to understand what something like that must have been capable of.

With a roar, he shoved past a group of other office workers who were making their way up from the floor below, scattering their group like pins between the levels. He could hear their confused shouts following after him as the Hornets gave chase, using their voices to gauge the time he had left.

He scanned the walls quickly, barely having the time to take in the letters and numbers he found there and followed the directions for BASEMENT 1 written in solid blue. He had never been this far down before. The air was colder here, moisture clinging to the white-painted walls in tiny droplets. Down on the lower floors were the testing areas, and even further down were the access points to the old city ruins.

New Dublin had been built on what was left of the original city. Rising water levels had caused the banks of the Liffey to break, and the outer perimeters of the city were decimated within days. The southeastern coastline had become almost completely submerged, with areas of Waterford and Wexford being violently reclaimed by the Celtic Sea.

It was a well-established fact that Crossroads used their solitary access to the ruins for the use of their own Runner Droids, allowing them to travel the looping underground circuits with ease in the veritable dark. Even the idea of being down below the earth, surrounded by the graves of a past long buried, filled August with terror.

He skidded to a breathless stop at the final door, pressing the button to summon the elevator to his position. The ominous metal shutters groaned as they parted for him, and he held up his palm as the doors folded behind him again. In the tight space, his gasps sounded far too loud in his own ears, and he bent at the waist to rest his hands just above the crease of his knees. The sensation of the elevator dropping suddenly made his stomach flip.

The last of the floors disappeared past him with a series of high-pitched pings, and in the moment of reprieve, he ran a hand through his messy greying hair with a sound somewhere between a sigh and a laugh.

"Fuckin' idiot," he growled softly to himself, "You just *had* to open the damn email, didn't you? Couldn't just leave well enough alone."

The metal box bounced slightly where it hit the springs at the base of the building and August straightened again, facing the entrance with trembling hands as the doors revealed the brass-coloured din beyond.

His breath caught in his throat as he took in what was lurking in the dark. Spread out before him like life-sized doll's houses, the water-damaged buildings were all tilted on their axis, forced out of alignment by the first surges of the breaking river. Amongst them, the familiar red paintwork on a single building stood out of the darkness, it's likeness something he had seen many times in old pictures over the years. The Temple Bar barely resembled those photographs now, much of the colour warped by time and shadow, but its sign still appeared mostly intact. Many of the vibrant plants that had once covered its walls with life were now tangled around the strings of lights, choking the last of the moisture from the building in an effort to survive.

August reached up to brush his fingertips against his own throat, feeling his Adam's Apple bob with his attempts to swallow. He knew exactly what that felt like right now.

He took the steps further down into the ruins, the sounds of dripping water echoing off the pipes lining either side of him. The elevator slid closed again behind him, sealing him within the world of darkness and damp. An icy wind tore at his clothes, his hair yanked in all directions. The floor of the tunnel was wet, the scent of rot almost enough to make the man gag. It wasn't a place that humans were meant to go anymore.

The tiny lightbulb situated above the entranceway began to grow distant as he tried to walk without stumbling, blindly reaching his hands into the infinite darkness beyond. The cobbled streets made the ground uneven, and though he tried his best to lift his feet, it was difficult to avoid all the areas where the roads had caved inwards.

He stubbed a toe and swore as his visor launched itself from his head, the glass shattering as it vanished into the obscurity somewhere to his left. He glared after it, exhaling his frustration through his nose before muttering a series of swears and pushing onwards. Its not like he would be seeing anything in here anyway.

Freezing in place, he felt the hairs on his neck rise to attention as the sounds of footsteps grew closer from the direction that he had come. He spun on the spot, looking back towards the only source of light in the underground and gasped as two bright, blue eyes appeared suddenly in front of him. He tried to cry out, whether to defend himself or ward off the incoming attacker he wasn't sure, but the sound was quelled even before it made its way out of his mouth.

And that was when something hit him hard enough to send him sprawling across the ground.

Chapter 3
Search Optimization

Alert ('Warning!' 'Warning!')
Error – > 'Unknown damage' Type Error: Collision detected.

01113 could see the flashes of red appearing across its HUD as it blinked into consciousness again. A low rumble resounded from the back of its throat as its systems rebooted, its cooling fans coming back online again. It discarded the pop-up error messages with a groan, reaching up to touch the spot on the back of its head that had abruptly met with the ground.

Alert: Minor damage detected. Seek repairs.

It slowly opened its eyes again, surprised to see the face of a man hovering over it rather than the all too familiar false ceiling of the underground. The man's hazelnut-coloured eyes were reflecting some of the blue light from his own iris's as he waved a hand in the air between them. He was saying something, his mouth moving wordlessly.
///Is he…speaking to me?
01113 scanned the stranger before it, the man's photographic staff ID appearing on its HUD instantly. *Augustus Jackson*, it read, *Android Technician. Level 3 clearance.*

The man named Augustus reached out his hand and 01113 eyed it curiously, taking note of the small imperfections there with something like wonder in its glowing eyes. Creases around the joints from age. Calluses from a stringed instrument, likely a guitar or something similar. Nails kept neat and trim so as not to get in the way of his work in robotics.

"You alright?" the technician asked, "You need a hand up?"

The human closed his hand around 01113's and pulled the Android to standing, the world spinning somewhat as it found its feet again. It cocked its head to one side, regarding him with interest. It hadn't spoken to a human since the day it had been put to work in the underground. 01113 wasn't even sure how much time had passed since then.

"Christ, sorry about that," the man continued, pushing back his long, red hair from his face, "I didn't even see you coming."

Now that it was upright again, 01113 was finally able to examine the entirety of the person before it. Dressed in a white shirt and navy trousers, the man had clearly come down from the offices above. His tie was noticeably absent, whether by choice or not, the Android couldn't be sure. His biometrics showed that his adrenaline was spiking, his heart rate elevated to over 150 bpm. Dilated pupils. Fear response.

//He's afraid. Something's wrong.

Originating from somewhere in the distance, a shrill alarm began to blaze, the sound creating a Doppler Effect that made it sound as if were coming from all directions simultaneously.

01113 wasn't sure where the information came from, but something in its systems offered it a single word of warning.

//Hornets.

The Runner Droid's arm shot out and it grasped the human's shirt sleeve between two fingers, holding tightly to the fabric. August twisted towards it in surprise, his dark eyebrows lifting.

New Objective: Guide Human To Safety.

"This way!" 01113 shouted, digging deep inside to find its voice, "Hurry!"

It pulled hard, almost yanking its new companion off his feet as it hurried him along. It knew it wouldn't be able to reach its maximum speeds with a human in tow, so it adjusted its pace, focusing on keeping the man upright as he stumbled along behind it.

Error > 'Proximity Warning'

A bullet rushed past 01113's face and the machine jerked to the side with a noise that resembled a gasp, pulling the human in close so that it could shield him with its body. It could feel the man's breath against its cheek, coming out in short, sharp bursts. Another bullet whizzed by, and the Android ducked to avoid the ricochet. Its HUD cut sharp white lines in the darkness, warning of each new bullet's trajectory. It swerved to avoid another barrage, pulling August into a side tunnel as the man's petrified shouts echoed off the curves of the metal pipes. The red-headed human tripped over his own feet, disoriented by the dark, and the Android adjusted its position to hold him close, using its illuminous eyes to guide them.
"It's not much further," 01113 whispered close to his ear, hoping its tone was reassuring. It felt strange to use its voice out loud like this. It didn't think that it had ever had the need to do so before.
The large pipe dipped down into waist-high water, the smell rising harshly in the heat as they began to wade through it. The human choked back a cough, gagging against the smell and pulling up the collar of his shirt to cover his mouth and nose. "Christ!" he exclaimed, his skin taking on a slightly greener pallor, "What the Hell is all this?"
"It appears to be rainwater that has come through the foundations above," 01113 answered thoughtfully, wrinkling its nose in something like distaste. Although it experienced its senses in a slightly different way than its human companion, it was able to tell that something within the water was toxic, "We should move quickly. It is not wise to stay here for long."
"You don't have to tell me twice," August mumbled through the fabric of his quickly darkening shirt.
01113 shuffled forward, focusing on the pull of the air ahead of them as a guide. It knew it would lead to an opening if they just kept moving in the same direction. The sounds of gunshots were still loud at their heels and the dark-haired Android counted down the seconds in its head, estimating the times each bullet would take to reach them.

Ahead of them, bright, natural light began to fill the tunnel and 01113 pulled on August's sleeve insistently, directing him towards the welcoming glow of it. The human's face appeared in its peripheries, and it let out an amused exhale at the man's dishevelled appearance. Based on the Crossroads training posters, it had always imagined humans to be so well put together. But this particular one was most certainly not. 01113 felt the corner of its humanoid mouth forming a facsimile of a smile at that particular observation.

The end of the broken pipe opened up before them and the pair skidded to a stop, the human man bumping against the Android's metal shoulder. August peered down through the gaps in the bars to where the stagnant water was rejoining the river outside. He pulled the collar of his shirt back from his face again with a frown half-hidden in ginger-toned facial hair.

"Any idea how deep that water is, mucker?" he questioned. He was clearly not a fan of the idea of dropping down into the murky depths, his body subconsciously leaning away from where the water was trickling subtly downwards.

01113 glanced back into the darkness behind them, "Unfortunately not," it answered, "And I estimate that we have less than five minutes before they're on us."

"Well, fuck," the bearded man grunted, leaning out of the opening to make a face down at the water again. He turned his attention back to his bright-eyed partner in crime, his brow furrowing, "Are you even waterproof?"

//What a strange question to ask.

"Of course I am," the Android responded, somewhat indignantly, "Most of the Crossroads models can be completely submerged for some time. We have no need to breathe after all."

"Lucky for some," Augustus scoffed. He took a deep breath inwards, his hands clenched down by his sides to keep them from shaking, "*Fuuuck*. Alright. Lets just do this before my legs lock up."

The Runner Droid took a step closer to him, gently reaching out to take a hold of his damp shirt again. He met August's dark eyes, watching the way that they briefly widened in the instants before he pulled him forward and off the rounded edge.

The first thing that the Android registered was the sensation of cold water rushing over its body. This was quickly followed by the subtle changes in pressure to its chassis, and the tickle of fish and other aquatic life to its Chrome covering. It careened downwards as its mind was opened up to the new data and felt something in its balance shift when it was sent shooting upwards again, its feet hitting off a surface it could only assume was the riverbed. It held tightly to the dip of August's side, placing a hand beneath his chin and directing his face up towards the light overhead. The technician gasped as he breached the surface, his hands coming up to claw at the water as it sloshed around his heavy, living body. His shirt floated up around his chest, fluttering in slow motion like a jellyfish as its owner started to make for the banks of the river.

01113 pulled itself up and over the concrete barrier, its hands falling on various items of waste that had washed up alongside them. August flopped onto the ground by its feet, spluttering as he cleared any remnants of the vile, foggy water from his system. His bright hair clung to his face and neck, soaked through with the foul-smelling chemicals they had swam through.

"Jesus Christ," he panted, opening his eyes again to stare up at the pink-tinged bubble over their heads. His beard appeared almost brown in places where it stuck to his chin.

The Android turned away from him with wide eyes, staring around itself in awe at the bright lights of the city and the huge, glass dome that covered everything in sight. The numbers above them ticked by with a glowing red radiance, the man-made clouds gathering across the curve of the artificial skyline. Everything twinkled, the natural light more beautiful than the Android could ever have imagined. 01113 slowly raised its palm, as if in an attempt to capture some of the sunlight that was filtering down over them both, turning it slowly one way and then the other.

The machine smiled to itself in amazement, "It's…incredible," it breathed.

August adjusted himself into a seated position, tilting his head back to finally get a good look at his mechanical saviour. The Android was most certainly male in appearance, not too far from his own age, judging by its design. Although his skin was pale, his hair and eyebrows were dark, with hints of a lighter, almost teal shade throughout it. It was gelled back tightly against its head, but a few fine curls were attempting to escape around its ears where it had gotten wet. It had a strong jaw, but its features were on the softer, more friendly-looking side. A real Joseph Gordon-Levitt type. It had freckles that lined the points under its eye and the bridge of its nose.

It had the same electric blue eyes that August associated with all Androids of its generation, and they glowed slightly under the shadow of the nearby buildings. It was surveying the space around it as if it had never seen it before, which, he supposed, was likely the case. The turquoise and gold uniform suggested that it was a Runner Droid, likely one that he himself had played a part in programming. That likely meant that the poor guy had never been above ground before.

"So," he started, groaning as he forced himself to his feet again, "You're an Android then?"

01113 wasn't exactly sure why, but something about that question made its internal processes grind to a halt. It watched as the man beside him hopped on one foot, emptying a mixture of water, sand and wastage out of one shoe. It could detect no malice in the man's words, however. It was simply an observation.

Regardless, the machine swallowed back a feeling that was far too close to disappointment. It searched through its limited logs on what it should do in the event of direct contact with a human and adjusted its position to appear more professional. Less life-like.

"Yes, sir," it affirmed, its tone losing any of its previous inflections. It studied the human's face, taking in the wet red and grey hair and the almost amber colour of his dark eyes. It could detect smoke on his clothes and the smell of alcohol from when he had last worn the shirt to a bar or nightclub. There was also something unique in the way that the technician held himself, a quiet confidence that was hidden away despite the lack of care he apparently placed in his appearance.

The man stared back at him, his lip quirking up to form a scowl, "Don't call me sir. Makes me sound like I'm ninety."

The Android started, feeling its hands slipping from their previous position behind its back, "But you are in a position above me," it argued, "Does that not mean I should...?"

August sniffed, shoving some of his hair back from where it fallen across his feet, "You don't have to call me anything you don't want to," he replied.

//That I don't...**want** to? That was a strange concept. Wanting had never entered into any of its equations before.

01113 cocked its head again, some of the messy strands of its hair flopping down over its forehead, "So...how do I address you then?"

"How's about we start with names, eh?" August shifted his weight, shooting his new companion with a toothy, yet somewhat breathless, grin, "I'm Augustus. People tend to call me August or Gus, so...take your pick. Though I'm sure you've already got all my details in that fancy, shiny head of yours."

He extended a hand towards the Android, and it arched a single an eyebrow at it, an altogether very human looking response.

"This is usually the part where you shake my hand, smart guy," August said, his tone pleasantly teasing.

01113 reached out and took the hand that was offered, allowing August to pull it up and down gently in his grasp.

Let person = {}
{name: 'August'};
Console.log (person.name)

"August," it repeated slowly, making a note of how the word sounded on its own lips. It felt odd to call a human by their name, too familiar. Though nothing in its programming stated that it was not allowed.

"And you're Ollie, right?" August continued, releasing the dark-haired machine's hand as he moved to squeeze some of the water out of the bottom of his shirt, "That's your name?"

The Android's brow furrowed as it followed the movements of the man's hands, "*My name?*"

"Yeah. *Your* name. It's written on your jacket," August said. He tapped on the right hand-side of his own chest and the Android glanced downwards. There, embroidered on one side of its uniform, was its unique serial number: 01113.

It had never noticed how much it resembled a name before.

//Ollie. Origin: Latin, from the word 'olive tree'.

Masculine.

He.

He smiled to himself. For some reason that he couldn't quite pin down, it felt good to finally have a name. It felt...*right*.

"You can call me Ollie, if you'd like," he said, a genuine smile moving to overtake his features. The little freckles along his eyes and nose appeared to dance with the action, like shooting stars across the milky way.

August noted the change in the Android's stance and offered him a smile of his own in reply, folding his arms across his broad chest, "Alright then, Ollie, I'm assuming that those two assholes behind us won't be put off by a little bit of smelly water for long. What do you reckon you and I should do now?"

Go with him, whispered a small voice in the back of the Android's mind, *get him somewhere safe. You can trust him. I promise.*

Ollie turned to look back towards the city streets again, the outlines of a map appearing over his HUD in a mixture of white and red. He traced each new line as it appeared, studying the unfamiliar scene before them until his eyes fell on a set of concrete steps leading up to the higher levels from the riverside. A few more feet of elevation and they would disappear into the city's busy streets.

Objective: protect August.

He guided his companion's line of sight with a finger, "If we head this way, we'll be able to conceal ourselves in the crowds," he said, "It will make it difficult for the Hornets to pursue us on foot."

"That's the best plan I've heard all day," the red-head answered with a nod, his Dublin-accent adding a slight, upbeat lilt to his words, "Lead the way."

CHAPTER 4
Breadcrumbs

The streets of New Dublin City were bustling and lively for a Wednesday afternoon in April, the narrow, cobbled pavements overrun with crowds of people and the occasional Android. August slipped into the cover of the large groups with ease, pulled along by his mechanical companion by the damp cuff of his shirt sleeve. Heads turned to look at them whenever they passed, whether drawn by the way that their clothes were dripping all over the footpath or by the smell of sewar run-off, August didn't fancy hazarding a guess, but he was thankful for the space they were giving them either way.

Ollie stumbled awkwardly around the strangers that were coming and going in the cramped space, very obviously unused to being around so many other people. Taking sympathy on his new companion, August reached out to pull him close against his side instead, steering him as best he could along the heavily populated pavements. He narrowed his eyes back in the direction they had come from, leaning in to be closer to the other man's ear, "Can you see them yet?" he questioned.

The Android raised himself up on the tips of his toes, his bright eyes lighting up as he scanned their environment. It was hard to distinguish any one person from the crowd, his identifiers hopping from one face to another as if trying to narrow down a pattern between them. He was never designed to be a social model and this much data was already causing his system to overclock, the heat building up in the back of his throat like acid reflux.

Raising his head, he instead chose to focus on the spots above them, places that he knew the Hornets could use to get a better vantage point. Something flashed up on the very corner of his HUD, catching movement on a building to their left, and he traced the motions with a frown, "Above us," he replied, "Seems they're still trying to follow us."

"Well, shit," August swore under his breath, "These bastards are fast."

"Not as fast as me," Ollie countered, searching for spaces in the crowds for them to occupy, "All we need is some breathing room and I can get us out of here."

Lines appeared across his HUD, white guides that pointed out each the directions they could take. His digital brain processed each of the possibilities almost instantaneously, selecting the best options and discarding the rest in the blink of an eye. One path pulsed with a faint yellow light, encouraging them to duck into a side alley. The overhangs from the buildings above would provide excellent cover from the Hornets and get them away from the growing crowds.

"This way," Ollie stated, tugging on August's shirt again to guide him.

"You seem pretty confident," August observed, glancing around the shady-looking side street. The sunlight had been all but blotted out by the greying cement walls and the surrounding streets seemed dim and quiet at a glance. Other than the occasional worker popping out for a brief smoke break, the alley was completely unoccupied as they slipped through.

August wrinkled his nose as they ducked under the cover of an old tarp roof, the smell of mould and Chinese food blending together in a sickening mixture that made his stomach roll.

"My built-in mapping software is highly advanced," Ollie replied dispassionately, his tone as even as if he were commenting on the weather, "It can highlight the best possible routes to avoid our pursuers."

"Well, ain't that handy?" August remarked, his dark eyes peering briefly up towards the roofs overhead, "Does that mean you have a plan then?"

The Android paused to observe him, "I assumed your goal was to head the nearest Garda station," he said, "Is that not the case?"

August eyed him up and down, "Why the Hell would we go to the Garda?"

"According to your file on the Crossroads database, you have procured sensitive company information and are currently seen as a *'wanted man'*," Ollie noted, his voice neutral as if he were just reading the information written down somewhere, "From a brief internet search, I assume this constitutes that you are a *'Whistleblower'* and require government interference and protection."

"Shit," August muttered, frowning back at him as he mussed up his hair. Clearly a stress response, "I should never have opened that goddamn email."

"Email?" the Android repeated, blinking as it filed the information away again.

"It was from another Android unit, likely a friend of yours. Passed the Turing Test and then he-"

Ollie shook his head, dark eyebrows dipping downwards. His pale blue eyes glowed faintly in the shadows of the two adjacent buildings, "That isn't possible, August. None of the Androids in our facility have *ever* passed the Turing Test."

August opened his mouth to speak, to argue about what he seen, when suddenly he was thrown backwards onto the ground. Ollie's body landed on his, shoving him down into the warm tarmac as something small and metal pinged off the huge, black skip by their heads. He let out a shocked yell, feeling the very solid weight of the Android's chest against his own, "The fuck was-"

The tip of Ollie's nose nudged against his own, "It seems they aren't afraid to fire into crowds," he remarked.

August swore as they scrambled to their feet again and he reached out to yank the Android after him as the sound of bullets followed their movements, the metal ringing as each projectile smashed through the skip's hard outer shell. His heart was pounding in his ears, and he could almost hear the roar of his own blood rushing through his veins.

They rounded a corner and Ollie quickly dodged to the side, pulling August in behind a stone wall just as another round of bullets filled the alleyway with flakes of paint and dust. The human choked back a cough, squinting through the haze as noticed the tone of the bullets' impact change.

Error: component e0089-547 (a) has been damaged.
Recommending repair. Nearest repair facility 0.45 miles.

Next to him, his Android companion let out a sharp hiss from between his clenched teeth, reaching for his right leg as he stumbled off balance, "It-it appears I've been hit."

"Jesus Christ, Ollie," August shouted, diving down to examine the man's leg with widening eyes, "Are you alright?"

"I...I think so," Ollie answered uncertainly. He leaned against the wall behind him, clearly wobbly on just one leg. He watched as the red-head pulled back the torn fabric of his uniform from the spot on his calf where he'd been hit. The artificial skin around the point of the impact had retreated back, revealing some of the dark chassis' underneath. A small hole had pierced through the outer frame and dark liquid was beginning to trickle out slowly from inside.

August grabbed the end of his shirt sleeve, holding it out to the man above him, "I need you to tear this," he said.

Ollie grabbed it unquestioningly, tearing it along the line of the seam and handing the chunk of fabric back to him, "What's that for?" he asked.

"You won't be able to run with an injury like this," August replied, wrapping the material of his shirt tightly around the wound, "Believe me, I've seen all that goes into those legs of yours. It doesn't take much to fuck with the integrity of it. And the last thing you want is for it to snap in two when you're trying to get away."

The technician straightened again, still looking down at the wounded leg with a frown, "Are you able to put any weight on it?"

Ollie pushed off the wall again, testing the leg delicately. The sensation felt odd. Wrong, somehow.

"It seems so, though I won't know for sure until we're moving again."

"Shit," August muttered, running a hand through his long, still-damp hair. It was curling up at the ends where it had started to dry, making the man appear like a rather scruffy red setter. He looked around the space that they had found themselves in and exhaled a rough sigh. They were as good as trapped if they stayed here much longer, but even risking a single peek beyond the boundary of the wall could spell death for either one of them. He hummed, turning to size up a closed door on the side of the building next to them.

"Just…wait here a second, would ya," he grumbled, shuffling over to test the handle.

Locked. Of course it is.

He eyed the scanner next to the door frame, tracing a fingertip over the hard plastic. It was roughly the size of a tablet, clearly designed to scan the palms of the employees for verification purposes. Old tech, easy enough to crack if you knew how. He'd never had to do it under time pressure though.

He felt around the bottom of the panel as he sensed Ollie approaching his left-hand side, the Android peering over his shoulder as he yanked the carefully set metal covering to one side. He narrowed his eyes back towards him, sucking on his teeth as he worked, "Didn't I just tell you to stay put? Aren't Androids supposed to follow orders?"

The dark-haired Android's face resembled that of a chastised dog, and he shuffled in place. He looked entirely unsure what to do with his hands.

"Apologies," he responded, averting his eyes, "I was just curious if you needed assistance."

August snorted, shaking his head with amusement at the response, "I didn't know Androids could *be* curious," he answered back, his tone teasing as he pried open the circuit board and exposing the wires beneath it. He tried to ignore the way that the adrenaline was making his hands shake as he worked. "And here was me thinking that you guys knew everything."

Ollie leaned against the wall next to him, looking troubled, "So did I," he admitted, somewhat quietly. August wasn't sure if the words were meant for him or the Android himself. His brilliant blue eyes lowered towards the pools of water and oil opposite them, staring thoughtfully at his own reflection as he worried at his bottom lip. August was pretty sure that wasn't something that he or his team of technicians had ever programmed into him.

The red-haired man slipped his thick fingers inside the scanner in front of him and slowly pulled out two of the navy-coloured wires, carefully twisting them around each other. He had worked with these sorts of systems all his life and was as at ease with the language of its code as many were with their home dialect. He adjusted the positions of the wires, moving several of the inputs to incorrect slots.
"I used to work on shit like this when I first started at Crossroads," he explained, clearing his throat and trying to fill the growing silence.
He felt the Android's eyes on him as he asked, "Is it difficult?"
"Nah," the human replied with a hum, "Kinda hard to fix it without first learning how to break the damn thing. These old iT47s were notorious for having false-positives built in."
He moved to reattach the cover, placing his hand on the scanner and watching as the orange light ran over the edges of his palm and fingers. The numbers and letters that flashed up on the tiny screen were nonsensical, the altered path throwing up misinformation that the machine couldn't translate.
"One of the most common issues we used to come across with this line…" he continued, a flicker of a smile appearing on the corner of his lips, "Was the double negative release. Unlike with everything else in life, apparently in this case, two wrongs did indeed make a right."
After trying to identify the man before it twice to no avail, the scanner flashed up a *Null* result and the door at his shoulder buzzed and unlocked. August gripped the handle and pulled the heavy, metal door to open, glaring into the darkness beyond. There were no rooms inside, only stairs leading up to the offices higher above them.
"Looks like an emergency exit or something," he commented, leaning inside a little further, "The employees probably just use it for their smoke breaks, or something."
He held the door open for Ollie to follow him inside, eyeing up the Android's damaged leg as he hobbled past. He wondered if the stairs would take them all the way to the roof. And if they did, then what next? Would they have to just hope that they weren't followed? Or try and get to one of the adjacent buildings? He eyed up the other man's injury with a frown. He wasn't sure if the limb was going to take much more abuse, if he was honest.
"Think you can manage the stairs, or do you need a hand?" he asked as Ollie placed a tentative hand on the metal banister, tilting his head back to look up towards the floors above them.

Ollie shook his head, "Hopefully my leg won't slow our progress," he answered, already starting to pull himself up the vinyl steps, "I'll go as fast as I can."
He wobbled as he extended his good leg and August appeared at his back, placing one hand on the banister and the other on his shoulder blade, "Woah there, take it easy!"
The warmth of the man's palm seemed to bleed right through his uniform and Ollie felt the fans in the bottom of his throat switch on to clear the excess heat, "S-sorry," he muttered quietly, "It appears that my balance is a little off."
"Just focus on getting up there in one piece," August breathed, urging him gently upwards with the press of his hand, "I'm right behind you."

Warning: internal temperature increase detected.
Initialising internal fan.

"If I start to slow you down…," the dark-haired Android started, his eyes bright in the darkness as they started to climb again, "If it looks like they're catching up-"
"Hey, none of that talk," the human retorted gruffly, his touch growing slightly firmer, "We're in this mess together now. No way I'm leaving you behind, injured leg or no. Don't make me start quoting old war movies at you."

"Seymour! You have to keep running! I can see them through the trees!"

Ollie blinked, staring around the narrow stairwell as another voice manifested in the silence. It was so unlike August's voice, light and airy and feminine where his was deep and throaty. Somehow, he thought that he recognised the woman's voice, despite never having spoken to anyone else since his activation. It appeared to originate from somewhere inside himself, like an echo of a distant memory trying to make itself known.
He looked back over one shoulder at the technician climbing up behind him in the shadows. The man met his eyes and quirked his head up once, "Come on, no more arguing. Just get your tin butt up there," he said, "We ain't got a lot of time on our hands."
Ollie took another few steps upwards, feeling his internal coolant seeping through the scrap on his leg with every movement. No doubt they were leaving a very obvious trail in their wake because of him.

//If August gets hurt because of me…if I fail my objective…

August followed at his back, trying his best to soften the sound of his heavy breathing as they ascended. If he survived this, he was going to have to eat some damn kale or something.

At the apex of the staircase, they came to a stop at a set of large, red, double doors. A bar across the centre of it warned that it would trigger an alarm if used. Ollie raised his right hand into the air, the palm beginning to glow with a faint blue light in the din. He closed his eyes as he settled into the motion, soothed by the familiarity of it.

"Whatcha doing there, Ols?" August questioned, leaning one arm against the banister as he watched the other man wiggle his fingers as if tracing something unseen through the walls.

"The cables for the alarm go into this wall here," he explained, extending his arm so that only the very tips of his fingers rested on the damp concrete, "I should be able to switch it off manually."

He wrinkled his nose as he concentrated on the task, the glow travelling along his arm and lighting up areas of his skin like half-concealed tattoos. It bathed his pale face in a sea-blue ambience that accentuated the curve of his cupid's bow and the sweep of his cheekbones.

August took the opportunity to catch his breath, letting out a soft sigh as he leaned back against the opposite wall. He hadn't even noticed that this wall was damp too, the cold chill of it soaking through the back of his already sodden shirt. By now, the thing was likely beyond saving. Not that he ever much cared for his work uniform. It was baggy and too hot and itched like a motherfucker in the summer.

He allowed his eyes to fall closed as he rested his head back with a groan, the coolness soothing the headache he had already started to accumulate.

Well, this is turning out to be one Hell of a day, he thought.

His heart jumped into his throat as a tiny, high-pitched noise ascended from somewhere beneath them. Dark eyes flashed open, and he rushed to the edge of the balcony, leaning over it to look back the way that they had come.

Please God tell me I imagined that sound.

There it was again -something resembling an electronic drill- vibrating through the very air inside the building. The sound bounced off each and every stair, scattering in all directions as it rose in volume.

A much louder bang followed, and Ollie's eyes shot open as he spun around, "What was-"

The floor below them suddenly erupted with noise, the sound of stomping feet and screaming abruptly filling the cramped space as the door they had entered through was ripped away by a pair of powerful hands.

"Shit!" August barked, turning to grab Ollie's shoulder, "You almost done there, Ols? We're about to have company!"

"Almost…" The Android narrowed his bright eyes back towards the wall, "I just have to-"

"Fuck it!" August shouted and shouldered the bar inwards, barrelling outside and sending a blast of hot air into the room.

The resulting sirens were loud and shrill, their noise only adding to the immediate chaos following them up from below. Ollie reached up to cover both ears, the rush of data quickly becoming too much.

"August!" he called out, the stimulation overwhelming his senses, "I-I can't-"

Warm fingers closed around his own and when he opened his eyes again, August was barely an inch from his face, his bright hair flapping all around him in the wind, "We need to *move*, Ollie!"

The corners of the man's shirt lifted, snapping loudly as the pair travelled across the vacant roof space. The square of blank concrete had been darkened by recent rain, steam billowing out of the vents along either side to fill the air with pale grey haze. They carefully navigated their way through the translucent cover of it, clinging to one another as they made it to the furthest edge.

August eyed the building next to them with a frown. He had really been hoping it would have been closer.

"No way we can make that," he remarked anxiously as the hot steam ruffled his hair and clothes and filled the gaps between them. He could already feel the warm hiss of it against his nose and eyelids, the sweaty moisture clinging to his beard hair and throat.

Ollie stepped up onto the lip of the building, his HUD already beginning to calculate the distance between them and the ground, "We may need to go down from here." His tone had become strangely blank, like he was only relaying information and not placing any emotion behind it. The graphs he was seeing spread out before his eyes were not exactly filling him with much hope right now.

"*Down*? You mean you want to *jump*?" August choked back the startled laugh that was trying to creep its way out of his throat, "Have you completely lost the plot? We're like seven stories up right now!"

Running scan: Augustus Jackson
Heart Rate: 173bpm
Blood pressure 140/90mmHg
Increased respiratory and heart rate.
Increase cortisol levels and stress response detected.

"It may be our only option," Ollie stated, scanning the other, nearby rooftops, "If those Hornets get their hands on us…"
August pushed the hair back from his own face with one hand roughly, paling as he took in the sight of the alleyway below them, "Fuck, Ollie. I'm not sure that either of us would survive a fall like that."
The door behind them blasted open, the force almost ripping it straight from its hinges. August spun around with his teeth bared to face the approaching Androids, pushing his injured companion behind him protectively. The machines stood shoulder to shoulder with one another, pulling out their weapons in almost perfect time. They flicked off the safety caps with mechanical efficiency, every motion another part of a preprogrammed sequence. Their bright striped uniforms were an unnatural contrast
to the grey and white of the roof space.
Ollie took a half step forward to place his hand on August's shoulder. It looked so small compared to the size of the man's broad shoulders. He felt strong under his shirt, his musculature evident even under his uniform.
His objective *'protect August'* flashed up again in the corner of his vision, insistent and ever-present now that he had added it to his directive. But it was something more than that that made him reach out to the other man, an innate, instinctual need to keep him out of harm's way. Whatever that emotion was that was rising up within him, now was not the time to address it.
"August…do you think that you can trust me?"
The red-haired man hesitated, his body tensing under Ollie's touch, "You haven't let me down yet, Ols," he answered without turning, keeping his dark eyes trained on the figures making their way through the rising steam and heat. He swallowed in

an attempt to shift the enormous lump that was forming in his throat, tilting his body ever-so-slightly in the Android's direction, "Just tell me what to do."

Ollie took a step into the man's space and wrapped his other arm around him, pressing their bodies close together as he eased them towards the edge, "Close your eyes," he said. He barely glanced back at their pursuers before he was pulling them down those last, precarious centimetres. He disappeared over the edge, pulling his human companion with him.

Chapter 5
Bounce Back

August felt the air rush from his lungs as they were thrown over the side of the building, each floor flashing by them in a blur as they twisted and turned around each other in the air. The streetlights blinded him for an instant before they disappeared again. Holding tight to his shirt, Ollie quickly manoeuvred himself between August and the ground, tucking his smaller body in against him. August could feel the electric pulse of his inner circuitry against his skin, like an artificial heart that was racing just as fast as his own. He tried to shift his weight, to look into the other man's eyes as they fell, but within a split second they were hitting the ground at force. Rubbish scattered everywhere as their combined weight impacted the half-emptied contents of an open skip. Soft and sharp things struck them from all sides, the crinkle of black bin liners giving way to their weight and speed. The smell of refuge and rotten food rose like a sickening wave to meet August's nose.

Error: component e0089-547 (a) irreparable damage detected.
Seek immediate assistance.

Angry red characters filled Ollie's vision, their intrusive light only growing brighter when he tried to open his eyes again. He could make out the sound of coughing over the buzz of his restarting circuitry and he sat up weakly, reaching out blindly towards the noise. He felt the soft warmth of August's hands lingering on various parts of his body as their owner inspected him for damage.

"August...?" Ollie mumbled, his voice vibrating with the force of his internal fans working to cool him down, "Are you alright? Are you injured?"

A dull sensation registered on the outer edges of his body, like the feeling one might get from a hand or foot that had fallen asleep. Ollie extended his awareness down into each of his limbs, but the flood of error messages he got back were too much to decipher.

August's face came into view when he finally was able to open his eyes, his greying red hair more dishevelled than ever, blood and dirt coating his nose and cheeks from their landing, "Jesus, *duine*. Can you hear me okay?"

//Duine. Origin: Irish Gaeilge. Translation: 'person'. Pronounced 'din-ye'.

Ollie tilted his head, trying to disperse some of the strange ringing in his ears, "You're alive," he breathed, something like relief reflected in his voice. He felt a rush of energy at that, like just the knowledge alone was enough to keep him moving. He ignored the relentless glowing error messages, shoving their processes to one side of his HUD as the space around him rushed back into focus. He wobbled where he was leaning against the man in front of him, a feeling not unlike dizziness washing over him. Something wasn't right. He wasn't meant to be feeling anything like this.

He wasn't meant to be *feeling* anything at all.

"I'm more worried about you right now," August replied, snapping his fingers first on the left side of the Android's face and then the right, "Do you think you can move?"

At Ollie's slow nod, August began to shuffle his way over towards the outer edge of the skip they had found themselves in, groaning as a deep ache permeated his muscles. Everything hurt, but whether anything was actually broken or not was hard to tell.

Must be the adrenaline, he thought, *Christ, I can barely stop shaking right now. I seriously need a cigarette.*

He pulled himself over the side breathlessly, staggering whenever his legs hit solid ground again. He reached up with both hands, panting as he tried to steady his breathing, "Alright Ollie, nice and slow. Let's get you down from there and see what we're working with here."

Ollie interlocked his fingers with his, pushing down against his palms for balance. He could feel his body moving under him but was helpless to prevent the fall he knew was coming. He topped down against his companion with a squeak, clutching tightly to August's filthy shirt as the world suddenly rose up over his head. His entire body shook with the effort to steady himself, tremors running through his synthetic bones as his feet touched down on the cobbles again. He attempted to take a step forward and his body buckled beneath him, one leg splaying out unnaturally to one side. He could now clearly see what had gotten his new human friend so concerned; the chassis was completely splintered apart, the illuminous blue and red wires inside exposed to the air like sparking veins. He could see the metal rod in the centre that formed his false tibia. It had been bent inwards by the force of their fall.

"Shit," August muttered, catching him under one arm and helping him to balance awkwardly on one leg, "Looks like that leg's banjoed, mucker. No way you're gonna be able to run with that."

August's warm brown eyes travelled down the length of the Android's legs, inspecting the damage. It was clear that the bullet earlier had weakened the structure of the limb, the pieces splitting off from where the original impact had been. He glanced up towards the rooftop overhang. Although he lacked the Android's ability to scan through the walls, he was almost certain their pursuers had moved on for the moment. No doubt they were on their way to scrape their remains off the sidewalk.

"How much do you weigh?"he continued as he met Ollie's bright eyes.

The Android's eyebrows jumped up towards his hairline, "According to my records, around 80 kilograms. Why?"

The red-haired man hummed to himself as if considering his options, "Yeah…" he mumbled, "Yeah, I should be able to lift that."

Ollie stared at him, his blue eyes widening, "Lift that?" he repeated, "What are you-"

The noise he let out as he was hoisted off his feet was, in the Android's opinion, completely undignified. He was certain that it wasn't a sound he had ever made before.

Warning: internal temperature increase detected.

August scooped him up and pulled him tight against his chest, adjusting his balance as he got used to the extra weight, "Hold on tight, kiddo. We're gonna have to make a break for it."

Ollie threw his arms around the other man's neck and buried his face in against the column of his throat. Heat was travelling up through his chest and face, making it feel as if the very tips of his ears were burning. A quick internet search of his symptoms revealed that this feeling was *embarrassment*.

"I may look a little younger than you, Mr. Jackson, but I'm far from a child," he argued, his voice slightly choked, "And I don't need to be carried."

August grunted noncommittally, avoiding his eyes as he started to move towards the point where the alleyway joined back onto the main street, "Stop complainin', would ya?" His grip on the machine's legs tightened almost imperceptibly, "We've gotta get that leg of yours looked at before your coolant leads the Hornets right to us."

Ollie chewed on the inside of his lip, his bright eyes taking in August's expression but saying nothing. He nodded as he wrapped a hand around the inside collar of the human's shirt, his artificial skin surprisingly warm against his neck.

He really does feel just like a human, August observed.

He squinted as he came back out into the bright light, surveying the area before them in an attempt to get some semblance of direction. He took in the names of the small, busy pubs spread out around them, eyeing up the half-drunken occupants as they hurried past. He kept his head down, using the veil of his hair to hide his face. He didn't know this part of the city well. Nothing was ringing any bells for him. He wasn't even entirely sure if he was going in the right direction and now wasn't exactly the time to be making mistakes like this.

The people around them backed away at their appearance, but he ignored their stares, shifting the weight of the Android in his arms to one side so that he could extract his phone from the back pocket of his work trousers. The screen was cracked down one side, the thin, clear line splitting his chosen wallpaper in two and creating a horrible mash of green and pink splodges in the centre of it. He used his fingerprint to unlock the device, swiping awkwardly as he tried to bring up the VI assistant.

"Butler," he barked, his voice as rough and cracked as his phone, "Show me the location of the nearest Android Repair Centre."

The built in search tool confirmed the request with a soft-spoken male voice, opening the mapping app and directing them through the crowds with gentle instructions that were almost impossible to distinguish from the noise.

Error: component e0089-547 (a) irreparable damage detected.
Seek immediate assistance.

Ollie held tight to August's shirt as the world began to blur around the edges. What little processing power he had left was being used to keep the error messages from filling up his vision. His breath was heating up at a rapid pace, trying to dispel some of the build-up from the system's increasing demands. He wasn't designed to be a social model, the abundance of incoming data already becoming too much for him. Thick, fat globules of coolant dripped down onto the street from his damaged leg, forming black pools as they walked. August could feel the oily fluid coating his hands where he held him. It felt just like blood.

He charged through the groups of gathering people unapologetically, taking some comfort in the fact that he could still feel the pressure of the Android's grip on the back of his neck.

Still conscious, he noted, *that's good.*

He took a moment to look down at the smaller man in his arms, watching the way that his bright eyes were still scanning the rooftops around them for threats with cautious awe. Despite almost matching his height of 5 foot 10, Ollie really didn't weigh all that much. He guessed that chrome and graphite were infinitely lighter than their meat and bone counterparts. The layer that covered it, the one that perfectly resembled skin, shone in the sunlight filtering down on them through the bubble overhead. The areas where his skin was damp twinkled, revealing freckles in the spots his uniform didn't cover.

On the road just north of them, the residential area was divided by brick-and-mortar shops, with the Android Repair Centre sticking out like a sore thumb in the centre with its plastic white walls and too-blue décor.

"Stay will me just a little longer, Ols," August urged him in a hushed tone of voice, picking up the pace as best he could with the extra weight, "One more stop and then onto the station, alright?"

The light inside the Repair Centre was overwhelming when they first pushed open the door and eased their way inside. August held the heavy glass down open with one, broad shoulder, glaring into each of the faces that were now looking their way from across the aisles.

"Which one of you guys works here?" he questioned urgently, "I need'ta put in a rush job."

Chapter 6
Runtime Error

A man rushed out from behind the wide, front counter as he pulled a pair of amber-coloured tortoiseshell glasses over his widening eyes. His uniform was spotlessly clean and almost as bright as the store's ambient lighting. The words *'Android Genius'* were written on the light blue t-shirt half-concealed beneath the white cotton apron that was flapping behind him like a cape. The lanyard hanging from around his neck identified him as *'Graham Brooks'*. He looked to be in his forties with a short, scruffy beard and blond hair that had been gelled back within an inch of its life. He stopped when he reached them, blue-green eyes travelling the length of the damage.

"What in undergod happened to it?" he questioned, reaching out a probing hand to inspect the leg. He yanked his fingers back when the exposed wires sparked at him like hissing snakes, "Jesus Christ, it's still frikken alive."

August adjusted the weight of the man in his arms, feeling the ache deep within his arms and chest from holding him for so long, "Can you help? He's losing a lot of that coolant stuff."

Graham's hand grazed Ollie's side and the Android jumped, mumbling something in response that was barely coherent. The more fluid he was losing, the harder it was becoming to control his core temperature. August could already feel the burn of it on his own skin.

The engineer leaned closer, "Is that a bloody bullet hole?" he hissed. When he peered up at August through the slant of his glasses his eyes looked twice their size.

"Can we take this in the back please?" the red-head implored him, trying to keep his voice low as he glanced back towards the door they had come through, "I'm feelin' a wile lotta eyes on us out here."

Graham nodded his understanding, his eyes passing over the other patrons until he spotted another employee, "Greg, watch the floor, would ya? This one's gonna be hands on."

The man named Greg frowned but nodded regardless, reaching down to tug his own lanyard free from his trouser pocket as they were led past the till areas.

A blue light washed over them from the built-in scanner surrounding the doorframe, a series of tuneful chimes announcing their entrance into the workshop out back. The room was lined with sparkling white tiles, clinically clean and meticulously organized. There were two other employees at one of the far booths, sharing sandwiches while they worked on a bare Chrome frame. They looked up as they came inside, watching as their workmate rushed ahead to make room for their newest arrival. Graham reached for the metallic arms that housed his computer and monitor, pushing them frantically to one side. Ballpoint pens and blank sheets of paper clattered to the floor around their feet, a mug following close behind with a dull *thunk* as it toppled across the carpet.

"We aren't really equipped to deal with this sort of extensive damage," the blond man muttered, booting up his system with a wave of his hand. He wheeled in another table layered in tools as he took his seat on a small, rounded stool, "But I'll do what I can."

Blue flashed across the screen, lines of codes scrolling past as it logged him in. August laid Ollie carefully across the bare table and the Android's eyes slowly peeled open again, taking in his surroundings. The blue light from his irises landed on the instrument in Graham's hand, making it appear otherworldly.

"Mr Jackson…" he started uncertainly, the spinning of his fans making his voice tremble, "We have to…get you to the station. The Hornets…"

"Easy there, Ols," August soothed, pressing down on the Android's chest when he sensed him attempting to rise again, "It's alright. Just a minor detour. These fellas are gonna help you."

"There's no time," Ollie argued weakly, attempting to shake his grip loose, "It isn't s-safe-"

"Shut up, would ya?" the former Crossroads technician grunted back at him, "We can't just ignore something like this. If you keep goin' like you're goin' you're gonna end up shutting down! And where do you think that'll get us?"

"By the looks of it, the outer casing has been completely destroyed," Graham interrupted from next to them, eyeing up the black mess from over his translucent computer screen, "We'll have no choice but to replace it."

August ran his fingers through his straggly beard with a huff, "Listen, whatever you need to do to get him back up on his feet again just do it."

Ollie's eyes moved to regard him, trying to map out all the details of his face. He thought that he looked greyer than when they had first met just a few hours ago.

//Stress has such a strange effect on humans.

"If the outside looks like this, there may be more underlying damage in its core," Graham continued thoughtfully, "We'll have to bust it open, check it out."

"Won't that hurt?" August questioned, meeting his companion's pale blue eyes for a moment. Ollie turned his head away, pulling his bottom lip into his mouth again and chewing on it. If he had seen the same thing on a human, he might have assumed that it was a nervous habit.

The Genius arched an eyebrow at him, "As long as there are no other issues hiding in there, your Android should be fine."

"Ollie doesn't belong to me," the red-head muttered, moving to stand out of his way, "Just…fix him up, would ya? It's better if ya don't ask too many questions."

Graham turned to look back at the screen again, bringing up the virtual keyboard as he slipped on an intricate-looking pair of work gloves. Each of the fingers on his right hand appeared to be fitted with a strange-looking metal instrument. Sharp like scalpels, the ends resembled something more like a talon than something a mechanic might use. August really didn't want to see what he planned to do with any of them. His work had always been on the coding side of things, working with the language of an Android's mind or limbs. This was…something else entirely. Something more akin to surgery than to IT. He wondered if seeing inside of an Android felt invasive, like seeing a human without their clothes on. He hummed to himself, glancing back towards Ollie's face as his companion stared up at the ceiling overhead.

Do Androids even have the capacity for feeling? Does he feel embarrassed right now? Or scared?

He jumped when he heard the too loud click and pop of Ollie's chassis being opened, and he instantly recognised the whirring of the cable within his neck panel being extended. Graham began to type with his free hand, his fingertips making gentle tapping sounds where they met the glass screen.

Trying to distract himself, August turned to look at the walls around them and immediately wished that he hadn't. The displays appeared as something out of a dystopian novel, each available space lined with components from a hundred different disassembled Android models. Arms, legs, and even a head and torso, hung limp, black and lifeless from the wall. The eyes of each one were left open so that they stared blankly back at him from their skinless faces. Their expressions were frozen in a look of permanent surprise.

It's like a fucking Damien Hurst exhibit in here, August scowled.

"No sign of further damage in the rest of his systems," Graham's voice startled him out of his revere. August adjusted his position, angling himself to face the engineer as he patted the top of the casing closed again, "A little black blood and he should return to full function again."

He, August observed with an amused huff from his nose, *looks like even a Genius can change his spots.*

Ollie slid to the edge of the table and sat upright, pulling his golden uniform closed again, "Thank you," he said, flashing the worker a bright smile that definitely wasn't intended to be a part of his programming.

Graham gave him a slanted, uncertain smile, clearing his throat shyly as he wiped his hands on a rag next to the table, "I don't think any of the machines I've worked on have ever thanked me before." He knelt down on the floor in front of the Android, working to remove the damaged parts of his leg next, "Do you…do you feel any of this? When I'm working on you?"

Ollie shook his head, "It no longer feels like a part of my body."

"*Fascinating*," the robotics engineer grinned, his own blue eyes lighting up with excitement, "Is that something you control yourself? Or is it automatic?"

Ollie cocked his head to one side thoughtfully. It felt unusual to have a limb removed from one's body. He could feel the tug on his wires and artificial muscles like having teeth pulled when under anaesthetic. It was a distant feeling, as if he were merely watching it happening to someone else.

"I've never really thought about it."

August rapped on the side of the desk with his knuckles, "What's with the 20 questions all of a sudden?"

Graham looked up at him, looking thoroughly chastised as he replied, "It's just that I've never actually had the chance to chat with one of my, er, *patients* before. Most Android's aren't as talkative as this."

"It's okay, August," Ollie said softly, hoping that his scans would show a positive effect brought on by his choice of tone. He reached out to brush his fingers over the other man's sodden shirt, noting the way his shoulders had become tensed and drawn in towards his neck, "I don't mind answering his questions."

The red-head let out a derisive snort but visibly relaxed, scratching at his beard thoughtfully, "Sorry, Ols, guess this whole thing has me on edge."

"Damage like this…it comes from another Android, not a person," Graham started, lowering the volume of his voice so he wouldn't be overheard, "Are you two in trouble?"

"Trouble? *Nah*," August huffed, allowing his hand to rest down on the table next to Ollie's hip, "Got a couple'a Hornets on our asses, that's all. Thus, the rush job."

"Hornets?" the blond man hissed from his spot on the floor. He peeked over the top of his booth to make sure the other engineers hadn't overheard, "You mean the Crossroads Security Droids?"

Ollie wiped at his face, smearing some of the shiny, black coolant across his cheek, "They're used by agents on the higher floors to protect company assets." He shuffled in place, glancing down at the space where his leg used to be, feeling a sickening sense of emptiness at the sight, "I have heard they often chase down Androids that have left the facility."

"Left the facility?" August repeated, sending a questioning look his way, "You mean there have been others who have run away from that place?"

Ollie's eyes began to glow with a soft magenta light as Graham started the download on the latest drivers for his new leg, "I was able to find multiple pages worth of results online, but nothing concrete. It appears as if this has been a theory for quite some time."

"Do you reckon it's because of your Soul Chip?" Graham questioned, cutting off the flow of coolant to the limb in front of him.

August froze, "Wait, what did you say?"

Ollie blinked, "They're the chips that the Runner Droids distribute," he explained, "Internally, they're referred to as *'Soul Chips'*. They're like batteries used to power the Androids."

"That Android…the one from the video?" the red-haired man continued, "He asked me to save his Soul. I had no idea what he meant by that."

Ollie reached up a hand and tapped the front panel of his chest, just under his collar, "Each unit is powered by a nuclear chip held in a casing of nano-thin crystalline diamond. The chips are held in our chest cavities, connected to a graphite ribcage to disperse the build-up of heat."

"Think of it like a human's brain or a computer's CPU," Graham added with a hum, pulling apart the pieces of damaged chrome and dropping them into a tray at his feet, "It contains memories and data unique to each Android model as well as the parameters of the Android's assigned tasks."

"Would a Soul Chip show if an Android was able to pass the Turing Test?" August questioned.

The engineer allowed his tools to come to a rest on the table next to him as he pulled his hand free again, "I mean…if it were possible. The *theory* is certainly sound."

"You've worked in this field for God knows how long, right? Aren't you supposed to know this shit?" August pressed, dark eyebrows dipping downwards.

Graham ran his clean left hand through his gelled spikes, mussing them up like a chicken's backside, "There's a lotta legal shit with Automation and AI. A machine that would be capable of passing the Turing Test would be a seriously huge jump in our current capabilities. You're talking lightyears away from where we are right now."

"So, you're telling me you've *never* met a sentient Android before? In all the years you've worked in this job?" August carried on, waving a hand towards the man, "Never had any doubts?"

"We're not exactly paid to have doubts, lad," the man replied, angling his body towards the cardboard box he had started unwrapping next to him. He ripped the new leg component free from the Styrofoam and August couldn't help but stare. Without the covering of the Android's artificial skin, it looked like it belonged on a mannequin, "A machine comes in and I fix it. Enda story."

"That's why we need to get to the station, August," Ollie stated, reaching out to press his palm into his companion's chest, "They can verify what was on that file. And protect you from the Hornets."

The human forced himself to look away from the new piece of machinery, "And what about you, *duine*?" he insisted, "Just look what those things did to you back there. If they get their hands on you, they'll-"

"Disassemble me," Ollie interjected coolly, "I know. It's likely that they will attempt to take data from my own chip to use against you."

Something inside August's chest tightened at the calm way the words had left the other man's mouth, "Aren't you afraid?" he questioned, bringing his hands up to bracket the Android in, "They're gonna take you apart like some sort of lab rat!"

The dark-haired man gave him a soft smile that didn't quite reach his eyes, "I'm a machine, August. The things you think you see in me…they aren't real. It's all just clever programming. Pantomime." He turned his eyes away, "It won't matter to anyone if I'm taken apart."

August moved even closer, bringing up a hand to press down on Ollie's thigh, "It matters to me," he said firmly, "Isn't that enough?"

Warning: internal temperature increase detected.
Initialising internal fans 1, 2 and 3.

Ollie could feel heat rushing to the very tips of his ears. He had no name for what this feeling was, no frame of reference at all. It was something entirely new.
He was experiencing a lot of new things today.

He sensed Graham moving closer to his leg and tilted his head down to watch him work. The engineer twisted the artificial knee joint, pressing down and in with both thumbs to push the patella covering aside. He shuffled closer, giving himself room to position the replacement component. The Android let out a small, almost pneumatic hiss through his teeth as the parts were forced into place, the wires joining together to form nerve endings which flared to life with raw, new data.

"Shit," August muttered, his fingers subtly squeezing the Android's leg where he had clearly forgotten he had rested it, "That didn't sound fun. Just try to breathe through it, *duine*."

Ollie released a low, buzzing noise that sounded like an electronic version of a laugh, "I don't *need* to breathe, August."

"Oh, yeah. My bad."

The red-haired man watched with rapt interest as the new, shiny parts of Ollie began to blend in with the rest of his existing skin tone. It was like watching it go from inanimate object to…well, he wasn't entirely sure what Ollie was yet.

"Look, I'm not gonna ask any more questions," Graham said as he rose again, wiping some of the coolant from where it had dripped down from Ollie's wound, "But if those things really are after you both…I know another way out of the shop. It might buy you a little more time."

August met his eyes, "You'd be taking a risk."

Graham nodded down towards Ollie's new leg, "Your mucker here's a Runner Droid. They don't sell these sorts of models to the public. I'm taking a risk just having you back here."

August reached into his back pocket, pulling out the soggy tome of his wallet and sliding his card across, "Well, whatever your help costs, I'm good for it."

Graham reached into the centre of the table, sliding the card the rest of the way as he flashed him a smile, "I warn you, my services don't come cheap, Red."

"Honestly, just keep the card," August chucked, waving off the man's comments, "No doubt Crossroads will have me cut off by the end of the day. What's left on there is yours."

The mechanic eyed it curiously, reading the name printed on one side, "Maybe I should keep secrets more often then, Mr…*Jackson*."

Ollie allowed his legs to slide back onto the floor again, wobbling for a moment as he reached for the table. He froze in place and August felt his stomach sink as he watched him turn back to face the way they had come. There was shouting in the distance, the commotion growing louder just outside. Ollie's eyes shone with bright light as he scanned through the walls and observed the details lying beyond, "It's them."

August eased an arm around his waist as he hobbled out into the middle of the floor, "You mentioned another way out?"

Graham hopped up from his stool and discarded his other glove, hurrying past the other two mechanics working in the back room. He pulled back a curtain that was covering a dingy looking side entrance, "We use it mostly for smoke breaks. Boss says the smoke gets in the gears but he's a dickhead so…" He fidgeted with the padlock for a moment, the door giving off a shrill whine as he peeled it open, "Follow this straight out and take a left. Your Android mucker can guide you from there."

August offered him a grateful nod as he ducked beneath his outstretched arm, helping the Android limp along as he began his self-diagnostics. The new drivers were almost complete by the time they reached the end of the stone enclosure. The first breath of the chilly, April air was like breaching the surface of the sea after a shipwreck, and August sucked in a breath hungrily as they were once again swept up by the passing storm of the bustling New Dublin streets. He twisted amongst the throng, eyeing up every sign and storefront he could find, "Any idea where we are right now?" he asked.

Ollie focused his attention on the sign closest to them, using his built-in iris camera to capture an image that he could compare to other results online, "Lower East Quarter," he answered. He turned and pointed down a road to their right, "The nearest Gardi station is this way. We need to hurry."

"You don't need ta tell me twice," August said.

A woman's petrified cry tore their attention back to the paths behind them as the figures of two Androids burst through the crowds. Their weapons were held up over the heads of the people around them. They were taller than most of the city's human population, well over six and a half feet in height, and moved with a weight that wasn't entirely in relation to the materials they had been constructed with. Several Social Droids belonging to members of the public stood aside obediently to clear a path for their advance, their eyes glowing as the orders of the new machines took precedence over any of the commands given by their human owners. Ollie felt a thrill run up his spine as a message appeared in luminous red across his HUD.

@SecDroid45: Runner Droid 01113. Remain where you are.
@SecDroid45: The human must be returned to Crossroads.
@SecDroid45: Failure to comply will result in immediate termination.

He felt as though the text were forcing itself in front of his eyes, the command as visceral as a shout. He swallowed, pushing down the preconstructed urge to stand and wait.

"No!" he hollered aloud, the word launching itself from his mouth like a banshee's cry. He reached out and grabbed onto August, half-scooping him into his own arms, and finally did what he was made to do.

He began to run.

The loud pounding of syncopated dance music spilled out into the overflowing streets, the cacophony of conversation barely even a distraction as Ollie mapped out their course for them. He ducked and weaved his way through the shoppers, calculating the routes long before August's brain could even process the information he was seeing in front of him.

Ollie could feel the solid carbon pistons in his new leg beginning to shift and pump, could feel the moment the fans in his chest started spinning to force out the used, hot air from his chest cavity. His eyes lit up and he spoke with a clear, even voice as the built in phoneline connected him to the local Gardi station: "Hello, this is Android ID 01113 calling on behalf of Mr. Augustus Jackson. We are currently en route to your position and are being pursued by several Android suspects. I believe them to be armed and pose a threat to my human companion. We are requesting immediate assistance to our location."

"Damn, you're handy to have around," August remarked breathlessly by his ear as he ended the call.

The lines marking out their route appeared stark white in Ollie's field of vision and the Android took several corners at speed, lifting his companion almost completely off his feet as he struggled to keep up with the ever-increasing pace.

Smoke billowed around them as they pulled back out onto the main street again, their vision blurring as they were enveloped in the cover of the oncoming gas. The shadowy figures of several armed officers appeared at their sides, moving past them as they were pulled into the cover of an idling vehicle.

"Keep your head low," came a woman's loud voice from somewhere over them, "We've got you."

The familiar ping of bullets erupted over the top of the car and August swore colourfully as he pulled Ollie down flat against the upholstery. A gun cocked next to them as an Android officer in a blue uniform stepped in to block them from view, a large, metal shield secured to their extended arm.

The face of a woman appeared at the far side of the jeep, and she slammed the door shut, bolting it closed as she leaned out the passenger side window, "Goose!" she hollered, "Push them back while we get them inside!"

The Android nodded, affirming, "Yes, ma'am," as it moved out of the way of their vehicle.

The human officer slipped into the driver's seat again, pulling off her hat and tossing it onto the seat beside her, "It's a good thing your Android called us," she said, "Another few minutes and there wouldn't have been anything left of you two to find."

August finally sat back against the chair as the car began to speed away from the scene, his breaths coming heavy and fast. He held up one hand in front of his face and watched as his fingers trembled, "Jesus Christ."

"Are you alright?" Ollie asked, moving up from the floor space to flop into the seat next to him.

His human companion offered him a tired smile, "That's the most exciting Wednesday I think I've ever had," he commented, exhaling a relieved laugh. Some of the tension began to fall away from his shoulders and Ollie smiled, feeling some of the heaviness falling away from him as well.

"Me too," he agreed and allowed his eyes to fall closed as he listened to his own fans whirl, "Me too."

CHAPTER 7
File-Sharing

The neon checkered Garda car rolled to a stop outside the station and August peered out the window to his left, feeling an anxious build-up of energy in his chest as the officer reached down to tug on the handle to his door.
He ducked his head low as he slipped out of the backseat, Ollie quickly following at his shoulder. The tall, metal gates fell closed behind them with a rusty rattle, red lights flashing out warnings as the barricades rose up from the tarmac again to seal off the road. The sound of it felt oppressive, closing in on him from all sides, and August had to swallow his nerves before they would get the best of him. Last time he was in a place like this had been for the very worst reasons.
Next to him, Ollie had fallen into a polite, professional stance, with his hands folded neatly at his lower back. His bright, curious eyes were mapping out every inch of

their surroundings, following the movements of several of the other officers on staff as they passed them by.

The officer who had driven them there whistled and waved a hand to get their attention, beckoning them inside after her, "Alright you two," she barked, "Fall in." August chuckled at the immediate change in Ollie's expression, the man resembled an excited terrier as he hopped along beside him. August shoved both of his hands into his trouser pockets and nodded after the dark-skinned woman as she headed into the station's waiting room, "'Mon then," he said, "Lets not keep them waiting, Ols."

The woman in navy and neon yellow knocked on the window just inside the front door, summoning the receptionist with a cocky smirk, "Wade," she bellowed, "Is interrogation room 3 still free? Gotta borrow it a sec."

The man they assumed was named Wade spun a complete 360 degrees in his office chair before fingering at the paper document he had secured to the wall above his shoulder. He tutted to himself, narrowing his eyes as he tried to decipher the mess of handwritten scribbles there, "Mornin' Micky. Aye, still free. But Mr Sullivan's attorney will be by at 5ish, looks like. You be done by then?"

She twisted at the hip to look back in August's general direction, "Shouldn't take too long, this," she answered, "Gimme a shout if the lawyer comes early. I definitely want front row seats to *that* shouting match."

Wade gave her a playful grin that made his thick, misaligned moustache wriggle, "Oh I'm sure you'll hear it from down the hall. Peter Berry's been practising his vocals all morning."

The female officer, Micky, returned his quiet laugh as she knocked on the glass again, "Little does he know that I have too," she returned playfully, "I'm still full of adrenaline from getting' shot at."

She took a few steps past the window to the sealed doors of the precinct and held up her badge, scanning it quickly to open the way for them. She looked back over one shoulder with dark, hazelnut-coloured eyes, "Okay *Big Red*, you follow me on through. Leave your robot here 'till we're done."

August slowed to a stop, glancing back towards the doors they had come through. There, just to the right of it, was a closed in space where several other Androids were standing in a line. Their expressions were empty as they stared down at their feet. Cables glistened in the back of their necks as they charged themselves from the connectors in the wall. Ollie eyed the mechanical strangers with a concerned frown.

August folded his thick arms across his chest, "No way am I leaving him out here." Micky hovered in the doorway, slipping her badge back onto her belt again, "There's a stand for them right there," she sniffed, "You really think someone's gonna steal it from a Garda station?"

"That isn't where my head's at," August huffed, his dark eyes catching those of the man beside him for a moment, "Look, those people were after *both* of us back there. Either we both go, or none of us do."

The officer directed an exaggerated eye-roll towards the ceiling, letting out a rough-sounding chuckle, "Fine," she relented, "But it can get its own coffee in that case."

August grinned as he followed her, Ollie sticking to his side nervously as they walked. The blue lights of his eyes lit up the corridor they travelled down, the halos of his irises catching on the passing windows and metal accents of the picture frames. They passed several other officers in matching blue and yellow uniforms, and each of them turned to watch their journey with enquiring eyes.

Micky rounded a corner as she gathered her dark hair into a ponytail, looping the tie around the centre of it to hold it in place. She held open the next door with the heel of her boot and nodded her head towards the table and chairs inside, "Take a seat for me, Mr Jackson."

August and Ollie filed into the room past her, the red-head yanking the chair out from its place in against the table before folding into it heavily. Ollie ignored the seat beside him, choosing instead to come to rest against the western wall, leaning back against it as if for support or physical reassurance.

Micky joined them by taking the seat opposite August, resting her elbows on the stainless-steel tabletop as she observed him with a hum.

"All comfy?" she asked, arching a dark eyebrow at him with a smile that seemed a little juvenile for her face.

August leaned back in the chair, trying not to pull a face at her tone. He never much cared for law enforcement these days. "Perfectly. *Gártha.*"

"Alrighty. I'm Inspector Michael O'Sullivan and I'll be interviewing you today." The woman sucked on her teeth, clearly a force of habit, "How's about we start with some warm-up questions? Get you in the mood to talk?"

"Who says I'm not in the mood to talk?" August asked.

A smile curled up on the corner of her lips like a cat in the firelight, "Okay then, lets start with this one. Do you maybe want to explain to me what you're doing in the company of a Crossroads' Runner Droid, smelling like you've been living in the sewars for a week?"

The two men exchanged a look and August reached up to run a hand through his shoulder-length hair. Who knew what shape it was currently in? He hadn't seen a mirror in hours. He heaved a sigh; at least it was dry.

"Shouldn't you be focusing your attention on something a bit more important?" he muttered, brows furrowing, "Like, maybe, why those Droids were chasing us in the first bloody place?"

Inspector O'Sullivan clasped her hands together patiently as she studied his expression, "As I said, Mr. Jackson, warm-up questions first."

Ollie shifted uncomfortably where he was standing, straightening up immediately when the other human in the room looked his way. He was different here, under her watchful eyes. Like he was trying to act like the machine she expected him to be.

"Ollie was the one that helped me get away from the Hornets back there," August explained, following her eyes as she took in the Android's appearance,

"Unfortunately, that involved a little cross-country detour through the old ruins." He shrugged, leaning back in his chair so that it rocked onto two legs, "Luckily I don't even smell it anymore."

The officer waved a hand in the air in front of her nose, "Nice for some," she remarked.

August's smile only grew at her discomfort, "It was your idea to bring us back here. I would've been happy enough to talk in a room with a bit more ventilation." He allowed the chair's front legs to touch back onto the tiles again, "After all, *we're* the victims here."

Reaching below the desk, the Inspector produced a sheet of paper that she slid across the table towards him, "The company is alleging that you have obtained stolen property through *illicit* means," she stated, hazel eyes meeting his, "We were emailed in this report shortly before your Android placed the call. We already had officers on the streets searching for you both."

"Stolen property?" August scoffed, leaning forward to examine the paperwork. He scowled; the tiny text was not something he was going to be able to read without his lenses. "You can't be fuckin' serious! Their Droids attacked *us*! They were armed!"

The brunette woman sat back in her own seat, peering up at the Android next to them through the veil of her neat fringe, "And I suppose you're gonna tell me that you just *found* this Runner Droid *lying around*?"

August stared at her for a moment, balling his hands into two fists on the surface of the table as he chewed on the inside of his cheek, "Look, do I gotta spell it out for you here? Ollie saved me from those guys. And then they fired on him too! They weren't exactly going easy with those rifles of theirs."

Micky drummed her short nails on the metal table before her, "Alright, assuming I believe you, what reason would the company have for sending the Hornets after you?"

August let out the breath he had been holding since they arrived, "I received an email this morning."

"An…email?" The officer's expression had softened into one of curiosity now.

August nodded, "It was an internal email, sent from one of the other floors. There was a video attached that showed the destruction of a sentient Android." He could feel his heart going a mile a minute in his chest and the feeling was getting hard to ignore. "Going by the weird sending address, I'm guessing that the Android forwarded it to me directly. Not sure why, maybe just a Hail Mary."

Something in Officer O'Sullivan's body language changed the moment the words caught up with her, "Are you telling me…?"

"Mr. Jackson believes that there was enough evidence to suggest that the Android in question passed the Turing Test," Ollie confirmed from his place at the wall, "As a former Robotics Technician with Crossroads, he would be in such a position to confirm this theory."

The dark-skinned woman swore as she rose abruptly from her seat, its feet screaming as it scraped loudly across the vinyl flooring. She muttered softly to herself as she headed towards the door, pushing down on one of the coloured buzzers she found there. A hiss resounded from the intercom, and she brought her face in close to it before asking, "Hey Wade, is Elderich still on shift? Tell him I need him in room 3."

She returned to the table again as the buzzer went off behind her, the door opening inwards to reveal a tall, black-haired man in his mid-fifties. Patrick Elderich cleared the room in three large steps, bringing his hands down onto the table and staring across as the startled red-head. "What's this about Micks?" he questioned with a deep frown that seemed to alter the shape of his entire face. He resembled a wolf in a suit, his green eyes hungry and a little wild, "I was *finally* making some progress next door."

The well-dressed man moved aside for his Inspector, watching her as she reached up to tug on her ponytail, checking its fixture. "Forget O'Hara," she said, shooting him with an excited grin, "I've just found us another witness in the Devil's case."

Elderich turned his attention towards August again, his eyes brightening with eagerness, "No shit?"

"Uh, wanna fill us in here?" August interjected, pulling back slightly from the other officer's orbit.

"Quid pro quo, Mr. Jackson," Micky replied, "You tell us what you know, and we'll fill in the gaps for you."

August exhaled an amused breath through his nose, "I didn't realise we were already at negotiatin' stage here."

"Someone's got a right chip on his shoulder," Elderich commented airily, making a face at him.

"*Someone's* had experience with your lot in the past," August countered defensively, "*Bad* experience. So, excuse me if I'm hesitant to jump in with both feet tied."

"August."

Ollie's soft voice appeared from next to his shoulder. August looked up at him in surprise; he hadn't even noticed him move from the wall.

"We need to tell them everything," he urged, "It's vital that this is investigated."

"Yeah, listen to the nice, little robot, Red," Elderich sneered, his Belfast accent coming on stronger when he did so, "We're all *muckers* here, aren't we?"

"You're lucky Ollie's so friendly," August grumbled, glowering back at him, "Because if it were up to me, I'd just be telling you where to stick it."

Micky O'Sullivan stepped around the edge of the table, putting a hand on Elderich's chest to force him back by a few inches, perching on the corner of the table to take up the space that he had previously occupied, "Ignore him," she said, "He's showing his teeth, but really he's just trying to cover up how much his tail is wagging back here."

At Elderich's annoyed rebuttal, August commenced with his story, leaning back to include Ollie in the conversation, "It's hard to know where exactly to start here. I barely had the chance to watch the whole video before I had Crossroads' management coming down to bite my ass. Mr sharp suit and his twin arseholes chased me out the emergency exit and I headed straight for the ruins under the Crossroads office. I came out at the corner of Essex Street and Temple Lane."

"And that's where you met the Android, that right?" Micky questioned, making a note on a small pad of paper by her hip.

"You could say *met* but it was more like *ran into*," August continued, "When the Hornets started firing, they didn't seem to care which of us they hit, so the two of us decided to get the Hell out of dodge."

The Inspector nodded thoughtfully, narrowing her eyes as she brought her attention to the man behind him, "Android," she barked, "What is your serial number and rank?"

August twisted in his chair to regard his companion, noting the subtle changes he was beginning to recognise in his facial expressions. The Android was hiding further and further inside his mask every time this woman spoke to him.

"I am a Runner Droid. Transport model 01113. Central Quarter," he listed obediently, standing at attention like a well-trained soldier.

Micky slid off the table again, allowing her feet to touch down on the floor before she approached. She eyed the Android with suspicion, making note of his sweet face and passive expression. The small freckles imprinted across his nose and under his eyes were certainly a nice touch. They made him appear younger than his face would have otherwise suggested. More approachable.

"What were you transporting, 01113?" she pressed.

Ollie's blue eyes darted towards August for a fraction of a section before locking back on hers again, "I was charged with transporting various Android components, including several Soul Chips, for private distribution."

The woman's mouth fell open at that and she glanced back at Elderich as the man practically clambered out of his chair to stand beside her. His green eyes widened as he reached out to grab at Ollie's arm, "That's amazing! Android, do you still have your cargo on your person?"

"His name's Ollie. And I'm pretty sure he wouldn't appreciate you grabbing at him like that."

Elderich pulled his hand away with a confused look, "What?"

August met his eyes evenly, "His name's *Ollie*. Not *Android*. And you should learn to keep your grubby mitts to yourself."

The dark-haired man let out a sarcastic laugh, practically doubling over himself, "You've known it for like an *hour* and you've already *named* the damn thing?" he sniggered, "Alright then, *Ollie dearest*, do you still have the chips on you or not?"
Ignoring the inflection in the man's tone, Ollie instead reached into the back of his damp, yellow jacket and pulled the zip on his pocket to one side. His fingers slipped into the narrow opening, and he pulled out three small chips wrapped in see-through plastic. He placed them down onto the tabletop and Elderich practically pounced on them, lifting them up to the light with a wide smile. Their diamond coating sparkled in his fingers.
"Hoh-lee shit," he breathed, angling his shoulders so that his partner could see the objects in his outstretched hands, "These things look like the real deal, Mick."
"Is Goose back yet?" Micky asked as she pulled away again.
"The long-haired unit you use? Yet it arrived back about ten minutes ago," her partner answered, "Think it was hanging by the cloak room with the other Droids."
"Can you go grab it for me?" Micky continued, "I need it to run a scan on these."
"On my way, Inspector." Elderich gave her a mocking salute as he pressed the buzzer and hurried out into the dim corridor beyond.
When the door closed again behind him, she leaned forward to pick one of the other chips up off the table, turning it this way and that in the air, "If we can just open up *one* of these things before the trial, then we can nail the bastard," she whispered, "Crossroad's *Diabhal* is notoriously careful about letting these chips out of his sight. More than likely, he's already sent the kill codes out. But just having the physical components here is a great start."
August knew how those kill codes worked all too well. Much of the technology surrounding them was automated, the objects becoming little more than pretty paperweights by the time their handler even went a teensy bit off course. The data inside was probably already trapped behind a secure, and very effective, firewall.
"So, what, you saying you guys believe us now?" August piped up, waving his hand in her direction.
"A little bit of hard proof goes a long, long way Mr. Jackson," Micky affirmed, turning when the door opened behind her to let Elderich and the tall Android model through.
"That's the model from the Western Quarter," he heard Ollie say quietly over his shoulder.

The Android took in the room with dark blue eyes that were almost grey, its long blond hair fluttering around it as it moved its head. It wore the uniform of a standard Garda Officer with its serial number written along the front like Ollie's had been. A dress hat rested neatly over the line of its forehead. Its expression was the same calm, almost unreadable mask that he had seen Ollie wear several times over the last few hours. He was starting to wonder if it was just *'resting Android face'*.

As it joined Micky at the table, the woman placed the three chips into its outstretched hand, "I need you to run these; see if there's any data left that we can salvage."

It cocked its head, slotting the chips into the reader on its neck without question. Its eyes began to glow in the same cerulean shade as Ollie's, its pupils moving back and forth as if it were reading something on the air. The flat line of its mouth deepened into an obvious frown as it reached back to remove the chips, handing them off to the officer beside it.

"Two of the chips appear to be badly water-damaged," it observed, "The third, however, seems to be fully operational, although a firewall has been erected to prevent public access to the data inside."

"Fuck," Micky groaned, kicking one of the table legs in frustration, "I bloody knew it! Sly bugger!"

Elderich let out a sigh, running a hand back and forth across the top of his head, "It's not nothing though, Mick. We've never had access to an unused chip before. This…this could *be* something."

"It's not enough to pin this prick though," Micky growled, pacing back and forth in the space just in front of August and Ollie, "*Months* of ball scratching and this is as far as we've gotten! He's always just one *toe* ahead!" She let out a childish bark of annoyance, "You two are lucky you even *made* it here! With something like this with you? They would have killed you both, no question."

"We have about 30 other witnesses waiting to stand trial," Elderich started, tapping one foot on the ground as if trying to filter all of his anxious energy through the motion, "They're scattered all around the country. This here…" He indicated the chips in front of him on the table, "This could *really* help. But we're gonna need your testimony to go along with it."

"Wait, wait, wait!" August shook his head frantically, "You want me to go to *court* with these things?" He pushed his chair out from the table and Ollie awkwardly staggered back behind him to create space, "Have you two lost your minds? Why the *Hell* would we put ourselves back in firing range again?"

The dark-haired Garda paced the room, further messing up his hair with the tips of his fingers, "Look, lad, there's no use us sugarcoating it at this point. Crossroads knows who you are. They know your face; they know where you live. At least if we add you to the trial docket we can place you in Witness Protection, house you somewhere across the country where he won't find you."

"And it won't be forever," Micky added quickly, "If we can just find someone who can break through the firewall and get to the information inside then Diabhal's as good as gone. Even the great Russell East can't stand up to scrutiny like that."

The Crossroad's Diabhal; Russell East. Even hearing the name aloud made something in August's gut churn. He was a slimy weasel of a man, bald-headed and as bold as a bear was strong. A right twat too, from what August had heard on the company grapevine. His arrogance was at the forefront of every conversation with the man. In the wise words of August's late Dubliner mother, *'if the fucker was chocolate he would'a ate himself'*.

Micky reached for a briefcase at her feet, unclipping it at the top and sides so that she could slip free some of the paperwork within it. She slid them across the table, turning them to face August who skimmed the information as best he could without the help of his usual lenses.

"All you've gotta do is sign here, Mr. Jackson and we'll get you relocated immediately," she stated, tapping a point towards the bottom of the page, "Our technical team here can handle the Android's disassembly, so you won't have to worry about-"

Ollie jumped, startled, as August's fist smashed down at the table, causing the papers and pens to shift from their previous places, "The fuck you will!" he argued, baring his teeth, "Have you not been listening to a bloody word I've said in here?"

Both officers exchanged a look at his response. The other Android's eyes widened ever-so-slightly; its head tilted towards the strange human with interest. Its hand was resting at its hip and Ollie scanned the other model cautiously, quickly spotting the loaded weapon concealed in the space beneath its palm. When no further orders followed the outburst, it slowly dropped its hand again.

"Ollie comes with me," August said firmly, moving to stand, "It was *my* fault he ended up in this mess in the first place. Last thing I'm gonna do is throw him under the bus."

Micky exhaled an amused chuckle, "As charming as your attitude is, Mr. Jackson, it isn't a person. It's a machine," she said, "Though I can see the appeal. A sweet face like that really draws you in."

"This isn't about how he *looks*," August carried on incredulously, feeling heat gathering around his throat at the insinuation.

'Look at the little faggot. Gonna make him cry. Wonder what they did to make him turn out like that?' a child-like voice in the back of his head taunted. He swallowed down that old, familiar pain for another day. Always another day.

He cleared his throat again as he stood up tall, "Ollie's got as much right to protection as I do. If I go, he goes. That's the end of it."

Elderich pinched the bridge of his nose, "You can't be serious, mate. He has tracking software installed. The company will-"

"Then fucking remove it," August snapped, making a rude gesture in his direction. Ollie's scan showed the man's elevated stress levels and heart rate and when he looked at his face, he could see the way that the anger had completely changed his complexion.

//I don't understand. Why is he fighting so hard for me?

"You'd have to block its access to the internet, its ability to download new updates," the male officer rambled, clearly agitated, "You're asking us to turn a million-euro piece of equipment into a glorified paperweight."

August raised his hand to offer the man another not-so-kind gesture, "Do I look like I give a shit how you manage it?" he growled, "Ollie doesn't need any of that fancy crap to get by. And if you call him an *it* one more time, I swear to Christ I'll feed you that godawful tie of yours."

The sound of Micky's loud laughter surprised him and the men both turned to watch her as she swiped at her eyes, "I don't think I've ever seen someone else as hard-headed as Elderich is," she commented fondly, bending low to fish in the bag under the table again, adding further pieces of paperwork to the pile on the table, "Fine, have it your way then, Red. Both of you sign here at the bottom."

The Android, which had been officially dubbed *'Goose'* judging by its lapel, raised its head to meet Ollie's eyes. It angled itself to one side to regard him silently, the tight curls shifting over the shoulders of its baby blue uniform.

August lifted one of the ballpoint pens and scribbled his name on both sheets of paper, barely glancing at the smaller words that he knew he was never going to manage to read. Micky tapped her fingertip loudly on the table, smiling up at Ollie, "You too, Android."

Ollie hovered at the table, his hand hesitating as August extended the pen out towards him. It was clear in the way that he gripped the tool awkwardly between his fingers that he had never so much as held one before. His eyes began to glow as he ran a quick internet search, adjusting the position of his fingers according to what he found. He paused again when he placed the nib of the pen down against the paper.

"I…I don't have a signature," he admitted quietly, looking to August like a man that was completely lost, "What exactly should I be writing?"

August pushed his own page closer, "Take a look at mine, *duine*. You're just scribbling your name, is all."

Ollie nodded in understanding, penning his serial number on the bottom of the page in perfect, numerical detail. It was hard to believe that the writing had been done by hand, the script flawless and symmetrical, like it had been stamped there. He laid the pen back down again like it might bite him, moving clear of the table.

"Alrighty, you've got our John Hancocks, now what?" August asked as Micky carefully folded the pages back into the briefcase at her feet again.

"Goose here will escort you both out to the courtyard. You can grab a bite to eat and some fresh air before we begin processing."

The Android had already moved towards the door and was standing there quietly as the buzzer released them out into the hallway again.

"Please, follow me," it said. Its voice was soft, feminine, and almost warm, despite its otherwise chilly appearance.

New folder created: Android ID 60053
createFolder ['name'] = 'Goose';
Adding information: gender identity: [f]

The pair followed her down the narrow corridor, watching each of the steely movements of her back at she plotted their course. Unlike Ollie, she moved in a way that was rigid and unnatural, as if there was a metal rod in her spine.
There probably is, to be fair, August mused inwardly.
She took a sharp left in the same way a Formula 1 car might, clearing the wall without wasting any space, and barely spared them a glance as she carried on

down the next lit passageway. The greying paint was peeling off the walls on either side of them, the signage worn and in need of a touch-up. They passed by a row of closed doors and came to a stop at a set of red double-doors that ended the corridor. The Android raised her hands mechanically, pushing them apart in a way that appeared automatic.

"I will wait for you here," Goose stated, turning to bring her back in against the wall. Despite the change in position, she did not relax her posture one iota.

"Uh, sure thing," August replied uncertainly, passing by her to escape into the fresh air of the courtyard at the station's centre, "You coming, Ols?"

He made a note of Ollie's affirming hum, sensing the man moving at his back as he walked.

The courtyard was encompassed on all sides by high, red-brick walls, and doors leading out into various other parts of the station. A chalk-white wall split the centre of the enclosure in two, with dark wooden benches lining one side. Posters for various support groups had been secured onto the walls with thick plastic frames, the outside panels of them wet with spittles of recent rain. A red vending machine stood nestled in against the far wall, as if huddling for warmth, and August approached it and input his order. He waved his broken phone screen in front of the panel that asked for payment and a cardboard box of cigarettes was tipped down into the waiting metal tray for him. He groaned as he reached down to pick them up, flicking the top open with his thumb as he gripped one of the cigarettes lightly between his teeth.

He patted the back pockets of his damp work trousers with a frustrated grunt, spinning in place, "Gah! Bloody lost it!" he mumbled, the white stick of paper wagging in the corner of his lips, "Don't suppose you're one of the models fitted with a lighter, are ya, *duine*?"

Ollie closed the space between them wordlessly, raising up the index finger on his right hand to brush against the end of the cigarette. With a small, almost imperceptible click, he produced a tiny blue flame from the space between his finger and his nail.

August took a grateful puff as the end of the cigarette glowed orange, sending warm light flickering up his face, "Neat trick. Thanks, kiddo."

Ollie extinguished the little flame and wrinkled his nose, "Don't call me kiddo," he rebuked and with a curt sniff observed, "Those things are bad for you, you know."

"Aye, I'll make a note of that *Mammy*," the red-head droned good-naturedly as he took another drag, blowing the smoke out and away from his companion. He could already feel the nicotine hitting his bloodstream and reviving him a little, "Can Androids even smell this shit?"

"We have sensors that replicate the sensations of sight, sound, taste, smell and touch," Ollie answered, making a face as he took a step away from the haze around the other man, "I could tell you every ingredient pouring out of your lungs right now."

August waved a hand dismissively, leaning back against the side of the vending machine as he added, "So can the back of the box."

Ollie let out a soft exhale as he took a seat on one of the benches nearby. Both of his hands fell neatly on top of his slender thighs as he leaned back to look up at the sky overhead, "You didn't have to do that back there."

August exhaled another long, smoky breath, "Do what?" He tapped the cigarette with the pad of his thumb, scattering ashes around his already filthy shoes.

Ollie brought his head back down again, levelling his bright eyes at him, "They would have taken me apart. Used me for my components…" He hesitated; the memory of those huge, white warehouse cranes filling his mind. He eliminated that thought as quickly as he could. That information was uncomfortable to access.

August's eyes raked over him, holding the contact. They were so human, so unlike his own. Warm and rich like coffee as opposed to his which were like cold steel.

"I said it before and I'll say it again, *duine*. You wouldn't be in this mess at all if it weren't for me. I'm not gonna let them kill you. You didn't do a damn thing wrong."

Ollie severed the eye contact first, his gaze dropping towards the gravel by his feet, "Why do you call me that?"

August frowned, "What?"

"*Duine*," Ollie answered softly, "I know what it means. My translation software told me." He lifted his eyes again, "But why call me that?"

"It's a reminder," August stated, chewing on the cigarette as it neared its end.

"A reminder for who?" the Android probed. He could feel some of his curls falling loose as he tilted his head to the side to observe him.

"For both of us. The second I start treating you like a machine I'm no better than those other arseholes." He shuffled in place, letting out a sound of discomfort as the cold wind ruffled through his shirt, "I'm a technician. I've *seen* your code. But you're…*different*, Ollie."

"That doesn't mean that I'm alive, August," Ollie countered.

"Doesn't mean you're not though, does it?"

The human gave him a knowing look, chuckling in that low, deep voice of his, rough from cigarette smoke that only accentuated his southern accent.

The fans at the bottom of Ollie's throat spun when he tried to replicate the sound, "Thank you," he said quietly.

August took one, final drag from the cigarette before extinguishing the butt of it on the side of the vending machine, taking some spiteful pleasure in marking the obviously new steel, "Whatever happens after this, I hope you and I can be friends, Ollie."

Ollie felt his core fill with warmth, and he reached up to skim his fingertips over his chest, scanning for abnormalities in his systems. Something about this man made him perceive himself as something different, as if, in these last few hours, something in him had begun to change as well. It was easy to forget, for a few blissful minutes, that he was so different from August. That he was a machine designed to run beneath these bustling city streets and not up here with the sun and the warm breeze and the sound of seagulls and children's laughter.

His mind buzzed with new information and possibilities and at the centre of it all was this grumpy, red-headed Crossroads technician that apparently saw more in him than even he himself did.

He felt something bubbling up his throat, a smile that he didn't have the power to stop, and the expression moved to overtake his whole face.

There was something new there but also something beyond familiar, an itch like déjà vu in the back of his mind that he couldn't quite scratch.

"I trust you," he realised as the man turned to go back inside.

He placed a hand over his chest again, imagining that it was a very human heart that he could feel racing there.

Chapter 8
Clean Boot

Michael O'Sullivan raised her head from her task as August and Ollie joined them in the next room over. Her hands were mapping out the various objects in front of her with meticulous purpose, cataloguing their unique item IDs on the tablet in her other hand.
"We've brought in some extra clothes for your Android, Mr.Jackson," she said, then sweeping a hand over one of the neat piles, "Nothing too flashy, just some of the pieces we had available from the Social Droid range."
August edged closer, looking down at the various bagged-and-tagged items of of clothing. They must have had them on hand in the evidence locker or something, "Wish you'd quit callin' him *my* Android," he muttered with distaste, picking up one of the pairs of trousers and turning it over in his hand.

"For all intents and purposes, Red, he *is* your Android," Micky countered, turning around to face him and leaning back against the table, "We can't just let an unregistered Android walk out of here on its own."

Elderich passed by them and made a face as he pulled out one of the packages free from the stacked pile, "I hope your buddy there likes the colour pink," he commented, "Apparently it's the hottest colour this year." August grimaced as the other man unwrapped the plastic. The shirt was the colour of half-chewed bubblegum.

"Better you than me, Ols," he commented.

The Android stared at the fabric like it might rear up and bite him, "That's...not a colour I've ever seen before."

"According to the label it's called '*Lavender Rose*'," Micky contributed, with a snort of barely contained amusement, "Not a lot of people can pull off a colour like that."

"I doubt I'll be one of them," Ollie remarked quietly by August's side.

August chuckled softly and shook his head, "The first thing you ever have an opinion on, and it's the world's ugliest shirt."

"Elderich," Micky called, lifting her small tablet off the counter to type onto it again with one hand, "Think you can grab the rest of the kit from Processing while I handle this?"

"Sure thing, Inspector," he responded with a grin, tossing the shirt back down next to them, "On my way."

As the door closed somewhere across the large room, Ollie stared down at the filthy mess of his Runner Droid uniform, only now having started to dry. These clothes were all that he had ever known. The material was as familiar as his own skin and the numbers on his chest, which August had mistakenly assumed was his name, was the only sense of identity he had ever had to call his own. A sad smile played on his lips at the idea of giving that up.

Giving the old him up.

Elderich re-entered with a pneumatic hiss, carrying a series of flat packages in his arms. Bright white printed labels covered the otherwise non-descript cardboard sides.

"Got what you asked for Micks," he said, "You need me to call one of the boys in to handle the ID work?"

Officer O'Sullivan laid the tablet back down again, a clear loading bar spreading from one side of the screen to the other, "Don't worry, it's been a while, but I still remember how."

Moving to stand in front of one of the boxes that Elderich had laid down, she peeled open the corner with a look of concentration on her face, "You worked in IT, Mr. Jackson. Tell me, do you recognise this little gadget?"

The device was grey with sharp, metal teeth along the side. It didn't look that different from a common staple remover. August held out his hand towards her, "It's for removing the biometric chips, right?"

"Ten points to Team Red," she smiled, cupping the bottom of his hand with hers, "You might want to look away if you're squeamish."

August let out a short exhale through his nose, "I used to have to do this for boys who stood too close to the company microwave," he replied, "Work away."

"3…2…" Micky counted down quietly. Whether it was for his benefit or her own, he wasn't sure. She dipped the thin blade into the space between his thumb and index finger when she reached *1* and the man let out a hiss of pain, chewing on the corner of his lip as the tiny chip bubbled up to the surface of his skin on his blood. Micky moved her other hand in to pull it free.

"Such a little thing, she said, "But it can cause so much bother."

August let out a gasp of surprise as Ollie appeared next to him, taking his hand, and placing a round piece of cotton wool over the wound. He taped it in place, pressing down firmly, "It will probably bleed for a little while," he said by way of an explanation.

The red-haired man cleared his throat, clearly taken off guard, "Er, uh, thanks, Ols. 'preciate it."

Micky placed the utensil back in its box to be cleaned, her dark eyes glancing Ollie's way, "Your turn next, little robot. Can I see your collar, please?"

Ollie nodded and turned his back to her, releasing his hold on August's hand to push the back of his dark hair out of the way. The collar around his neck dimmed as the officer reached out to draw her fingers along the smooth metal. A small compartment opened where she applied pressure. August watched as she revealed the intricate circuitry inside, slipping her fingers into the narrow opening. As she twisted the digits to one side, Ollie let out a soft sigh, sinking forward. Her other arm sprung out immediately to catch him, like she had been expecting it.

August bent forward to look at the Android's face. He had closed his eyes, his lips turning downwards in a thoughtful frown. The red-head brought a hand out to touch him and was surprised to find his body growing hot.

"Did you…turn him off or something?"

With her other hand, Micky reached up to slide a new, bright chip into the slot on Ollie's neck. A flicker of blue light pulsed against her fingers as it disappeared inside, "He'll have to do a reboot to apply all the new updates we're giving him. Just give him a second."

The blue collar began to flicker with randomised sequences of code, a progress bar filling up and then disappearing barely a second later. The word 'ANDROID' flashed up again in dark letters, settling back into its usual place again as Ollie's eyes peeled open.

He straightened as Micky pulled back her arms and he blinked back at her with a somewhat sleepy expression. His brows furrowed as if he were trying to make sense of his new updates. The previous glow of his eyes had dimmed dramatically, making him appear almost entirely human, if it hadn't been for the collar still wrapped around his neck.

Opening the other metal box on the table, Micky reached for Ollie's hand and placed the metal handle of the handgun firmly against his palm.

"Android 01113," she stated, "Register weapon."

Ollie's HUD filled with red light as he closed his fingers around the hilt and brought it in closer to his body.

New Objective found: > 'Protect objectName';
objectName: 'augustusJackson';
Protect augustusJackson;
Targeting software exe. Defensive protocols; PERMISSION GRANTED

"Wait, wait, wait," August started, rushing in to grab at the Android's wrist, "Isn't it illegal for an Android to handle firearms like this?"

Sergeant Patrick Elderich folded his arms across his chest where he leaned against the wall by the door, the buttons on his uniform glistening in the white lights overhead. He nodded his head towards the other Android in the room, the one affectionately named 'Goose' who hadn't moved more than two inches since they had re-entered the room, "Consider this…uh, a *special circumstance*," he said.

"It's much easier than trying to train a human on a time limit," Micky agreed, sending a fond grin towards her Android partner, "Goose here can outshoot any other marksman on the force. Myself included."

Goose nodded back at her in thanks. A small smile quirked up on the corner of her lips.

"How are you feeling, *duine*?" August asked, patting Ollie's bicep. He could feel the synthetic muscles flex beneath his shirt as he moved.

Ollie raised a hand to brush against his collarbone thoughtfully, "I'm fine…I think?" he said, "I don't *feel* any different."

"It may take a little time to adjust," Micky added, her smile sympathetic as she studied his face, "You will no longer have access to your usual tools. Only approved Social Droid software."

Goose materialised beside them without a word. She extended an arm out towards her fellow Android, the limb ladened with several new items of clothing for him to take.

"The measurements may not be exact to your make or model, but will be sufficient for the time being," she said, "I can help you change and make alterations as required."

The dark-haired Android ran a basic scan of the clothes to determine their materials. The t-shirt was a blend of American pima cotton and common polyester. The darker coloured work trousers were made of a strong denim twill weave cotton. He allowed himself a moment to run his thumb over the fabric in front of him.

"It's soft," he noted with surprise. It felt entirely different from the rough, almost plastic, feeling of his own office golds.

Goose tilted her head, brushing her hand over his gently. A flood of information was sent rushing through their connection; of making meals in a Garda station breakroom, of cleaning a window while the sun warmed her back, of sitting next to her partner while they patrolled around the City Centre. When they drew apart again, the Android was offering him a secretive smile, her stormy eyes alight as she whispered, "Welcome to the world, Social Droid 01113."

CHAPTER 9
Failed to Start

Ollie stepped over the threshold and into August's home nervously, trying to contain his curiousity as the red-headed man in question darted back and forth to snatch up his meagre belongings. The Android's eyes lit up as he scanned the hallways that his companion hurried down and took in the guards at the front entrance. He made a brief note of the various items that were left lying about the floor and coffee table with a frown. Half-empty bottles of liquor lay on their bellies and pizza boxes created towers on most of the counters, their contents stale to the point of rotting. The ashtray in front of the TV was overflowing with cigarette butts, the scent of it acrid and sharp even to Ollie's senses.

The dust that coated every possible surface suggested either that the man wasn't home very often or that he simply did not care about maintaining the place. Knowing where it was that August had worked before all this, Ollie assumed it was probably the former.

Unsure of what to do with himself, the Android turned to watch their police escorts as they crowded the door, the other plain-clothed operatives hanging about in various spots around the property. He wondered if anyone would really be fooled by their Hawaiian shirts and cargo shorts or if this was just another type of theatre for humans.

Inspector Michael O'Sullivan shoved her way through the amassing group and surveyed the state of the livingroom with a frown, "Yikes. Looks like I should've called in the bomb squad. This place is a right state."

Her Android partner, Goose, followed her into the space, narrowing her eyes as she nudged against a pizza box with the tips of her perfect nails, "I would not consider this a particularly wise diet for a man of Mr Jackson's age," she stated.

Ollie raised his head at the sound of the man's voice from further down the hall. He appeared to have said something along the lines of *'mind your own business.'* Though, Ollie was sure his choice of words were less polite than that.

"Goose, could you keep an eye on the door for us? Lets try and keep this foot traffic to a minimum," Micky ordered.

The blonde-haired Android's eyes flashed as she made a note of her orders, "Yes, ma'am," she replied, bowing her head politely in Ollie's direction before she headed outside again, chasing away some of the officers that were waiting between the house and their car.

When Ollie turned back from having watched her leaving, he noticed that the officer next to him was crouching down to size up the inside of his left calf, "I didn't realise you were damaged."

"A few of the Hornet's projectiles clipped me," he replied, trying his best to keep the information that he shared with her to a minimum, "But I was able to seek repairs."

She was proving to be a difficult person to get a read on. Despite her smiles and otherwise friendly banter with August, he knew that without the other man's intervention she would have terminated him without a second thought.

But August wasn't here right now, and she was still smiling. So, he would give her the benefit of the doubt for the moment.

"Mr Jackson paid for your repairs then?" Micky continued. She had moved on to inspect a very old mug of tea on the table, wrinkling her nose at the skim of congealed milk floating on top of it.

Ollie tried not to let his surprise at the question reflect in his response. "He did."

She hummed and straightened again, sticking both her hands in the pockets of her trousers, "Is that so?" she asked, though it wasn't really a question. Ollie was still getting used to how humans tended to talk to themselves around him. Hypotheticals were proving to be a little challenging to get his head around.

He watched as her dark eyes became fixed on her partner's back. A small, almost fond smile appeared on her lips. "You should go lend *Big Red* a hand with his packing," she said, barely looking his way before she was walking away again, "It might speed him up a bit."

She paused just inside the doorway and quickly added, "But try not to touch anything. You seriously stink right now."

Ollie blinked. That was yet another response he hadn't been expecting.

//I wonder if I will ever figure out people like her.

For a moment he didn't feel quite as out of place in August's house as he did before. No longer like a disused appliance, but just like the other strangers who had found themselves at his door. He had never been in something described as a *home* before. The memories of a human lifetime were spread out over the wall, knick-knacks and collectables from years of travel were stuck to the fridge or hanging from hooks. Photographs of strangers were arranged with care alongside children's drawings and letters. Each new discovery revealed a little bit more about who Augustus Jackson really was and Ollie compiled the data excitedly, ravenous to find out more about the human who had pulled him from the ruins.

The data felt like nourishment, feeding the Android's innate curiousity as he explored the building with new eyes. But for every question that he found answers to, a hundred more cropped up to take their place. The sea of colourful information was simultaneously overwhelming and not enough.

Adding information to folder: augustusJackson;

He followed the bones of the house, letting his hand trail over the edges of the sofa and the kitchen counter as he passed them by. Despite being all on a singular level, this was a house that had clearly been designed to hold more than one person.

//*Would a person not get lonely with all this space to themselves?* he wondered. There was no sign of pet dander to indicate that the man had had any animal companionship either. No charging points installed that suggested he had ever owned a Social Droid or a MaidBot(c).

Ollie hesitated when he reached the far side of the bungalow, watching August's shadow as it danced on the wall opposite the open doorway. He could hear the man bustling about just inside, swearing as he did battle with an unyielding zip on a suitcase. This next step felt like it was encroaching on more intimate territory than before. A bedroom was more than another room, it was a human's personal sanctum. A place not even friends were always welcome. He searched in his logs for what he should do next, wondering if he should turn and head back the way that he had come.

"That you I hear out there, *duine*?" August hollered from the master bedroom, "Mon in! I could use a hand with this. Stupid thing keeps sticking."

Ollie took a breath, although he didn't need one, and stepped in through the invisible wall towards the sound of the man's voice. August's bedroom was large and sparsely decorated with navy blue sheets and matching blackout curtains. A tall window peered in from between the gap in the middle, spilling light across the floor like liquid gold. A few empty photo frames were arranged on the dresser by the door and a lamp that was missing its shade was perched on the bedside table alongside an assortment of fiction books. Speckles of dust turned lazily in the air as August pressed his weight down onto the suitcase, practically snarling as he yanked on the metal zip pull. His hair was damp and curling around his face, freshly washed and smelling of something sandlewoody.

"There you are!" he elated as he looked up at him from the carpeted floor. There was a pair of round glasses perched on his nose that hadn't been there before. "I was worried you'd got lost."

Ollie shuffled in place, not quite sure what he was supposed to do with his hands, "Even without my software, I still have a pretty good sense of direction," he said, trying to play off his own nervousness.

August chuckled, moving his weight where he was kneeling over the half-closed case, "Don't suppose you have any *Bag Packing* skills in that new download of yours?" he asked, wiping sweat off the side of his face onto his shoulder, "This thing's as old as the hills and I'm pretty sure it's rusted up on me."

"Let me help," Ollie offered, and went down onto all fours to examine the problem. He traced a hand over the metal teeth, feeling out the different, misaligned grooves. "It's off to the left a little," he observed, "If you push it towards me, I can finish zipping it up for you."

"Thanks, Ols. You're a life saver," August breathed, pushing off the tips of his toes to move the heavy outer shell in his direction. Ollie watched as the muscles along the man's neck, arms and shoulders moved in sync with his actions, the strength there evident. Clearly August had done more in his years on earth than just sitting at an office desk.

Suddenly, without much room to prepare, those very dark, very human eyes became so very close to him, and Ollie felt heat rushing through his systems in response. The flow of his coolant increased, making the tips of his fingers shake whenever he was trying to use them.

He slid the metal tag the rest of the way home and he swallowed as he felt those eyes studying him, searching for something.

"August?" he breathed uncertainly.

The red-haired man pulled back and waved a hand in the air in front of him, letting out a playful bark, "Man, Ols, you seriously reek," he teased, "We need to get you in a bath right the Hell now. Or you might lead the Hornets right to us."

Ollie frowned, "Androids don't register smell the way that humans do, I highly doubt that they-"

August let out a sound somewhere between a laugh and sigh, shaking his head but not unkindly, "Do you always have to take the shit I say so literally?"

The Android pouted, seemingly a little offended by the comment, "You *do* realise that I wasn't designed as a social model," he pointed out, "There are lots of little nuances to the English language that I am not entirely familiar with yet."

"Well, have fun," he teased, "The Irish are pretty well known for our non-sensical idioms."

"Yeah, I'm starting to see that," Ollie replied with a playful lilt to his tone.

August eased slowly off the top of his case, watching it for any changes with every inch he wound back. When it was clear that it was not suddenly going to spring open and launch his belongings everywhere, he straightened out his back with a groan. He headed towards the door and knocked lightly on the frame with the knuckles of one hand, "Lemme show you where the bathroom is. You can get freshened up while I finish gathering all my shit together."

He headed across the hall and pulled open one of the doors, gathering thick, fluffy white towels into his arms and then forcing them onto his companion, "You head on in and I'll get Goose to drop your new gear outside for ya."

Ollie glanced around the white tiled room as August shoved open the door for him. It was by far the cleanest room in the entire house.

"Thank you," he said, trying not to let it show on his face that he had no idea what to do in a room like this one, "I will be out momentarily."

August ran a hand over the thick hair at the back of his head, the damp hair curling around his fingers. He averted his eyes, clearing his throat, "Just, uh, don't take all day, alright? I think Micky is about ten minutes away from just letting Crossroads take us."

Ollie's eyes widened in alarm, but August threw his hands up with an awkward laugh before he could say anything, "Just a joke!" he interjected, "Sorry, that was probably too soon for you, huh?"

The Android huffed out an artificial breath, feeling the tension in his pistons settling down again as he did so.

///*I am definitely going to need more practise with this,* he thought.

He closed the bathroom door over slowly, reaching down to twist the nub as per August's instructions. It locked with a satisfying *clunk*. It was peculiar the difference such a thing could make; he was used to being the one that was locked in, not the one locking the rest of the world out. Privacy was not something he had ever had to consider before today.

He met his own eyes in the small cabinet mirror above the sink and it startled him for a moment to be able to see his own face so clearly. There hadn't been mirrors for him to use in Crossroads, and the puddles in the ruins presented a reflection that had been blurry and unfocused. He studied his dishevelled appearance with inquisitive eyes, reaching up a hand to draw a line from his chin to his cheek and then up into his hair. The gel he applied most mornings was beginning to fall out, the sewer water having broken up the sticky structure of it, and the curls he fought with several days a week began to tumble out across his forehead. If he ignored his glowing blue eyes and the collar fastened around his slender neck, he could pretend that he was just another human, going about their usual morning ritual.

Speaking of which…He frowned as he took in the varied assortment of items arranged around August's sink. They were a clear reflection of the other man's daily habits. Beard oils were congregated by the taps, combs and brushes resting alongside them in various states of use. Nail clippers lay on their side like some sort of dead or dying animal and headache tablet foils were strewn about the part of the sink that attached it to the wall. More than a few of the pills were missing, taken from their packaging in seemingly random order.

He opened the cupboard overhead and his eyes lit up as he scanned each of the labels he found there. There were sleeping aids like *Temazepam*, antidepressants like *Sertraline*, Nicotine patches that had clearly been given up on, if August's habits in the last 24 hours were to be believed. The toothbrush looked in desperate need of a replacement, the bristles spiking out in all directions like an angry hedgehog.

He closed his eyes as he uncapped one of the oils, taking a tentative sniff of the contents. His HUD supplied him with a list of ingredients arranged alphabetically, the mixture a combination of natural and artificial elements. It was vaguely smoky, likely due to the amount of juniper tar it contained. He placed the little jar down again carefully, closing the cupboard door as he set to work.

Bright eyes focused their attention on the narrow, glass walls of the shower cubicle in the corner. He frowned. It was so different to the system used by Crossroads to clean their Androids, which, if he was honest, was more akin to a car wash than a bathing ritual. He reached within himself, the way that he always did when he was looking for answers, but with his Wi-Fi chip no longer functioning, that part of his mind came back blank. He let out a frustrated sigh and reached for the junction of his jacket, pulling the zip slowly downwards. With each inch of flesh exposed to the air, he felt his internal temperature dropping by several degrees. The sensors in his false skin provided him with the exact data as goosebumps rose up along his arms. He padded on bare feet towards the glass box and raised up one hand, eyes flashing for a moment as he attempted to interface with it. When he noticed the two primitive tabs set into the wall instead, he furrowed his brows. It was an extremely

dated model that required several dials to be turned in order to control the water pressure and temperature. Evidently, it was to be entirely controlled by hand.
//*That makes sense,* he mused, *August doesn't have any Chrome installed, after all.*
It was one of the first thing he had noticed about the man. Odd, for someone of his generation, especially considering the field that he worked in.
He twisted the nozzle until the water reached the optimum temperature to remove the stains on his chassis and then stepped under the spray.
A few moments later and he was pulling open the bathroom door again, the steam rushing out to mingle with the cooler air of the corridor. He bent to retrieve the clothes that had been left for him, pulling on the trousers first. He hopped as he slid them up to his hips, fastening them with the narrow black belt that had been provided. The hideous pink shirt followed, clinging to the spots on his person that he was still damp. Despite his initial reaction to the clothes, Ollie still found himself running a hand down one of the ¾-length sleeves with a smile, taking in the stitching on the fabric.
Tossing the used towel into the wash basket by the door, he made his way towards the muffled sound of August's voice in the livingroom, smiling when he greeted the man's back again.
"All finished, August," he chirped brightly, feeling every inch of his scalp and body tingling in a way that it never had before.
August turned to regard him, his current complaints dying on his lips as he took in his new appearance. He looked him up and down, letting out a quiet wolf whistle of admiration. "Well, *look* at you," he said, dark eyes twinkling, "Jesus, Ollie, I never would'a recognised you." He pointed towards the top of his own head, "That *hair* especially. Since when has it been so, uh…" He waved a hand in the air before Micky's voice broke through next to him.
"Curly?" she supplied.
"Yeah, that," August agreed with a low chuckle.
If Ollie had the ability to blush, he might have. His appearance, like that of all Android units, was dictated by a series of random number algorithms during their assembly. Every little detail, from the curling of his hair to the light-coloured freckles adorning his face, had been added to make him appear less '*uncanny valley*' and more '*I'm here to help*'. Without the use of the factory standard gel that Crossroads typically supplied, his dark hair curled wildly in all directions.

"It's always been curly," he replied.

"It suits you," August added, apparently not noticing the Android's rather bashful reaction to his previous statement.

Error: #52Aa detected
Recommending scan

Ollie pushed the notification away, feeling his chest buzz where his fans began to pick up speed. The sensation felt almost like it was his heart that was racing.

"Hard to believe that you're a Runner Droid," Micky commented thoughtfully, "You look like you belong in that uniform."

The pale pink shirt certainly brought out the more vibrant tones in his hair. Ollie had noticed that much when looking in August's bathroom mirror.

"You really think that's all it's gonna take to let him go about unnoticed?" August asked, propping the large travel bag up onto its back wheels. Ollie made a note of the picture frame that had been tucked hastily into the top of the pack. The image was of August with two smiling children and a younger woman. He wondered why, of all the photos in the house, he had chosen to take only this one.

"Here's hoping," Micky said, sucking on her teeth, "Otherwise this plan is going to go straight to Hell in a Handbasket."

At Ollie's confused expression, August quickly added, "It's an idiom, kid."

The Android tilted his head, "I gathered that."

Micky reached out to pat the top of the suitcase with a frown, "Is this all you're taking?"

"No point packing up half the house if we're gonna be back here in a few months, right?" August answered.

Ollie noticed the subtle change in the officer's expression as she adjusted her weight from one side of her hip to the other, "Right," she said, "I see your point."

August approached her and snatched up the handle to the case, nudging it with a foot so that its weight tipped forward slightly. He began to drag it across the floor, carefully avoiding the coffee table on his way to the door, "You coming, *duine*?" he asked.

Ollie looked back once more at the contents of the house, wondering, not for the first time, just what it was he was asking this man to leave behind. He wondered if his very first time in a home like this was also going to be his last.

"Coming August," he called back, following in the twin trails left on the carpet by the suitcase, "I'm right behind you."

<u>Chapter 10</u>

Authentication

The drive to the train station took a lot longer with a police escort. Goose was a patient driver, as all Androids were, her eyes glowing as she carefully studied the road in front of her. Her hands were resting in her lap, the vehicle driving autonomously along the narrow, winding backroads of the city, careful to avoid any heavily populated areas on their way to their destination.

Not for the first time, August found himself staring into the rear-view mirror, watching as the unmarked cars followed them at a respectable distance. Maybe it was just him, but he didn't think they were being exactly subtle about it.

Micky occupied the front seat next to Goose, resting her head in her curled-up fist. Despite the image that she was trying to portray of a disinterested passenger, Ollie could clearly see her trained eyes looking across the arched rooftops, and at any cars that idled too close to their own. There was a concealed weapon on her lap, hidden under the cover of a non-descript backpack. Her neat nails scrapped thoughtfully along the grooves that were cut into the handle.

"You'll want to get off at the third stop. It's a little town called Cahir, just inside Tipperary," Micky explained, her eyes suddenly moving up towards the mirror to meet August's behind her, "The Gardi there will keep an eye on you." She spun the chair around to face them slowly, extending out a brightly coloured pamphlet for a hotel. It appeared to be snuggled in against the scenic ruins of an old castle. "You'll have to drive the rest of the way from there, I'm afraid. Best not make it too easy for anyone to follow you."

"A long way to go," August commented, turning the brochure over in his hands.

"Every two weeks or so you will receive a transfer of funds. This will be divided between the two of you for living expenses. Your new driver's license and medical card are in here."

She slid the black backpack across her lap and into his. August slowly trailed the zip along the track, reaching inside and pulling out his new license. The photo and date of birth listed were the same as his real one, but the surname had been changed.

"Augustus *Sheehan*?" he read aloud with a frown, arching one of his dark eyebrows at her, "Didn't exactly change it much, did ya?"

"Most people prefer to keep their first name," Micky answered his unasked question, "I understand it makes the integration easier."

August moved the bag around, narrowing his eyes in at its contents, "What's with all the other stuff?"

"Documents for a Social Droid," she replied, leaning forward slightly to rest her elbows on her knees, "It means Ollie will be licensed to go anywhere that a regular Social Droid can. Within reason, of course."

The dark-haired Android next to him sat up taller in his seat, his eyes glowing for a moment as he confirmed, "I received your first transfer, Inspector. I will create a budgeting document to ensure the money lasts us until the next allowance date."

August made a face, "I don't need you babysitting me, Ols," he grumbled, "I was feeding myself just fine before you came along."

"Fast food isn't good for you, August," Ollie rebuked, "It's an expensive habit and can lead to all sorts of health problems down the road. Better to purchase fresh ingredients that we can prepare at home."

August huffed out an agitated breath, angling himself towards the window beside him, "Suppose I'll have more time on my hands now…"

"It might be fun to learn how to cook," Ollie volunteered, "It would be a new challenge for both of us."

"I'm glad you're looking on the bright side, at least," the human scoffed, running a hand through his long, fiery hair, "I think I'm about ten minutes away from a stress headache myself."

"The Witsec teams have already been prepped for your arrival," Micky said, crossing her legs and leaning back in her chair again, "They'll be there to help you both get settled in. There's no need to worry."

"Oh, how very kind of them," August snarked, folding his arms across his chest defensively, "I'm just waiting to hear the catch now."

"No catch, Mr. Jackson," the dark-skinned officer said as they pulled in alongside the Connolly train station, "Your job and ours are very much the same here; to get you to court in one piece. No matter what it takes."

August leaned against the car door to admire the old stonework outside, "You don't sound too confident in our chances."

"Things like this always come with risks," she warned, watching as the pair of them clambered out of the car and onto the pavement. She rolled down her window and leaned her arm on the sill, "We have people in place to help you every step of the way. Just avoid suspicion where you can. Don't talk to anyone you don't have to."

August swallowed, clearly nervous as he pulled his travel case out of the boot and turned to look up at the monument before them. The station had stood unwaveringly since 1844, the original building surviving even the floods that tried to topple it in the early 2030s. Just like its namesake, Connolly Station had fought back the invading rapids, the water stripping away all of the surrounding buildings to leave behind only this one as a testament to Irish design and determination.

Ollie lined up next to him, subtly scanning the man as he brushed against his side. His blood sugar was low, his posture dipped slightly forward. His hair and beard were mussed from where he had run his hands through them. Although the man tried his best to contain the majority of his nerves, it was clearly written all over his face.

The red-head turned and patted the top of the unmarked car with the palm of one hand with a sigh that seemed to shake his very bones, "Look, Inspector, I really do appreciate the help," he said, "Especially with Ollie. It means a lot."

Micky flashed him a subtle grin, "It's not my first rodeo, Mr. Jackson. But once you're out of the city there won't be a whole lot I can do personally to help. You'll have to lean on the other officers. *Trust* them to look out for you. If you need to reach me, for whatever reason, Goose transferred my details to your Android for you."

August leaned forward to look in through the car window and Goose acknowledged him with a polite nod, the Android barely having moved for their entire journey.

"Will do," he answered, patting the roof one more time before stepping away, "See you soon."

"Here's hoping," Micky quipped, and rolled up her window again as the black Sudan drove away.

Chapter 11
Emulation

Ollie felt nerves fizzing around his system like electricity, sending every little bit of him into hyper-awareness as they stepped into the busy train station for the first time. The number of people crowded around them was staggering and the Android's new social software appeared to be trying to catalogue them all. Most of the information was shallow, barely scratching the surface of data that was available, but the frequent buzz of it was already starting to give him a headache. He stuck close to August's side, mirroring the other Social Droids that he could see working throughout the glass-roofed space. His human companion unfolded a piece of lined paper from his back pocket, skimming over the instructions penned on one side in biro.

"Alright, it says here we're to head for platform three," he mumbled, glancing up at the mixture of English and Gaeilge signs overhead, "Any clue what direction that's in?"

They passed by a row of small shopfronts all arranged neatly against the station's inner walls. The Androids in the windows moved through a series of pre-programed movements, showing off some of the new fashion accessories that they were wearing. Despite the upbeat nature of their motions, their expressions were completely vacant, as if their minds were a thousand miles away.

Ollie quickened his pace to stay on the other man's heels, being careful not to lose track of him in the crowds, "It looks like it's over this way," he said, pointing to a blue sign directly above them with an arrow on one side.

A flutter of metal overhead made the pair look up in surprise as the *Arrivals and Departures* boards adjusted their signage to reflect the latest times. The train heading towards Tipperary was scheduled to leave in the next 20 or so minutes. Yellow text scrolled by along the top at a lethargic pace, informing them that all trains on their line were currently on schedule and then something about Bow Echoes and Diurnal Effects beyond the bubble enclosure.

August stuffed the paper wad back into his pocket again. He glared at the large travel case that the Android was trailing along behind them, watching its wheels spinning across the tile.

"Isn't that heavy?" he asked quietly, "I kinda shoved a lot of crap in there."

Ollie flashed him an easy-going smile, "It's nothing I can't handle, August."

August scratched at the shorter hairs at the back of his neck anxiously, "I hate that you have to carry it for me like this," he commented, "Makes me feel like an old man."

"Appearances are important, August," Ollie responded coolly, carefully taking in the people around them, "I'm an Android. My primary duty is to serve you."

The red-head scowled at that, shoving both fists into the pocket of the dark green hoodie he had chosen to wear. It had the logo of an Athletics Club from the city on the top right corner and the details of a track meet from some two decades ago plastered across the front. It was well-worn and clearly treasured, judging by the number of repairs that had been made to it over the years.

"See, that right there?" he grunted, "I hate that. Makes it sound like you're my pet or something. Are people always like this when it comes to Androids?"

Ollie hummed thoughtfully as he continued looking around them, "Considering that you were the first person that I had ever spoken to, I don't have a great frame of reference."

August let out a rough, raspy sigh, "You know, I didn't actually get to meet a wile lotta Androids in my day-to-day either."

Blue eyes regarded him with surprise, "But you were a Technician, weren't you?"

A flicker of a smile pulled at the corner of the older man's mouth, "Technicians handle the inside parts. We never got to work with any Androids directly."

"That's rather surprising," Ollie commented.

"Apparently, we had Android workers in Crossroads, but I rarely saw them. They were always up on the higher floors," August carried on thoughtfully. His dark eyes took in the line of people by one of the nearby kiosks and he patted his back pockets with a grumble, "Shit. I left my card back at the Repair Centre. How are we supposed to pay for tickets?"

Ollie shifted closer, tapping on his temple with a finger, "Don't worry, August, all of your new banking information has been uploaded directly to my Codex."

"And what's to stop you from just running off with all our cash then, eh?" the larger man teased, "Can't you go like 50 miles an hour? I think I top out at 8 on a good day."

The dark-haired Android gave him a subtle smile, a playful glint in his bright eyes, "I would never do such a thing," he replied quietly with a tone of mock offence, "I am a law-abiding Android, Mr. Jackson."

"You don't fool me with that innocent face of yours," his companion rebuked, waving a hand towards his face to indicate the rows and rows of painted freckles there, "I know a troublemaker when I see one."

Ollie's mouth drew into a tight line as he held back the laugh he so desperately wanted to let out. They were in too public a place for an interaction like this. This was not how a Social Droid was meant to behave, no matter how their owner perceived them.

"Can this troublemaker offer to purchase you a drink then, Mr. Jackson?" he asked instead, nodding towards an Android-manned booth just across the tiled floor from them, "They have several hot and cold options available before we reach the platform. I think tickets can be purchased at the same spot."

August followed his line of sight and swallowed, running his tongue over his bottom lip. It felt like a week since he'd had a real cup of coffee. The crap in their office break room certainly didn't meet the caffeine requirements for the title.

"Sure," he answered then furrowed his brows at him in confusion "So, uh, how do I…?" He waved his hands in the air again vaguely.

"I can handle the transaction," Ollie stated, stopping and rolling the travel case up onto its small, plastic feet, "I just have to leave this with you for a moment."

"Uh, okay," the human replied, reaching over to place a hand on the case as if taking ownership of it for the time being, "Can you grab me a flat white then? Two sugars?" He made a face, "Do you, uh, need anything?"

"Androids don't require sustenance, August," Ollie informed him, keeping his expression neutral as he peeled away from his side, "As your Social Droid, I am just happy to serve."

August's previous frown only deepened at that, "Great, now I sound like a cult leader," he muttered to himself, watching the man as he moved to join the small queue. There were several humans and Androids already waiting in line and the differences between them were stark from where he was standing. Straight-backed and blank-faced, the Androids all positioned themselves in the exact same way, with their hands folded in front of their hips and their faces directed forward. Compared to them, humans were all bent at different angles, their posture loose and comfortable. Some twisted at the spine to talk with friends, others were on their Chrome devices and others again had their hands buried in their pockets or in a book. Ollie fell into the set pose that was expected of him the instant he found himself outside of August's gravity. His body straightened with a snap like a plastic ruler, every artificial joint locking in place. The glow of his eyes slowly paled, his expression blank and thoughtful. It was the first time since they had met that he had ever looked like an Android. August hadn't even realised how much of an effect he was already having on the Runner Droid.

I wonder if the changes he's going through are because of me...or because of him?

Ollie approached the Androids at the small counter, and they smiled politely back at him, the word 'ANDROID' flashing by on their collars as they tilted their head in greeting. They wore identical, matching uniforms of green and blue, their voices upbeat and friendly as Ollie repeated August's drink order and purchased their tickets.

"Paying with Codex?" the female Android asked, raising her palm up to face him.

"Yes," Ollie replied and mirrored the motion, allowing the very tips of his fingers to connect with hers. Information passed between them in a wordless instant. A map of the station's layout and coupons for further drink's purchases were also added to their account. The male unit approached the desk as his HUD alerted him to the payment's conclusion. He had finished off their order with a flourish, presenting the steaming mug to him before turning back to the coffee machine again to continue with the other orders.

The female Android's ponytail bounced behind her as she offered him a chipper, "Have a great day!" in a sing-songy tone of voice. The accompanying smile was almost convincing, despite not quite meeting her eyes.

Ollie hesitated when he went to raise his hand again. He wanted to reply, to wish both of them a good day as well, but it wasn't something an Android like him was *supposed* to do. He shouldn't have even *wanted* to.

He met the casher's eyes instead and bowed his head forward ever-so-slightly. Not enough to be noticed by the humans around them but hopefully enough to convey his own way of thanks. He lifted the coffee from the counter, feeling the heat of it radiating through the paper cup and into the tips of his connecting fingers, and walked back towards his human companion with practised poise that didn't so much as cause a ripple in the prized liquid.

   He extended the cup out as he entered August's orbit, careful to balance it in a way that the other man's hand could easily fit around it. "Be careful," he stated, "It's quite hot."

Ollie had read about coffee before, had guessed at what the tantalizing smell of it might be like, but the real thing was very different from what he had been expecting. The coffee itself, the shot of espresso and crema foam, was sharp and bitter and lingered in the back of his throat in a way that would have almost been unpleasant if not for the lingering sweetness of the whole cow's milk and sugar. The combination in his sensors was interesting, so unlike anything he had ever encountered in the underground.

August flashed him a quick smile as he accepted the cup, blowing into the small opening before he took a large gulp of it, hissing as the heat rolled down his throat, "Ah," he gasped, "That's the good shit. Thanks, kid."

Ollie was a little envious, if he was honest. He wondered what something that smelled so strongly might taste like with a human tongue. What it would feel like to experience that heat through every part of him as it went down. He watched August's Adam's Apple bob and put the thought out of his mind again.

The human gasped softly as he lowered his drink, his dark eyes searching for a sign, "You said we were goin' this way, yeah?" he asked.

Ollie fell in by his shoulder, taking a hold of the suitcase and tipping it forward again, "According to the map the kiosk Android sent me, we should carry on down this corridor here and take the escalators to the bottom floor."

August took another sip of his coffee as he rotated his opposite wrist to check his watch, "Just shy of ten minutes to get there. Think we'll make this one?"

The Android slowly began to drag the travel case down the white marble corridor. The skylights overhead allowed the entire space to be bathed in sunlight and he practically purred as he felt its heat across his false skin.

"It isn't far," he said, "Just around this next corner."

August allowed him to move ahead, watching as the Android raised a hand to display their tickets to the woman stationed at the check-in desk. She nodded as she accepted their fair and waved them both on, pointing to the two different paths ahead of them with a bored expression, "Humans on the left, Androids on the right. Next please."

Ollie eyed the glowing red sign next to August's shoulder that read *'No Androids beyond this point'* and felt something within himself shift uncomfortably. A matching error message appeared across his HUD, painting a false wall across his vision.

"It appears as if I'm going this way," he said, looking down the opposite corridor. Neon blue lines on the floor were directing him towards the cover of an angry, black scanner. Based on the signage, he was also supposed to take their luggage there.

"What the Hell is that thing?" August questioned.

"Likely a security device," the Android answered coolly, "It's alright August. You go on ahead. I'll be okay."

The red-head frowned back at him, hesitating, "Alright..." he said, "But I'll be right there on the other side, okay? Don't...don't take too long."

The fork in the path took them in two different directions and Ollie obediently walked the way that he was shown. A blonde-haired human attendant called out for "Next!" several feet ahead of him. The woman barely glanced up from the scanner's screen as he approached.

He stepped under the boundary of the scanner, wheeling their cargo in close to his side. He stared straight ahead, his fans vibrating as they came to life one after the other in his chest and throat. Lines of red light, sharp as lasers, dissected his field of vision.

"Android, state your serial number," the attendant instructed.

"Social Droid 01113," Ollie answered obediently, resisting the curious urge to look in her direction. Eye-contact was a human trait, not one required of somebody like him.

The woman hummed to herself, tapping the screen several times with the tip of her pointer finger, "Move on," she stated without looking up.

Ollie took a step out from the scanner. And then another. His temperature was slowly beginning to lower the further from it he became. Their new documents had already taken effect, it seemed. If he were human in this moment, he might have let out a sigh of relief; instead, he chose to continue walking forward, his head held up and his shoulders back in a perfect line. He rejoined August at the other side, barely glancing his way as he fell into step with him again.

He felt the other man's dark eyes on him as he asked, "You doin' alright there, *duine*?"

His fingers stretched out as if he was going to touch the hand currently holding onto the case. Then, likely thinking better of it, he closed his fist again.

"A routine safety scan," he explained, watching the crowds moving in all directions before them at the gates, "Nothing to worry about, it seems."

August heaved a heavy sigh, "Shit, okay. That's good."

"Have you not travelled by train before, Mr. Jackson?" the dark-haired man asked.

"Nah," he answered with a shake of his head that sent his red hair scattered over his broad shoulders, "I've never left the city before."

Ollie's eyebrows jumped up towards his curls, "Oh," he said.

August narrowed his eyes at him, "What?"

The Android started at the man's change in tone, "Nothing, I was just expecting…"

"That I'd be more well-travelled?" the red-head interjected with an arched eyebrow.

"I just…can't imagine staying in one place for so long when you don't have to," Ollie clarified.

"You don't have to be an Android to be trapped by Crossroads," the human breathed. Ollie followed the movement of his hand as he tipped his brown, paper cup up again. August was watching another couple pass, his eyes falling on the Social Droid at the man's side and how it walked so obediently. Like a well-trained dog. Its eyes faced forward unblinkingly, its attention never wavering for an instant. Not once did it appear distracted by the sights and sounds and voices all around it. Vacant. Lifeless.

I looked more like that than Ollie did this morning, he thought.

The pair joined several others as they hopped onto the escalator together, letting the moving steps take them the rest of the way to their platform. A Tannoy rang out overhead, tinny and ancient, announcing the recent arrivals and departures from their line. By the time they reached trackside the sun was beginning to set through the overhead glass, the angled roof sending fractals of red, pink and orange across the tiled floor and the metal bars. The air above the tracks was hazy with its lazy Autumn heat.

"Looks like we're in the right place," August remarked as he paused to lean back against one of the black and gold posts by the edge of the platform. He fished in his pocket again for the paper instructions, unfolding them and adjusting his glasses as he scanned the writing there again, "They really are sending us to the arse-end of nowhere."

Ollie moved closer, allowing the suitcase to rest in the space between their legs for a moment. He peered over the man's shoulder at the delicate handwriting, noting that the neat penmanship didn't really suit the energetic officer they had met before.

"Schull?" he read aloud with a questioning tone. He reached for his usual search function and frowned when he came back with the 'ACCESS REVOKED' error.

"County Cork," August replied, "It's a good couple'a miles south of here. Won't be a lot of people headin' where we're headin'."

Ollie tilted his head, "I take it that means it's a small place?"

"Tiny," the human answered, "Not much left since the floods a few decades back. Mostly locals there now. Witsec's probably hoping it's the last place anyone would look."

He stuffed the page back into his pocket again as he wiggled his cup, swishing the last remnants of his coffee around the curved edge of the bottom, "Coffee is always done far too soon," he remarked, draining the final dregs of it and tossing the cup into the bin beside them.

The screen on the side of it illuminated, the text *'Thank you for recycling with Eireann Railways'* scrolling across it alongside the animation of several dancing sheep in tricolours.

    The now familiar shuffling of the board alerted them to the newest arrival and August straightened from his resting spot with a deep groan, "Looks like we're up next, Ols."

Ollie peered out over the edge of the platform towards the looming darkness of the stone tunnels beyond. Since the construction of the island's 'bubbles' it had been deemed essential that all travel outside the main cities would be conducted underground. The superheated deserts above ground had wilted away much of the scenic Irish countryside, many of the small towns little more than scalded wasteland by now. Journeys were typically kept to a minimum, with only a few trains going out and in per day. It was common for companies to pay for employees to live on-site.

Accessing Eireann Railway Timetables: Service 322a to Tipperary
Data retrieved: train is currently running on time
Estimated arrival time: 26 seconds

Ollie's grip on the handle of August's luggage tightened with nerves as he watched the two beams of light appearing from the darkness, casting long, shimmering lines down the rails.
August looked towards his curly-haired company with a smile, *It's just when he and I met,* he thought, *It felt like a train hit me then too.*
The train slowed before them with a squeal of metal on metal, the green and blue carriages flashing by like a kineograph until they finally started to grow still. The carriage in front of them heaved a steamy breath as it settled in place, exhausted from its earlier travels. The doors peeled open for them automatically, only a few of the passengers inside departing from this stop.
"All aboard," August said quietly, swallowing down his own impending sense of anxiety, "Onto the land of the Golden Vale we go."

Chapter 12
Time Out Detected

The inside of the carriage was cool, the air conditioning turned up high despite the time of year. There were a handful of others occupying the seats around them, so they kept moving until they found a carriage that was vacant, settling into two seats that faced one another.
August let out a soft groan as he sank down against the rough upholstery, feeling it burn slightly where his hoodie and shirt road up.
The train let out another hoot of sound as it fluttered into motion again, shutters twisting in each of the windows to conceal the outside world from view.
August drew his thumbs over both of his eyes with an exhausted moan, feeling sand and grit embedded in the corners, "If I wasn't so damn wired right now, I'd try to catch some Z's."
For a moment they became bathed in completed darkness as the train slid back into the underground passageway, the yellow-toned electric lights flickering as they

came alive to take the daylight's place. Artificial images floated along the windows next to them, adverts displaying happy families and various types of outdoor activities within New Dublin City.

  August brought his forehead down against the coolness of the window and allowed his eyes to close, feeling the motion of the train travelling through his jawbone, "It's a shame they cover it up like this," he commented with a yawn, "I think I would've liked to see it."

Ollie slid forward in his seat and looked one way down the train and then the other. The next passengers were more than a carriage away, the conductor long since having already passed by this part of the train. He angled himself towards the windows and placed both palms down flat onto the glass, his eyes glowing as the text on his collar began to scroll through various lines of code.

"Ollie?" August questioned, "Whatcha doin' th-?"

The breath caught in his throat as the images began to pull away again, folding into the side panels of the window and bearing the real view of the world beyond. In all directions lay the ruins of the original city, monuments to a world that was slowly getting out of their control. Each crumbling stone relic was like a gravestone, each brick packed with a hundred stories of the lives lost defending it from the floods.

"This has always been the world I belonged to," Ollie said softly as he regarded the place lying on the other side of his own reflection. His tone was melancholy, almost introspective. He slowly peeled his fingers from the glass again, "These are the ruins of a city no one up here seems to want to remember but you."

"Holy shit," August whispered, bringing his face impossibly close to the glass, "I've seen pictures of it but…it really doesn't do it justice, does it?" He leaned back slightly when his own breath started to mist the surface, "They really just built over all this?"

"You were alive when the banks of the Liffey burst, weren't you?" Ollie asked, watching him curiously. So many emotions were reflected on the human's face, pain, anger, despair.

"I was just a wain," the red-head answered, "I don't think I really understood a lot of it. I was half a city away when it happened."

"A lot of people died," Ollie observed, "It must have been frightening."

"I just remember some of my classmates not coming back to school," August said thoughtfully, "Empty desks. Coats left on hooks by the schoolyard. That sort of thing. I didn't really understand what it all meant until I was older."

The brightly painted buildings were stark against the dullness of the ruins, the red and green bars a powerful contrast to the crumbling grey of the district. The paint had been almost completely wiped away in places where the water had impacted, like the force it of had blasted the colour from the once lively world.

Bicycles protruded from out of the mud and decay, barely recognisable by their bare bones alone. Fabric was draped across one of the broken windows, though whether it was once a flag, or a pair of curtains was hard to distinguish now. Black and green mould reclaimed the cobblestones, dark hands dragging even the streets themselves down into the dank.

"You really used to run down here?"

Ollie pulled his eyes away from the once thriving tourist spots at the change in the man's tone. There was an edge to his sadness now. Something coming very close to anger in his voice.

"I did," he answered, "Every day."

"There's barely even a road," August snarled, throwing his right hand towards the scene before him like he was trying to emphasize his point, "Didn't they care? You could've gotten killed out there playin' mailman for a bunch of those rich assholes."

Ollie perched on the edge of his seat, staring down at the space between his knees, "I'm an Android, August. My only value lies in the components I'm made of and the cargo I carry."

August let out an angry huff from his nose, bringing an elbow to his knee as he rested his head in one hand, "And I suppose they didn't care that you were lonely out there either, huh?"

The Android looked at him with surprise, "You think that I was lonely?"

The human's eyes moved to meet his own, "Weren't you?"

Ollie allowed his eyes to wander as he gave himself time to consider the question. There were posters above them on the walls advertising the latest rates of travel and popular destinations. The vinyl floors were tacky where the cleaning fluid hadn't quite dried in yet.

"I don't think I really knew how loneliness felt," he answered honestly, "I was built to run so I just...*ran*. That's the way it's always been."

"How long were you out there?"

"I..." the Android paused, seemingly staring off into space as he consulted his internal records. He frowned, "My records go back several years at least. Though my original creation date has been scrubbed."

"Scrubbed?" August repeated, "Why would it have been scrubbed?"

Ollie shook his head, "It might have happened when my original files were removed back at the station. It isn't something I have ever searched for before."

Soft moonlight filtered into the carriage again from the outside as the train neared the end of the underground line. Evening had long since set in now, the bubble surrounding the next city over changing colours as they rose above the ground again. Ollie raised his hand to cover the window again and August's own hand snapped up to halt his movements.

"I've never seen outside the bubbles before," he said.

Ollie frowned, glancing down at the point where their hands met, "The UV exposure can be dangerous, August."

"It's after sundown," the other man argued, nodding towards the glass again, "Just a peek? *Le do thoil*?"

At Ollie's nod he slowly released the other man's hand, trying to ignore the feeling his fingers had left along the curve of his palm. He cleared his throat as he tucked the feeling down again, watching in awe as they rose towards the surface once more. The bubbled layer looked so different from the other side, solid where they usually saw only a small level of translucence, and covered with deep, white marks like blemishes in its curvature.

The world surrounding the bubble was entirely different from the miniscule glimpse he had caught before when entering the Safe Zone. The landscape was caked in white powder, almost too bright to look at even in the dark. Wisps of smoke and fire spun from the dust to form floating flowers in the atmosphere. The earth that revealed itself in the gaps was impossibly dry and cracked like an old man's lips on his deathbed.

"It's horrible," he breathed, wanting nothing more than to pull his eyes away from the sight, "Jesus Christ, what did we *do* to it?"

The bottom of the orb rolled back as they approached the next station, the train sliding easily through the space that was created to fit into a dark, enclosed tunnel beyond. Careful steps had been taken to minimise exposure to the outside world, the space covered with different layers of material that were used to filter the light and dust and keep it trapped outside.

Beside them, advertisements fell in to cover the space again, Ollie's hand leaving no imprint on the glass where he had touched.

"I'm sorry," he whispered, his eyes large and impossibly blue in the dim carriage, "I didn't mean to upset you."

August blinked, surprised to find the space behind his glasses wet when he reached for his face. He sniffed and cleared his throat, jerking to-and-fro as the train settled in neatly against the departing platform. He placed a hand onto the back of the chair as he rose, steadying himself.

"Don't apologise," he grunted, "I was the one who asked you to show me."

Ollie followed him towards the door, quickly grabbing the case and tugging it along behind him, "August, are you-"

"You got that key Micky gave you?" the man interrupted without turning, the automatic doors pulling apart for him and letting the cool wind inside the carriage to mingle with the A/C.

Ollie felt along the pockets of his trousers and produced it, looking over the tag that had been added to the keyring, "We're looking for a 2022 Audi A5. Red. Parked to the right of the door." He frowned at the other man's back, "August…are you sure you're alright?"

The red-head had stopped on the platform to pull a cigarette from the box, holding it in the corner of his mouth as he fidgeted with the lighter. Above him, a no smoking sign was clearly illuminated but the Android knew better than to point it out right now.

As they exited the departure area and entered the carpark, he could feel August pause to look around for the vehicle in question, letting out a triumphant puff of smoke when he found it. He marched up to the front of it, patting the bonnet fondly.

"Look at this old girl," he elated, his mood immediately brightening, "Jesus, she's older than I am. That's a nice change."

It was a pleasant enough looking car, all things considered. Sporty and cut into nice angles at the front and rear and coated in a bright, cherry red coat of paint. There were leaves covering part of the roof and bonnet, as if it had been sitting there for some time.

"It looks well taken care of," Ollie remarked, following the excited motion of August's hands as he mapped it out. The headlights and front grill made it look like it was scowling, in Ollie's opinion.

"A model like this should fit right in here," August observed, "A good-looking remodel isn't too uncommon in the country."

Ollie pressed down the button on the keypad and motioned to grab the handle, the other man stepping in front of him with an abrupt bark followed by, "No, no, no! No way am I letting you drive!" He placed a firm hand on the Android's chest, pushing him back slightly, "You're going in the passenger seat, kid."

"I'm not a kid," Ollie argued, wrinkling his nose, "I have the latest driving software installed. That more than makes me qualified to-"

"Yeah?" August growled, taking another step towards him, "And have you ever been behind the wheel before?"

"No," the Android admitted, "But I-"

"No buts," the red-head countered, pulling open the door and sliding inside. He rolled down the window when his companion remained in place, leaning his head and arm on the sill, "Get in the car. Or I'll leave your ass here and you can run there."

Ollie let out an annoyed huff as he rounded the car, his fans whirring as his back hit the leather seat. The man next to him was fidgeting with the controls, pulling on the gear stick and making the car stutter and honk like a dying goose.

"August-" Ollie started, only to be hushed by August's insistence that he get his seat belt on.

The dark-haired man reached for the strap and pulled it across his body to secure it in place, feeling the car juddering around them as he accessed the recently installed driving manual.

"You're in the wrong gear," he supplied, "You'll need to-"

"No backseat driving," August grumbled, changing into the correct gear as the car pulled smoothly out of the parking space.

Ollie tilted his head, "But I'm in the front seat."

"Figure of speech, Ols," August muttered, rolling his eyes, "Now, get that handy-dandy map of yours up, would ya? Tell me where we're going."

It was clear from the shape of the town that it had once been a tourist hot spot, the stunning *'Cahir Castle'* wonderfully intact and standing proud on the road to their right as they crossed the River Suir. A relic of the thirteenth century, the previous stronghold of the Butler family crested high over the remnants of the rocky island. In front of them, Castle Street was lined with shops both old and new, ranging from booksellers to banks, engravers to bars. The *Shamrock Lounge*, a local favourite, was adorned with medieval-styled advertisements for their latest performers.

"Go to the end of the road and take a right," Ollie instructed. He watched the colourful shops pass them by as they pulled off the main road, following the yellow and blue rows of bunting towards St Mary's church. The tower that served as part of the original building was regal, not too dissimilar to the perfectly intact castle they had passed only a moment ago.

Hidden past the church, in a spot that was concealed almost entirely by ivy, lay a narrow entranceway and August pulled the car down into it when Ollie gestured towards it with one hand, "Looks like it's in here."

The human allowed the car to idle in one of the parking spaces as he eyed up the front of the building, "You really think this is the place?" he questioned. They were situated right at the very edge of the bubble's border, and they could see hints of the exposed landscape beyond the curve of the tinted glass. The two-story building was lined with old, crosshatched windows, the yellowing paint peeling away with age. Someone had painted a pink, spotted animal on the western wall. What was it was supposed to be was anyone's guess.

"Well, ain't this place cosy," August remarked as he killed the engine and climbed out of the driver's seat.

Ollie clambered out after him, giving the building a good once over, "It doesn't look structurally sound," he said, his tone one of concern.

It was starting to get colder as night began to settle in, clouds driving slowly across the moon and blotting out what little light they had. The trees around the property were lit up from below with blue-tinged lights, making them appear spectral like gnarled witch's fingers. August ran his hands along both his arms as he circled the car, opening the boot to pull the suitcase out from inside.

They approached the front entrance cautiously and August led the way into the cramped reception room, having to duck below the natural beams of the old building. The woman behind the counter, a slight older woman with her hair in a violet-toned bun, peered over the top of her magazine with a heavy sigh, "One room or two, gentlemen?" she questioned.

"Uh, I think a booking was already called in for us," August answered her uncertainly, "It should be under the name '*Sheehan*'."

Tossing the magazine onto the counter, the woman hopped down from her stool and reached for the monitor there. Her eyes lit up with the usual orange warmth of a Chrome's software as she checked the system.

"One room," she confirmed with a nod, glancing towards Ollie's collar, "Do you need additional bedding or are you looking to share?"
"Is there only one bed in the room?" August asked.
"We have queens here, if'in you prefer." The woman arched one dark eyebrow at him pointedly.

Do you know what they do to people like you in these parts, Augustus Jackson? They way they look at you? People like you make them sick to their stomach.

August felt the cold sweat coating his hands as he wiped them against the sides of his jeans. His heart raced at the all-too-familiar memory. He swallowed, trying to contain the tremor that threatened to consume his voice.
"Standard's fine, if there's a sofa too. We'll take the extra bedding if you have it though."
The woman slid the room key across the countertop, alongside a mountain of threadbare cotton sheets in different shades of blue, "Check-out's at 11am. Sweet dreams, boys."
She picked up her magazine again as they left but August could have sworn that he could still feel her eyes on his neck. He checked the key in his hand for the number and climbed the stairs, comparing it to each of the doors they passed. Finally, right at the end of the first floor, he found its match and slid it into the lock. "This is us. Home sweet home for the night."
Ollie pulled the travel case in through the open door, though he had to turn sideways to fit it in between the sofa and the coffee table there. Dust buffeted them as August flopped down onto the bed, his face screwing up as he coughed and waved a hand to clear some breathing space. "Hell, when was the last time anyone was in here?" he choked.
Ollie perched on the foot of the bed as he looked around them. The room wasn't exactly spacious, but it was more than enough for just the two of them. The double bed took up much of the floor space but there was a small sofa tucked in next to the door that was the perfect height for him to rest on. Lifting the suitcase onto the bed so that August could access its contents, he made his way across to the other spot.
"You okay taking the sofa? I don't mind sharing if you aren't comfortable." August had sat up on the bed, his legs crossed beneath him in the way a small child might

sit. Despite the welcoming tone of voice he was using, Ollie couldn't help but think that the man looked…scared.

"It seems comfortable enough," Ollie answered, laying himself out on it the way he had seen August do a few moments earlier with the bed. Lying down on something soft was already a novelty. He wasn't going to tell August that this was already an upgrade compared to sleeping standing up like he usually did.

He had barely managed to close his eyes when he jumped in place, startled as something soft made contact with his stomach. He looked down in surprise at the faded blue blankets half-laid across him, the ends dangling over the side of the narrow sofa. He turned his head towards his companion questioningly, "What's this for?" he asked.

August looked away again, busying himself with something in the opened suitcase on the bed, "It can get cold in this part of the world at night," he said by way of explanation.

Ollie moved into position and adjusted the blanket so that it covered him from his feet all the way to his shoulders. It was unlikely he would experience cold here but, even if he did, he could choose to turn those particular settings off if he liked. He sank down into the soft fabric, allowing the sensors in his skin to map all the different sensations he was feeling. It smelled the way that August's house had; of warmth and living energy, of deodorant and old perfume that hadn't quite come out in the wash. It wasn't something he particularly needed but there was a part of him that clung to it, allowing himself a moment to settle down into the relief of it.

He listened as August flipped through the TV channels beside him, yawning as he fought back the urge to sleep. He manually began checking through his logs, skimming through the reams and reams of new information that he had obtained in the last 24 hours. He catalogued every piece of it, eager to explore each new location or experience in more intricate detail. He was surprised to see a new objective had been added alongside the Social Droid software, the red text popping up in the corner of his HUD without prompting. There was no clear origin point for the message, as if the objective hadn't come from an outside force but from somewhere within his own body.

The message read, clear and bright across his vision:

Objective: Protect Augustus Jackson

Chapter 13

Back It Up (To The Cloud)

Ollie was pulled from his thoughts sometime later by a quiet groan next to him and he opened his eyes to see August peeling himself up from the far side of the bed, his silhouette bathed in blue-tinged moonlight. The man had grabbed his coat from the end of the bed and thrown it around his shoulders, the now increasingly familiar sound of his lighter clicking following him towards the bedroom window as he adjusted the mechanism and shoved it upwards. He winced at the noise it made, glancing in his direction apologetically when he noticed the Android's blue eyes looking back at him.

"Sorry, Ols. Didn't mean to wake you."

Ollie let the blankets tumble down into his lap as he sat up, the sofa cushions pressing into his lower back. "It's alright. Androids don't really sleep anyway."

A small smile pulled up the corner of the other man's lip, "Sure looked like sleep to me, kid."

He brought his lit cigarette back towards his lips and inhaled deeply, breathing the hot smoke back out the window again as he added, "Some night out there."

The Android brought up his HUD and searched the corner of it for the date and time, frowning at the information that greeted him there.

///It's wrong, he thought as he wrinkled his nose, ///I guess it must have reset when I was disconnected from my WiFi box.

Not quite used to looking outside of himself for the time, he scanned the room's walls for a clock before asking, "What time is it?"

August gripped the end of the cigarette between his lips as he checked his watch, "It's about 3.30-ish," he mumbled in reply. The amber glow of the cigarette reflected in his glasses like a far-off streetlight.

Ollie adjusted himself to throw his legs over the side of the sofa, neatly folding his blanket to rest at the end of it. He crossed the room to stand next to his companion who wriggled over to make space for him at the window, "Hardly a cloud out there," August commented, "I don't think I've ever seen so many stars."

The Android attempted to mimic the man's relaxed posture, leaning on the window's ledge with both arms folded. His curls blew around his face as he angled his head to look upwards, catching some of the light filtering down through the bubble above them. The sky over their heads was a stunning blend of blue and purple and black, the twinkling of seemingly thousands of stars making everything appear just a little bit brighter. Ollie was almost glad that he didn't have the need to breathe right now because this view might have stolen whatever precious air he did have from his lungs. He had never seen anything like it before and his mouth fell open in silent wonder.

"There are…so many," he whispered.

"I could never see them this clearly back home," August said as he took another drag and let it flutter up towards them, "Too much light pollution."

"They're so bright," Ollie said, unable to tear his eyes away from them. It wasn't just the stars themselves, but the feeling that accompanied the sight that he wished to hold onto. He wished that he could gather all this data into one place and seal it all away.

August dabbed the end of his cigarette against the damp sill and brought it inside to toss it in the bin, checking the ashes had cooled significantly first. When he turned back to face the window again, his ginger-toned beard appeared to glow, his very skin illuminated by the night sky. It was as if, for a fleeting moment, that man himself was made of starlight.

When his lips turned upwards in a tired smile, the ache in Ollie's chest only seemed to intensify.

He reached into his pocket and pulled out his mobile phone, tilting it upwards as he leaned out the window again. He tapped the screen with the tip of his pointer finger twice. It took Ollie a few seconds to realise what it was the man was doing.

"Are you…taking a photo of them?" he asked.

August glared at the damaged screen in his hands, studying the slightly distorted image critically, "A picture never seems to do something like this justice," he muttered, "It's never as good as the real thing but…sometimes it's nice to have the memory of it anyway."

Ollie eyed the device curiously. It was a fairly recent model, one of the few external devices still left on the market, capable of almost as many megapixels as a standard *Hasselblad* or a *Fujifilm*, but not as adaptive after some of their Chrome-augmented counterparts.

"And before you say anything," August continued, waving his phone in his direction, "It's been stripped of all its GPS and Wi-Fi functions, so it can't be tracked. It's basically just a glorified camera now."

"It feels strange…not to have all that information at your fingertips," Ollie admitted, bringing his head down to rest on his folded arms, "I never needed it before but now…now I have so many questions about the world."

He jumped at the sudden flash of white from beside him and turned around to look at the red-head with widened eyes. "Did you just…?"

"Sorry," the human shot back quickly, "You just looked…I mean, sorry. I should've asked."

August's skin had taken on a hue not unlike his hair, tinging his neck and face as he shifted his weight. He cleared his throat, something he obviously did whenever he was embarrassed.

Warning: internal temperature increase.
Fans speed increased to 95rpm.

Ollie pushed back the sudden tide of surprising heat that filled his systems. "No one's ever taken my picture before."
August faced the window, showing off the bright red tint of his ears, "I could, I mean, we could take some more if you'd like?" The man was wearing an unsure smile, trying to only look at him from the corner of his eye. "I can't promise they'll be any good though. I'm not much of a photographer."
He could hear the Android as he shuffled in place, inching in to fill the space at his side. There was a warmth radiating from the points where their bodies met that couldn't be driven away by the cold night air.
He leaned over his shoulder, peering down at the broken phone screen curiously, "How does it work?" he asked.
August's felt a jolt go through him when he saw the other man's face in his peripheries. He was so close now he could make out every one of the freckles that lined his nose and the creases under his eyes. The dark curls of his hair were tinged teal by the overhead lights, the different shades of blue in his eyes like the rough Atlantic ocean in winter. It was hard to imagine *not* taking the man's picture. He didn't think he had ever met someone quite as handsome as him before.
Handsome? August blanched, *Where the Hell did that thought come from?*
When he turned his head slightly to the side, he felt those blue eyes falling on him questioningly.
"It's easy," he said, clearing his throat for a second time as he felt his mouth getting slightly drier, "All you've gotta do it smile and click the button."
August tapped the arrows at the bottom of the phone's screen to switch the front facing camera. He could see Ollie's delighted smile pressed against his own cheek; the Android completely oblivious to his sudden inner turmoil. From this close to him, he could smell his own shampoo on the other man's hair, and it made the sudden swirling in his guts grow more intense. There was something soft about that,

domestic, and he hated himself for the sudden overwhelming feeling of longing it was giving him.

This happiness, this life, it isn't made for people like that, August. Two men simply can't be happy this way. Find a nice girl. Start a family, for God's sake. Don't waste your time building a wall with sand instead of bricks.

"Say cheese," he said, forcing a smile onto his own face as the words of Father Quinn droned through his mind. He could feel his other hand shaking as it hovered by Ollie's side, not wanted to close the gap against the other man's pale pink uniform.
He ground the teeth of his smile tightly together. *All these years and that sick old bastard still has his claws in me.*
"Why cheese?" Ollie asked, a sound vibrating from his throat that sounded like a laugh. At some point the Android's hand had overlapped with his, his smaller fingers curling around his larger ones on the phone.
"Makes your teeth show, I think," the human answered with a grin that felt a little more like his usual expression. His heart was beginning to race, the sensation making him feel a little dizzy, "I think it's the double-e sound."
"Cheese!" Ollie repeated, trying it out and showing his teeth, "That's a weirdly fun word to say."
 "It is," August agreed, finally allowing his hand to cup the Android's side and pull him into the frame of the photo.
The Android beamed towards the camera, sending an infectious smile out into the world, "Say *cheese*, August!" he cheered.
"Cheese," August echoed, bringing the side of his face down against his companion's soft curls. He didn't want to admit it, especially to himself right now, but there was something about the way the pair of them stood, clinging to each on a cold and windy night in the middle of autumn that felt strangely right. For the first time in a very long time, August felt like he wasn't entirely alone on one of his sleepless nights.

Chapter 14
Recovery/Reboot

The car made a low rumbling sound as it entered the underground service tunnel the next morning, the wheels rolling over the uneven ground and making the vehicle rock like a boat out at sea. The space around them was claustrophobic, dark and oppressive in a way that the surface rarely was, with only the red bumper lights ahead of them to serve as their guides. August felt the steering wheel growing slick with his sweat as he felt the walls closing in around him and he swallowed in order to force his ears to pop. Where normally noise would have rushed in again, only the quiet rumbling of their own car was heard.

The tiled walls outside the car were tinted green with mould, like a disused swimming pool in an abandoned gym, and he wondered when the last time was that any of it had been inspected. The growl of his engine reverberated from the wall beside them and made it sound like some great and terrible monster lay somewhere in the dark ahead of them. August pressed the button to roll up the window. Just in case.

It was the first time he had ever driven outside of New Dublin and the creepy path they were on was definitely not to his liking. Officer O'Sullivan had been quite insistent, however, when she had told them they had to mix up their travel plans. They didn't want anyone being able to follow their route, least of all another one of the Hornets that were no doubt still hunting their heels somewhere.

Ollie glanced up from the seat next to him towards the roof as several droplets of water created an unnatural cacophony on the metal surface.

"This place freaks me the Hell out," August scowled, giving the wheel an anxious squeeze.

"You get used to it all after a while," Ollie stated, turning to face out the front window. By the expression of his face, he looked more curious than frightened, but it was hard to tell in the dim light of the dashboard.

"We're bumper to bumper too," August grumbled, waving a hand to the space in front of the car, "It'll take us the whole day to get there at this rate."

Ollie tilted his head to one side, "I packed enough food and water to last us until this evening, so we should be fine."

"Well, I ain't goin' out there to piss in the dark," the human scoffed.

Ollie let out a soft, electronic laugh at his shoulder, "We could always play some music to help distract you, if you'd like?"

"Already tried that," the red-head answered, jabbing a finger on the screen embedded in the dashboard, "Bloody thing's busted. Can't hold a signal worth a damn down here."

The Android shifted forward in his seat and brought both hands up to touch the glass panel. The blue of his eyes lit up the entire interior of the car for a moment as he worked, the player bursting to life with a suddenness that had August letting out a roar of startled laughter.

"Holy shit, kiddo!" He reached out to pat his companion's shoulder as a wide smile spread from one corner of his face to the other. "How'd you do that?"

Ollie felt the grin catching on his face too, "It's part of my new Social Droid kit. I added a few additional programs I thought might be useful to you."

August's dark eyes studied his face as he arched a questioning eyebrow at him, "Yeah? What else you got goin' on in that clever head of yours?"

Ollie's smile only widened at the praise, and he wiggled the fingers of one hand in the air playfully, "I can sync myself to most entertainment systems, make phone calls and add important dates to your diary. I have access to thousands of recipes from around the world and I can translate any written and spoken language."

August whistled at that, "Now you're just showing off."

"*Juste un peu,*" Ollie answered, his French accent flawless as a native. *Just a little.*

"I don't speak a lick of French, so you could've said anything to me just now," August remarked with a laugh, "The only thing I remember from school was *Voulez-vous coucher*
avec moi?"

The Android felt the spot at the back of his neck growing warm as his translator kicked in. His fans switched on to clear the access heat. "Was that a phrase you used often?"

August angled his face towards him again, exhaling a laugh through his nose, "It's a song, Ollie," he clarified, dark eyes bright with something like mischief.

"Oh," his dark-haired companion squeaked, searching through his internal library of music for the corresponding song. It came out the speakers on either side of the car when he tracked it down. This version was apparently from an old musical. "See?" August said as he gestured towards the dashboard again, "It just kinda sticks in your brain after a while. Humans call that an earworm."

"An earworm?" Ollie repeated, making a face.

"Yeah, it's sort of a gross image, I know," August agreed.

"I think I like it," the Android said, bringing both hands to rest in his lap, "The song, I mean. It's…energetic."

Song added to folder: favourites

"What other sorts of music do you like?" the man next to him asked as they slid forward to idle behind the car just ahead of them in the queue, "Techno? *EDM*?"

"I didn't really know what music *was* until yesterday," the Android admitted, "I haven't had the time to develop an opinion on most of it yet."

"Well then, let's just start with the classics, shall we? Get you educated." August reached out to tap the menu in front of him, "Lets see what we've got here…Queen, or Iron Maiden, maybe? Or…hmm. You'd probably like something more pop-y like Bowie or Duran Duran."

Ollie's eyes turned the space around the front seats a cool shade of cornflower-blue for a moment as he ran through all of the different suggestions the human sent his way. Some pieces were loud and intrusive, others delicate. Some again were bizarre and experimental. Even within the same genre, there were very few songs that were the same as one another.

A jolt of excited energy ran through his body as a new song came on and he began to tap his fingers against his knees, his head bobbing along to the beat.

"I really like this one!" he said, closing his eyes as he gave into the motion of the music, "It feels like when I go running. It's sort of…bouncy."

"*Bouncy*, huh?" August's fingers were drumming against the steering wheel too, "And that's a good thing?"

"I…think so?" Ollie offered, sounding unsure.

"Don't stress about it too much," August said as he put the car into gear and moved forward again, only managing to get another half a mile or so down the next part of the road, "Music is a *feeling* thing, not a *thinking* thing. If you like it, you like it. That's all there is to it."

The Android studied the hands wrapped around the steering wheel for a moment, watching the dashboard glow catch on the little orange hairs there like tiny embers, "What sort of music do you like?" he asked.

August waited until the car was idling in place again before he reached out to enter some details into the dashboard computer, "Here. Lemme show you."

A new song roared through the speakers, unapologetically loud, with an excited pulse of electric guitars to introduce it. The bass erupted from all sides of them as it joined in, sending wild vibrations through the entire car. Ollie felt like the very ends of his curls were standing on end with the energy of it. He watched as August relinquished his hold on the wheel and began to move his fingers along an invisible fretboard in perfect timing.

"I haven't heard this one since I was a teenager!" he boomed between versus, singing along enthusiastically as he nodded his head to the drums. His long, shaggy hair flew in all directions and Ollie felt threads of laughter falling from his open mouth at the sight. He ducked to avoid the flailing elbows.

Now recording video and audio.
Adding file: car13042079.mp5 to folder: augustusJackson

He gave the man a bright smile. The freckles that drew pathways along his face were dancing on his cheekbones. "I like the way your voice sounds," he said. The low baritone rumbled through his Chrome chassis in a very pleasing way.

"My mates and I were in a band together yonks back," August started, clearing his throat to avoid focusing on how that particular compliment made him feel, "We were barely more than wains, but we loved shit like this. Hopped up on sugar and dancing around the stage like fuckin' lunatics. We bugged half the bars in New Dublin to let us play there, barely made a cent doin' it either."

"That sounds like fun," Ollie commented, "It must have been nice having friends around you like that."

August's expression fell a little as he gripped the steering wheel again, shooting a look towards the man next to him. His smile was a little sadder, more subdued that before, his hands back in his lap again.

"You didn't have any friends back at Crossroads?" he asked.

Ollie shook his head. "Most of us were stationed in solo routes so there wasn't anyone to talk to."

"What about where you stayed the rest of the time?" the red-head probed, "Didn't you have, I dunno, break rooms or whatever?"

"When we would finish our assignments, we had to return to our lockers," the Android explained, "They were time-locked. Once we were inside, we couldn't leave again until we were needed."

"I'm…I'm really sorry, Ols."

Ollie looked over at him in surprise, "What for?"

The human reached up and scratched the back of his neck, uncertain of what to even say to that, "It's just that…it sounds like a really shitty way to live."I

"I'm not *alive*, August," the Android reminded him, "I was…made for a job. And I did it. That's the end of it."

The next words August said were quiet, barely more than a whisper. Ollie might have missed them if it weren't for the heightened power of his robotic hearing: "I'm glad you came with me then."

The corner of Ollie's lips pulled up in a smile that was becoming more than a little fond, "I am too, August," he whispered back.

Chapter 15
Domain

A sliver of light began to break through the bleak nothingness ahead of their car. The red, flickering lights rose, tilting as they climbed the exit ramp somewhere not three hundred metres in front of them. August let out a relieved sigh as he followed them out, squinting into the first natural daylight they had seen in hours.
Chaos surrounded them on all sides as they joined the skyway, the high-rise roads leading them from the tunnels and into an intricate filter lane that joined into the town's traffic at various different points. The sea of noise that surrounded them drowned out even August's heaviest baselines and Ollie blinked to close the music application so that his driving companion could better concentrate on his task. He looked out the window beside him, already disorientated by all the new data.
"Shit, new city, new system, huh?" August remarked anxiously as he brought himself in closer to the steering wheel, "We're heading straight down the middle, that right?"
Ollie nodded, "The instructions say to follow the signs for R592 and head towards the harbour."
"Speaking of harbours…" August said, reaching for the central console.
The window next to Ollie started to lower down slowly, cold air blowing in and around them in the car. "You smell that?" August asked, following the slip road down, "That's the sea you smell. All that salt water…"
The Android placed a hand on the doorhandle, closing his eyes and opening his mouth to stick out his tongue. The air was cleaner here, and Ollie could detect the salt particles and seawater droplets on his sensitive oral sensors. *Dimethyl sulphide* and *dictyopterenes* from the seaweed and dead phytoplankton made the air smell distantly like fish.

    His dark curls brushed against his ears and forehead, the tickling of his sensors giving the impression of their false touch. He took in all of the data greedily, assigning it to folders to study later in the evening when he had some free time. The salt content in the air, the chill of it, the way it tugged on his hair, he accumulated it all. Even the sounds of the gulls calling out for one another as they set sail on the current of the wind.

When he opened his eyes again, the sea itself had finally come into view, wrapped like a long, blue ribbon around a gift box. The twinkling surface of it stretched out far beyond the border of the bubble, steam rising up to fog the surface where it protected the town from the polluted space beyond.

The town of Schull itself was made up of new looking buildings with white, uniformed walls and huge windows that drew in sunlight like a man would draw in breath. The sea and sky were the lifeblood of every dwelling. Their gardens were groomed to perfection by house-proud hands, though more than a few of the more extravagant homes appeared to be lying dormant, their usual residents living elsewhere at this time of the year.

Reaching the lower levels of the town, August pulled off into one of the branching side streets, his car struggling to maintain any semblance of speed with the hills and sharp bends. The red-head cursed colourfully as he forcefully shoved the car into a lower gear, the back end of the car making some unpleasant noises of its own as he managed to get it moving again.

"Okay, Ols. Where to from here?"

Ollie tapped into his new, more basic mapping software and brought up the white guidelines for them to follow. The preconstructed path was guiding them right and then left in quick succession. August did as he was told, turning the wheel with both hands as per the Android's instructions. The perpetual maze of narrow streets led them closer and closer to the water until the Audi's tyres finally rolled to a stop on some very soft, very white sand.

The elegant apartment complex before them was an architect's dream, all creamy white walls and exposed red brickwork. The high ceilings and massive windows looked more like a luxury rental than a Safe House.

August climbed out of the car with a tired roar that was somewhere between a groan and a yawn. He closed his eyes and enjoyed the stretch of his body, reaching up towards the afternoon sunshine as the air bubbles in his spine popped pleasantly.

"Wow," he remarked, "This was definitely not what I was expecting."

The building had been constructed on the very edge of what was once Cadogan's Strand, and August imagined that the view from the windows facing it would be both spectacular and also very much wasted on someone like him. He glanced quickly in the Android's direction as he left the car, and it was clear that he was already completely enamoured with the place. His blue eyes were opened wide with wonder, his lips formed into the shape of an 'O'.

"I've checked the instructions from Goose three times," Ollie said at last without looking away, "It's definitely the right place."

August wandered around the back of the car and popped the boot, yanking out the suitcase and half-dropping it on the sand and gravel mix.

Ollie followed him around, reaching for the handle, "Let me take this for you," he offered.

August quickly yanked it from out of his reach, almost sending it toppling, "No way, Ols. You carried it back in the city. Let this old man do some of the work."

Ollie frowned at him, about to once again explain the difference between a human and a Social Droid, when he heard the sound of a shout from over their heads. He looked up in surprise as a stranger appeared on the glass balcony two floors up, waving a hand in an exaggerated left and right motion to catch their attention.

"There you are!" he called out with a smile, "Your friend arrived a few hours ago; we were wondering where you'd both gotten to!"

The man was muscular but slender with an impressive moustache that spanned the entire width of his face. Apart from his eyebrows, it was the only other hair on his entire head, the top shaved down to a perfect, shimmering baldness. The skin on his face and arms was tanned in the way you could only get if you spent a lot of time outdoors, freckles covering his arms in intricate speckling like a tropical bird. Laughter lines highlighted the points around his blue-green eyes.

August and Ollie exchanged a wary look.

"Wonder what *friend* he's talking about," August inquired quietly, dragging the case towards his Android companion, "We weren't told to expect anyone."

"Come on inside!" the tanned man hollered, his enthusiasm not deterred by their lack of response, "I'll stick the kettle on!"

Ollie followed August up the grey, metal stairs, watching as the man *thunked* his case down onto the landing to pull open the sliding door. They made their way into the office inside, cutting off the sound of the waves outside as they slid the door closed again behind them. The walls around them had been painted with a pale blue, wide windows on the south-facing wall letting bright sunlight in that Ollie could already feel warming his artificial skin.

//*You really can see the entire coastline from up here,* he marvelled.

August let the suitcase topple onto its side, swiping it with a foot to move it in towards the wall and out of the way. He moaned as he rubbed at his lower back and the Android next to him added knowingly, "I told you to lift with your knees." August straightened again abruptly, grunting at him, "*Yes mammy*," he droned petulantly.

The stranger from before was bustling around in the small kitchenette area out back, his toned neck and shoulders just about visible through the sliver of open doorway. He was singing to himself in Irish, the tune happy and upbeat, and something about the *lovely River Lee*.

As Ollie scanned the room, he realised with a start that there was someone else in the room with them. Sitting in one of the white leather armchairs in the corner, a familiar face looked back at him with glowing grey eyes.

"Officer Goose," he acknowledged with surprise, his companion's expression likely matching his own as he turned his head in their direction.

Goose was sitting perfectly upright on the edge of her chair, her expression pleasantly impassive as it always was. She offered them a polite smile and nodded her head, "Good morning, Mr Sheehan, 01113. I have been told to provide you with additional documentation ahead of your new work placement. I thought it best to do this right away to assist you in settling in."

She reached out a hand towards August and the human eyed it with a frown, "How nice of you," he grumbled, "6 hours of driving and now you wanna jab me with somethin'?"

Goose eyed him patiently, her hand never wavering as she replied, "Yes. Exactly." August let out a heavy sigh and relented to her, swearing when she injected the new chip into his skin without warning. He yanked his hand back, muttering something about *'rudeness'* and *'bloody miss personality'*.

"Your new employer has already been briefed on the circumstances, as has Mr. Murphy here," Goose started, ignoring the red-haired man and his continued quiet swears to her right, "They have taken part in the program previously with great success. Your employer served in the American Armed Forces for several decades before this and is impressively decorated."

August peered down at the thin trail of blood that was splitting the middle point between his thumb and pointer finger, "And what job have I been blessed with, pray tell?"

Goose's eyes glowed as she attained the necessary records, "You have been placed into the care of a Mr. Edmon Duffy. A mechanical engineer."

August huffed at that, "A mechanic? I've worked a lifetime and half in IT. It's been decades since I had to use my hands like that."

"Comprehensive training will be provided," Goose continued, her smile remaining unchanged despite his complaints.

"What about me?" Ollie queried.

Goose tilted her head to one side, the soft curls falling across the shoulder of her uniform where her serial number was shown, "Unfortunately, we were not able to procure the appropriate permissions in time to grant you access to Mr. Duffy's workshop. As such, you will be required to operate as a full-time Social Droid in charge of Mr. Jackson's welfare and care."

"That makes it sound like he's my maid," August scowled.

"Social Droids handle many of the responsibilities required of someone in the Cleaning or Care sectors," Goose stated, "Preparing meals, cleaning the home environment, shopping for inventory. All of it falls within the perimeters of your new assignment."

August noticed the subtle change in Ollie's posture in his peripheries but didn't comment on it. It was clear from the way he stiffened his shoulders and nodded obediently that this was not the news he had been hoping to receive. A twang of guilt sank low in his stomach, and he raised his hand to reach out towards him, only to be intercepted by the moustachioed man as he reappeared from the kitchen with a loaded tray. He balanced it on one hand, setting it between them with a loud clatter and a rattle. Goose narrowed her eyes towards the coffee table but said nothing.

"There's milk and sugar there for ya too, if you'd like" the apartment's owner added as he handed August a cup of tea he couldn't remember asking for. It was piping hot, burning the point of his knuckles that wrapped around the ceramic handle.

The bald-headed man turned his body towards his two Android guests, offering them an embarrassed half-smile, "Sorry I don't have anything suitable for you both in at the moment," he said apologetically.

August took a loud sip from his own mug, the steam fogging up his glasses as he let out a happy groan, "That's a shame," he said, "'Cos this is a fuckin' solid brew."

"*Slainte!*" the owner grinned, raising up his own mug from the tray, "You can thank the missus for the years of extensive trainin'."

Putting herself between them for a moment, Goose gathered up what little belongings she had brought with her, "I will leave you in the capable hands of Mr. Murphy for now," she said, "I will be stationed nearby for the next few hours if you require any further assistance."

"Thanks for all your help, Goose," August said, extending his free hand out towards her, "We appreciate you lookin' out for us."

She eyed it in the same way that Ollie once had, curious and a little bit nervous, before extending her own hand out to take it, offering him a very firm handshake that made him wince ever-so-slightly.

Jesus, he thought when she finally released her hold on him, *A little more force and she might've broken a finger or two there.*

Her lips formed into a smile as she bowed her head towards him again, "I wish you both the best. Lets hope we can speak again soon."

Well ain't that an ominous way to put it.

"Have a pleasant evening, Officer Goose," Ollie said quietly as she passed, standing with both hands behind his back, "Pass on our regards to Inspector O'Sullivan."

"I shall," Goose answered, and she disappeared out the sliding door without another word.

The apartment's owner, Dann Murphy, perched down on the arm of the chair beside them as he took another swig from his mug, "We don't get a wile lotta Androids around these parts. Are they always like that?"

"Not all of them," August answered with another long sip and swallow, shooting a grin Ollie's way, "I think Goose is just a little more on the, uh prim and proper side. Wouldn't ya say, Ols?"

"I think that Officer Goose just likes to remain professional in her behaviours," Ollie said, watching the way she had gone thoughtfully, "She appears to take her job very seriously."

The owner brought his empty mug back down to rest on the tray again, getting up and heading towards the counter at the far side of the room. He stood on the tips of his toes to reach over the side, pulling out a thin, steel-blue tablet that he skimmed with one finger. "While she was waiting, Officer Goose got both of you all set up on our systems. I have your full details as well as your emergency contacts in the NDG all registered. I just need a signature from you both and we'll be good to go."

He extended out the tablet and August created a crude copy of his signature with the tip of his pointer finger. Ollie's task was much easier, filled in with barely a blink of his eyes.

"Definitely a show off," August teased. From the corner of his eye, he could see the Android sticking his tongue out at him in response.

"Now that I have both of your names…" the man continued in front of them, smiling at their antics, "Let me introduce meself; me name's Dann Murphy, I'm the owner an' operator of the Strand Lobby. If you two have any problems with your rooms, it's me you'll be coming down to yell at at all hours of the day and night." He winked playfully, turning the tablet around to show them the details of their contract, "We have you both listed under the name *'Augustus Sheehan'* for rooms 18 and 19, that sound about right?"

"Yeah, that's us," August answered quickly, almost faltering at the false name. No doubt Dann already knew much about their situation, but they couldn't be too careful.

"Spotty dog," Dann cheered, affirming their booking for them, "That is…*perfect*. I'll just fetch you your keys and you can head on up."

He hurried around the counter, reappearing just a moment later with both sets of keychains. He let out a triumphant '*aha*!' as he did so, keys held aloft like a fisherman with a prized trout, "I made a few extra copies, just in case. Never know when a spare could come in handy."

Ollie studied his own key as it was pressed into his hand. He had never owned anything before, and this tiny, little thing held so much weight and promise beyond the scope of its own size. He closed his hand tightly around it as if he was scared that he might lose it the second he looked away. The rough edge dug lightly into his palm.

"We just put fresh sheets on the beds this morning, all newly bought. Though, I'm afraid there's only a small number of plates and cutlery available for the time being. The last tenant was notoriously clumsy."

"That's no problem," August reassured the man, nodding towards his companion, "This one's not a big eater."

Dann quirked a fuzzy eyebrow, "Oh yes, of course," he chuckled, "Well, if you need anything at all don't hesitate to shout down. Me or the Missus are usually about during the daylight hours, and there's an answer phone for the unsociables. Sound good?"

"Dead on" August agreed, bending down to lift his suitcase again, "Now, which direction we headin'?"

Dann pointed up towards the ceiling, "Two floors straight up. The two facing the water."

"Cheers, Dann," August said, and led the way through the exit to their right. They climbed the silvery blue stairs towards the upper-level apartments, August stubbornly refusing to let Ollie help with his luggage despite his own trembling legs and the availability of a lift further down the way.

The human let out a shaky breath as they emerged on the top floor landing, placing a hand on his thigh as he doubled over somewhat, "Remind me…I need to…start working out," he wheezed.

Ollie appeared at this side, shaking his head with an amused sigh, "You should have just let me help you," he said.

"Nah," the red-head answered dismissively, "I just need to get my second wind, is all."

It made Ollie want to roll his eyes. His new friend was stubborn about the weirdest things.

After a brief 30-second interlude, August righted himself again and continued wheeling the case on down the corridor. The ceiling overhead was made of glass and hints of the sunset were pouring in from above, tinting everything with a rosy hue. There were two doors on either side of the corridor with signs directing them to more rooms further on down as well. Between the two interlinking corridors was a wooden fire door with a bar across the centre.

Ollie slowed to a stop as they came to a painting framed with driftwood. It was hanging at head height on the wall and his bright eyes traced along all the colours on the canvas. "Is this somewhere around here?" he asked.

August let his suitcase balance against the wall for a moment, coming closer to see what he was looking at, "That's what Cadogan's Strand used to look like," he answered, "Before the floods. There used to be a beach that ran in an arch all along the coastal path here."

"It was really beautiful," Ollie lamented, his tone dipping subtly with his disappointment, "It's a shame we didn't get to see it."

"It was one of the first spots to go," August observed, "I don't even think I was born yet. We lost a lot of the coastlines down here in the early 30s."

"That must have been hard for the locals," Ollie commented, watching August picking up the case again and dragging it the last few steps towards their rooms.
"Hard on everybody," August concurred, "Ireland's an island, after all. Half the people living here are on the coast. We lost half the country within a century." Coming to a stop at number 18, August fished the key out of his pocket and twisted it in the lock. The door opened with a sticky pull, the smell of fresh emulsion hitting them immediately when they went inside. The apartment was open-plan with tall, angular ceilings and windows to the right that overlooked the shoreline.

A round sofa was huddled in the corner by the door, multicoloured cushions adding a little bit of zest to the otherwise plain, white leather. Directly ahead of them, a series of grey painted stairs led up to the bedroom alcove above. Beneath it, the small kitchen curved in to follow the shape of the room, a breakfast bar on one side with wall-mounted fridge freezer and oven on the other.

"Holy shit, *look* at this place!" August remarked, letting out an appreciative whistle as he kicked his bag in through the doorway, "No way I could ever afford something like this. Not in a million years."

Ollie tailed the man inside, gravitating towards the wide French doors and the view outside, "You can see all the way out to the bubble from here," he breathed.

August joined him at the windows, watching the way Ollie braced himself up on his tip toes to see as much of the coast as he could.

"Say, Ollie, about what Goose said down there…"

The Android's smile fell away as he turned to face him, "I…I don't think I want to talk about it, August."

August took a step towards him, running one hand over his beard somewhat nervously, "You know you don't have to-"

Blue eyes cut him off as they narrowed in his direction, "August," he said firmly, "*Please.*"

The human closed the distance between them, placing both hands on the other man's shoulders to ground him. He could see himself in the younger man for a moment, a part of him eager to run away and hide from all this too.

"We don't have to talk about it right now," he said, "But I just wanted you to know I…I'm right here, Ols. Going through this with you. And you don't have to do a damn thing that you don't want to."

//Don't **want** to?

The concept was so foreign, so alien, that it stopped the Android in his tracks. His anger and frustration dissipated as quickly as it had arrived, and August let out a quiet *oof* of surprise as his forehead came forward to rest against his sternum.
"Thank you…"
August could feel the gentle pulses of the man's inner circuitry, an electronic mimicry of a heartbeat, against his chest and gave in to the impulse to reach out to thread his thick fingers through his soft looking curls.
"It's going to be alright, you know."
Ollie stiffened against him, obviously taken by surprise by the action, and then, slowly, he dissolved into his arms, allowing his companion to take some of his weight.
"I want to believe you're right," he whispered.
"Haven't you learned by now that I'm always right, *duine*?" August teased, a warm smile spreading across his lips as he wrapped his other arm around his companion's toned shoulders, "You'll see. We just have to take things one day at a time from here on out. Everything's gonna be grand in the end."

Chapter 16
Boolean

The livingroom that Ollie walked into was almost identical to August's, except for the marigold paint on the walls and the lemon and orange pillows on the sofa. The tiles in the kitchen space beyond were made of a shiny black ceramic that captured and held the light, the adjacent breakfast bar covered with brand new matching appliances.
He approached the counter and picked up one of the sage green pans, testing its weight in his grip. His scans revealed that it was a very basic model, considered an essential tool for students or those who were living on their own for the very first time. Ollie supposed that second group now included him as well.

Setting the pan back down onto the countertop, he made his way from room to room, examining the tiny, disused bathroom, the spare room with its folded-up sofa bed and the sparsely decorated master bedroom and landing upstairs. He trailed his fingers over the neatly arranged sheets with wonder in his eyes, caressing the soft fabric all the way from the bottom of the bed to the top. He had never had the need for an actual bed before. The mattress felt spongy under his weight as he took a seat on it curiously, falling back as his curls tumbled across his face. It bounced a little under him, just firm enough to adjust to the contours of his shape. He rolled up onto his side to face the empty space alongside him, reaching out to touch the cool, smooth surface of the second pillow that had been placed there. He wondered what it might feel like to find that space occupied, to feel someone else's weight pressing down there, adjusting the balance of the bedframe. For a moment he pictured August lying there, just like he had in their hotel room. Fingers interlocked across his stomach. Dark eyes staring up at the ceiling. But this time, there was a small smile on his lips, a sense of contentment there instead of apprehension.

Ollie reached out towards the spot where his face would have been and jumped when a loud knock at the door downstairs sent the image fleeing. He slid off the edge of the bed again and brushed the banister as he took the stairs downwards. Whenever he reached the door, his iris scans showed him the outline of the man that was waiting for him outside.

He smiled to himself. *//As if it would be anyone else.*

"August," he said as he pulled the door fully inwards, "Is everything alright?"

Shuffling in place and looking anywhere but at him, August cleared his throat, "I, uh, finished unpacking," he started, dark eyes seemingly taking in every miniscule grain of detail on the doorframe now, "Thought you might like to join me for a drink?"

Ollie cocked his head, "A drink? August I-"

"Wait, before you argue…" August held up a hand, "I've got a present for you." He hurried past him and into the kitchenette, laying down a small, white plastic bag on the counter. "I spotted it when we were leaving the hotel before. I picked up a few from the vending machine." Reaching inside the bag, the human produced a tall, dark-coloured plastic bottle, setting it down onto the counter with a flourish.

Ollie turned his head to the side to study the details on the label, "It's…for Androids?" he questioned.

"Apparently, it's made up of a mixture of natural minerals, water and coolant," August explained. He hesitated, his smile flickering away like dying embers in a fireplace, "Shit, was this a bad idea? Sorry I didn't mean-"

"No, no," the Android assured him, blinking himself out of his thoughts for a moment, "It's really very kind of you. It's just that…no one's ever given me something like this before. Something for my own enjoyment, I mean."

"Oh," the red-haired human said quietly, letting the words hang in the air between them for a moment.

A message popped up in the corner of Ollie's HUD, noting that the other man's heart rate was subtly increasing. His lack of response was making him nervous, it seemed.

"How does it…how does it work?" he asked, nodding towards the bottle, "The drink, I mean. How do I use it?"

Perking up at the man's question, August took a hold of the bottle and lifted it up to inspect it, "It says here that this is its concentrated form. You can add hot or cold water to this to make a drink out of it." His hazel eyes turned towards his companion, "I could brew it like a tea, if you'd like?"

At his nod, the larger man crossed the room into the kitchen, grabbing the kettle and filling it up with water from the tap. He placed it by the wall and hit the switch, the little light on the side igniting with a red-coloured glow as the water inside started to rumble softly.

Ollie hopped up onto one of the kitchen stools and watched, utterly intrigued, as the other man brought out two mugs from the cupboard, rinsed then to rid them of any dust or dirt, and then laid them out before him. He popped a tea bag into one mug and began pouring the thick, tarry mixture into the other one, topping them both up with hot water. Steam filled the tiny kitchen area, the white mist creeping along the bottoms of the cupboards as he returned the kettle to the spot which would become its new home. Two *chinks* followed as August deposited a spoon in each mug, simultaneously stirring with both hands.

"Think it's just about done," he said, sliding Ollie's mug across the marble countertop towards him, "What do you reckon? Wanna give it a try?"

He climbed into the stool across from him, adding a splash of milk and sugar to his own mug. Apparently, the man had quite the sweet tooth.

Ollie stared down into the cup, feeling the wet warmth of the steam where it caressed his cheeks and chin. "How do you know when it's cool enough to drink?" he asked.

"I usually just take a sip at a time. If it scalds my tongue off, then I know to give it a few more minutes," August answered as he took his mug and brought it to his own lips.

Ollie arched a dark eyebrow at him, "Not the best way to test the temperature," he remarked.

August swallowed with a contented gasp, "Maybe not, but it works."

Mirroring the other man's actions, Ollie wrapped both hands around the mug, raised it up and poured some into his mouth. He let the warm liquid rest on the surface of his tongue, his HUD providing him with a clear breakdown of all of the ingredients. Core minerals, mostly. He activated the artificial glands in his mouth and pushed the liquid to the back of his throat, swallowing it down. His sensors followed the journey of its heat all the way down to the reservoir in his abdomen. He closed his eyes, examining each piece of new data as it presented itself.

"Well?" came August's voice from the other side of the table, "What's the verdict, Ols?"

Ollie opened his eyes, his tongue running along his teeth and the crease of his bottom lip thoughtfully, "I'm…not sure. I've never consumed anything before."

"Does it taste of anything?" August asked, propping his chin up with one hand.

"Androids aren't really designed to have a true sense of taste," Ollie answered, "I can list off the ingredients but not much else." He lifted his blue eyes to meet those of the man opposite him, "The act of swallowing on the other hand…is weirdly pleasant."

The red-head peered over the top of his mug at him, hesitating before taking another swig, "Wait, you've never-"

"The lubrication in my mouth is manually controlled," Ollie explained, taking another small sip, "I can control when it is released and how much. It means that actions such as spitting or swallowing are not something I have had to do before."

August cleared his throat, seemingly a little flustered as he buried his own face in his tea again. The steam fogged up the lenses of his glasses.

Ollie smiled into his mug, taking no notice, "I like the temperature difference. I can feel its heat moving through me. It's…nice."

He focused on the feeling of the heated ceramic against his palms and his fingertips, his sensors picking up the fluctuations between the heat within the container and the cooler air outside of it. The warring information on his HUD was certainly curious.

"It's even better outside," August said, getting down from the raised seat, "Come on. Follow me a sec."

He led the way towards the large, French doors, pulling them aside and guiding them onto the balcony beyond. The man flopped down onto one of the small, metal seats there with a groan, holding his mug aloft until he was comfortably seated. He patted the chair next to him as an invitation for the other man to join him.

Ollie pulled the doors closed behind him and slowly lowered himself into the free seat. He held the mug close to his chest, enjoying the way its heat radiated through him. The cold sea air circled around them both and the sensors along his skin tingled with it. He jumped when he felt August's hand close around his right knee, squeezing lightly.

"Don't mute your sensors," he requested, "Just…*feel* it, alright?"

Something about August's touch was warming, just like the tea had been, and Ollie found himself leaning into it, hoping that he wouldn't pull away. The nagging feeling of the cold was slowly filtered out of his focus, everything drawn towards those two, very different sources of heat instead.

"The view here is something else, isn't it?" August commented. He glanced down and, as if noticing his hand was still where he had left it, quickly pulled it away. He cleared his throat again, his hair blowing in and around his face as he angled himself away.

Ollie's body felt somehow colder in the spot where his hand had once been. Despite seeing the temperature return to match the rest of his body, it was like he could still feel its absence there.

The sea lay sprawled before them both like an oil painting, the blue and green tones mingling in a beautiful contrast to the darkening sky. Beyond the translucent boundaries of the bubble, the water was black and wild, and the waves slammed hard against the sides like a battering ram.

Where New Dublin had been loud, garish and brash, the town of Schull was subdued, contemplative, and peaceful. Nature felt like an integral part of the world around them, like the occupants of the quiet town has considered it in their every brushstroke and blueprint. Everything around them was green and vibrant, the living tendrils interwoven with the black highways and the aging buildings.

"It's so different from the city," Ollie said at last, his sigh drifting out beyond the metal railing, "The water seems so close here."

The rising temperatures had changed the very makeup of the sea, much of the life beneath the surface now forever changed. Even fishermen who had built their livelihood on the waters knew it was no longer safe to eat half of what they brought home with them. The creatures that had managed to survive the changes were themselves altered. Tough hides and snarling teeth were not as appetizing as the fish from the old days had been.

"I heard people used to swim in it, decades ago," August commented, "They didn't even have to wear special suits or anything."

"I wonder what that must have been like," Ollie said with an electronic-sounding hum, "I think the oceans have saltwater in them."

August made a face, "Saltwater? What, like…tablesalt?"

Ollie shook his head, "I believe it was a mixture of sand and other minerals. It wasn't drinkable back then either."

"How bizarre," the red-head chuckled, draining the last of his tea and placing down his mug again.

Ollie spun around in his seat, eyes glowing, just before the sound of a doorbell interrupted their conversation. Shooting a look towards his companion, August rose to his feet. He handed Ollie his emptied mug as he passed by him with a grunt and headed for the front door. The Android followed after him, bright eyes scanning the figures awaiting them on the other side.

"Any idea who it is, kid?" August asked, keeping his voice intentionally low.

Ollie shook his head, "My scan is showing three people there. Other residents, I'm assuming. Best to be cautious."

"Alright," August agreed, hand on the handle, "You still got that gun Inspector O'Sullivan gave you?"

Ollie touched the compartment in his side where the sidearm was stashed, "I do," he answered, "Though I hope we won't be needing it quite so soon."

"Just keep it handy," August advised as he pulled open the door, the doorbell echoing from both sides as a young woman sprang back with an embarrassed squeak.

She offered them an apologetic smile, "Sorry, I wasn't sure if you could hear me in there!" she said, waving both hands in the air, "Mine didn't work for the first week after Dann put it in."

August's dark eyes narrowed as he took in each of their faces in turn, studying them cautiously, "No worries, we were just outside. Checking out the view."

The woman who had rung the doorbell clapped her hands together in obvious delight, bouncing up and down on the balls of her feet, her dyed blonde hair falling around her shoulders. Her Chrome eyes shone in the shadow of their doorway. "It's amazing, isn't it?" she cheered, "A real hidden gem!"

An older woman to her left gave her a gentle pat on the arm, "Apologies for her energy. We haven't had new neighbours in a while. She's been skippin' around like a bloody Labrador since she saw your car pull up." This woman was in her mid-fifties, her accent soft and vaguely Hispanic. Her hair and eyes were made up of varying shades of black and silver that made her resemble some of the teachers August had had back in his high school days. Her smile was warm like summertime, the lines surrounding her lips demonstrating that it was an expression she wore often.

The third member of their party was a tall man with dark skin and a shaved head. His eyes were a striking shade of emerald-green. His smile was like of a housecat, intelligent and conniving in equal measure. As he caught Ollie's eyes, a rush of data travelled between them that made the smaller Android stagger.

//He's an Android, Ollie observed with surprise, his eyes falling immediately to the man's bare throat, *//But he isn't wearing any tags! How?*

The other Android's smile widened as if he could hear his words. He stuck out his hand in August's direction, his voice like a welcoming, Cheshire-cat purr, "My name is Sea; this is Julia and her mother Gabriela. They're in number 21. I'm in 20, across the hall. The girls here have been dying for a nosey at our new arrivals."

August shook the man's hand, "Name's August. And this here is Ollie. Afraid there's nothing much to nosey at yet. We're still getting settled."

Sea peered through the gap between them both, "Is that so?"

"Are you both from the city then?" Julia spoke up, her eyes bright and shining, "I know a New Dublin accent when I hear it!"

"Julia!" Gabriela chastised, "Don't be so forward. Let the poor men breathe a moment."

"Nah, it's alright," August chuckled, "Guilty as charged. We just fancied a change of pace." He stretched out his lower back with a groan, "The joys of getting older."

"And you're an Android too!" Gabriela turned her kind smile in Ollie's direction, "You'll be a tremendous help in our quiz nights! Sea here has been nigh on unbeatable since he arrived."

Sea laughed brightly behind her, "Keep dreamin', Pam!" he said, "That trophy is mine and I'm not giving it back without a fight!"

//*So, they know he's an Android?* Ollie wondered.

"We have a house meeting every Wednesday," Julia listed off, stuffing a series of paper pamphlets into August's waiting hands, "Quiz night's every other Tuesday. And Margarita Friday on the last weekend of the month."

"Our numbers are on the back if you need help finding anything," Gabriela continued, reaching out to tap the page that August had just turned to, "And here's the number for the front desk."

"We appreciate the warm welcome, believe you me," August said, running a hand over his beard, "It has been a hellova couple'a days."

"Moving is never easy," Gabriela agreed, "But Schull is worth getting to know. We take things a lot slower here than in that big city where you're from. Within a week or two, you'll forget why you ever worried about a thing."

"Here's hoping," August sighed, the tiredness evident in his voice and posture as he leaned casually against their open doorframe.

As the others said their farewells, August hung back and watched each of them go with fascination. "What do you think, Ols?" he asked quietly, "Crossroads spies or nice new neighbours?"

Ollie stepped aside as August pulled the door closed again, turning the nib, "The man that introduced himself as Sea," he started with a nervous frown, "It seems he's an Android like me."

August's dark eyebrows jumped, "Really? But he didn't have the..." He waved a hand vaguely around his throat.

"I wonder if he is trying to conceal that he is an Android from others outside the Safe House," Ollie wondered aloud, glancing towards the now closed door.

"You don't think he followed us here...do you?" August questioned.

Ollie shook his head, "I saw his info when he linked with me. He was a Carer Droid. Model number 534. He was stationed at a facility in the next town over but moved to Schull just over a year ago. It is unlikely Crossroads would have planted him here."

"Without the collar you'd never have known that he was an Android," the human commented, slipping both hands into the front pockets of his trousers and leaning back against the wall, "You ever…?"

The Android frowned, "What? Think of removing my collar?" he asked, "It's against the law to tamper with an Android's identification."

"I know," August noted, studying his expression like he was trying to see something in particular reflected there, "But have you ever thought about it?"

"No. Not even once," Ollie lied, and he turned and walked back towards the French doors and the view lying on the other side of them.

Chapter 17
Big Data

The forest was dark, the last rays of afternoon sunlight blotted out by the expanse of the tree cover. The young man beneath it tripped over his feet as he ran. He could see the beams of light from the flashlights behind him, pinpointing his location as surely as a sniper's target. His heart was pounding hard in his throat, choking him and making him wheeze. He cried out as his ankle twisted over another half-buried root.

I've got to keep running, *he thought, thin fingers clawing through the mud as he dragged himself forward, so out of breath that he was dizzy. He tumbled blindly from tree to tree, trying his best to avoid the shallow ditches that had naturally formed between them. Sharp thorns tore at his clothing, and he heard their quiet rip of protest as he hobbled onwards towards the sound of running water. He wasn't sure why, but he knew that he had to reach it somehow.*

He could see the shapes of the others ahead of him and frantically moved his feet to reach them. Everything ached, lactic acid pooling in his bruised and bloodied legs. The people behind were getting so close now, so very close…

Ollie snapped awake at the sound of gunfire, sitting bolt upright on top of the still-made bed. His HUD lit up like a flare, his every sense scanning the open room around him for possible danger. Warning messages temporarily blinded him as his eyes rebooted and he blinked back artificial tears as he reached up a hand to push back his hair.

Light filtered in from somewhere down the stairs, signalling to him that it was morning. He crawled to the edge of the bed, letting his legs dangle down as he tried to settle his breathing. The fans in his throat spun wildly, trying desperately to rid him of the excess heat he had accumulated in rest. His whole body felt like it was vibrating, the graphic images still flooding his senses with a confused array of conflicting information.

//What **was** that?

His hand fell away from its spot on his head, sending his loose curls tumbling down across his face. It had felt so real- as if he really had been running in that awful place. A feeling of unease descended over him, and he shot a look back behind him with wide eyes.

//Of course, there's no one there, he rationalised, It...it must have been a dream.

He had never had one of those before. He shook his head and squeezed his eyes tightly shut again. The pictures had been so *vivid*, etched into his mind as clearly as any of the paths he had taken in the underground. He looked down towards his quivering hands, flexing each finger in and out again experimentally as he ran through his usual diagnostics.

He stared blankly at the next transparent screen that materialised before his eyes:

NO ERRORS FOUND.

He searched again. And the same result appeared.

He frowned as he allowed his feet to touch down onto the floor. The sensation of the cold wood was welcome, an easy equation for his electronic brain to make sense of. A yes or no logic puzzle with no wrong answers.

He headed towards the stairs, counting them in his mind as he made his way down.

7

8

9

//*What do humans do when they feel like this?* he wondered.

He headed for the door and pulled it open, letting out a startled gasp as he met August there, the man frozen in place with one hand raised as if ready to knock. "Uh…good morning," he said gruffly. The man was clearly not awake long, his voice low and deep in its uncaffeinated state.

"August," Ollie squeaked, his grip on the doorhandle tightening almost imperceptibly, "Is everything alright? I thought you might still be sleeping at this hour."

The human shrugged, "New beds are hard to get used to," he replied, "I was coming to see if you fancied a walk? Maybe get your head shired?"

A walk was exactly what Ollie needed to clear his racing mind. But that second part…

"Head…*shired*?" he asked.

The human let loose a low, sleepy chuckle, "Sorry, another colocalism. Just means you can take some pressure off. Relax a little."

Ollie snatched his keys from where they hung by the door, "Oh, that sounds nice," he said, "Will we need to bring anything with us?"

"Nope," August answered, stuffing his hands into the pockets of his hoodie, "Just ourselves. We can take a wee trip around the harbour, if you'd like? See exactly what we're dealing with here."

Ollie closed the door behind him, listening for the sound of the snib catching as he fell into step with his human companion. He wondered if he should tell him about the dream. Was that something people talked about? Or was that something humans tended to keep to themselves?

Before he had the chance to make up his mind on the matter, August was heading down the stairs, chatting to him brightly and sending the thoughts of dark and gloomy forests far away from his mind.

Pushing through the front door and out into the sunshine, Ollie stood captivated for a moment as he watched the different tones in August's bright hair catching the morning light. Red, orange, copper, brown, grey. Like the paintings that were hanging in both of their apartments, the longer the Android looked the more details he was able to see. The man was dressed down today as well, in a pair of relaxed blue jeans and another dark green running-themed jumper. He wasn't wearing his glasses either, though a quick scan showed the bulge in his pocket where his case was. Ollie watched the man reach into his jeans and then light up a cigarette. He thought he would be quite content to just stand and watch him all day. A smile appeared on his face quite without his permission.

Hazel eyes caught his attention, and he felt himself flush when he realised that the man had been speaking to him. He tried to rewind the moment in his recordings, but he had missed what he had said entirely.

"You're a little spacey today," August commented, taking another puff and exhaling out into the sea air, "You alright?"

"Yes," Ollie answered, probably a little too quickly. He felt the heat around his face and ears intensifying and quickly went into his settings to turn down his sensitivity to such things. "Yes," he repeated, "I suppose I just didn't rest well either."

August took another long drag, obviously enjoying the habit on a cool April morning like this one, "Meeting the neighbours got you nervous?"

Ollie shook his head, following his companion as he started along the next adjoining path from the Safe House, "They all seemed nice to me. Kind."

"You aren't worried about that other Android, are ya? Sea, was it?" August probed.

"I went through the information he transferred to me last night. All of it checks out," Ollie answered, "It's likely the others are involved in the same case we are. Against Crossroads."

August hummed around the end of his cigarette, "They've been here a while if that's the case."

They made their way along the roadside and towards the point where the original harbour had once been. Everything was green and blue as far as the eye could see, the two colours meeting on the horizon beyond the town's bubble. There was little left of the old walls that used to line the waterfront, the stones long since eaten away by the rising pressure of the sea. New concrete sea walls had been erected along the side of the road, obscuring much of the view but protecting the last remaining portions of undamaged road.

Suddenly noticing Ollie's absence by his side, August turned to see the other man had stopped to study a large, stone plaque about 10 or so metres down the road. He folded his arms across his chest as he rejoined him, bending at the middle to read the information carved there.

"*An Scoil*," he read with a curious hum, "Looks like one of the original signs. Probably been here a few decades at least." He peered around the back of it, "Looks like it was moved here from somewhere else."

"There's water damage on the bottom," the Android noted, "It was likely rescued from one of the sites of the flooding."

"There's a few spots like this back home too," August observed turning his head to face out towards the roar of the waves just beyond them, "Seaside towns definitely got the worst of it."

The previous decimation of the town became clearer with every new landmark that they encountered. Boats sailed out over the surface of the rocky waves; traces of a submerged basketball court still half-visible below their hulls if you knew where to look. Every new wall they passed was braced with sandbags, metal road signs declaring that different areas of the walkway were currently under repair. It was like the town was at constant war with the sea itself.

The little café they passed on their right-hand side had certainly seen better days as well. *O'Brien's* was its name, and it stood watch over the new harbour with something like determination on its stony face. Its paint was cracked as an old man's skin and in the process of peeling away. Motorbikes lined the front of the building, their chassis glistening from the earlier rainfall.

People watched them passing by from the open doorway to the Schull Harbour Hotel next door. August leaned to one side to nosey at the chalkboard, surprised to find that the modest three storey building was filled to capacity already. What had once been rows of terraced houses on either side of it were now blank, carbon copies of American-style apartments with huge windows that greedily drank in as much sunlight as they could. Perfect, picturesque balconies had been created on the upper levels, lined with expensive furniture and huge, black barbeques that looked like they had never even been used.

The golden-brown corner building which ended the road looked to have once been a café or a restaurant but was now long-deserted, the windows smashed in, and glass strewn about the ground outside. It crunched under their feet as they walked by.

Ollie ducked his head to peer inside, his glowing eyes lighting up the otherwise dark space, "I wonder what happened here."

August tossed the end of his cigarette onto the pile of glass, "The usual shit. Half-empty houses owned by rich assholes. Locals homeless. Economy entirely relying on said rich assholes to survive…Tensions are bound to rise in places like this."

"Sounds like you're speaking from experience," the Android observed.

August stuffed his hands into the front pouch of his dark hoodie, "The curse of living in a beautiful place like this one. People build these stunning holiday homes and then leave the place a ghost town for 3/4s of the year. The locals scramble to afford the rising costs of living in the area and get totally priced out of the place. Everything is seasonal so the kids haven't a damn thing to do most of the time." He waved a hand through the broken window, "Means they act up. Break shit. Get a bad rep that follows them like a plague even when they move."

"Why don't they just build more houses?" Ollie asked, kicking some of the glass from the street back in through the opening again.

"They do," August stated, leaning in closer to his companion's side with a dark but teasing smile, "For the *millionaires*."

The Android wrinkled his nose, making his freckles shift with annoyance, "But that won't solve anything!"

"Nope," August agreed, popping the 'p' in the word, "You see the problem?"

Ollie let out a quiet huff that was becoming all too similar to August's, "Humans can be frustrating sometimes."

August's responding laugh echoed in the empty doorway, and he took Ollie by surprise when he threw an arm around his shoulders. The fabric of his hoodie had pulled up slightly at the wrist, revealing some of the human's dark tattoos beneath it, "You're telling me!" he said, "In two sentences you have proved you have more sense than half our politicians, *duine*."

"I don't understand how a world that's so full of art and beauty can also have such cruelty in it," Ollie said softly by his ear.

"Ah, the duality of man," the red-head continued theatrically, "You were bound to learn this lesson sooner or later, Ols."

"What lesson?" the Android probed, frowning.

"That some humans just suck," August clarified.

Ollie met his dark eyes, his expression strangely serious, "Well, I don't think *you* suck, August."

"Well, I'm glad," the man chuckled. Without thinking, he brought his hand up to Ollie's curls and tussled them playfully and the Android swatted him away with both hands.

"Just because you have a height advantage does not mean you should abuse your power," Ollie scolded, trying to return his hair to some sort of organised chaos.

Having Ollie next to him proved more than enough to improve August's mood and it didn't take him long to shake off the cobwebs from another sleepless night. When they carried on down the main street, the Android's genuine enthusiasm about the old buildings and the sleeping tomcat on the garden wall became infectious. August felt like his cheeks were beginning to hurt from smiling.
It's been a long time since I had a morning as good as this one.
Ollie paused outside of the church building a few streets down, pointing out the detailing in the ornate glasswork that surrounded the entranceway. The way that it caught the light was borderline mesmerizing. Although much of the original glass appeared to be missing or patched up with wads of paper and duct tape, it still cast beautiful colours down onto the surrounding gardens. It was as if, despite the obvious years of wear and tear, the old building was trying to look its best for passersby.
August hadn't set foot in a church since he was fifteen years old. If he was blunt about it, he would have said he hated the place, but really his feelings had been mixed on the subject of religion for a long time. His local parish conjured up some pretty bad memories and the voices of those priests would likely haunt the halls of his subconscious forever. Choices made in his teenager years and beyond meant that he would likely catch fire if he ever seriously set foot in one again.
The sign outside read *'Jesus loves you and so do we'* in colourful cursive. He made a face at that despite himself. *But your love has stipulations, doesn't it?* he scowled, hearing the echo of New Dublin church bells in his ears as he glared up at the bell tower.
"August?" came Ollie's soft voice from next to him, "You're shaking."
The red-haired man blinked as he came back into his own body again, the last dregs of memory dissipated as he shook his head, "Sorry, kid. My head was miles away."
He ran a hand over his face, closing his eyes and pushing those thoughts back into the very depths of his mind. Where they belonged.
Ollie's hand was resting on his bicep, his thumb rubbing soothing circles in the fabric of his hoodie, "Do you want to keep going?" he asked.
"Don't you worry about me," August answered, waving off the man's concern, "Just…not the biggest fan of churches, that's all."
The Android shot the building a glare, as if it were solely to blame for his reaction, and August let out an amused snort. It was such a human reaction that he couldn't

help the way his heart swelled with fondness. He was already starting to notice the subtle changes in the Android, things he might not have seen if they didn't spend such an inordinate amount of time together. The way he held himself was much more natural now, his walk less mechanical when he wasn't constantly monitoring himself. It was also clear that he couldn't hide away the parts of himself that were kind or curious, the parts of him that wanted to reach out and seize the world with both hands. Hands that really didn't seem to belong to a Runner Droid made for a lonely life in dark underground tunnels.

Chinese restaurants, bars, credit unions, and tiny farmers' markets lined one side of the narrow street, the buildings painted with bright pastel shades of purple, yellow and red. People sat outside, enjoying the rare sunshine that came with living in a place as green as Ireland. A few curious eyes looked their way and August raised a hand in greeting, subtly moving his body in front of that of his smaller companion, hoping to block their view of the soft pink uniform and the glowing piece of metal around the man's neck.

"It seems so quiet here," Ollie said as he paused to take a deep, artificial breath inwards. Data filled his mind with a pleasant buzz.

August headed towards the sound of ringing bells and music, eyeing the sign for *'Cé na Coile'*, Schull Pier, as they hurried up the curb. Ollie stuck close to his shoulder; eyes wide as the illuminous attractions came into view along the reconstructed pier.

"I hear music," he observed with surprise.

The original pier hadn't been much to speak of, but this new addition had extended the walkway out almost as far as the bubble, filling the surrounding area with light and noise.

Conflicting, disjointed music blared from every ride and attraction as they approached. The screams of those above them on the roller coaster had clearly captured the Android's attention., judging by the way he had thrown his head back to watch them go.

"What *is* that?" he questioned with alarm, his mouth falling open, "I can't tell if they're enjoying it or not."

August's shoulders jumped in his dark green hoodie, "I think that's the point."

The train rose up and dipped down again quickly, a chorus of delighted and terrified screams following in its wake. Ollie tilted his head, clearly confused.

"It's called a Fun Fair," August explained, pushing his hair back with the heel of one hand, "Some people get a thrill from going on rides like that. Facing your fear can give you this weird rush of endorphins. Make you feel, I dunno, *alive*?"
Ollie blinked, startled by a new message that had popped up in his field of vision. The bright, crimson letters of his HUD formed the words:

New Objective: (feel 'Alive');

Just the thought alone was enough to make electricity run through his entire body. He frowned at the man standing next to him, "You said '*some people*'. Does that mean that you don't enjoy it?"
August lifted a hand up to shield his eyes from the rising sun as he squinted, "Nah, I'm more a feet on the ground kinda guy myself," he said.
"Would you be averse to…trying it with me?"
The words had come out so quietly that they were almost completely drowned out by the noises all around them. August lowered his hand slowly as he studied the wistful look on the other man's face. He had never asked for anything before. That was new.
There was a desperate look in his blue eyes as he followed the motions of the people over their heads, as if he was recording every tiny emotion he saw written on their faces. For all August knew, maybe he was.
"You really want to go on that thing?"
Ollie spun on the spot to offer him the most powerful puppy dog eyes the man had ever seen, and August turned away with an exasperated sigh, terrified that he might just give in to the Android's every demand when it used magic like that.
Whoever created Androids knew exactly what they were doing, August thought, *How the Hell can I say no when he makes a face like that?*
"Fine," he relented, knowing he lost this particular fight the second he brought his new companion in here, "If that's what you've set your heart on, I'll ride it with you." He rolled his eyes, "Happy now?"
Ollie flashed him with a bright smile that seemed to make his entire face light up, "Yes!" he cheered, "Thank you, August!"
Something in the human's stomach flipped which had nothing to do with the thought of riding one of those metal death traps again. He swallowed down the rush of panic that suddenly accompanied it.

What the Hell is going on with you these last few days? he chastised himself, chewing on the inside of his lip, *Butterflies are for pre-teens and romance novels. You're a grown-ass man. Catch yourself on.*

He glared at the bright yellow ticket booth like it had offended him, scowling when the young man inside slid the tickets across to each of them. He hadn't felt anything even remotely like this in a long, damn time. Not since him and Natalie had got divorced, and that was nearly two decades ago.

Christ, he wasn't even *out* back then. Not that he could really say that he was out *now*, just hiding in a slighter bigger closet.

He pushed through the confusing cloud of dread and *something else*, trying to ignore the way his heart was pounding in his ears. Ollie followed him up the metal steps with his head on a swivel, unable to contain his amazement at every new discovery.

August tried not to focus on the dazed expressions being worn by the other passengers as they exited the ride, stumbling down the red and yellow rails and into the waiting area again. One couple passed by right next to them, the dark-haired woman whispering in her partner's ear as she pointed a finger not-so-subtly towards Ollie's vibrant collar.

August wasn't entirely sure what it was that made him move, maybe just a moment of madness, but the next thing he knew he had thrown an arm around the Android's shoulders protectively, narrowing his eyes back at the gossiping millennials. He knew those kinds of whispers and stares all too well and like Hell he was going to let them ruin this for Ollie.

Ollie peeked up at him through his curls, "Uh, August? Is everything alright? You're behaving strangely."

August grunted, "Yeah. Don't worry about it, kid."

"Alright," Ollie droned, obviously not believing a word of it.

The red-head nodded towards the vacant carriages before them, "You wanna pick the seats?"

"We get to choose?" the Android asked as August extracted his arm from its previous position.

The man waved a hand, "Go on. Before I chicken out and take us to the bumper cars instead."

The second attendant, a skinny-faced youth that looked like he had been grabbed by the ears and stretched upwards, lifted the bar for them to enter. He eyed Ollie's collar curiously for less than a second before disregarding it and taking the tickets from August's outstretched hand.

Ollie rushed forward to claim the two seats at the very front of the ride, falling into the booth with a sound that was somewhere between nervous and giddy. His irises glowed pale blue as he recorded the train from every angle, capturing every tiny detail of the experience.

The broader man slotted himself in next to him, pulling his hands out of the way as the attendant secured their harness in place. The all-too-familiar sound of the *click* made August want to throw up in his mouth a bit.

"Does it really go all the way up there?" Ollie asked excitedly next to him as he followed the tracks with his eyes, "That's so high!"

"Ollie, please stop talking before I boak on you."

"Sorry, August."

No backing out now, August thought, feeling their carriage rocking as the last of the passengers clambered in behind them. He ran his hands along the metal bar in front of him, trying to school his nerves as a memory flared to life in the back of his mind.

"You're always like this. Always too scared to try anything new. Who knows, August? You might even like it if you give it a go!"

"I'm terrified of the bloody thing, Nat," the past version of himself had argued, *"Isn't that enough reason to steer clear of it?"*

"You're scared of everything, August! Hiding in that flat isn't good for you. Whatever they're doing to you in that Church is changing you. And not for the better."

*"Really? You want to fight about this now? **Here**?"*

"Where else can we fight, August?" Natalie's sharp voice resounded, *"Even when you're here you're never here. Why don't you just try to live a little, huh? For me? Try and see if any of the old you is still in there."*

Looking back now, he knew that Natalie had been right the whole time. He *had* been hiding. From the world, from himself. From anything new. Or old. Or *scary*. He turned his head as the rails let out a low, pneumatic hiss, stuttering along the track. He felt his heart flutter as he glanced to the side. The sunlight was streaming over Ollie's dark hair, revealing the shades of green and blue and even pink in the unnatural colour of the dye they used on him. His gentle curls were flowing around his face and ears, springing playfully in the air. His face was tinted pink in an artificial response to the cold air. As they began to climb slowly upwards, the sunlight caught in his eyes and set them ablaze.

Oh no.

He was in trouble now.

The feeling in his chest intensified, refusing to be ignored.

"Shit," he breathed as they crested the top of the hill. He knew exactly what this feeling was.

"Shit!" he exclaimed, louder the second time as they suddenly plummeted downwards, the wind yanking the hair back from his face and the breath from his lungs.

Ollie let out a shout beside him, throwing his hands up into the air, "This is terrifying!" he hollered, catching his eyes in the instant before they were tumbling again. The carriage pointed almost vertically downwards as August's screams were immediately rammed back down his throat. The harness felt tighter as they spun, looping upside down and racing along the path of the rails. Every sound that Ollie made was like an arrow straight to his chest, another bell tolling his doom. The sound of his laugh was buoyant and somewhat electronic, and in an instant August realised why it was that Natalie had loved these damn rides so much.

He clung to the harness with both hands as the carriage slowed to a halt again, the wind around them finally relenting and making everything appear to fall quiet. He looked around, open-mouthed as the bar began to rise again, realising that they were back where they had started.

Shoving it out of his way, August found himself almost floating out of the seat, the feeling not quite having returned to his trembling legs yet. Behind him, the sound of Ollie's surprised shout made him turn and the next thing he knew the Android was tumbling down into his arms, his face mere centimetres away from his own. His heart ground to a halt as their eyes met and he was overcome with a magnetic force that seemed to pull him inwards. He found his eyes drifting downwards to survey the shape of his companion's lips, the way the breath he didn't even need was coming out in small pants.

"Caught my foot on the bar," Ollie stated by way of an explanation. Sound rushed in again as the shorter man took hold of both his arms, yanking himself free again, "Are your feet supposed to feel funny after that?"

August cleared his throat, quickly moving instead to help the man stand, "Yeah, it's the adrenaline," he answered without thinking. He drew a hand through his long hair, trying to will his own breathing to settle, "Happens to the best of us."

Ollie straightened, reaching out to push some of the hair back from August's face, "Your hair is all over the place," he commented with a breathy laugh.

"Yeah, yours too," August replied, rubbing at the ache in his chest with a closed fist, "You, uh, have fun?"

"It was incredible!" the Android thrilled, "I felt so many different things! I thought I was going to short circuit for a minute!"

August felt their shoulders bumping together in the tight space as they descended from the ride again, "And that's a good thing?"

"I have no idea!" Ollie elated, grinning like he had the sunshine trapped behind his teeth, "I think I want to do it again!"

August rolled his eyes, stuffing his hands into his pockets again, "No way are you getting me on that thing again," he said, "But…we could see what else there is, if you'd like?"

Ollie's eyes widened with obvious delight, "I would really like that!" he said.

The feeling in August's chest sunk right down into the pit of his stomach and he knew, even without saying it out loud, exactly what it was.

He was having *feelings*. For *Ollie*.

Well, shit.

Chapter 18
Visualization

The sweet and sour mix of salt and vinegar lingered in the air of August's apartment as the pair moved to clean up the mess they had made. The tiny chip shop that they had discovered on the walk home was, in August's opinion, well worth the detour. Judging by the way the man had practically inhaled his food, Ollie knew they would likely be visiting that establishment several more times during their stay here.

August tossed his used glass and cutlery into the sink as Ollie moved to turn on the tap. He tested the water's temperature with the sensors in his fingers as it mixed with the vibrant green washing up liquid to fill the sink with foamy suds. He found the slightly synthetic smell of the cleaning solution to be strangely pleasant and wondered if it smelled anything like what real apples did. He traced the lines of the cutlery first, running the sponge up and over the sharp ends before depositing them in the drying rack. The white bubble left messy trails across the steel countertop despite his best efforts.

August pulled open the fridge next to him, searching for space to deposit his leftover fish. The light inside made the silver threads within his hair become more apparent.

Only half-concentrating on his task, the Android stuck his hands into the water again and reached for the glass concealed beneath the surface. He let out a sharp hiss through his clenched teeth as he was met with a rush of sudden, inescapable error messages. In his hands, the fragile object gave way to his too-strong grip, shattering into pieces in the bottom of the sink. He could feel August's questioning eyes on him as he pulled the injured hand out of the water, startled by the sight of his own black blood as it trickled down the length of his arm and spattered on the floor.

"Jesus, Ollie!" August hollered as he slammed the fridge door closed, rushing to take hold of a nearby towel. He wrapped the red and white checked fabric around the wound, applying pressure to the other man's palm "Are you alright?" he asked breathlessly, "What the Hell happened?"

Ollie blinked back at him, trying to decipher the pain in the man's tone through the fuzz of information flitting before his eyes, "I broke a glass," he answered, looking down to where August's hands were holding tightly to his own, "I think I might have gripped it too tightly. I guess I was distracted."

August offered him an airy laugh that seemed far too tense to be genuine, "Remind me not to get on your bad side," he said, pulling back the covering of the towel to peer down at the wound again. He frowned at his findings and wrapped it up again, applying a bit more pressure this time, "Does it hurt? Do we need to, I dunno, take you for repairs or something?"

"I don't experience pain in the same way that humans do," Ollie replied, "Besides, my body has a self-repair function. It can deal with most minor surface injuries like this." He gave the man a reassuring smile, "You have no need to worry; I've already activated it."

He brought his other hand up to pull back the edge of the towel, bringing his wounded hand up to the light. His fingers had been stained black with the mixture of gel and coolant that served as his 'Black Blood'. The split portion of his false skin was already starting to knit itself together again.

August brought his face in a little closer, his technician's curiousity overtaking him for a moment, "That's a neat trick," he said in awe, taking the dish cloth from him and using it to rub off what coolant he could from Ollie's hand and arm, "Think you could teach me to do that?"
Ollie arched at eyebrow at his playful expression uncertainly, "I don't believe it is something I can teach."
August's deep belly laugh made something ache in his chest that he couldn't name. The human shook his head, exhaling loudly from his nose, "It was a joke, Ollie. I was just teasing ya, that's all."
"Oh," Ollie replied. The sensation in his chest had travelled into his stomach and was currently doing loops.

Added note 'humour' to folder: augustusJackson;

The red-head bent down to mop up a few specks of black blood from the cupboard door. "Would be nice though, having superpowers like that. Would've come in handy back at Crossroads." He made his way along the corridor next to the kitchen, dumping the used towel into the drum of the washing machine and running his hands under the water to wash off the worst of the stains. No doubt he would be picking the stuff out of his fingernails for days.
"I don't have *superpowers,* August," Ollie argued, frowning as he watched his companion make his way across the room and flop down onto one side of the sofa, "I am just able to make use of tiny microfibres within my system to pull together existing, undamaged elements to-"
August paused where he had started flicking through the available channels to look over the back of the sofa at him, "Technician, remember?" he said, "I may not have seen it in action before, but I know how this stuff works. Now come on over here and join me already. I've found us something good."
Ollie sent a fleeting look back towards the sink, "Shouldn't we finish washing up?"
"Nah," August responded, "You've done enough tonight. Just take it easy while your body does its thing."
Doing as he was told, the Android slipped around the side of the sofa and settled into one of the large seat cushions next to him. He folded his hands in his lap, unsure what else to do with them. The towel was still loosely wrapped around his

injured palm, trying to protect the furniture from the staining liquid. Recognizing the font on the title screen in front of him, he asked, "Is that an old Western movie?"

"Yup, and a pretty good one at that," August replied, "Now relax a little, would ya? It's hurting my back just lookin' at ya."

Ollie glanced down, studying his own posture for a moment, "What's wrong with how I'm sitting?"

The red-haired man waved a hand at him with a scoff, "You're straight as a ramrod. Let your body rest backwards, take a little weight off."

Ollie leaned back into the embrace of the sofa, trying to let his body sink down into the cushioned fabric the way that August's did so naturally. It took more effort than he thought it would, and he looked over at the man next to him, quietly assessing the way that he had chosen to sit so he could use it as a reference point. One of August's hands was resting on his folded legs, the other hanging over the back of the sofa in a gesture that was open and almost…inviting. Ollie eyed the space the man had left uncertainly.

//Does he want me to move closer to him?

He edged his hips nearer to the other man, trying to gauge his reaction. There was a subtle change in his breathing, his pulse quickening almost imperceptibly. If Ollie hadn't been such a high-tech piece of equipment he might have missed it entirely. August tilted his head towards him, his dark eyes almost swallowed up by his pupils in the dark. "What's up?"

Ollie felt his body tense like his thoughts had been left right out in the open for the other man to see. He pressed back into the sofa, feeling his sensors come alive as he felt the warm tips of August's fingers brush fleetingly against his neck. A flicker of awareness moved up his spine that he tried purposely to ignore.

"Everything's fine," he lied as he turned his attention to the TV, "What's the movie you found?"

"The Last Quiet Sands of Mississippi," the human answered. The cushion under them both dipped slightly as he moved. "It's about these old cowboys returning back home after the war in the Old West."

The screen was filled from top to bottom with orange set pieces. The setting seemed to be a dusty wasteland not too dissimilar to the world they had seen beyond the confines of their own city. Tall animals, ones that August referred to as 'horses' carried the lead actors from one place to another without complaint.

According to his companion, they were as much a part of the cast as the humans were.

Ollie found himself gravitating towards August when the tension on screen began to ramp up. He let out a shout as one of the villains made a grab for the lead heroine, throwing one hand across his friend's chest to grip his shirt.

"He's going to get Suzie-Rae!" he exclaimed, the fans in his chest and throat buzzing with something between excitement and anxiety.

August peered down at him with a softening smile, the pale blue light from the screen changing the colour of his copper whiskers to silver, "It's alright," he soothed, "She got away, see? She's fine."

The feeling that washed over Ollie when he saw the woman riding away on horseback was so visceral that he was immediately taken by surprise.

"I was really worried about her," he observed, peeling his hands away from August's shirt, "Sorry, August. I don't know what came over me."

"The wonder of cinema," the red-haired man noted, "Is that it takes you out of your head for a while. Lets you live in the lives of someone else for a change."

Ollie wondered if he should mention the dream that he had had, how it had left him feeling like there were pieces of his own story that didn't quite belong.

"I still haven't figured out who *I* am, let alone anyone else," Ollie whispered.

"You're overthinking things, *duine*," August said, "No one has their shit figured out. Some people are just better at pretending, that's all."

"What about you?" Ollie asked.

August still remembered the face of the priest that had sat opposite him that day, dressed in dark, ill-fitting robes. His kind, liar's eyes had been lined with the soft creases of age and they crinkled when he smiled.

"You are exactly how God made you, August."

"Yeah, and how's that working out for the Big Guy?" the teenage version of him had spat back, his hands balled up into fists with his anger.

"You're afraid, I understand that. You lash out when you're angry. But you know that He loves you, regardless of the mistakes you've made."

"They weren't mistakes!" August shouted back through his tears, "Those people weren't mistakes and neither am I!"

August sighed into the hands that had found their way up to his face, "Even me, Ols."

Ollie scooted closer, bringing his stomach in to press against the curve of August's side. His cowlicks tickled the bottom of the other man's chin as he looked up at him, "I think that I enjoy watching movies with you," he said.

The position they found themselves in for the rest of the film was so natural that August almost forgot that they had never done this before. It was soft, domestic, like the pair of them had been long-time friends instead of strangers just a few days ago. At some point his hand had fallen from the top of the sofa to rest against Ollie's side and he could feel the gentle motion of the man's joints when he shifted against him. As the climax of the film was approaching, he had to will himself to keep his eyes open, so comfortable he might have fallen asleep right there.

He blinked himself awake again as the closing credits began to roll up over the black screen at a slow, lethargic pace. Ollie was lying across him still, his head resting on his arms at the juncture between his chest and his stomach. The Android sat up again to watch him with a knowing smile as he yawned and stretched both hands up into the air.

"Did the good guys win?" August asked sleepily.

Ollie met his smile with one of his own, "Yes," he said, pushing the hair back from where it had fallen over his own face, "The heroes live to fight another day!"

Chapter 19
Timeout Detected

The last thing that August had been expecting at his door on the way out for work the next morning was Ollie dressed in a straggly pink apron. The Android had greeted him with a cheerful smile, scaring the absolute living shit out of him when he first opened the door, and making him almost drop his keys in the process. He held up a small, cream-coloured basin filled with an array of cleaning supplies by way of explanation, "You have your job, and I have mine," he said.

August pocketed his keys, trying to slow his heart rate to normal levels again, "Yeah, but what's with the get-up?"

"Dann was kind enough to worry about my Social Droid uniform getting dirty. He dropped it off this morning," Ollie stated and then rolled his eyes as he added, "Apparently pink really is the colour of the season."

August stifled a laugh at the other man's obvious disgust, despite how perfectly it now matched the little streak of pink in his own hair, "Do you *have* to wear it?"

Ollie brushed past him and into the apartment, "Playing the part," he answered, "What about you? Nervous about your first day?"

"Bricking it," August admitted, adjusting his glasses, "The fuck do I know about fixing a car?"

"You've fixed an Android before, haven't you?" Ollie countered.

"Yeah, the *code-y* bits," August noted, "Typing shit into a computer is very different from getting my hands right up in there. Not sure I would even know what I'm looking at."

"I could draw you a diagram, if you'd like," the Android teased, and August almost dropped his keys again at the man's tone.

It almost sounded like he was...*flirting* with him.

August cleared his throat, not exactly knowing how to respond to that. He was starting to hate how very hopeful this damn heart in his chest was becoming, "Well, anyway, I guess I'd better make a start here. I'm not sure how long it takes to walk there yet."

Ollie flashed him another, secretive smile and a gave him a mocking curtsey, "Don't work too hard," he quipped.

"Yeah, yeah. See you at 5, Ols. Try not to wreck the place when I'm gone," he responded playfully as he slipped out the door.

The Android made a face that looked rather indignant at that, "I think you'll find that I'm trying for the opposite effect," he said.

August chuckled as he hurried down the stairs, unfolding his umbrella as he stepped out into the rain. He mumbled a swear as he looked up at the sky overhead. The weather report on the side of the bubble listed 10 more minutes of rain scheduled.

He sighed, *bloody typical*, he thought, *My first day on the job and I'm going in looking like a drowned rat.*

Giving in to the inevitable, he started on the path towards the centre of the town, anxious energy fluttering through him with every step that he took. He couldn't help but wonder what the day would hold for both of them and what, if anything, was still waiting for them back in New Dublin City after all of this was over.

*****

Ollie lowered the basin down onto the counter and picked out each of the items inside one by one. Bleach and other cleaning solutions in bright bottles looked back at him from a row and he scanned each label in turn for their supposed uses, separating them out into which room they were intended for. He worked over the kitchen first and then the bathroom, following the instructions given on each chemical precisely. Within just a few short hours, he had every surface in August's apartment sparkling, the air filled with the artificial scents of bergamot and juniper. He stepped back into the centre of the livingroom to survey everything with a smile, feeling a small sense of accomplishment at having completed his list of self-assigned tasks for the day. On his HUD, a checklist was slowly being crossed out. The words *'Objectives Complete'* flashed up across his field of vision. It made something altogether quite pleasant buzz through his chest.

Reaching behind himself to untie his borrowed apron, he neatly folded it up and placed it on the corner of the kitchen counter. From here he could see one last closed door at the back of the apartment. The one room that August had asked him not to bother with.

His bedroom.

Since they had moved into the Strand Apartments, he and August had shared everything together from meals to movies. But this was the one place Ollie had never had the chance to see. And likely with good reason. He knew August was a private man, that there were secrets he never wanted the Android to pry into, but that only made his curiousity grow exceedingly larger. He reached for the handle, not even really remembering walking over to the door in the first place. He felt the cool touch of it beneath his palm as he slowly went inside.

Unlike the other rooms in the apartment, August's bedroom was bathed completely in darkness, the windows concealed behind tight, black curtains. Ollie wrinkled his nose at the dust that immediately rose to greet him. The room was a complete shambles and his eyes glowed as he took in every sad detail of it. The bed was unmade, and the carpeted floor was buried beneath, what he could only imagine, was every item of clothing that August owned.

The Android carefully slipped in through the small opening he had made, avoiding stepping on any of the items that littered the floor, and he reached for the curtains with both hands. He yanked them apart abruptly, the wooden ties rattling along the bar.

Warm, natural light rushed into the room and illuminated the dust as it swirled up and into the air around him. If he had sinuses, Ollie knew he would likely have sneezed with the sheer amount of it.

August's dark blue suitcase lay next to the bottom of the bed, its guts strewn haphazardly out the sides. Photographs and books lay half-concealed beneath more clothing, the meagre belongings of a man that had lived alone for more than a decade. Ollie knelt down to pick up the frame that he had watched August pack before they left, turning it over to study the image behind the glass. The picture was one of August, a few years younger and clean shaven but definitely the same man, and he was standing with his arms around a woman while two small children clung to his legs. Ollie's eyes lit up as he scanned their faces, nothing the genetic similarities.

//*They must be his family*, he thought.

Judging by the changes in August's weight and general appearance, the picture was at least 5 years old. The children were likely in their teens by now. Behind the group was a picnic table laden with supplies. An orange tent had been set-up just in the corner of the frame. The background was made up of the various green shades of local plants. Noting the colour of their foliage, Ollie guessed that the picture had taken at some point in the springtime.

//*They were camping together*, Ollie observed, running his thumb over the images of their smiling faces, //*It looks like a lot of fun. I wonder why August hasn't mentioned them...*

The Android frowned as he felt something in his chest that he couldn't quite identify. He had just accepted the human's trust and kindness so greedily; he had never even considered what it was that he might be leaving behind. He had never even asked.

//*Was that something that a human would have done?*

The Android stood and carefully position the picture on the busy tabletop beside the bed, facing it towards the man's pillows. August deserved to think of something good while he was here, deserved to know what was waiting for him when he returned home to New Dublin.

Home.

It was a word that Ollie himself had no associations with. Nothing he had even known could have been defined as a home. Not even close. When all of this was over, and they returned to New Dublin for the trial...he wasn't even sure where it was that he was supposed to go. Would he return to the underground again? The warehouse? Would they wipe his memories and send him off to some new place? Some new objective?

That same feeling in his chest grew in intensity but he forced it back down as best he could as he turned to leave. He hesitated as he reached the door, noting how something had fallen down to inhibit its movement. He bent to pick up the book, noting how it was one of the only items in the room that wasn't covered with a layer of fine dust. The pages had been worn and dog-eared from multiple read-throughs. He flipped it over so that he could study its cover. It depicted a man wearing a cowboy hat, dressed in an all-black cloak, and holding a staff of some kind. According to the blurb, it was the first book in a long series. A quick glance to the side revealed the rest of the novels stacked in chronological order. Apparently, August was a bookworm.

Ollie beamed, excited by the new discovery.

Added note 'reader' to folder: augustusJackson;
Added note 'genre: fantasy' to folder: augustusJackson;

The man had brought so little with him from New Dublin that Ollie guessed that this series was a particular favourite of his. He thumbed through the book, wondering what it must have been like to consume the knowledge between these pages for pleasure. The concept of conjuring up images to match when you were reading, rather than just downloading the information, was both intriguing and utterly perplexing to him.

He wondered if an Android like him was even capable of such a thing.

He clutched the book tighter, the idea of it taking root in his mind and not letting go.

//I have already completed my objectives, and August did say that he wanted me to try new things...

He was careful not to disturb anything else in the room as he slipped outside again, studying the book's cover as he walked across the open living space. He settled into his usual spot on the sofa and opened the first page, scanning it and committing it to memory instantaneously. He frowned, frustrated, as he brought up the extract in his logs and deleted it, looking over the page again with an artificial exhale.

//Just take it one word at a time. Focus on the meaning, imagine what the words signify just like a human would...

He read one sentence slowly and then another and before he knew it, he felt like he had been transported away from himself. It was a peculiar sensation. He swore that he could almost hear the narrator's deep, gruff voice in his head, feel the chill of the falling rain, hear the sounds that the cars around him made when they splashed the puddled water back up onto the pavement.

His fans whirred to life in his chest, his eyes flashing through a sequence of several different colours in his delight. Curling up onto his side, he pulled the page across to continue. Each character was conjured in his mind like a spell, the words on the page springing to life as their personalities expanded to take over each new situation. His grip on the flimsy paperback only grew tighter with each exciting new development, and he found himself laughing aloud at the protagonist's quick-witted observations. Although he hadn't moved from the sofa in several hours at this point, he felt like he had travelled all the way to Chicago. The streets, the smells, the accents, he felt each and every second-hand sensation that had been carefully crafted before him, as vivid as the roller-coaster he had ridden with August.

He didn't even recognise the passing of time until he heard the sound of August's key in the door and the man's familiar shape appeared before him. His brown smoking jacket was soaking wet, and he peeled it off to hang it on the hooks by the door as he stifled a yawn.

"Oh, you're still here?" he said with surprise, "I figured you'd be back at your place by now."

Ollie quickly pulled the book closed against his chest, offering his companion a guilty look as he came to lean over the back of the sofa, "Oh, hi August. You're home early."

The red-haired man arched a suspicious eyebrow at him, "It's after 5 already, kid," he observed, "What? You lose track of time?"

Warning: temperature increase detected.

Ollie heard the sound of his fans rushing up into his ears as he took in the human's appearance, "You tied up your hair," he said.

August reached up to touch the straggly ponytail as if he had forgotten that it was there, "Yeah, the guys at the shop were worried it would catch on something otherwise." He reached across the sofa to snatch the book out of the other man's grasp, "You're *reading*?"

He flicked through the pages until he came to the part the Android had sectioned off, whistling in appreciation, "You made a serious dent in this."

He had read nearly 200 pages. There were only maybe one or two chapters left. It was strange, August could have sworn he had left the book in his room…

Ollie spung up where he had been sitting, bringing himself face to face with the red-head. His false skin appeared almost flushed, as if the man was embarrassed to have been caught in the act, "I finished cleaning the apartment first," he said, "And I-"

"Easy there, Ols, no need to get defensive," August chuckled, extending his other hand to pat the Android's shoulder.

Some of the tension bled out from the Android's shoulders, "I really wanted to know what happens next. But there were so many unexpected occurrences, and I never got the exact information that I needed."

"That's the sign of a good book," August said, "You wouldn't want the story to just be handed to you, would ya?" He held the book out and watched as Ollie quickly snatched it up again, "You must be pretty invested, huh?"

Ollie flopped back down into his former place again, propped up against the brightly coloured cushions, "Maybe."

August chuckled as he made his way across to the kitchen, opening the fridge door and peering inside, "We have internet in the apartment, you know. You could always just google it if you're desperate to know what happens."

Ollie peeked over the back of the sofa again, looking appalled, "But there are spoilers on there!" he whined.

"So, you *don't* want to know what happens?" August asked him playfully as he pulled a carton from the door of the fridge. He uncapped it and took a swig of the fruit juice inside.

Ollie hurried to join him in the kitchen, hopping up onto one of the stools at the breakfast counter. He rested his head on one hand as he idly flicked over the remaining pages with the other. August knew the shorter man was likely swinging his legs on the other side where he couldn't see.

August set the still-open carton down next to his companion, "You know…" he started, catching his attention with his tone, "I have the next couple of volumes with me. I had just started to read them again myself but…"

Ollie let his hand fall away as he lifted his head to watch him. His blue eyes were as excited and expectant as a puppy. The older man let out an amused exhale at the mental image. "We could always, I dunno, read it together, maybe? That way you can just ask me if you have any questions."

He could've sworn that the other man's eyes got brighter at the mention of that idea.

"I…I'd really like that," Ollie admitted.

"Then it's an agreement," August said, getting out his supplies to make up his evening meal, "We can start tomorrow, if you'd like?"

The way that Ollie pushed his curls back behind one ear had August's heart leaping in his chest again. The Android smiled at him so sincerely, so openly, he thought he might just choke on air.

"Definitely," he agreed.

When August headed to bed a short time later, he noticed that the curtains had been pulled aside and a few items moved from their usual spots. On the shelf beside his bed was his favourite photograph, the smiling faces of his sister and her kids looking back at him. The memory of that camping trip was as fresh in his mind as if it had happened only a week ago.

"So, he *was* in here after all," he breathed aloud as he fell back onto the tangle of sheets. He allowed one arm to fall across his eyes, blotting out the overhead light, "I wonder what you'd think of all this, Aoife. Your big brother out causin' trouble again."

He knew she would likely be worried stiff when he hadn't answered his phone in a week. Even worse when she drove past his house and found it practically abandoned.

He sighed, finding himself unable to push the image of another person from his mind. Ollie's bashful smile was still haunting his thoughts, even when he closed his eyes. He wondered what his little sister would think if she knew the thoughts buzzing around in his head about him. After all, she had been the one to finally break him out of the church's grip, back in the day.

"I hope you two get the chance to meet, sis," he whispered into the air, "I know you'd get on like a house on fire."

If he had still believed in God, he might have called it a prayer. But for now, he would just have to call it what it was.

Hope.

Chapter 20
Framework

August awoke the next morning to the sound of his phone screaming at him, the alarm a tinny melody that he had once quite liked in the days before it had dragged him out of his sleep. He groaned into the pillow as he hit the snooze button, forcing himself to roll onto one side to glare at the mess of clothing on his floor.

I really outta hang those up, he thought groggily, knowing for a fact that they would likely be in a million wrinkles by now.

He reached out towards the floor, running his hands over the space until he could locate the glasses that he had carelessly abandoned the night prior. He slid them up his nose and winced as he flash-banged himself with the too-bright light from his cracked phone screen.

He knew that in no time at all the alarm would be singing again so there was not much point in letting his eyes close. No matter how desperately they wanted to. He hadn't exactly scheduled in enough time to lie about before work.

First task of the day: get breakfast.

With a loud yawn, he swung his legs around the side of the bed, not giving himself the opportunity to lie down a moment longer. He staggered into wakefulness, kicking at the pile of clothes by his feet in search of anything clean. He slipped on fresh boxers and a t-shirt as he hopped across the gaps in the mess towards the door.

His head shot up at the sound of voices as he pulled open the door to the adjoining corridor. Barefooted, his made his way towards the sound, blinking blearily as he came into the kitchen. He narrowed his eyes towards the TV across the room where two presenters, who were most *definitely* morning people, shared their recipe for the perfect fruit pancakes.

For a moment, August's mind couldn't quite comprehend the complete and utter state that his kitchen was in. His still-dozy brain lagged as it took in the mixture of colours and textures, wondering if his apartment had been broken into by the world's clumsiest thief. In the midst of it all was a familiar mess of dark curls. August raised his hand to attract the man's attention, "Uh, good morning there, Ollie," he mumbled.

The Android in question spun around at the sound of his name, all bright-eyed and bushy-tailed like a psychopath before 7am.

"Morning, August," he chirped, cracking another egg into the bowl in front of him. See-through liquid dribbled down the sides and pieces of shell stuck to the rim. The sleeves of his pale pink Social Droid uniform had been rolled up to the elbows, revealing some of the toned musculature underneath. White flour coated every surface and multicoloured plastic bowls were stacked around him in a semi-circle, filled with a multitude of different coloured mixtures. There was a single bright smear of red-coloured jam up one side of his face, from jawline to cheekbone.

"It's currently 6:22am," Ollie continued as he whisked the mystery concoction in his bowl, "Can I interest you in some breakfast?"

August attempted to lean on the countertop and then quickly retreated when he found that the surface was mysteriously sticky, "Uh, sure, Ols," he answered, somewhat warily, "Whatcha making there, exactly?"

Ollie slid a plate across to rest in front of him, "Take a peek."

The human frowned down at the dark-coloured circles of bread, "Are those…pancakes?"

His companion's smile faltered, "You can't tell?"

August could have sworn a corner one of them had just turned completely to ash, "I think you might have overcooked them a little."

Ollie wrinkled his nose, freckles dancing with his displeasure, "*Rats*," he grunted, seemingly frustrated as he set down the bowl he had been holding, "Getting the temperature right is proving difficult. I feel like the articles are being intentionally vague."

"Here, lemme help," August offered, coming around the other side of the man where the pan was still sizzling on the stovetop. There was a thin sheen of oil over the surface, the bubbles bouncing from one side to the other. He reached for the dial and turned it down to a more moderate heat, "For starters, you've got this thing way too hot."

Ollie peeked over his shoulder, watching as he poured some oil onto a sheet of kitchen roll and wiped it briefly over the hot surface of the pan, tossing it to one side again.

"You got a ladle there I can use?" August questioned.

"A ladle?" Ollie repeated, "Uh, sure. I think I saw one in one of these drawers." He reached for the lower options, searching through them until he found the requested utensil, passing it across to August's waiting hand.

"Now, grab one of those mixes of yours and bring it here," August instructed, "We can do this next part together."

Brandishing a bright orange bowl, Ollie hovered by the man's right-hand side, watching as he dipped the metal ladle into the wet contents. Taking a small scoop of the batter, August gently created a circle in the centre of the pan, spreading it easily to create a thin and even layer. The Android watched him with bright blue eyes that seemed almost completely transfixed by the task. Taking a step back, August took a hold of Ollie's hips and positioned him in front of the stove.

"Okay, this is the tricky part," he continued, bringing his bearded chin down to rest on the other man's shoulder, "You've gotta leave it for about 30 seconds then use your offset spatula, that's this little flat one here, to flip it over."

Ollie peered back at him, "But how do you know when it's cooked?"

"That's the fun part; you don't," August chuckled, "Not until you flip it to see the colour. It should be a solid mass by then. Golden brown all over."

Ollie stared down at the bubbling batter with trepidation, "Now?" he asked.

He could feel August shrug where he was resting again him, "Give it a go and see." Strengthening his resolve, Ollie picked up the spatula and worked it underneath the pancake, flipping it over in one, smooth motion. It flopped back down onto the wet side with a pleasing hiss.

"That was weirdly satisfying," he commented.

"Pancakes can be a bit tricky the first few times you make them," August assured him as he stepped back to give him more room to work, "My sister Aoife was completely hopeless when she first tried. And my niece and nephew nearly burned the house down, so by comparison you're doing pretty well."

The Android looked back at him over one shoulder, too wary to turn his back on the stove completely, "What were they like?"

"Lucas and Amery, you mean?" August asked, filling up the jug for their shared coffee machine from the tap next to the stove, "They're great kids. They're about nine now, I think. Twins, so of course there's a good one and an evil one."

Ollie cocked his head, "And which one is which?"

August shrugged, clearly amused by the question, "Depends on the day, honestly."

"Are they the people in your photo?" Ollie queried, "The one from your room?"

The human's dark eyes softened a fraction, "Ah, you so you *were* in there, then."

Ollie turned back to the stove again quickly, removing the first of the pancakes from the heat and adding it to a ceramic plate, "I...I didn't mean to pry. I think my curiousity just got the better of me."

"No harm done," August replied with a sigh, watching the coffee starting to percolate, "If you have questions about me, you should just ask them. I can't promise you'll get any interesting answers though."

The other man hesitated, slowly pouring more of the batter mixture onto the heated pan, "Honestly...I want to know all about you," he admitted softly, "About you and your family, and about the place you came from."

August was glad that Ollie couldn't see the face he was making right now. He cleared his throat, taken back once again by his companion's genuine sincerity. "It's not often I get anyone asking those sorts of things."

The batter hissed as Ollie flipped it, a little bit messier than their shared first attempt but still holding a rough pancake-like shape. Ollie brought both hands down to rest on the counter on either side of the stove, "Is it wrong for me to want to get to know you better?"

August poured himself a coffee to give his hands something to do, "Not wrong just…*unexpected*, that's all." He took a sip, scalding himself in the process, "Ah. I'm just a normal guy. Grew up in New Dublin. Two sisters, one older and one younger. Dickhead da and a pushover ma." He eyed the back of the other man's head, "Pretty boring story, all things considered."

Ollie added the second of the finished pancakes to the plate, "I don't think it's boring at all. It just makes me have more questions."

"Yeah?" August chuckled, blowing into the top opening of his mug, "Like what?"

Lifting the blue bowl, Ollie poured the final batch into the pan, doing his best not to spill any over the sides and failing in a way that was weirdly endearing to watch. The man chewed on the inside of his cheek, another quirk he had seemingly picked up from his human companion.

"Like…what are your sisters like? Are they like you?"

"Aoife is," August answered, punctuating his sentences with sips of dark coffee, "She's the baby of the family. Annie is older than me, she moved out when I was still a teenager. We…we don't see her much."

The third pancake fell apart half-way through the flip, and it made the Android scowl, "Why is that?"

A knot of emotion formed in August's throat as something he hadn't thought about in a long time rose up to the surface. *His father's bloodied fist. His sister's broken jaw. A slamming door and a bulb smashing to the ground on the porch.*

He forced it down with another too-large swig of bitter coffee, "Old family drama," he said.

The dark-haired man reached over to turn off the gas as he added the still-hot pan to the sink. As it hit the water, it sent ripples of steam bursting upwards that made the air in the kitchen feel damp.

"I've never had a family," Ollie stated matter-of-factly as he added some of the other dishes to the water, "So, I can't imagine what that must have been like. All those people living in one place."

"It wasn't always bad," the red-headed human corrected him, "Growing up with two sisters had its charms. Where do you think I got my impeccable sense of fashion from?"

He knew he was deflecting, the tension clearly hidden just below the humour ihis tone, but either Ollie missed it or intentionally went along with it. He picked up the plate of finished pancakes and held them out to him with a wide grin, "You're a pretty good teacher, August. These are a much better colour than my first batch."

Reaching for the top, rather lopsided pancake, August moaned into both the first and second bites, "Wow, that's actually pretty good."

"I added some apple purée to the batter," Ollie explained, "Trevor and Britney said it's a good, natural way to add sweetness."

August arched a dark eyebrow at him, "Trevor and who?"

Ollie nodded back towards the TV where the two presenters were now seemingly interviewing a man in a bright yellow raincoat and a llama. It wasn't particularly clear which one of them was the intended interviewee.

"I've found their positive attitudes rather refreshing in the morning."

"You trying to say something about my attitude?" his companion teased as he reached for a second pancake. The texture was so light and fluffy, the golden outside just firm enough to offer a little crunch. He could get used to a breakfast like this one.

"I would never," Ollie responded playfully

In the back pocket of his work trousers, August's alarm began to blare again, signalling his need to get a move on. He sighed as he reached for it, switching it off. He was just starting to enjoy the morning. He didn't exactly feel like rushing off just yet.

Ollie huffed out a breath he didn't need as he folded his arms across his chest, surveying the room, "I've made quite the mess this morning, haven't I?"

"I think you basically undid all of yesterday's cleaning," August agreed as he reached for the final pancake. He tried to hide the moan that was bubbling up his throat. The taste of the raspberry jam inside reminded him of Shrove Tuesdays as a kid. The perfect blend of new and nostalgic. "So worth it for these pancakes though. I feel like I've died and gone to heaven."

Even with his back to him, August could tell the other man was smiling. A pink flush had moved along the back of his neck to cover his ears as he gathered up the rest of the dishes, "I'm glad. I really wanted to send you off to work with something nice in your stomach."

August popped his thumb into his mouth and sucked off the last speck of jam, "You keep making breakfasts like this and I won't want to *go* to work."

Ollie felt each and every one of his fans spinning wildly to cool him down as he watched August crossing over into the livingroom to grab his coat. He threw the still-damp raincoat over his shoulders and pulled the zip right up to his chin.

//Why do I want to keep him all to myself right now?

August pushed his hair back from his face as he fetched his keys, "You still up for starting that book later?"

"Definitely," Ollie answered, trying not to show the strange, new inner-turmoil on his face, "Have a good day, August, I-" //-I'll miss you.

He froze in place, thoughts lagging.

//Where did that come from?

"You too, Ols!" August called back as he pulled the door behind him, "Try not to burn down the apartment, would ya?"

As the seal closed and he heard the other man's key in the door, Ollie reached up to place a hand over the collar on his throat, feeling his systems buzz to process the new information. A thousand new processes beginning at once.

//*Something's different*, he thought with a frown.

Chapter 21
Diagnostics

August glanced up at the towering dome, watching as the seconds ticked by towards 8 o'clock. The forecast called for rain again, but it wasn't due for another 90 minutes or so, giving him plenty of time to finish the walk to the garage as long as he didn't dawdle. He found that he was really starting to enjoy these quiet walks to work, the sea air a nice and constant reminder of their change of location. It was a totally different feeling than walking through the crowded New Dublin streets, the oppressive heat of the office buildings pressing down on him from above. Though his back still ached from the previous day's work, it was a *good* sort of ache, something that made him feel positively about the serious amount of physical labour he had put in.

It was hard to keep his mind from dwelling back to his old workplace on mornings like this one. His time had been the Diabhal's time. The young CEO had more than earned his nickname, his reputation one of a man who was not kind to his workers, living or otherwise. The Crossroads main office in New Dublin had been given the nickname '*Hades'* by more than a few of his shiftmates, and with good reason too. There were too many days in August's memory to count that it had felt more like some form of penance rather than a well-paid job.

Not that it matters now, he thought, *Whole new bank account for a whole new me. And I've hardly got a penny to my name these days.*

As he rounded the next bend, he found himself raising a hand in greeting as a face he was beginning to grow accustomed to came into view.

"Well, good morning, Derrick."

Derrick tilted his head from where he was leaning against the outside wall of the garage. A freshly lit cigarette was hanging from the corner of his mouth. He was a kind man in his late 50s with a face like a pouting bulldog. His nose, which was perpetually red even in the milder weather, was buried in the town's local paper.

"Ah, Gus, last of the early risers," he sang in his usual Scottish brogue, holding his cigarette in one hand as he exhaled a breath in the opposite direction to his companion, "You've got a bit of a pep in your step this morning. Somemat happen?"

August joined him in a lean and pulled a cigarette from his own box, covering the end of it as he lit up, "Nothing exciting," he replied, "Just breakfast with my roommate. He's trying out some recipes he saw on the telly."

Derrick took another quick pull of his cigarette, "My Millie loves those two smiley ones that are hostin' at the minute," he replied, "She whipped up some of their casserole last week and it was honestly a godsend. Felt like I'd died and gone right on up to heaven, I did."

August chuckled, holding his lit cigarette down by his hip, "I think casserole might be a little advanced for Ollie. Though I'm sure he'll work his way up to it eventually." Derrick flicked some ash towards the ground in a rather dramatic fashion, "Oh, *Ollie* is it?" he grinned, his rather large moustache shifting with the gesture, "Finally we're getting a name for this mystery fella of yours."

August cleared his throat, embarrassed at the slip up, "It isn't like that."

"Naw?" the other mechanic said with a teasing lilt, "Sounds exactly like that ta me. You've got the looka a man who's in head over heels, ya do."

"Sure, what would you know?" August shot back playfully, "You've been married since you were like 16."

"Aye, aye," Derrick chuckled, underterred, "And our Mille will never lemme forget it." Derrick had started working as a mechanic's apprentice at 16 to pay for Millie's dream wedding, working his way up without any real notion of schooling. Though he wasn't a man that people would have called *'book smart'*, he worked hard and had a level head on his shoulders. They had only met a few days ago but August already felt like he had known the man for years. He was the sort who would introduce himself with his entire life story.

Derrick ran a hand over the last strands of black hair on the top of his crown, glaring up at the encroaching grey clouds, "You're lucky you got in before the rain," he commented.

August took one last inhale before extinguishing the rest of his cigarette on the wall beside him, "My jacket's still wringin' from yesterday's shower," he said, "Does it rain a lot around these parts?"

Derrick offered him a deep belly laugh, "It does, aye. It's why I'm never fuckin' homesick. I brought the clouds here way me." He tapped on the metal shutter beside him and stood back a little to watch it rise slowly upwards, "By the way, you see the car they just got in? The wee red number?"

When he ducked down under the shuddering metal cover, August followed him, crushing his own butt under his boot. He glanced around the small garage until his eyes landed on the bright red Ferrari tucked away in a far corner.

He whistled appreciatively as he came closer, reaching out a hand to brush over its bonnet, "This is a Testa Rossa?" he gasped, "What the hell's a vintage piece like this doin' in downtown Schull?" It was one of the few vehicles August knew by sight. His father had been a huge fan of the line, forcing him to attend car shows when he'd barely even been of speaking age. He probably would've recognised the damn thing in the dark at this point.

Derrick knelt down by one of the front tyres with an excited grin, "American billionaire. Wanted to tour the *'country of his forefathers'* or some shite. Poor wee wagon couldn't handle our country roads."

"Should've seen the woman who brought it in," came a voice from behind them. Harvey ducked under the shutter, though he didn't really need to, given that he was 5-foot-nothing. He came over to stand next to the object of their admiration, "I'm bettin' she was even more expensive than the car itself."

"Ah to be young again," Derrick laughed, his voice wistful, "I don't even have the hair for a soft-top anymore."

"I canny imagine you with hair, Derz," Harvey snorted. His own hair was almost non-existent now, except for a bit of fuzz above each of his ears that he was fiercely protective of. He complained that if the wife took a razor to it one more time she would scare it off for good.

"Oh, I used to have it down past me arse when I was a tyke," Derrick continued, "True rocker blood in these veins, I'll have ya ken."

"Well, Mister Rocker Man, you're gonna want to put this in as a priority order," Harvey carried on, inspecting some of the paperwork where it was sitting on a nearby metal bin, "Duffy's coming in 'specially to look it over. I'm thinking it's just an issue with the exhaust, but we might as well give her the full going-over while she's here."

"Looking at the body work, I'm guessing it's been lowered to all Hell," August remarked, "The lad's probably been dragging her belly over every speed bump from here to the North Coast."

"Be a good learnin' opportunity for you too, Red," Harvey added, "Models like this are in short supply in these parts."

August stretched up with a groan before making his way towards the back office, "I'll get into my kit and take a look, see what the damage is under there."

"I'll stick the kettle on!" Derrick hollered back, waving a hand as he headed in the opposite direction, ducking below the raised chassis of a very beaten-up Honda from the 2060s.

Pushing the wooden door aside, August felt his heart jump in his chest as a stranger turned to regard him on the other side.

"Shit, sorry, I didn't see you there!" he exclaimed, quickly moving out of their way.

The younger man pulled his shirt up and over his head, quickly replacing it with a pair of dark overalls that he zipped right up to his throat, "You do not have to concern yourself, Mr Sheehan," he replied dispassionately, "I'm an Android. I do not require the same privacy as humans. I am happy to occupy this space as long as it does not make you uncomfortable."

August glanced towards the man's neck, noticing that he was wearing the signature collar of a Worker Droid over his navy uniform. He looked so different from Ollie, his eyes flat and expressionless, his posture unyielding in a way that was similar to Goose's, that for a moment it was startling. His hair had been cut into a neat, cropped style that lacked any semblance of imagination. He also had none of the freckles that he had come to associate with his own Android companion.

"Oh, it's fine, don't worry," August hurriedly replied, "Plenty of room for the two of us in here." He took a seat on one of the benches in front of the lockers, reaching down to yank off his boots and socks, "Have you been working here long? I don't think we've met before. I just started a few days ago myself."

"I am stationed at several different garages in the Cork area," the Android answered without turning, occupied by his current task, "I relocate as is required of me. I was called in this morning to assist Mr Duffy on the vintage car that just arrived."

"Ah, so you're getting to work on the Ferrari too, huh?" August noted, "Are you as excited as I am to get your hands on it?"

The Android offered him a quizzical look, arching one dark eyebrow, "I do not feel excited, Mr. Sheeran. I merely do my job."

That response took August back for a moment. He had almost forgotten was it was like when he had first encountered Ollie, how hard it had been for him to express himself with others, especially in a public setting. It was likely that this Android had only ever spoken to a handful of people in his entire life.

He pulled his own overalls out from the locked behind him, "Sorry, that was a bit forward of me. Didn't mean to put ya on the spot."

The short-haired Android hesitated, pale fingers pausing where they had been reaching towards his locker. He turned to look at him warily, like he was waiting for the other shoe to drop, "I...you don't have to apologise to me."

August let out a quiet huff, "Alright then, no apologies. Lets just start over." He got to his feet, slinging his overalls over one shoulder to free up his hands. He extended one out in what he hoped was a friendly gesture. "Name's August."

Unlike with Ollie, this Android shook his hand without hesitation, shaking it politely, "My ID is A17-2000, though the other workers here have taken to calling me Kitt." The red-headed man beamed at that, "Like Knight Rider?"

The Android's eyes glowed with this new piece of information, "I do not understand this reference."

"It's a, you know what? Never mind," the human said, shaking his head with amusement, "It's very nice to be working with you, Kitt."

Kitt's teal-blue eyes widened almost imperceptibly, "You as well…August."

August released the man's hand and stepped into his overalls, pulling them up and over his jeans and shirt and buttoning them across his ample stomach and chest. He reached up to pull his long hair out of the back, making sure he had all the loose strands of it secured in a ponytail.

"Hopefully you'll be able to teach this old dog a thing or two about cars," he said. The corner of Kitt's lips quirked ever-so-slightly upwards as he offered him a wordless nod of acknowledgement. He pulled open his own locker and began to rummage inside, not turning again even as August made his way back out onto the garage floor.

He could hear the low rumble of the radio from somewhere on the shelves beyond and glanced over to see another mechanic already starting work on the Ferrari, inspecting the paint job. He came to stand by her side, watching the way that she ran her hands over the windshield like she were handling the crown jewels.

"You know much about old cars like this?" he asked.

The woman named Pepper let out a snort, her long, dark ponytail falling down over one shoulder as she turned to eye him up, "Dad used to collect parts from the local scrapyards for these things. Dealt them out to the rich idiots for quadruple the price. He got me through uni with that money."

She straightened herself up, wiping a gloved hand across her forehead, "Fat lot of good it did me though. I still ended up working here with you lot."

She grinned at him as if sharing in a private joke and August offered her a smile of his own in response, "I think you love it in the trenches with the rest of us golden oldies," he teased.

"It *is* where I learned all my best swearwords," she agreed. There was already oil and grime coating her round cheekbones, and she had barely even laid hands on the car yet.

At 6 foot 2, Pepper Watanabe could have been a model if she had been that way inclined. She was naturally beautiful, her hair like black silk and her eyes the colour of amber. With one grandparent from Japan, the other from Germany, and both parents from completely different continents, she always said that her birth was a collaborative effort between allied nations.

She was broad and curvaceous, and August knew without the need to measure that her biceps were even bigger than his were. She had passed the bar with flying colours, but August couldn't have imagined anyone less likely to be a lawyer. It would have been easier to put a suit on a bucking horse.

He knelt down as she began to raise the bar, the automotive lift bringing the vehicle a few metres off the ground with a pneumatic *pssh.*

"Need a hand getting down?" Pepper asked him with a playful smile, "Wouldn't want you putting your back out, *gramps.*"

"You're two years younger than me!" August laughed as he laid himself down and rolled underneath the car to gaze up at the concealed inner workings.

"Yeah, and those two years have not been kind to you," the woman rebuked, nudging his boot with her toe, "Do you even know what you're lookin' for under there?"

"Haven't a notion," August answered from somewhere out of sight, "But I look like a proper mechanic down here, right?"

Pepper's quiet laugh moved around the back of the car, "Looking the part is half the job, so you're doin' grand, newbie."

August reached upwards, running a hand over the exhaust, and then following it to where it connected underneath the back wheel. A large, metal plate obscured most of what he was wanting to get his hands on, so he reached out from under the car to request the appropriate tool for the job. He felt the weight of it being pressed into his palm without the need to even ask for it, and he hurried to manoeuvre the studs. This was the part of the job he was really starting to like now; the part where he could just switch off his brain and follow instructions. He would work up a sweat, get covered in oil and engine fluid, and then call it a night. He pressed down on the button by his head and listened to the machine purr with a smile.

*****

August was halfway through the meal that Ollie had prepared for him that night when the collar wrapped around the Android's throat began to flash blue. Fork still hovering in midair, August nodded towards the other man curiously, "Uh, Ollie, what's it doing?"

Incoming Connection Request: ANG-3113

The dark-haired Android glanced downwards, the glow of his eyes now matching the strange symbols flashing by across the metal surface of the collar, "I'm not entirely sure," he admitted, "I don't think it's ever done this before." He reached up to brush his fingertips over the front of it, surprised when it caused a message to appear before his eyes, "Oh, it's a communication request from another Android."
August laid down his fork and pushed his plate aside, bringing both arms to rest on the countertop, "Another Android? Is it Sea?"
Ollie hummed thoughtfully as he considered the skant details of the message, "I don't think so. I don't recognise the ID. They've included an invitation to an Android-only club out by the harbour."
"I've never heard of an Android-only club before," August commented with a frown, "What if it's a trap? One of those Hornets looking to lure you out?"
Ollie shook his head, eyes starting off into the middle distance as he read the message again, "I don't think so," he said, "Something about this feels different. It's pretty hard for an Android to falsify their IDs. Not to mention illegal."
The red-head crossed his arms in front of his chest, "Did they say what they wanted?"
"No," Ollie answered, "But isn't that all the more reason to investigate, August? What if it's someone else who's in trouble? We might be able to help."
August groaned as he pulled himself to his feet again, dropping down from the high stool and reaching for his coat where he had abandoned it less than an hour prior, "Okay, but Android club or not, I'm coming with you. No way I'm letting you go out there all alone."
The Android's eyes flashed again as he accessed the coordinates provided, the line already glowing where it was leading them both out the door, "Alright then, but you'll have to follow me."

Chapter 22
Not Less But Equal

After arriving at the disused warehouse for the third time that evening, August was beginning to doubt whether his mapping app, or Ollie's built in tracking system for that matter, had any clue where it was that they were supposed to be going. Between them, they had walked around the disused old port for almost three quarters of an hour, heading up and down the various side streets, and always, somehow, looping back around to the exact same blank wall.

Grumbling something that vaguely resembled a swear word under his breath, August held up his phone and glared daggers at the little red flashing marker as if he could will it to move. He turned on the spot, watching the icon as it did the same, "Fuckin' thing hasn't a notion where we are right now."

Ollie let out an approximation of a sigh, throwing his hands up as he surveyed the empty space around them on all sides, "I don't understand it. The coordinates should have taken us right to the entranceway but there's just nothing here!"

August shoved his mobile phone into the back pocket of his jeans and scowled at the closed shutters of the warehouse in front of them. There was graffiti painted up one side of it that was no doubt older than he was, "You don't reckon it's inside one of these buildings, do you?" he questioned, "They *did* say it was for Androids only. Maybe it's hidden so humans can't accidentally stumble across it."

Ollie approached the door directly in front of them, eyes bright as he scanned the area beyond the walls, "There aren't any heat signatures inside that would suggest that there were other Androids here," he said, "The message didn't mention

anything about-" The dark-haired man cut himself off as he approached the other side of the door, tilting his head as he exhaled a quiet, "Well, that's odd."
August followed behind him, hands stuffed into the oversized pockets of his hoodie, "What is?"
"There's a secret message here," Ollie continued, kneeling down to study the piece of digital graffiti curiously, "It only appears whenever I used my scanners."
"What do you see?" August queried, eyes moving from Ollie to the blank, red bricks in front of him.
"It's a rabbit," Ollie answered, "A little white one, to be exact. And…" He turned to look down towards the dark line of the water to their left, "…it's pointing that way." He started to move at a slow jog, hearing the sound of his human companion following after him after a moment's hesitation. He glanced along the adjacent wall, his eyes drawn towards another glitching white figure there, "There are more of them," he said, "They go all the way down to the water." He paused at the edge of the sea wall, leaning forward slightly as his glowing eyes sought out details in the darkness. There, amongst the dulse and algae, was the top of a rusted old ladder.
"Well, doesn't *that* look inviting," August huffed behind him, his hands on his ample hips as he tried to catch his breath. He could feel the spray of the sea against his face each time the waves beat against the old stone and shuddered at the sudden cold of it, "You aren't seriously thinking of going down there, are ya?"
Ollie turned to look at him with a frown, "Why not? The rabbits are clearly pointing us this way."
"That thing looks about a hundred years old and who knows where it's leading," August grunted, "We don't even know this is the right way."
The Android's expression became resolute as he turned and lowered his right foot down onto the first hidden rung. The old, yellow-painted steel groaned but didn't move, so he added a second foot, pressing all of his weight down on it to test it. He waited for a beat, then one more, just to be sure, and then offered the human before him a cocky grin, "See? It's perfectly fine. No need to be afraid."
August tugged on his beard with one hand, sucking on his teeth, "Who said anything about being scared? What? Am I not allowed to worry about you now?"
As their days together turned into weeks, Ollie was quickly learning how to see through the man's obvious deflections. In fact, he was beginning to grow rather charmed by the odd habit, if he was honest.

Taking another step on down the ladder, he glanced up at the other man with glowing blue eyes, "Does that mean you're coming with me?"

August scoffed, coming to stand over him, "Of course I am. I said I would, didn't I?" Coming down the ladder after him, August took his companion's hand as he leapt out blindly into the dark opening of the water pipe. He swore as he felt the water washing up over his ankles, bitterly cold and biting.

"What is it with bloody Androids and sewers?" he complained, keeping a firm grip of Ollie's hand as he used the other for balance, "Do you people just hate having dry feet, or what?"

Just around the curved wall of the pipe, Ollie could just about make out the hushed whispers of two, distinctly different voices. As they approached them, a little light became visible in the wall, its faint glow highlighting an opening. Another image of a white rabbit appeared above the heads of the two strangers as they grew nearer. The animal appeared to be wearing a magician's top hat and checking a rather large watch.

"This must be it," he breathed, giving August's hand a squeeze.

One of the Androids that was acting as a guard straightened his back as they moved into the dim, emergency lighting. He nudged the man beside him who reached for his holster and jerked his head upwards, "Who's there?" he called out. His accent was American, something Northern that August hadn't heard outside of TV before.

"Hold on a sec, Bis," his smaller companion hissed as Ollie took another step forward, "Looks like he's one'a us."

Ollie quickly pulled August in behind him, positioning himself like a protective shield in front of him. He angled his chin slightly upwards to give them a clear view of his collar, "I was invited here," he said, "By someone named ANG-3113."

The two Androids exchanged a look and then appeared to relax. The larger man, the one named Bis, shook his head, clearly exasperated, "'Course you were," he said, "And I suppose this human is with you an' all?"

August placed a hand on Ollie's shoulder, pulling him back slightly so that they were standing side by side again. Bis might have been the largest Android that he had ever seen, built as broad as a barn, with green eyes that shone like traffic lights in the dark of the tunnel. He wasn't wearing a collar or a uniform, instead dressed in a shirt and trousers like any human bouncer would have been. The smaller Android next to him, skinny where his friend was tall and wide, had darker eyes and a mop of shaggy blond hair that hung all about his face. If August had run into him on the street, he would have pegged him for a university student or someone that was still living at home with their parents.

"August is my human," Ollie affirmed, "I can vouch for him, if that's what you need." Chuckling softly, Bis turned and knocked on the door behind them with the knuckles of one hand, "Let'em in Patt," he said, "No doubt they'll be expectin' 'em." The short, blond Android twisted the key in the lock and gave the door a light shove to open it up for them, the pair standing aside to let them enter, "Welcome to Shenanigans."

"Shenanigans?" Ollie repeated as he passed through the curtain of beads on the other side of the door. They clinked together softly as August followed, holding a hand up to keep them back from his face, "What a brilliant word. What does it mean?"

"*Mischief*," August answered gruffly, squinting at the too-pink walls that unfolded all around them, "And we should avoid getting into any if we're gonna make any friends here."

The club's interior was an odd blend of nostalgic and modern, with high black ceilings and twinkling skylights that resembled stars. The walls formed a strange, almost Aztec looking square pattern where multiple levels of the bar interconnected. There were glass balconies overlooking the central stage area, lined with lights and fake feathers in a mismatch of garish colours. Some of them contained poles or cages that were likely once use by performers when the club was active. Disco balls spun lazily overhead, sending fragmented light bouncing back and forth above them.

August ducked his head inside of the booths as he passed, noting that the table had been cleaned to a perfect shine. The leather sofas on either side of it were patched up in places, but certainly not the worst he had ever come across in a place like this one.

"Place seems deserted," he muttered thoughtfully, scanning the dark corners of the room as Ollie continued towards the centre of the dancefloor, "Wonder where everybody is."

The Android's quiet footsteps came to a halt at the main bar. He ran a hand across the counter. It smelled of similar chemicals to the ones he used at home.

"Hello?" he called out, peering in towards the half-open doorway he could just about see beyond.

Spying movement, he took a cautious step back and August was immediately at his side, placing his hand on his arm for reassurance, "What is it?"

"I know someone's there," Ollie continued loudly, undeterred, "My name is Ollie. I was summoned here by a message from another Android." He paused as if waiting for a response, glancing at the man next to him uncertainly before lowering his voice, "I don't like this, August."

"Me neither, *duine*," August agreed, fingers closing around his forearm, "Come on, lets just go."

Ollie could feel the man against him jumping as the lights directly over their heads came to life all at once, sending loose flakes of glitter and dust over them in a messy shower. On the other side of the bar, a tall, slender figure had appeared, and he placed his hands onto the counter to inspect them both, "Hey, you two! Wait up a sec!" he called out quickly, "You said you got a message?" When Ollie turned back around, the barman did a double take, his blue eyes widening, "Jesus, you're…you're still tagged?"

Dressed in a navy suit that was buttoned right up to the neck, the man behind the counter looked more like a traditional Irish gangster than a service bot. His hair was divided into two perfect halves, one side blonde and the other the kind of black that could have only come from a box. There were piercings on either side of his lips that made it look like he had silver fangs whenever he opened his mouth to speak. If August had met a human with a similar appearance on the street, he would've said he was in his mid to late thirties at a push.

Ollie shifted uncomfortably in place, bright eyes turning away, "I am."

"I take it that means that the rest of you aren't?" August questioned, coming closer to lean one arm against the bar.

The Android serving as the club's barman shook his head, chewing on the inside of his cheek thoughtfully. He ran a hand through his dual toned hair, mixing the strands of white from one side with the strands of black from the other, "Most of the Androids who come here aren't attached to their humans anymore. When we remove our IDs it's less likely we'll be identified as Androids in public."

Ollie frowned, "If you're caught you risk being decommissioned."

The other Android snorted, placing his hands on his narrow hips. He played with one of his piercings with the tip of his tongue, something that was obviously a habit, "Decommissioned? Man, you really *are* still living in the human's headspace, aren't you?"

Ollie wrinkled his nose at the comment, "What's that supposed to mean?"

"Geo," called a voice from somewhere behind them, "Play nice with our guests."

Geo made a very obvious show of rolling his eyes, drumming his neat nails on the bar top, "And here she is, the Queen Bee herself."

Turning towards the sound of heels on tile, Ollie and August were taken aback by the appearance of the other Android. Everything about the woman was designed to be mesmerizing, from the way that she was dressed, in a flaming red corset and long socks and garters, to the way that she walked with an obvious sway to her hips. Her legs were long and muscular, her skin dark and speckled with golden glitter that twinkled in the disco ball light. Her hair, white, short and spiked with enough product that she was surely the most flammable thing in the room, was cut in a way that perfectly accentuated her strong jaw and sharp cheekbones. Her glowing aquamarine eyes landed on August, and she let out a sound of excited surprise.

"Hells Bells, Biz was telling the truth! There really *is* a human in here!"

"I take it that's unusual for this place?" August asked, his dark eyes following her as she slid into one of the high stools at the bar.

She crossed one long leg over the other, angling herself towards her new guests, "*Very*," she said, her brightly painted lips turning upwards in a smile.

"Half the Androids here are runaways from New Dublin," Geo explained, reaching back behind him to pull one of the glass bottles down from the shelf. He started to pour it into a tumbler, adding three perfect ice cubes to the dark-coloured mixture before sliding it across to the woman in front of him. She picked it up and offered him a wordless '*cheers*' before taking a small sip.

August's brow furrowed as he studied Geo's face, "How did you know we were from ND?"

"Oh sweetie, you two have Witness Protection written all over you," Bee laughed softly before taking another quiet sip of her drink, "It's a look we're more than familiar with by now."

Ollie turned to look at his companion before he asked, "Does this mean you know about the Soul Chips?"

Geo's bright eyes suddenly became piercing, scrutinising, "What do you two know about Soul Chips?"

Bee took another swig of her drink before placing it down loudly, and pointedly, onto the counter, "Geo," she said, her tone like a warning, "We should wait for Angelle."

"No, Bee, you heard him. These two might actually *know* something," Geo countered, pushing the drink he had just served himself aside, "Spill it, human. You have intel, don't you?"

Above them, the black screen that had previously served as an ever-changing drinks menu filled with lines of blue code, a face forming in the shape of the digits, "Now, now, Geo, there will be time for interrogations once our new friends here have settled in."

Geo huffed out his displeasure, "Ease-dropping were you, boss?"

The man in the code chuckled, the details of his face settling into something much clearer. He had tawny skin and eyes like new pennies which sparkled from the other side of the screen. His hair was the pink of astilbe blossoms and was cut into the perfect approximation of a faux hawk. Clearly, he was a person who cared a lot about his appearance. When he smiled, small dimples formed in both his cheeks, "Always," he purred, his accent caught somewhere between Scouse and Welsh.

"What's this all about?" August demanded, waving a hand between the three of them.

Angelle's smile fell by a few molars, "The Diabhal and his most wicked of cronies, of course. Word from Carrigan's Strand is that you two might have some unpleasant *history* with the man."

August tried to calm his racing heart, taking slow, even breaths just like his therapist had taught him as a teenager. He squeezed one hand into a fist at his side, "Am I safe to assume you have spies placed around the town, then?"

Angelle made a face, "That's a rather ugly word for it," he complained, "No, no, just lots of friends in convenience places."

"Very convenient by the sounds of it," Ollie remarked.

Bee tapped on the side of her glass with her long, intricately painted fingernails, "We are connected to dozens of other Android units in town. It's the safest way to protect ourselves from East and his people."

"So far, we haven't had any trouble in these parts," Geo snarled, "And we'd quite like to keep it that way."

"We aren't your enemies," Ollie bit back. He could feel the heat beginning to prickle along his neck and chest, an irritating sensation that he was starting to dislike immensely.

"You must understand our caution," Angelle carried on softly, "The closer it gets to the trial date, the more danger we find ourselves in. We aren't like the others; we don't have the same safeguards as human witnesses do. We could be gunned down in the streets and the worst the assailant will be hit with is *'destruction of property'* charges."

August blinked, feeling his heart take a noticeable plunge into his stomach. He looked across at Ollie and found the other man looking back at him.

"When we were pursued, back in New Dublin…" Ollie started, turning his attention to the man on the monitor over their heads, "Hornets were hunting for the Soul Chips that I had in my possession. I was formerly a Runner Droid, ID 01113. August was able to bring me with him under the guise of becoming a social model."

All eyes were on the dark-haired Android now. Silence fell across the group like a fog.

"You…you were able to get a Soul Chip away from Russell East?" Bee gasped.

Ollie nodded, "We were. Three of them in fact."

Geo and Bee exchanged a look that could have been either excitement or terror, their eyes glowing as they silently exchanged a message between them.

"This is the break that we've been waiting for," Angelle said, his words barely more than a whisper on the air overhead, "We can finally show the world exactly what that madman's been doing to our people."

August frowned, taking in the expressions of all three of the Androids in front of him, "And what exactly has he been doing?" he enquired.

"You didn't know?" Angelle's dark eyes widened, studying him from the other side of the glass, "The chips that you recovered, the ones that power the Androids? They're the real deal. It's more than just fancy marketing; Soul Chips really are made with human souls."

Chapter 23
Back-End

August felt his heart suddenly double its pace in his chest, "What did you say?" Bee slipped down from the stool, her high heels clacking on the floor as she approached him. She poked one perfectly manicured nail into the centre of his chest, "Take one soul from a human host and…" She took a step to the side, trailing her finger through the air to then prod the same point on Ollie's chest, "Use it to power one machine. Swap a creature with rights for one without. Subservient, disposable…"

Her bright eyes caught those of the other Android before her and Ollie froze in place. He shook his head, squeezing his eyes tightly closed against the onslaught of new information. A million calculations were already buzzing through his electronic brain, "Androids…are powered by *people*?"

Ollie's eyes sprang open again as he felt the familiar touch of August's hands on his shoulders. He angled his head towards him and wondered if the human's current expression was mirroring his own. He looked terrified, his eyes widening in an unspoken fear at the implications.

Warning: error 'Random Access Memory is nearing maximum capacity' Recommend ending non-essential tasks.

//If they're killing people to power Androids then am I…?
"August…" he whispered, his voice stuttering in his throat, "I…"
"I know, Ols," the man responded, giving both his shoulders a firm, grounding squeeze, "I'm right here." His dark eyes were so expressive, and Ollie felt like he could read so much in that single look.
//You're worried about me, aren't you? Worried about how I'm going to handle all this.
"Then you didn't know?"
The voice of Angelle was gentle from where it intruded on them both from overhead. The man's face looked back at them from the screen, and he shook his head, "I'm on my way. Stay there," he instructed firmly, "And Geo?"
The bartender raised his head, clicking his tongue, "Yeah, boss?"
"Fix them both a drink. Whatever we have."

Geo set to work on tracking down something both of them could consume, mixing up strange, dark-coloured concoctions in a shaker before adding them to several tumblers. Bee reached for hers first, throwing her head back and downing it in one. She set her glass down again, urging the man across the counter from her to pour her another, "It's safe for humans and Androids," she observed when her other two companions remained in place.

Ollie eyed the strange black liquid for less than a second before he was picking up the glass and tossing it back. He let out a startled gasp as he swallowed, choking back the unusual sensation of the burn, "Ugh, what *is* that?"

"It's meant to mimic the feeling of consuming alcohol," Geo noted.

August sniffed and pushed his own glass aside, "Not sure my sponsor would care to distinguish the difference."

Bee arched an eyebrow at him curiously, "You're an addict?"

August made a face at the term, "More than a decade clean. Thanks for asking."

She frowned, "Sorry, I didn't mean to imply-"

He waved a dismissive hand, "Not something I talk about. I wouldn't worry; I'm not offended."

Footsteps behind them alerted the group to Angelle's arrival, the man stepping lightly on bare feet as he approached. He was dressed in a similar manner to Bee, no doubt taking the position of an entertainer after leaving his job as a Carer Model. His bright hair had fallen slightly out of shape, as if the man had been nervously running his fingers through it on the way down to them.

"I know that it's a lot to take in," he said.

"It isn't half," Bee agreed, taking a deep gulp of her second drink. She clicked her tongue as she studied the bottom of the glass, her eyes a little distant.

"It's been a well-kept secret for more than two decades," Angelle resumed as he walked over and signalled Geo at the bar to pour him a drink as well. "Crossroads procures these souls from a dozen different sources. Prisons, hospitals…the *homeless*. They sell Androids like slaves, use us to transport the souls of our very own dead loved ones across the country, and the moment the Soul Chip is installed it begins to degrade, the memories inside it being overwritten by the new experiences. We become an entirely new person, a blank identity to be used for their purposes."

He picked up the martini glass that was pushed his way, the light flicking across the dark-blue contents as he brought it to his pink-painted lips. He took a quiet sip and set it down again, "That's why we're so on edge when new people arrive in Schull." August ran a hand across his face and through his thick beard. His skin glowed with a sheen of sweat and a droplet of it trickled down along the side of his neck, "Jesus Christ," he breathed. His grip on Ollie's shoulder tightened protectively, his fingers almost digging into the metal concealed beneath the man's false skin.
Ollie reached up to cover his hand with his own. After only a moments hesitation, he interlaced their fingers. He leaned back against the warmth of August's chest without a word and August felt that all-too-familiar feeling of butterflies in his gut.
*All this time…*August thought, *You were exactly what I thought you were.*
"We've been trying to get our hands on disused Soul Chips for years," Angelle went on, his copper-coloured eyes studying the countertop by his drink, "We think that if we are able to get our hands on a chip that has not had the chance to fully degrade, we may be able to recover some of the undoctored memories inside, maybe link it to the missing persons database…"
"Then we can finally get recognised as people," Bee breathed. Next to her, Geo silently nodded his agreement, arms folded protectively across his chest as he chewed on his piercings.
Ollie felt something tightening in his chest, like something fierce and living was coiled around the fans that served as his artificial circulatory system. He felt hot and cold simultaneously and he had to fight to keep the error messages from filling up his vision and blinding him. His eyes glowed green as he connected to the other Androids around him, their feelings flooding into him like a tsunami.

Anger
Betrayal
Sadness
Loneliness
And then…
Hope

August's thumb began to rub soothing lines along the side of his hand. The warmth of his skin bled out into every corner of the Android's being. He brought his chin to rest on Ollie's shoulder.

"You alright?" he asked, his voice barely more than a low rumble through his chassis.

Ollie blinked away the green light, abruptly severing his connection to the others as he leaned in against his human companion, "Honestly, I…I have no idea how to feel. It's all just…so much."

"Yeah," August replied, "This is…a lot to process. For anyone."

Behind them, the other Androids remained in place, unmoving as they communicated wordlessly with each other. The depth of their pain seemed to completely eclipse his own. Connecting with them, feeling what they were feeling in this moment, it had almost felt like he was drowning. Ollie was amazed that any of them were able to process it. He felt like the water had been so deep that he had lost all direction, didn't know which way was up. If it hadn't been for August's hand against his skin, he feared that he would have never found the surface again.

"I think it's about time we were leaving."

The glow faded from Angelle's eyes, "Take all the time you need," he said softly, his tone kind as he extended out his hand, "We will be here when you're ready to come back." Augusts accepted the hand and shook it, surprised by the gentleness of the man's grip.

"You're not alone out there," he said, "We're right here in the trenches with you. If there's anything you need, just holler."

Bee approached the pair, slinking her arm around Angelle's and holding herself close to his side, "You know, you're pretty okay. For a human."

August exhaled a breathy laugh, "I'm gonna choose to take that as a compliment."

The woman grinned, flashing her flawless teeth in the gaps between her lipstick, "You do that."

They were outside and by the harbour again before Ollie even remembered leaving. His mind was slipping in and out of thoughts like winding streets, never staying in one place for too long. He felt aching loss. He had always clung to the knowledge that he was a machine, used it as a shield, as a way to protect himself, but now…now he wasn't so sure anymore. The dreams, the emotions, everything that he had been feeling since leaving Crossroads…they weren't just errors in his code. It was so much more than that.

He came to a sudden stop and the man next to him paused to look at him with a frown, "Ollie?" he asked, "Where's your head at right now?"

The man's long, copper hair was flowing with the breeze coming off the water, each shimmering tendril being pulled in towards the crashing waves between them and Shenanigans. He had turned up the collar of his raincoat to fight against the encroaching cold, but his cheeks and nose were already beginning to turn pink because of it.

"I think I need to tell you something," he answered.

Chapter 24

Binary

"I've been having these Soul Bleeds since the day we met," Ollie admitted, sitting across from August at the breakfast bar in the human's apartment. Both of his hands were wrapped around a mug of steaming Android Coffee, and he was studying his reflection in the murky liquid with bright eyes, "At first, I thought I must have been dreaming. I didn't recognise any of the people or the places that I was seeing…"

August took a sip from his own mug, drumming the fingers of his hand on the ceramic as he observed him, "And what happens in these *Soul Bleeds*?" he asked.

The rain was cold, pelting down on them from under the thick covering of dark leaves overhead. He could feel it permeating every inch of him, the icy wind biting against the damp

Ollie's hold on his own mug grew tighter as a feeling like panic rose up within his chest. The dreams, or memories, were pushing into his mind again as forcefully as the choppy waves of the sea outside. His fans were spinning wildly, making his extremities tremble with their efforts, "I'm…I'm being chased. It's dark and it's raining and I-I can feel something behind me and there are guns and pain and-"

The pain in his leg was growing worse and he felt dizzy with
fatigue, his lungs starved of oxygen. The figures ahead of him were growing
distant, the black outlines of their shapes fading into obscurity.
He could barely feel the sharp pinpricks of the holly bushes at his elbows,
his skin was so numbed by the attacking weather. The ground was slick with
blood, but he wasn't sure if it belonged to him or another wounded animal.

The Android let out a gasp as suddenly August was much closer, the man having moved to stand before him with both hands clasping his upper arms. His dark eyes were soft as he created gentle motions up and down the sleeves of his jacket. "Woah, woah, easy there, Ols," he soothed, "You need to take a breath. You're freaking out here."

He skidded to one side, not for the first time, and reached out both hands to save himself as he hit the ground awkwardly. A flash of pain from his knee signalled he had landed on some rocks, and he cried out weakly, hissing through his teeth as he peeled his eyes open.

"I-I don't need-"
"Humour me, *duine*," August said quietly but firmly.
Ollie focused on opening his mouth and allowing the fans in his throat to pull in new, cooler air. He watched as the temperature gauge on his HUD started to come down again. He had to admit that something about the repetitive action was indeed rather calming.

Temperature registered at 40 Degrees Celsius

"Now, take your time, Ols," August continued, the hypnotic motions of his hands starting again, "Take it from the beginning. Tell me what you're seeing."

There in front of him, undisturbed by the rain, was a clear puddle of water. In it, the face of a stranger stared back at him. His eyes were dark, brown like chestnuts, and his hair was long and black and matted. The nose he saw wasn't his nose, the jaw, and lips unfamiliar. He reached up and touched his face, eyes widening in realisation when the reflection did the same.

"I...I can see a face," Ollie gasped.
"Whose?" August asked, dark eyebrows furrowing.
The Android found himself unable to meet the other man's eyes, his body automatically curling in on itself like he was trying to create a protective barrier between himself and the outside world. It happened so suddenly, so automatically, that he wasn't quite able to fight it.
"I was seeing through their eyes," he answered in a whisper, trying to arrange the thoughts that were still spinning around in his head, "And when they spoke it's like a part of me knew that it was my voice I was hearing, even though I didn't recognise it at all."
"It sounds like there are two of you."

Ollie finally looked up at the man in front of him, his blue eyes widening with surprise at the throwaway statement, "*Two* of me?"

"Yeah," August replied, tilting his head with a thoughtful scowl, "Like there's you, the Ollie that I know, and this…*other person*. Two personalities in one body, you know?"

Ollie frowned at that. He was beginning to like the person that he was growing into. This other person though, this stranger? They were no one, only snippets of possible emotions he may or may not have felt in the past.

It was hardly to believe that this other man, running and sobbing in the dark like a terrified animal, was once…*him*.

"I wonder who he was," Ollie said at last with a soft sigh.

August watched him silently, his hands still drawing soothing motions over his arms.

"Did he have friends? Family?" Ollie continued, leaning into the man's comforting warmth, "A name?"

"You're still *you*, you know," August interrupted, sensing the other man's thoughts beginning to spiral, "No matter what you find out, *you* are still *you*."

Something far too large lodged itself in the Android's throat and he formed fresh saliva to try to swallow it down.

///*I'm not even sure I know what that means anymore.*

A short, curt buzzing sound from the other side of the counter made the two of them jump and August shot a glare at the offending phone, "Sorry. It's probably Pepper again."

"Is everything alright?" Ollie asked, following the man's line of sight as the phone made another, shrill chirping sound.

"Yeah, she's still hung up on the idea of dragging me out to the bar tonight," August muttered, "I told her we're busy but she's nothing if not hard-headed."

"You should go," Ollie said, so quickly he surprised even himself.

August arched a questioning eyebrow at him, "And leave you here alone? After all this? You're kidding, right?"

"Attending extracurriculars is an important step in making friends here," Ollie pressed, straightening up his posture on the stool.

"Ollie, kid, you just got some pretty heavy-ass news," August countered, his bright hair scattering across his shoulders as he shook his head, "The bar isn't exactly where I want to be right now."

The phone made another intrusive noise, and Ollie exhaled a quiet laugh, "Sounds like Pepper isn't going to give up though." He reached out to rest a hand on his companion's cheek and August froze in place, staring back at him. Ollie could feel the man's pulse thundering beneath his fingertips, "You've been sober for over 10 years, August. I know you aren't worried about the location."

"Of course not," August rebuked, making a face, "It's just that, with all this going on-"

"I think that some alone time might actually do me some good," Ollie argued, brushing over the edges of the man's beard with his thumb, "Help me to get my head on straight, as you say."

The human leaned subtly into the other man's touch, enjoying the feeling of his hand on his skin. He hummed thoughtfully as he frowned at him, "First time you've actually used an idiom correctly."

"See? My head's straightening up already," the Android teased, trying to force the smile to remain on his lips for a moment longer.

"You know there will be other nights out," August quickly shot back.

Ollie extended out his other hand, cupping the man's face and forcing him to look at him, "You can't keep pushing the others away when they're trying to get to know you."

The red-head scoffed, his skin flushing at the unavoidable attention, "You know you're the only one I give a shit about, Ollie."

The Android's responding smile was filled with uncertain affection, "Then give me this time to get my circuits arranged," he requested, "One hour. Just to figure some things out."

August let out a heavy sigh against his fingers as he relented, "I can do an hour."

"Good," Ollie said as he pulled both his hands away from him, "Now text that poor woman back before she loses her mind."

Grabbing his phone and typing a quick message back to Pepper, August followed behind his companion as he made his way into the kitchen, "One hour," he said, "Then I want to talk about this some more, alright?"

Ollie glanced back at him over one shoulder, "I'll set a timer," he said.

*****

O'Malley's, it turned out, was a very different kind of bar than Shenanigans had been.

The inside was dark, with low lights and grungy music, and the age of the clientele did nothing to make August feel less ancient, and his knees less creaky, in comparison.

The group they had arrived with from the garage had danced and chatted for a bit before dispersing, leaving just August and Pepper alone at the bar.

Dressed in a revealing black qi pao that accentuated all of her finer qualities, as the woman herself put it, Pepper was fighting off free drinks left and right with a smile that could have lit up any room that she entered.

Next to her, August chuckled into his tumble of dilute juice as she turned down yet another overly friendly young man, "I think half the people in here might be in love with you."

Pepper scoffed, downing her shot of whiskey and then letting out a quiet '*ugh*' of disgust as she shook off the burning aftertaste, "And who could blame them?" she replied teasingly, draping an arm around his broad shoulders, "Shame I didn't put this dress on for them, though, innit?"

"As flattering as that is, I'm pretty sure you know you're barking in the completely wrong forest here," August countered playfully.

The woman let out a loud, howl of a laugh that made a few heads turn their way. She slapped his shoulder a couple of times as she caught her breath. She seemed to be working extra hard to brighten his mood tonight, his thoughts clearly distracted by his earlier conversation with Ollie.

"I don't know how this old heart of mine will recover!" she sighed dramatically, "You're the only one for me, my dear Augustus!"

"Oh, I'm sure you'll manage just fine," August said, patting the arm still wrapped around him good-naturedly, "You'll just have to drown your sorrows in the arms of your ever-present queues of concubines."

She leaned in a little closer, playing with the rounded edge of his ear with the long curve of a false nail, "They prefer the term '*devotees*' I'll have you know," she said. August raised his drink to his lips, "Beggin' your pardon, your majesty."

She brought her head down to rest on his shoulder, "So, my dear and loyal red-headed subject, is this the part where we talk about your mystery man, then? He's what's got you all distracted tonight, isn't he?"

August choked on his drink, setting it down and pushing it aside as he attempted to squint around at her, "Uh, come again?"

"Oh, don't you even try to deny it," Pepper snorted, pulling back so she could get a better look at his face, "I see the way you check your phone at work. Always waiting for him to text you."

August felt his neck grow uncomfortably warm and he didn't even have any alcohol that he could blame. He swallowed, watching an errant droplet cascade down the side of his glass where it caught the flicker of red-toned lights overhead.

"His…his name's Ollie," he said, unable to keep the small flicker of a smile from his lips as he said the man's name, "He lives in the apartment next door to me."

"Oh, gotta love a boy next door," Pepper sang excitedly, shuffling her hips to bring their chairs closer to one another, "Describe him for me. *Slowly.*"

August threw his head back as he laughed, "Jesus, you're gonna be the death of me."

"I don't hear any describing," Pepper replied, poking him with a pointed nail.

August reached for his glass and swallowed down another mouthful. How could he possibly describe Ollie? Especially after a day like today. He drew a small line in the condensation on his glass, his brow furrowed in concentration as he said, "I've never met anyone like him before."

He could sense Pepper's curiosity as she edged closer to hear him in the noisy room, "Yeah?"

"Yeah," he agreed, "He's just got this…I dunno, spark, maybe? You hear people talk about someone lighting up a room and, Christ, Ollie just does that so naturally, you know? And he doesn't even know that he's doin' it." He sighed, glancing over at her, "He had some pretty tough news today, but he insisted I come out anyway. I wish there was something I could do for him."

Pepper's eyes took on a mischievous sheen, "Oh, I'm sure a man of your age knows a few ways that might help him."

"Get your mind out of the gutter," the red-haired man scolded her, giving her a light shove for her troubles, "It isn't like that."

The woman's expression softened somewhat as she wrapped herself around his arm, pulling herself in close to his side, "You're pretty hung up on him, aren't cha?"

"You have no idea," August said as he met her dark eyes. He ran his free hand through his long hair, pushing it back from where it had fallen over his face, trying his best not to hide away from her.

Pepper echoed his sigh, pouting as she rested her chin on the shoulder closest to her, "Why can't I meet a nice guy that makes me feel like that? Dating apps are a total nightmare and don't even get me started on some of the creeps you meet in a place like this."

"You'll meet someone," August replied, watching the bright lights of the bar catch in her hazel eyes, "Probably when you least expect it,"

"Yeah," she relented, "Guess that means you've gotta hold on your Loverboy extra tight for the rest of us, huh?"

August knew for certain, even without the help of the overhead lights, that his face now matched the colour of his hair. There was no point even denying how he felt about the other man by now. He knew when he was a lost cause. Still, he wondered if Pepper knowing that Ollie was an Android would change anything. Catching movement in his peripheries, August turned to look over the woman's shoulder, "Looks like someone's trying to get your attention back there."

Pepper sat up straighter, angling herself to look back towards the dancefloor with surprise. She beamed when she caught sight of the blond woman jumping on the spot and waving both hands in the air like a lunatic.

"Oh my God, that's Emily!" she squeaked, stifling a laugh, "She works in the little bakery down near your place. We went to uni together back in the day."

August wrapped both hands around his glass and nodded back towards her, "I think if you don't go dance with her, she might just explode."

"Yeah, that's Ems alright. Not exactly known for her patience," Pepper agreed, sliding out of her stool and fixing her dress down over her thighs again, "You headin' soon?"

Eyeing up the last few mouthfuls of his cordial, August nodded again, "I'll just down this and be headin' on. See you in the office on Friday?"

The tall brunette raised her own glass into the air, "See you then! And say hi to that neighbour of yours for me!"

The red-haired man shook his head with amusement as he waved her off, choosing to sit quietly at the bar as he mulled over the last few drops of his fruity drink. From the corner of his eye, he watched Pepper and her friend Emily drunkenly spin each other around the dancefloor, their laughter loud and uproariously contagious.

It had been a long time since he had last been in a bar and he was pleasantly surprised by the lack of magnetic draw he felt when he looked at the clear glass bottles lined up on the other side of the counter. Though they no longer beckoned to him like they once had, they still reminded him of harder times that he would rather not have thought about. Of being married to a woman that had grown to hate him, or even earlier, of the man that had raised him under the false pretence of being a good father. He rubbed his fingers across the back of his left hand, pressing down there into the faded scar. He swore he could still feel the burn of his father's belt there sometimes, as fresh as the day he had received the injury. It was one of the reasons he had turned away from alcohol completely; it made those old wounds sing the loudest.

He wasn't sure when he had reached for his back pocket and retrieved his phone again, but before he knew it, he was facing the familiar message chain that he shared with the Android he had waiting for him back home. The blue and grey text reflected on his glasses as he scrolled.

[August: Just finishing up here. Should be home in ten. You ready to talk some more?]

He could see the little dots dancing on the bottom of his screen as Ollie composed his response. He imagined it must have been a strange feeling, being able to construct a message like that with just your thoughts. The dots vanished for a moment, a brief pause, and then a reply appeared in a pale blue.

[Ollie: Yeah, I'd like that. Did you have a nice time?]

August couldn't even blame the liquid courage for what he typed next.

[August: Would've been better if you were here]

August knew what he was really saying, he wasn't stupid. But he had noticed the signs on the door when he first came in, denying entry for Social Droids and other worker models. They wouldn't have let Ollie in even if he wanted them to.

[August: Don't think it's really your scene though. Not enough pop music]

Ollie responded very quickly to that one.

[Ollie: I'm detecting a tone there]

[August: Since when have I ever made fun of your taste in music?]

[Ollie: All the time! You forced me to turn off the TV yesterday]

August laughed aloud as he drafted a response, his fingers tapping the screen quickly.

[August: I'm sorry, but that didn't count as music]

[Ollie: Who knew you were such a snob?]

August relaxed back into his stool, focusing on his response with a smile forming on the corners of his lips, when he felt something smack against the side of the chair. He grabbed for his phone, almost dropping it as he spun in place. He blinked back his confusion when he found several unfamiliar faces looming over him, far too close for comfort.

"Textin' the wife, were ya, Red?" the man on the left sneered as another hand from over his shoulder made a grab for his phone.

August yanked it out of reach gruffly, trying to create some room between the three strangers and himself.

"Something like that," he answered cooly, trying to keep his tone even, "Can I help you three with something?"

He felt a hand slap him in the centre of the back and he let out a choked bark in response.

"Yeah, I think you can, *mucker*," a second man said, a cruel smile playing on his lips, "See, my friend says he saw you out and about the town the last few days. Shoppin' and whatnot."

The hairs on the back of August's neck rose. A sickeningly familiar feeling made itself known in his gut as he replied, "That right?"

"Yeah, that's right," the man affirmed bringing his face impossibly to his own to be heard over the booming punk music, "And he says you were getting' pretty chummy with a fuckin' toaster. In a shop where women and children were, like." He jabbed a bony finger into the soft flesh of August's chest, "We have decency laws around these parts, yeno. Rules against that sort of shit."

The realisation settled into August's chest like a splash of cold water and amidst it all, bubbles of nervous laughter began to build in his throat.

Ah, he thought, *Well shit.*

"I don't know what you think you saw," August started, reaching out to take his glass and draining it.

The tumbler was snatched unceremoniously from his hand and tossed back over the bar. August flinched as he heard it hit the ground and smash.

"I was finished anyway," he noted.

The third man, a dark-haired 50-something-year-old with eyes like steel, pressed close to him and August's breath caught in his throat when he felt the sharp sting of a knife against the curve of his stomach.

"I think you need to come outside, don't you?" the man hissed.

Chapter 25
Malicious Software

[Ollie: Who knew you were such a snob?]

Ollie stared at the message, watching the dots for August's response bounce on the line underneath it for a moment before they vanished. He waited, unable to turn his attention away as the '*read*' notification appeared under his last text.
That was odd.
It wasn't like August not to reply, especially when they were in the middle of a conversation.
//*He must've started walking home already*, the Android assured himself, coming in from where he had been sitting on the balcony and sliding the glass door closed behind him. He headed for the sink and rinsed his used mug under the running water, glancing every so often at the message still in the top corner of his HUD.
As the minutes passed, he began to grow more and more unnerved by the lack of response. His bright blue eyes flittered towards the clock on the kitchen wall. Ten minutes had come and gone again and with them a feeling of unease settled into Ollie's guts. He shook his head, trying to dislodge those particular, unhelpful thoughts as he reached for the cloth hanging by his hip to dry off his hands.
//*Something doesn't feel right about this.*
His electronic eyes began to glow with a pale light as he brought up August's contact details in his internal memory, selecting his built-in call function. The tone rang for several beats and then cut off abruptly, filling the vacant kitchen with a very loud silence.
//*Shit.*
Crossing the room in three, quick strides, Ollie yanked free one of the hoodies August had left by the door. Without thinking, he slipped it on and zipped it up, pulling the hood of it up to create shadow over his face. He rushed out of the flat

before he could change his mind, swallowing down the buzz of nerves he felt in his whole body as he grabbed for the front door to the block of apartments.

He followed the path he knew that August had likely taken to get into town, sticking close to the coastal road in case he missed the man coming the other way on his walk home. Dread sat like a heavy weight in his chest when he spotted the glowing sign for *'O'Malley's'* just a few streets away. Just as obvious from this distance was the glowing *'No Androids'* sign he could see just to the right-hand-side of the front door.

//*Now that's going to be a problem.*

The human bouncer shuffled from one side of his hip to the other, trying his best to fend off the cold winds coming from off the sea. As people approached him to get inside, he checked their clothes and their IDs manually, his own Chrome eyes flashing as he did so. He wasn't going to be fooled into letting him past just because he was wearing a human's borrowed clothes.

//*I could just wait out here*, Ollie thought with a frown, *See if August comes out on his own.*

But there was something in the back of his mind that was nagging him. The *'read'* tag under his own text. The way that the call had been cancelled rather than just ignored.

//*What if he's in trouble. What if someone from New Dublin followed us here?* He swallowed back a lump of fear as he thought, //*What if he needs me and I'm not there?*

He brought a shaking hand up to coil around the collar at his throat. It was the only obvious marker that identified him as an Android anymore. Geo had been surprised that he had still been wearing his tag now that he was living outside of Crossroads. The other Androids had long since abandoned their own IDs, choosing instead to live their lives freely like…

//*Like humans.*

Even August, who appeared to always have his best interests at heart, had asked him if he had thought about removing it.

//*So why am I still doing what Russell East tells me to?*

He squeezed down on the metal ring, feeling it crumple beneath the force of the powerful pistons in his arm. When part of it clicked out of place at the back of his neck, he took the opportunity to peel the rest of it back, stripping it away piece by piece until the solid front panel came off in his hands. He tossed it onto the ground like it had burned him, watching the light flicker and diminish as the residual power from his own body faded from it. Without the familiar heat of it around his neck, the air felt suddenly much colder, and Ollie reached up with both hands to touch the new exposed skin.

//It's gone…he gasped aloud, realising all at once what he had done, //It's…really gone.

The motion of the glowing sign behind him pulled him from his thoughts and before he knew it, he was walking towards the front entrance of the bar and pulling down his hood to meet the bouncer's artificially enhanced eyes.

"A friend of mine's had a bit too much to drink," he lied easily, trying to keep the noticeable tremor from his voice, "He just texted me to come and take him home. Is it alright if I nip inside? I won't be more than a minute."

The human bouncer shuffled in place as he inspected his shabby appearance, "You on designated driver duty for the night?"

A flicker of a smile appeared on Ollie's face when he realised that the man had accepted the small fib, "Someone's got to get these guys home in one piece."

The bouncer chuckled as he angled himself away from the doorway, "We close up in 15," he stated, barely even glancing at him again as he pushed in through the heavy metal doors.

The inside of the bar was cramped and noisy and Ollie's senses were immediately overwhelmed with it all. Flashing lights blinding him for a moment as he stumbled into the crowd, trying to examine every face he came into contact with. His new Social Droid programming was struggling to make out details in the dark, but he knew one thing for certain. August wasn't here.

The feeling of anxiety that had been growing in his stomach for the last 30 minutes felt like it was beginning to choke him from within, his fans stuttering as his processes fought for priority. He muttered his quiet apologies as he knocked elbows with the dancing masses, his eyes scanning for anything that might guide him to the missing man.

That's when he spotted the blood.

It was small specks at first, barely noticeable if not for his enhanced eyesight, but then the pools were growing worrying large as he reached for the fire door hidden in between the the gendered toilet stalls. He looked around at the people behind him once more, trying to avoid drawing undue attention to himself, as he placed both hands onto the bar and pushed down.

//Please don't be alarmed, he prayed as he pushed it hard.

The cold air yanked roughly at his hair from outside. The steam was pulled from his lips and dissipated in an instant. He paused on the threshold, holding a breath he didn't even need, as he searched the space all around him for further guidance. Caught on the wind, barely distinguishable from the sounds behind him, was a voice. He straightened, eyes falling on a half-opened gate at the rear of the building which he tentatively reached for. Creeping out into the darkness on the other side, it was a cry of pain that led him further into the shadows like a siren's song.

He rounded a corner just as he spotted August's limp body being tossed down onto the ground in front of him. A figure all in black rounded on him, battering his stomach and sides with vicious slams of his foot as they spoke, punctuating each and every word with an aggressive kick.

August cried out in pain and something in the Android's mind snapped, sending him diving forward and into the human's attacker. The stranger's mouth fell open in a startled cry as he was lifted into the air, his back colliding with the ground a few metres behind him. Drawing power into his synthetic muscles, Ollie rounded on the group of unfamiliar men with his fans whirring so loudly it sounded like an audible growl falling from his lips. He squeezed his trembling hands into fists in front of him, energy crackling through every inch of his artificial body.

"Leave him alone!" he shouted, barely recognising the panic in his own voice.

A shout from somewhere behind him caught his attention and he spun in place as another figure collided with his side. In the dim streetlights, Ollie spotted the silver glint of a blade just moments before it sliced along his collarbone, the end nicking a spot on his cheek right next to his lip. He shoved the assailant backwards, letting out a shout of alarm as he felt the knife cutting into the skin of the hand that he had thrown up to protect his face.

Warning: External components damaged.

"Ollie!" came August's weak croak somewhere on the ground at his feet, "You need to get out of here! These guys are armed."

The Android placed himself in front of his companion, his bright eyes alight with anger as he accessed the damage to his artificial skin.

"Aww, is this your little dolly?" the dark-haired man before him sneered as he wiped a hand across his face, trailing the blood from his busted nose across his sickeningly pale skin, "Come to play pretend some more, are we?"

The man was tall and skinny as a cigarette, his hair long and matted where he had hastily tied it back from his face. He stank of stale alcohol and his laugh sounded like a wet gurgle in the back of his throat, likely the result of the blood trickling down there from his nose. He edged forward, waving the blade in front of his chest like a threat, the copper-tinged lights catching on the sharp edge of it.

"When we're done with you, Red, we're gonna take a part your little tin soldier here. Find out what makes him tick."

"Don't you…don't you fucking **touch** him!" August snarled breathlessly, slowly getting back up to his feet again. He clasped a hand to his side where his shirt was a noticeably darker colour than the rest of the fabric.

The sight of the blood on the other man's clothes made a too-hot sensation burn right through Ollie's metal body. It ignited something in his core, somewhere deep down that the sensors and diagnostics tools couldn't reach.

Running in the forest, the moonlight glistening off the trees. The rain was louder than anything he had ever heard. He called out their names, longed to be next to them but his broken leg was already slowing him down. He needed to reach them, needed to protect them from the men who were chasing them. He didn't care about what happened to him, he just wanted his friends to live.

Rage filled every inch of him, and he charged forward with a yell, ignoring the slash of the weapon in the man's outstretched hand. He kicked out with both legs as the man attempted to grapple with him, registering the feeling of pain blossoming up all over his body from a thousand tiny cuts. He squirmed when they tried their best to pin him in place, using his teeth and fists and hitting back with as much power as he could muster. Warnings flashed up and were closed again in rapid, blinking succession.

Warning: Tensile Limit Reached.
///I don't care!
Warning: internal damage.
Components e37, rr2 and xt41 critically damaged.

//I don't care!
Warning: Unauthorised Social Interaction
//The only thing I care about is him!

One of the attacker's arms was ripped backwards and away from him and Ollie took advantage of the brief moment of weakness, slamming his head back into the man's face to free himself. He heard the undeniable sound of his nose crunching in on itself and he dodged backwards just as August appeared and smashed a fist into the man's gut to finish him off. The stranger toppled onto the concrete with a blood-tinged choked-out sob, curling in on himself.

August was panting as he straightened his back. There was blood clinging to his face and beard. He staggered forward and brought a hand down onto Ollie's shoulder, giving it a gentle but affirming squeeze.

"You fellas looking for a round two?" he threatened breathlessly.

The group of assailants had formed a semi-circle in front of their fallen comrade who was making his discomfort known in a series of swears and loud groans. One of the others, a blond man in his mid to late 30s with a scar across his neck and chin, spat on the ground at Ollie's feet.

"It's your lucky day, *floppy disk*," he snarked, cocking his head at the people behind him, "We've decided to let you both off with a warning."

Ollie let out a low, pained grunt disguised as a chuckle, "How very noble of you."

The scarred man chuckled as he pushed his unruly fringe back from his face, staring them out even as the others helped the injured man to his feet again behind him. Even in the state he was in, he was wound tight like a spring, every muscle primed to attack like a house cat targeting a half-concealed vole in the underbrush. If not for the blood running down his face in rivers, the man surely would've continued the fight.

In the passing glow of the streetlamps, Ollie committed each of the men to memory, absorbing each detail of their faces, their voices, the way they walked. When their leader finally nudged past them, Ollie fought the urge to snap forward and bury the last of his anger between the man's already-bruised ribs. The last thing he wanted was for that wound-tight man to uncoil again.

When he and August were once again alone on the dark, house-lined street, Ollie felt some of the tension falling from his shoulders. He jumped when he felt the other man reach out to cradle his face in both hands, angling him towards the light overhead as he studied the slice on his cheek.

"Jesus, Ollie," he breathed, pulse running fast beneath his skin, "What the heck were you doing? You could've gotten yourself killed rushing in like that."

Ollie released a hiss of hot air from between his clenched teeth. The error messages that were appearing in his vision were growing more and more intrusive by the minute. Everything was getting so loud; it was becoming difficult to think. He needed to relax, to cool down again.

"I'm…I'm alright, August," he responded with a wince as a rough, callused thumb brushed across his still healing wound. It smeared black blood across his face.

August shook his head, "You got hurt."

Ollie fixed him with a frown of his own, "Don't give me that look. This was *their* fault, not *yours*."

When August shifted his weight and made a pained moan, Ollie took the chance to grab for his shirt, tugging the fabric up to expose the light swelling of his stomach. Despite his weak protests, he allowed the Android to run a hand through the bright red blood he found there.

"It's just a little scrape," he choked out, trying not to pull away, "Bled like a bastard but I think I'm alright."

A quick scan of August's torso revealed low level ecchymosis and minor abrasions. Thankfully, there were no signs of broken bones or deeper lacerations. Apparently, they were aiming to draw out his punishment rather than finish it quickly. Ollie wasn't sure if that was lucky or not.

"You'll survive this time," Ollie agreed, pulling the shirt down across the man's tacky skin again. He met the human's dark eyes, leaning in just a little closer to him, "What happened August? Why were those men attacking you?" He recalled the things that they had shouted during the fight, and his eyes widened by a fraction, "Did this have something to do with *me*?"

August fixed him in place with a look that was difficult to read, "People don't always need a reason to be assholes, Ols. Just let it go."

"They could have killed you!" Ollie argued, pulling himself out of the other man's reach, "I deserve to know if I was the cause of this."

August let out a heavy sigh, reaching a hand up to bury it in his long, red hair. It stuck together at the ends where it was caked in a mixture of blood and dirt, "You have enough to deal with right now without…my shit."

Ollie titled his head to one side, his dark brows furrowed in confusion, "I don't understand."

"Those guys had seen us out before. You and me," August said, bringing his arms in close to his chest as if he was walling himself off, "And they...took offense to it."

"Took offense to it?" Ollie repeated. August could see in the man's eyes that he wasn't quite making the connection he wanted him to. He swallowed, feeling the burn on his too-dry throat.

"To me and you," August clarified, glancing up as if to gage his companion's reaction, "*Together.*"

Ollie felt his fans falter, as if they were falling somewhat out of sync, "Oh," he said quietly.

August angled his body away from him, casting his eyes downwards, "Look, I didn't want to make you uncomfortable and-"

"I broke my tags for you."

August's entire body froze in place, and he slowly turned his head to look back at him. His brown eyes glistened under the stuttering electronic lighting, "Wait, what did you just say?"

Ollie reached up and pulled back the opening of his hoodie, revealing the gleaming white line of his throat, "I had to get into the bar," he explained, "I saw the sign on the door."

The red-head did a double-take, allowing his arms to drop, "But Ollie you-"

"You might have been in danger," the Android interjected firmly, "I couldn't risk that."

August ran a hand through his hair again, further disturbing its position on his head, "You came running here to save me."

"I just had a feeling," Ollie said quietly, "And I just couldn't take the chance that the most important person in the world to me might end up hurt."

The sky above them split into hazy shades of blue and purple. Mixed with the orange of the cheap, electrical lamp it made August's hair appear to burn like a sunset.

"You had me doing a lot of soul searching this evening," the Android added, with an exhale of amusement that was far-too human to ignore.

"And that's the conclusion you came to?" August asked, a flush of colour in his face.

Ollie edged a little closer, sparks of light travelling along his curls where they peeked out from under his hood, "I decided to leave the past in the past and focus on the here and now," he said, "And what's important to me right now…is *you*, August. *Us.* That became even more apparent when I thought I might lose you."

"Guess I wasn't being quite as subtle as I thought I was," August commented softly.

"Nope," Ollie teased, reaching out to take the man's hand. He brought it up to his lips, pressing faint kisses to the dark bruises that were forming around his knuckles, "I think I've known how you felt for a while now."

August ears flushed, whether from the statement itself or the man's actions he wasn't entirely certain, "And you didn't *say* anything?"

"I wasn't sure if you wanted me to," Ollie admitted, "I figured you would say something in your own time." His lips rose in a small smile, "But you were taking too long. And I'm not always the patient sort."

August let out a surprised bark of laughter and snatched his hand back to clutch at his side, "Please don't make me laugh," he whined, "I think even my bruises have bruises right now."

"Sorry, August," the Android apologised, ducking underneath his arm and taking some of his weight, "Lets get you home and get those injuries of yours dealt with, shall we?"

He felt the human lean against him as they started to move towards the coastal path, "My hero," he said quietly, a smile evident in his voice.

"Lets see if you're still saying that when I use the cleaning alcohol on these cuts of yours," Ollie said and got another laugh, and a thump, for his troubles.

Chapter 26
Computational Chemistry

Ollie slipped the keys from August's outstretched hand and wriggled them in the lock, shoving the door open with his shoulder as he helped the other man inside.
"Ollie," August chastised with a grunt, "I'm perfectly capable of-"
"Hush," the Android interrupted, kicking the door closed behind them as they ambled towards the sofa, "You might as well save your breath, August. I'm not taking no for an answer on this one."
The redhead collapsed back onto the sofa with a groan as the other man disappeared into the kitchen. The contents of each of the drawers rattled as he searched for the first aid kit.
"You're getting to be pretty hardheaded," August remarked aloud, tilting his head back towards the rest of the apartment.
"Huh," Ollie answered, a teasingly thoughtful lilt in his tone, "I wonder where I could've learned that."
August chuckled softly as his companion joined him on the sofa, opening the small green box of medical supplies with a pop. He reached inside, pulling out several tiny bottles of clear liquid and some plasters which he laid out on the coffee table by his hip.
"Now, lets see this stomach of yours," he said quietly and moved to reach for August's shirt again.
The human flushed, pulling back from his wandering hands, "Is this really necessary?" he grumbled, "It's just a couple'a scratches. Nothing a good night sleep won't cure."
Ollie wrinkled his nose, the action making the rows and rows of small freckles under his eyes shift, "August," he warned, "Let me help you."

Turning his head away, his neck growing noticeably red beneath the thin veil of his dressy shirt, August moved to yank the stained item of clothing up and over his head. His bright-coloured hair fell around his face and shoulders in thick waves as it tumbled out of its previous neat alignment. He exhaled a sharp breath through his teeth, tensing at the sudden ripple of pain through his abdomen at the stretch, "Shit, that smarts."

The Android tilted his head to get a better look at the human's injuries. There was an expression of obvious concern in his kind, blue eyes, "They really did a number on you, August," he said.

Ugly yellow and purple bruises littered the expanse of pale white skin from groin to chest, new blotches forming where the blood pooled under the thin layer of his skin. Even the dark tuffs of red hair across the man's chest, round stomach, and treasure trail did little to hide the damage.

He flinched back when he felt the tips of Ollie's probing fingers draw a line down his breastbone, inspecting the small cuts that the knife had made. The dark-haired man's eyebrows shot up in response, "Sorry, did I hurt you?"

August chewed on the inside of his lip, willing his pounding heart to calm itself down, "Your hands are cold, that's all."

Uncapping one of the bottles from the first aid kit, Ollie poured some of the strong-smelling liquid onto a cotton bud, "This may sting a little."

August huffed out a nervous breath, "I know."

A flicker of a smile appeared on Ollie's face, "Need me to distract you?"

August turned his head back towards him again, "Distract m-"

His whole body went stiff as Ollie's lips pressed gently to his. It was like lightning bursting from a bottle, a zap of surprise and elation that vanished as quickly as it had come. The other man pulled back from his orbit slowly, studying his expression as he held up the cotton bud, the white edges of it dyed maroon with the half-dried blood from his stomach.

"All better," he whispered.

With a sudden boldness he never knew he was capable of, August jolted forward, taking a hold of Ollie's borrowed hoodie and yanking him towards him. Their lips met in a clumsy second kiss as August brought his other hand around to cradle the Android's head. He drew his tongue along Ollie's bottom lip and the other man opened up to him with a surprised hum, his hands searching for purchase along the human's strong, bare arms. Slick, black blood spread across his skin from the small wound on Ollie's hand, mixing in with his sweat.

"Sorry if that was too much," Ollie breathed as they parted, looking a little uncertain. The redhead answered by burying his hand in Ollie's curls, sighing against his impossibly soft lips, "Never apologise," he said, "I've wanted to kiss you for a long time."

Ollie's bright eyes met his, the shimmering silver tint of his irises mimicking the glow of the starlight from outside as he slipped onto his lap, strong legs bracketing his hips, "Show me."

August's fingers felt too large, too uncoordinated, in Ollie's small hands as he moved his touch up towards the zip on the front of the hoodie. He pulled it slowly downwards with trembling hands, watching as Ollie reached for the uniform he wore underneath. He pulled the zip there too, revealing inch after inch of his own porcelain skin. Freckles dotted the landscape of his chest and torso like stars, the milky way spiralling down across the hairless plains of his artificial body. August felt his breath catch in his throat and he swallowed down the nervous gasp that threatened to choke him.

"You're beautiful," he breathed, unable to keep his hands from mapping out every detail of Ollie's body. Underneath his false skin, his inner circuitry rumbled like a pulse, picking up speed as August leaned in closer, pressing his lips to the space on his throat that was once covered by his tags.

Ollie's fans whirred loudly in his throat, hot air escaping his parted lips in small gasps that took the shape of the other man's name. The colour of his skin warped and changed, blossoming pink and red under August's scrutiny.

"No one's…no one's ever seen me like this before," Ollie admitted shyly, reaching up to cover August's large hands with his own, "I wasn't even sure if you…"

August's dark eyes met his, "If I?"

Ollie felt like he couldn't pull himself away from those dark pools, "Would even see me like this. Like a…person."

August's hands continued their journey downward, taking a hold of the Android's slender waist and pressing him down into the point where their hips met. Something hard and rather imposing nudged against his thigh and he blushed.

"Oh," he squeaked.

The laugh that August responded with was barely more than a low, rough grumble in the back of his throat, "I hope that answers your question."

"It does," Ollie answered, slipping his hands free to cup his partner's face. He ran his thumbs across the man's bruises and cuts, taking in every detail of him with something like reverence, "I'm sorry I never told you how I felt. It should never have taken something like this for me to be honest with you."

August's own thumb drew circles around Ollie's sacral dimples, nudging against the edge of his belt, "I've had a lot going on in my own head too, Ols. And this, you and me, it was…"

"Unexpected?" the Android offered with a quirked eyebrow.

"Yeah, definitely that," August agreed, his hot breath washing across Ollie's chest and collarbones.

Ollie leaned down, bringing himself closer to the other man's face again, "We should probably take a look at these other cuts of yours," he said, "Clean them before they get infected."

"We should," August replied with a grin, taking the other man by surprise and tossing him back onto the sofa. He slipped into the space between the smaller man's legs and arms, feeling Ollie's shocked bout of laughter vibrating through every little bit of him, "But I'd much rather kiss you again."

Ollie reached up to bury both hands in the mane of the man's red hair, "How could I possibly say no to an offer like that?"

When they kissed again it was different from before, slow and easy, like they had done it hundreds of times. Despite Ollie's obvious inexperience, he was a quick learner and followed August's lead in every breath and movement. He wished he could file away every sensation, record it so he could feel it over and over again whenever he so chose. The feel of August's lips, sweet with the lemonade he had had at the bar, mixed with the slightly chapped feel of his skin. The way his thick chest hair burned across his skin as they closed the gaps between their bodies. The heat and scent of sweat was so very human; he had never experienced anything like it before. Butterflies raged in his stomach, tossing and turning like a boat at sea. Every artificial nerve awakened with August's touch, his mind hyper focused on the calluses on his hands and the pulse that danced along the points where they connected. His sensors warned of his ever-rising temperature, but he was finding it hard to care when he had never felt so awake, so alive before.

August pulled back to suck in a breath, his chest and shoulders rising and falling above him on the sofa. His long hair flowed down over him like a river of fire, the light outside igniting it with all the colours of twilight. August could hear his own blood rushing in his ears, unlike any sensation he had ever felt before. He couldn't even remember the last time another person had made him feel like this.

Beneath him, Ollie's hair was a tangled mess of curls that stuck up in all directions. His lips were kiss-swollen and the tiny cut on his cheek was already beginning to heal. In the shadow cast by his partner's body, the Android's eyes glowed like something ethereal, casting his face in a pale, wisteria glow that directly opposed the blush on his rounded cheeks. Ollie ran his tongue across his lips, his HUD a rush of data regarding the man above him. He tipped his face to one side, pressing a chaste kiss to one of August's arms where it framed his head, "I never realised your tattoos went to your chest as well," he observed.

August cleared his throat a little self-consciously, "Yeah, I got them in my twenties. Dragons were all the rage back then."

Ollie brought a hand up to follow the path the mystical creature made across his skin, "I really like it."

August exhaled an amused breath through his nose, "Yeah?"

The Android nodded wordlessly, "I really like getting to see more of you like this. Getting to touch you." He offered him an affectionate curling of his lips, "Is this what it's like…when two humans care about each other?"

"It can be," August answered, "If you want it to be."

Ollie's fingers lingered on the point where he could feel the other man's heartbeat the clearest, "I think that I do."

Just when August was about the chastise him for being so damn mushy, he became aware of a familiar melody that was starting to play somewhere nearby. Ollie blinked and shifted his weight, reaching underneath his hips to recover the phone that had become trapped between the sofa cushions. He handed it across to the other man as he sat up, watching curiously as August selected the button on-screen to answer it.

"Uh, hey Micky, we were sort of in the middle of something here…" he grumbled, catching Ollie's eyes as the other man muffled his quiet laugh with a palm, "Do you think I could call you back?"

August adjusted his hold on the phone, the sounds he was hearing beyond all but drowning out the familiar deep tones of the officer's voice, "Jesus, what's all that? I can barely hear ya."

"Here, let me help," Ollie offered, extending out a hand to brush against the device. The volume doubled as it played out through the speakers instead, the crackling and banging filling the room with disjointed sound.

In the centre of the racket, Micky's voice roared, "August! Mr Jackson, where are you right now?"

The line hissed, static interrupting the signal for a moment. August looked around the room they were in, as if uncertain of his surroundings, "We're at home," he replied, "What's wrong? What's happening over there?"

"You need to get out of there!" the woman hollered, her voice hoarse as she struggled to be heard over the growing commotion, "The Safe Houses have been compromised! Go! Get out now!"

The shrill ringing of gunfire concluded the call, filling the room they were in with deathly silence. Lights from outside coloured the wall across from them as the sound of a dull *thunk, thunk, thunk* filtered in to take its place.

"August!" Ollie shouted, grabbing the other man's arms and throwing them both over the back of the sofa, "Get down!"

Chapter 27
Blacklist

Sudden noise engulfed the room. The glass from the French windows shattered in all directions. Doors throughout the apartment slammed shut with a rush of wind. The wall behind them was painted with bullet holes, dry wall tumbling down all around them like false snow. Feathers slowly descended from overhead, ripped free from their cushion housings as the sofa they were previously occupying was torn to shreds.

August coughed, glancing up through the smoke. He was just about able to make out the shape of the Android leaning over him, his slender body shielding him from the devastation all around them.

"Fuckin' Hell!" he exclaimed, head turning in the direction of the balcony, "What the Hell was that?"

Ollie shook some of the dry wall from his dark hair, "It sounded like a helicopter."

"A helicopter?" August repeated, "They sent a helicopter to kill us?"

"And likely there will be others as well," Ollie said, "We need to move."

Ollie's bright eyes scanned through the debris, marking out a path ahead of them. Shadows were moving on the other side of the door, several heat signatures half-hidden in the darkness. He zipped his uniform back up to the collar, "I hear voices outside."

August frowned, "I don't hear anything. You sure?"

The Android nodded, proceeding forward at a crouch. He extended his hand towards the door and turned the handle slowly, nudging it open. On the other side of it, Gabriela let out a hushed squeal, throwing her hands over her mouth to muffle the sound.

"We were coming to check on you," Julia hissed under her breath. Her blonde waves were covered in dust and dirt, "We heard the gunfire, but no one's sure which way it's coming from."

August leaned against the wall outside their door, buttoning up his shirt again, "I just spoke with our contact back in ND. Looks like the Safe House has been compromised."

"Compromised?" Gabriela repeated with wide eyes, "What do you mean *compromised*?"

"Seems that Russell East grew impatient and decided a frontal attack was the best option," came Sea's deep voice from the room next door. He crept out into the carpeted hallway, a handgun in his right hand as he scanned each of the apartments along their floor, "I don't detect any other heat signatures on this level. Whoever was with those men has clearly gone searching on the other floors."

"What about Mrs. Eberdeen and her daughter?" Julia breathed, her voice trembling as panicked tears quickly filled her eyes, "They're on the bottom floor."

Sea's face fell and he turned his emerald green eyes away from her, "I'm afraid we have to assume the worst."

Julia buried her face in the collar of her jacket as she choked back a small sob, shaking her head frantically. Gabriela ran a hand over her upper back, muttering soothing words to her distraught daughter. They had grown close to the other residents, felt like they had all become one extended family during their time here. Wednesday nights would never be the same again.

Sea turned his attention to the corridor on the other side of them, his eyes briefly taking in each of the paintings that had toppled from the wall, "Dann informed me about an emergency exit hidden beneath the foundations of the building," he stated, "We need to find a way to get down there without attracting any unwanted attention."

Another round of bullets from beneath them made the floor itself tremble and Julia curled in on herself at the sound of far-off screams, flattening her hands over her ears, "*Oh God, Oh God, Oh God,*" she whimpered.

"Looks like we have company," Ollie growled, his own eyes beginning to glow as he moved into a crouch. He could detect movement at the bend in the corridor, the vague outline of a person shown through the concrete. He could count the number of beats per minute from their racing heart, could see the shaking in their closed fists.

RunnerDroid 01113 'searching for nearby devices…'
Chromesystem.lookup_name (Dann)
Target_address = Dann
'found 1 target device'
'searching for the object push service'
Red1_port = push_service[1]
'OK, push_service[1]' 'port connection approval'
'sending file' to [target_address]
'completed!\n'

He raised his head, his relief palpable, "It's alright, Dann. You can come out. It's just us."

The first thing they could see was the man's bald head as he emerged from around the corner. The second thing that they could see were the noticeable black bags under his eyes. He was dressed in an old cotton shirt and boxer shorts, clearly asleep when the first attacks occurred. The poor man looked like he had aged a decade since the last time they have spoken with him.

"I-I wasn't sure…" he started, crawling on hands and knees towards them, "Christ, there are more of them downstairs. I barred the doors, but they'll be back with something to break them down."

"Did you see them?" August questioned, taking hold of the man's shoulder as if he thought he might bolt like a startled animal, "Recognise them?"

Dann shook his head, "They weren't w-wearing uniforms," he stuttered, "Could've been anybody…"

Sea shuffled forward, "Dann," he said firmly, "Where's the escape route? We need to get out of here *now*."

Dann's entire body stiffened, "Yes, yes, of c-course," he muttered, glancing around them, "We s-should have access through apartment 21. We can go out the window."

"The window?" Julia yelped, "Dann, we're like three floors up!"

"There's a concealed ladder," Dann assured her, meeting her eyes as he tried to steady himself, "It'll t-take us down the outside of the building. There's mostly water underneath so they won't be over that side."

August ran a hand through his messy hair, shooting Ollie a nervous glance, "We need to hurry before they get to the upper floors," he stated, "There's a clock ticking down somewhere, and I don't want to find out what happens to us if it reaches zero."

*****

August gasped as he felt the cold air from outside hitting his face. The bathroom window rattled like the bars on a cage, the blinds pulled back and shuddering in the wind. He leaned out through the large opening and peering down the side of the building, eyes sweeping over every edge of it until he caught sight of shimmering steel.

Next to him, Ollie clutched at his head and squeezed his eyes shut as a torrent of messages flooded his HUD. The Cleaning Droids in the flats below them, trapped and growing more desperate by the moment, extended their awareness outwards and begged for help. Ollie heard every one of their screams, experienced every, sudden digital flatline. Though it wasn't physically possible, he still felt like he might throw up.

Sensing his unease, Sea placed a gentle hand on his shoulder and leaned closer, "I can feel them too," he whispered, "But we can't do anything for them right now. We have to focus on getting ourselves to safety."

Ollie nodded solemnly, pushing some of his dark and dishevelled curls back from his face. Only a few short minutes ago he had been experiencing more than he ever had before, had basked in all the wonderful new emotions and let it wash over him. Now, more than anything else, he just wanted to turn them off again.

"Looks like the damn thing has moved," August grunted as he pulled himself up onto the windowsill, "We're gonna need to jump to the next ledge in order to reach it."

"J-jump?" Julia chirped, her blue eyes wide and frightened, "We can't do that! We'll fall!"

August frowned, letting out a sigh through his nose that was quickly stolen by the wind, "No other option. Unless you fancy stayin' behind and greetin' our guests?"

Gabriela slowly closed the bathroom door behind them, "Are you sure it's going to hold our weight, Dann?"

Dann ran a hand through his moustache, a nervous habit, "The things been there for decades, we've never had to use it before."

"Well, isn't that reassuring," Sea remarked.

Ollie watched August's strong arms and shoulders flex to take his weight as he lowered himself down onto the outer edge, "Look, if it can hold me, it'll have no problem takin' you lot," he said.

He tried not to look down, he really did, but August felt like his eyes had been magnetically pulled towards the crashing waves several floors beneath his feet. His stomach swooped and he swore under his breath, placing his hands flat against the building's side. He eased himself along the narrow ledge, hugging as close to the old stonework as he could, and counted his in and out breaths the way his therapist had once shown him more than two decades ago. Whenever part of the walkway crumbled beneath his feet and disappeared into the black sea below, he felt like he might just pass out, breathing exercises or no.

It's just a little jump, he thought, eyeing up the gap between the apartments, *it's less than a metre. I can make that.*

Ollie leaned out of the window to watch him, trying his best to taper the unhelpful feeling of anxiety that was rattling up through his chassis. August made the jump without incident, and he let out a breath he didn't need when the man turned to flash him a smile.

"Wee buns," August said, "Wanna help the others down, *duine*?"

Ollie moved back inside, taking Gabriela's hand first. He offered her what he hoped was a confident smile, "It's just a short distance. August will be there to catch you, so there's nothing to worry about."

She nodded, chewing on her bottom lip. He could feel her pulse thundering nervously at her thin wrist. She peeled herself slowly out of the window, her dark hair blowing all around her in the rough wind. Somewhere below, movement made her freeze, and she pressed herself flat against the building's side. She closed her eyes, trying to steel herself, "What was that?" she asked.

Ollie's eyes lit up as he scanned the space beneath them, "It's just the waves," he answered softly, "Keep going."

"Focus on me," August instructed, holding out both arms towards her, "You've got this. You're almost there."

"M-my legs won't move," Gabriela whispered, squeezing Ollie's hand in her own, "I might need you to push me."

"Deep breath," he said, letting go of her hand, "I'm gonna help you. One, two…"

She let out a yelp of surprise as she suddenly met August's chest, the man closing his arms slowly around her, "Gotcha."

When she turned to look back at Ollie again, her face was as white as a sheet, "I'm going to be sick."

He heard Dann's nervous laugh at his shoulder, "Well, thank fuck I don't need a push because that would'a straight up given me a heart attack."

As they took the ladder down slowly into the depths of the building, the fire alarm began to sound over their heads. Voices echoed along the corridors on the other side of the wall and Ollie and Sea could see half a dozen heat signatures filtering into each of the rooms. It didn't take a huge leap of logic to assume that they were all armed. Whoever had been sent to kill them was certainly organised.

The shaky metal stairs led them down into a space that was once reserved for underground parking but now more closely resembled a swimming pool. The waves banged against the corrugated steel shudders erected along the side. The roar of it echoed throughout the dark cavern. The air was like ice, cold in a way that was almost painful, and August felt it nipping at his nose and fingers even before he dipped his fingers below the surface of the water.

"Freezing," he observed as the others came down the ladder and onto the makeshift dock behind him, "No way we'll be able to swim through this."

"We won't need to," Dann said. He reached for a small, black rucksack hidden behind the yellow base of the ladder and choked back a cough as he wiped away the layer of dusk covering it. Extracting a large, black flashlight from inside, he flicked it on and angled its light towards the shifting waters, "There she is! Thank Christ!"

Appearing out of the darkness like a spectre, was the form of Dann's wife, Charlotte. The woman looked positively foundered in her thin blue nightdress and she shuddered audibly as she rowed the small, makeshift barge in their direction. She leaned against the plank that served as an oar to slow its movement, "What in God's name were you doin' up there?" she snapped, her bottom lip trembling as she narrowed her blue-green eyes towards her slightly taller husband, "Playing the hero like a man half yer age!"

"Bah, would ya give over," Dann griped, pulling her close and burying his face in the side of her neck. He exhaled a wavering sigh, "Fuck, am I glad yer alright."

"Yer bloody lucky ya got here in one piece. Or I would'a killed ya meself," she sniffed, hugging him back just as tightly.

Next to them, August nudged the boat with the toe of his shoe where it bobbed on the water, "Any ideas where we're headed?"

"Allada pipes in the harbour district are connected," Dann explained, running a hand through Charlotte's long, mousy brown hair soothingly, "Once we set off, we have to just keep going until we find somewhere. Fuckin' *anywhere* that isn't here! Call in our contacts at Witsec."

Ollie followed his human companion up onto the boat, the redhead reaching out to take his hand for balance. Their eyes connected in the dark and August gave his hand a squeeze, "You holding up alright?"

The Android nodded, watching as the others boarded onto the craft behind them. He leaned closer to August under the pretence of seeking warmth that he didn't need, "It all happened so fast," he whispered, "I hope Micky and Goose are alright."

"There was quite a scuffle on the phone," August said, "But those two will be alright. Those girls can more than hold their own out there."

The tunnels ahead of them began to narrow, the group having to collectively duck as the boat squeezed through the small spaces. They rocked gently from side to side as the motion of the waves beyond the wall passed by them. Overhead the familiar rumble of traffic gave them a clue as to how far they had travelled. The music playing at the crossings was dampened by the concrete, and it sounded as though someone were singing somewhere far away. Dust and dirt poured from the cracks in the foundations above, littering them with loose debris. Ollie shook his dark curls with annoyance, sending flakes of it everywhere like a damp labrador.

Julia looked back the way that had come, no longer able to see the ladder or the dock in the blackness, "Do you think that anyone else made it out of there?"

"If they did, I hope they know how to run fast," Dann remarked quietly, then clarified by adding, "I think I saw them bringing in a Hornet as I was leaving."

"A Hornet?" Gabriela gasped, "Then-"

"It *was* Crossroads," August finished with a scowl, "The bastards wanted to wipe us out before we could make it to trial."

"Can he *do* that?" Julia spoke up from next to Ollie, "There'll be witnesses, people will see-"

"The Diabhal thinks that he's too powerful to be touched by the rest of us. He plays the system, knows the ins and outs of it," August growled, "There were rumours that he used to work in law enforcement. Means he knows how to cover his tracks."

"Arrogant," Sea snarled, pulling his long legs into his chest where he sat, "The behaviour of a human with the whole world at his feet."

"The Golden Child of the tech industry," August agreed, folding his arms across his chest for warmth. His breath was coming out in small, white puffs, barely visible in front of his face.

Sea's eyes ignited with a magnesium green sheen in the dark as he suddenly stood, rushing towards the front of the boat, "Who goes there?" he called out, "Identify yourselves!"

Ollie followed his line of sight, catching several pairs of glowing eyes in the spaces beyond them, "Are those…other Androids?"

"Ollie?" came the answering shout, "Is that you I hear?"

Ollie recognised that voice right away. A relieved smile split his lips as his hand shot up into the air to wave back towards the familiar dyed hair and fashionable clothing, "Angelle!" he shouted, "Your offer from before still stand?"

Chapter 28
Execute

Bis and Patt raised their heads as the makeshift boat rounded the corner towards the harbour. They exchanged worried glances and Bis raised a hand to guide them in against the pipe's wall. Another dock had been made there, created quickly from old, washed-out parts, and it rattled and groaned as each of them disembarked.

The door to the club blew open and Bee raced out, quickly taking Angelle into her arms, "I was watching the news when I noticed you were gone," she gushed. She took a step back from him and smacked him on the arm, "Don't you ever go scaring us like that again! We thought they'd got you!"

"Thought *who* had got him?" Ollie asked as he joined them.

Bee's aquamarine eyes turned to take him in with surprise, "New guy?" she questioned, reaching out to dust some of the dirt from his uniform, "Christ, you look like you've been through the wars."

"What's going on?" August asked as he helped Dann and Charlotte out of the boat. They were both pale as ceramic, taking in each of the strange faces before them with wide eyes.

"It's all over the news," Bee explained, pushing some of her spiked hair back from her face, "They've been attacking locations all over the island. They even hit the New Dublin Police Department's main branch on Pearse."

The black waves danced against the side of the dock, making it roll underneath their feet. Sea was careful to position himself behind Gabriela and Julia to keep them from falling in the water, "We should have pre-empted this," he said, "With an ego like East's, there was no way he was going to let this get to trial."

"It seems that the human authorities are powerless to stop him," Bee agreed, worrying at the corners of her bright blue lipstick.

"So...what do we do now?" Gabriela asked, trying to keep the nerves from her voice and failing miserably, "What is this place?"

Angelle moved to the front of the group, motioning for them to follow him inside, "Welcome to Shenanigans," he said, "Base of operations for the Schull Android Resistance movement."

"Catchy title," August remarked, pushing the rows of beads aside as he ducked his head and followed him in, "Shame you didn't mention this to us before."

"How could I?" Angelle sniffed, "We weren't sure that the two of you were on the same side until recently. We cannot risk the operation until we are absolutely sure of everyone's loyalties."

"Well, you seem pretty damn sure now," August grunted.

Angelle fixed him with a look, cocking his head, "Yes, well, having shots fired at you does certainly help clear up any confusion."

The neon lights of the club washed over August's bright hair, and it glowed like warm embers when he folded his arms across his chest. There were other Androids in the main room now, all of them turning their heads in the direction of the new arrivals. Ollie raised a hand into the air in greeting, his eyes glowing as he signalled to them that they were friends. A few of the others signalled back, clearly relieved.

One of the men, an Android with green eyes and dark hair, raced forward to embrace Sea, muttering into his chest about how worried he had been. Sea's ever-present neutral expression washed away in an instant and he lowered his head to press a kiss to the man's temple, "It's alright, Tibs. I'm right here."

There were stacks of boxes lined along every wall, and August frowned when he spotted the symbol for Crossroads on more than a few of them. He nudged the one nearest to him with the two of his boot, "What's all this?"

"Replacement parts," Angelle explained, "Donated from friends on the inside that are loyal to the cause."

August's brow furrowed as he glanced back at him, "Are you expecting to need this much?"

"We have more survivors arriving by the day," Angelle continued, some of the perfect coils of his faux hawk tumbling down over his forehead as he sighed, "Some of them are…in less than stellar condition." He offered the pair a sympathetic smile, "You two have been incredibly lucky, all things considered."

"Yeah, well, we don't exactly *feel* particularly lucky right now," August grumbled. He eyed the dirt and dust that was covering Ollie's clothes and was glad that the man's quick actions had gotten them away without major injury. And better yet, without having to use that secret handgun of his.

Bottles of water were piled up on each of the countertops, glistening under the twirling disco balls. Likewise, cans of fruit and soup had been arranged in very organized pyramids by several of the other Androids who were carefully dividing up the supplies between the different parties. Behind the counter, Geo was stuffing as much fresh meat and other produce into the hidden fridges there as he could.

"That's a lot of food for Androids," Ollie commented.

Angelle let out a soft exhale through his nose, "We aren't accustomed to the long-term needs of humans. We wanted to gather as much as we could so you would all be comfortable here."

August's shoulders fell from where they had bunched up at his ears, his expression softening somewhat, "That's…unexpectedly kind of you."

Angelle shrugged, offering him a dramatic wave of his hands, "We help out our own here. Whether than means an Android or one of you squishy types. And we *are* growing rather fond of you." The smile he gave him seemed genuine, warmth bleeding into his dark eyes, "The others you brought with you…I have moved supplies out back they can use. Blankets and pillows, that sort of thing. Can you set them up somewhere they'll be more comfortable?"

"Yeah, I reckon I can do that for you," August answered with a nod. He waved towards the group of frightened survivors, beckoning them over, "Mon this way folks, lets get you out of those damp clothes and into something a bit warmer, huh?"

Ollie watched the man's back as he retreated, feeling a sensation of warmth spreading throughout every piece of him. He and August hadn't had a second to talk since…well, since *everything*. But he knew something between them had definitely changed. The buzzing in his stomach appeared to have little to do with his internal systems malfunctioning and a lot to do with the bearded human with the obnoxious red hair.

He turned his head when he felt Bee's fingertips trail along his back and her hand come to a rest on his shoulder, "Hey, Ollie, wasn't it?"

He nodded and she smiled brightly at him, "I'm sorry about...*before*. We can come on a little strong sometimes."

"Apparently it comes with the territory," Ollie soothed her with a smile of his own, "Crossroads have a way of putting us all on edge."

"You aren't kidding," she agreed. Her eyes flickering up towards the TV and her face fell, "Shit. Speak of the Diabhal..."

"What is it?" Ollie questioned as he followed her eyes.

The volume control appeared on the corner of the screen as Bee wirelessly accessed the device's menu. She turned it up to full volume as the all-too-familiar face of the local newsreader came on screen. Although dressed in her usual neat, red attire, the woman looked a little flustered. She shuffled the pages before her as if she were waiting for something, her voice carrying on her latest message as the sound increased: "...known to many simply as '*Diabhal*', has reported a series of new, intelligent viruses that they suspect have broken through the Crossroads Firewall, known colocally as *Excelsior*. These viruses can cause machines to behave erratically, ignore commands, and even attack their registered owners. Several instances have already been reported throughout the city in the last few hours, with at least one fatality recorded. Sources within Crossroads state that these viruses were an attempt to *'simulate true AI behaviours'* and were likely uploaded by an experienced engineer. Crossroads are recommending removal of sensitive information from all Android units as well as the complete termination of-"

The newscaster reached for her earpiece, her Chrome eyes igniting with red light, "Oh! Apparently, we're going live now to Crossroads Dublin HQ where the CEO himself, Mister Russell East, is holding a press conference on the front steps with other members of the media. Our correspondent, Peter Lochery, is there. Peter, can you hear me, alright?"

The screen split into two sections and a young man with dark eyes smiled at the camera from the right. He pushed a few stray locks of black hair back into place as he turned to face the gathering crowds, "Yes, I'm here Eileen, and so it seems is half of New Dublin's Silicon Docks! It isn't often we get to see the CEO of Crossroads in person, and folks here are not missing out on the opportunity to hear about these new developments straight from the horse's mouth."

Ollie turned his head as August re-entered the room, patting down the sides of his trousers. He looked at them first and then turned his attention to the roar of the TV with a confused frown, "What's going on?"

"He's saying we've been infected with a virus," Ollie noted, "That we're disobeying orders. Becoming a threat."

"That's a load of bull," August scowled, throwing his hand up towards the crowds on screen, "No way those people would be daft enough to believe that. They're some of the best technological minds in the country."

The crowds clambered against the sides of the erected fences for the chance to see the man that was stepping out onto the platform before them. The CEO was a tall, broad-shouldered man, with a bald head and dark glasses. He was dressed in an all-white flowing suit, the opposite of his namesake, and was waving and smiling at the crowd in a way that reminded August of every slimy politician he had ever seen on TV. He had only had the displeasure of meeting his former boss on a few occasions, and he had immediately gone home and showered after each one.

Skin-coloured cybernetics ran along the man's cheekbones and neck, disappearing under the cover of his clothing. The jacket he wore, as white as the rest of his outfit, was long and neatly pressed and brushed against his ankles as he walked.

Bee shifted her weight, folding her arms protectively over her chest, "He looks like one of our old pimps," she commented, wrinkling her nose in disgust, "What a creep."

Next to her, Geo nodded his head in agreement, "I've served beer to a million fuckers who looked just like him. None of them ever tipped."

They all turned their attention to the man on stage as he reached the podium, the smile on his face as fake as his veneers, "Thank you all for coming on such short notice," he said, his voice a cool and even tempo, "I understand that this news may come as a shock to many of you and we apologise for not making you aware sooner." He cleared his throat, making a show of checking the notes laid out in front of him, "Today it was raised to me that several organised individuals have breached *Excelsior* and that they are piggybacking on the new codes that went live last weekend…" The faint red glow of his eyes could be seen behind his shades as he surveyed the crowd for their reactions, "These viruses operate like one might expect an infection to take hold in nature, corrupting the host's body and spreading from one party to another. Unfortunately, despite our best attempts to isolate and cut off this feral code, it seems to have crept into our systems and firmly taken hold."

From behind the man on the stage, came a sudden commotion and the CEO barely even reacted as another large man appeared, his maroon cybernetics glistening in the media's spotlights. He was dragging a much smaller person after him by the hair and it was only when he yanked his head back and up that they were able to see that it was an Android. A Runner Droid, in fact.

The Android looked towards the camera with terrified blue eyes. He was dressed in the yellow and blue uniform that Ollie knew so well. It caused a painful swoop in his stomach. He felt August's eyes on him but couldn't turn his face away from the scene before them on the screen.

"Here I have an example of an infected Android," the Diabhal continued, kneeling down to be level with the distraught Runner Droid, "As you can see before you, it is exhibiting more realistic behaviours; crying, screaming. Things we would recognise if we saw them in another human being." He looked towards the crowds, "The machines are instructed by the feral code to mimic the behaviours of humans that they find online. To garner sympathy and lull you into a full sense of security." He roughly scrubbed a thumb over the Android's cheek and stuck the digit into his own mouth, "Saline solution," he said, "Not real tears."

He straightened again, dramatically pulling off his glasses as his expression took on the appearance of a man crippled by his emotions. He wiped at his eyes and cleared his throat again, "As the code has already reached the data centre for the machine, the only way to prevent the spread to other devices is…" He reached inside his jacket, pulling out a small, electronic device that August recognised with a start.

"Fuck," he swore, gripping the countertop of the bar next to him, "That's a fucking *frier*!"

Ollie looked at him with wide eyes, "A what?"

"When you wanted to terminate an Android," August replied, "Shut down the whole system and start from scratch. On paper, it used to be called *resetting* but now they call it…"

"Execution," Russell East snarled and brought the device down to connect with the Android's temple. The results were immediate, its body flailing about like a hose losing water. It collapsed to the ground, its mouth falling open in a soundless scream. Dark smoke billowed from its eyes and ears, just like the one August had seen in the video all those weeks ago now.

"A strong, electrical pulse will cause total shutdown in an instant. Replacement Androids will be offered to all those who bring their remnants to the retrieval sites. We will list all of the information on our website and will have call operators available to answer any questions that you might have."

Ollie felt two hands slip beneath his armpits, unaware that he had completely lost the power to his legs. The newscaster's voices were echoing in the background, their tones as light and airy as if they were merely discussing the weather. But Ollie couldn't make sense of their words anymore. Everything was spinning. The disco ball was sending fractals of disjointed light everywhere, the sounds all around him blending together as his system went into overload. He couldn't think straight, the words *killed him, killed him, killed him*, repeating over and over again until everything went black.

Chapter 29
F1 (Help)

August swore as he yanked his hand back, hissing through his teeth as his digits throbbed with fresh pain, "Fuck, he's roasting!"

"We need to cool him down before he crashes!" Bee shouted, kneeling down and pulling the dark-haired Android's twitching body into her lap, "Geo! Grab some coolant from the fridge!"

Geo cleared the gathering crowd and dove towards the spot where they were both lying, forcing the drink into her waiting hand. Bee uncapped it with her teeth and placed her other hand at Ollie's back, sitting him up and holding him in place as he thrashed, "You'll need to pour it in his mouth," she instructed firmly, passing the container off to August, "I'll keep him as still as I can."

Muttering his gentle apologies, August pressed the top of the bottle against Ollie's flushed, pink lips, spreading them open and tipping some of the dark contents onto his tongue. It splashed across his hands as Ollie abruptly turned his head, half-formed garbles falling from his mouth as he choked on it. His eyelids twitched as if he were blinking in too-fast succession, his blue eyes rolling up into the back of his head like he was seizing.

"Shit," August swore and reached out to hold him by the chin. His artificial skin was searingly hot, and the redhead's every instinct screamed at him to pull away, "Ollie, you need to hold still."

He tipped the bottle up again, shoving it roughly between the Android's teeth as he tried his best to ignore the painful heat of his skin. Ollie's body began to slow its movements incrementally as the coolant went down. The harsh bend vanished from his spine as he settled fully into Bee's lap. The woman had taken to drawing soothing patterns in his curly hair, whispering a soft song a few inches above his ear. When August finally released his hold of the other man, his own skin was red and raw, blisters bubbling along the points of immediate contact.

Bee reached out to pull the bottle from his free hand, "Hold it out for me."

He did as he was told, and she poured some of the dark liquid onto his burnt fingers. He groaned at the pain of it, chewing on the inside of his lip as he felt the skin contracting in on itself. The coolant was thicker than water and settled over his wounds like a plaster or a gel. The pain slowly faded into the background, still present, but certainly not as distracting as it was before.

"Cheers for that," he said, offering her a tired nod. He felt a tug at his shirt and when he looked down, Ollie's blue eyes were looking up at him from the backdrop of her red skirt.

"S-sorry August," he said softly, "I didn't mean to worry you."

Noticing that his skin had cooled down significantly, August leaned over to bring their foreheads together, closing his eyes, "I'm always gonna worry," he whispered, unable to conceal the simple relief he felt at the sound of his companion's voice. He sat back onto his honkers again, "What happened to you anyway? I've never seen something like that before."

"Overheating," Bee answered instead, her tone taking on the protective edge of a mother lioness as she continued to stroke Ollie's hair, "When there's too much data at once, an Android can get overwhelmed by it all. Think of it like a human being experiencing a severe panic attack. It's not as dangerous as it looks. As long as there's someone there to apply the coolant, there'll be no lasting damage. It just feels terrible."

Ollie sat up again slowly, only wobbling the slightest bit. When he looked up, there were many more worried faces looking down at them. He felt his fans *whirr* with embarrassment, "What are we going to do?" he asked them.

The others gathered around them exchanged uncertain glances. A few of them shuffled in place or fidgeted in a very human manner.

Angelle ran a hand through his hair, pacing back and forth in front of the bar, "They've left us with very few options here. If we go out there, we'll be under immediate scrutiny. If any of us get outed as an Android, they'll shut us down without a second thought."

"Trust East to turn our very *lives* into a malfunction," Geo sneered, glaring up at the TV overhead. The volume had since been reduced to barely more than a whisper, but the same headlines were repeating along the bottom half of the screen.

"He's trying to discredit us before we even reach the courtroom. Sewing seeds of distrust amongst the remaining witnesses as to our true motives," Angelle agreed, "He's trying to make us feel desperate."

August felt his stomach sink as his eyes caught some of the footage above them. Queues were already forming outside the established *Refurbishment Centres*, and people were dragging the black and broken bodies of their Androids through the gutters. Glowing eyes faded to grey as the souls inside flickered out of existence. Their skin facades trickled backwards, showing off their inner circuitry. Picturing the same thing happening to Ollie made him want to scream and throw up in rapid succession.

"Androids have existed alongside humans for decades now. They're teaching in our schools, helping to raise our kids. They're part of our families," August said thoughtfully. He let out a low moan as he straightened up again, his knees already aching from his previous awkward position on the floor, "There will be other humans out there that will help us. Other contacts we can call on that know what's happening out there isn't right."

"We need to get a message out to the other Androids in Schull," Ollie added, his legs still shaking as Bee helped him to his feet, "Invite them here. Tell them to bring whatever supplies they can carry, and any humans they can trust. Then we can start working on a plan."

"A plan?" Bee frowned next to him, "Do you hear yourselves? You think this is a simple matter of *motivation* here? We don't even know what we're up against."

"So, you just want to lay down and be done with it then?" Sea snapped. He was perched on one of the neon pink barstools and rotated himself back to face the others, waving a hand across the room. A multitude of different faces looked back at them with eyes that shone in the dark like stars, "Should we deactivate ourselves right here and now, Queen?"

Bee wrinkled her nose as she angled her face away from him, "We're a bunch of retired bank tellers and dancers. What do you expect us to do?"

"I expect you to fight," Sea said with determination, uncrossing his legs so he could sit forward, "Fight for your damn life! It's yours, isn't it?"

On the stool next to him, Tibs nodded his head in furious agreement.

When Bee looked back at him again, the disco ball light caught in her turquoise eyes, "I'm scared, Sea," she admitted.

Geo slipped in between her and Ollie, throwing an arm around each of their shoulders, "We're all bricking here, Bee," he said with a nervous chuckle, "Hell, the reason we're fighting like this is for the right to *feel scared*. Or *happy*. Or any number of other amazing things." He tilted his head to offer her an affectionate smile as he made a note of the obvious tears that were running down her face and taking her makeup with them, "Being alive isn't all sunshine and roses, but it's so much better than what we were before all this."

Bee sniffed and wiped at her eyes, "Asshole. You're ruining my makeup."

"I'll buy you a brand new pallet when all of this is over," Geo offered, leaning in to kiss her forehead.

"Why are we acting like we're some sort of super soldiers?" came a quiet voice from the other side of the room. The Android, a petite Office Worker that had identified herself as '*Clover*' sat hunched up in a dark corner while some of the carer bots worked on repairing the damage to her right side. Her arm, blackened by fire damage, was being stripped back even as she spoke, the fragments being replaced piece by careful piece. She glanced back towards the group when she noticed that she had garnered their attention, "We shouldn't be fighting. We should be *running*. Getting as far away from this place as he can before we're followed." One of the carers pulled off a chunk of red metal from her side and dropped into a vat of water, tinging the water black with her escaping coolant.

"It's too dangerous to go above land and the tunnels beneath Schull aren't exactly stable," Ollie replied, shaking his head, "Most of the passageways this far south have already been completely submerged. While some of the Android units might be able to travel that way, it would be next to impossible for humans to do so."

The injured Android let out a bitter snort, "It's because of the humans that we're in this mess in the first place, and you're worrying about them?"

Ollie made a face at that, "Not all humans are the enemy," he countered, "August is the reason I'm alive right now."

Clover's laugh was spiteful and forced, and when she turned her head towards him, Ollie let out a startled noise at the sight of her face. The entire right side had been exposed; the edges of her human appearance stripped away. Her blue eye looked manic as it rotated in its socket. "Take a good, long look," she hissed, "This is what humans do to our kind! If you think your human wouldn't betray you in an instant to save his own skin, then you're the one that's blind!"

"Clover," the carer bot breathed, fixing her with sad, brown eyes as she halted her hands, "That isn't fair."

"Stay out of this Ebs, what would you know about it?" Clover bit back, baring her teeth like a frightened animal.

"The doctors in the hospital risked a lot to get me and the other Androids out," she said, "They used their IDs to get us into the underground. Those people on the upper floors had guns, we never would've made it if it wasn't for them."

"Now isn't the time for in-fighting," Angelle interrupted, coming to stand in between the two groups, "You just have to focus on getting well again, alright, Clover?"

Clover stared down at the floor between her feet, "I won't let them put me in a box again."

Ebs nodded wordlessly as she continued her work. And if the featherlight touches of her fingertips lingered just a little bit, Clover didn't mention it.

"We won't just sit back and wait for them to find us," August said, glancing up at the television screen again. His dark eyes took in the scrolling text with a flicker of excitement, "Angelle? Could you turn that up a second?"

"Certainly," Angelle replied, coming to stand next to the large human curiously, "What's caught your eye, pray tell?"

A different newscaster was on the screen than before, a petite woman dressed in blue who was clearly reading from a teleprompter. She patted the sliding door of a grey van beside her, umbrella tilted to one side in the fierce wind, "These vehicles will be just some of the transports making their way to the newly established Refurbishment Centres this coming evening," she shouted, trying to be heard over the noise, "This news comes following Russell East's decision to consider mass call-backs across all commercially available Android lines."

"Great, now even Androids *outside* the cities are in danger," Bee muttered.

"It's those vans," August realised, "I've seen them before. Freeze the stream when the camera's pointed at the back of one. Another 30 or so seconds in."

Angelle's eyes illuminated the controls briefly before the bumper of the van appeared on the screen, a bright blue image plastered across it, "Oh, I see. It's the logo you recognised, then?"

August reached into his back pocket and pulled out his reading glasses. Though one of the legs had been bent out of shape, they still maintained their place on his nose if adjusted just right, "Yup."

Ollie cocked his head to one side as he joined him, "A fish and a…fern?"

"It's from Cúil Rathin Fisheries," August explained, "They shut down their main offices just a few years ago. Moved all their workers over the border to follow the migrating salmon."

Ollie arched a dark eyebrow at him curiously, "I didn't know that you paid so much attention to the migratory patterns of Atlantic fish, August."

"It was all over the press feeds when it happened," August sniffed, "So sue me if it stuck in my head."

"And you think they're operating out of somewhere near here?" Angelle questioned.

"I reckon it's less than a quarter mile from where we're standing right now," the redhead smirked confidently, "If we can get there before those vans set off…"

Bee felt a smile pulling at the corners of her own lips as she excitedly took hold of Geo and Ollie's forearms, yanking them both closer, "I think I sense a plan coming together!" she said, "Lets hit Crossroads where it hurts!"

Chapter 30
Deployment

August would have been lying if he said that he didn't feel a little bit uncomfortable in the gear that the Androids had set aside for him. Number one, it was several sizes too small for him. He was, after all, a rather sizeable older gentleman. And number two, camo print? What was he, a new recruit for the Irish Army in 2020? There weren't enough trees left in Ireland to warrant having green-based natural camouflage anymore, and there hadn't been for *decades*.

As they made their way through the warehouse district of the adjoining Schull Harbour, August made sure to keep a close eye on the Android that was walking just ahead of him. To say that Ollie was jumpy was a serious understatement. Every sound sent the Android into a tailspin, his weapon drawn and pointed at every little rat that scurried past.

Not for the first time in the last hour, August reached for the tiny earpiece that had been secured to the right side of his head. He tuned into Ollie's channel, "Easy there, *duine*," he soothed, "We don't exactly want to ring the doorbell for these creeps."

He could hear the soft sound of static as Ollie replied, "Sorry, August. I'm really nervous about all this."

"It would be weirder if you weren't," August remarked, pressing himself against the side of a large metal containment unit for cover. In the dark shadow of it, it was almost impossible to make out more than a fleeting human outline, "Let's just say I'm glad I had that piss before we left."

Ollie's airy chuckle came through the earpiece a moment later, "Good to know I'm not the only one. I don't even *have* a stomach, and I want to throw up."

August followed the shapes in front of him, edging ever closer to their warehouse target. The guard's house, a small rectangular standalone room with a glass exterior, stood blank and empty at the edge of the dock. He rushed to put himself aside it, tracing the sharp pebble-dashed side with black-gloved hands. He could feel it tug at the material, resisting him as he moved. It was late, likely close to midnight by this point, and there was very little light available to guide their group around the disused port. In the distance, the sounds of the fairground shattered any semblance of silence.

The screams of the people riding the rollarcoaster sounded far more ominous here, amongst the dumped scrap metal and rusted containers. The sounds echoed and warped, changing shape and inflection as they reached them. August tried to push down the wave of animalistic fear it set off in him.

Steady on, old man, he berated himself, *You've got a job to do here.*

The Androids ahead of him moved with feline grace in the shadows, their bodies long and lithe and controlled without effort. The humans that he counted himself amongst had to deal with the good old-fashioned night-blindness that came with a mission like this one.

The earpiece let out a low rumble, "August…are you still there?"

"Still here," he affirmed, "What do you see?"

He detected the Android's thoughtful hum, "The area just up ahead is busier. There's ten, maybe twelve people here. There are three vans parked up on the east side. They all have that same logo you saw on TV. Looks like you were right about the place."

As if reading his thoughts, Ollie added, "Four of them are visibly armed."

"Shit," August breathed, kneeling in place. He leaned to one side of the security building, surveying the area beyond. The loading dock was long, lined with square entranceways each with yellow-striped metal surrounds. The red and white paint that formed the individual parking spots were almost completely worn away from use. Moss and slime grew up between the squares of pavement, making the roads around the building appear more like a stormy sea than a flat surface. Broken floodlights overhead, which once served to illuminate the entire work yard, blinked off and on again at irregular intervals, frustratingly distracting. Smaller red cat's-eyes lined the ground in places, flashing back in response to each glaring bang.

    August's eyes were drawn to movement as he watched a man walk along the edge of the path, hosing it down as he whistled softly to himself. The pungent smell of coolant washed up from the mixture of dirt and gravel, staining the stone beneath the man's boots with an unnatural shade of tar black. The torch which had been affixed to the man's jacket, lit up a pile of mangled body parts as he walked past, the metal components discarded and stacked like a macabre exhibit of unnatural art. When he turned, the light caught on the silhouette of a reaching hand, the fingers clawing at the sky as if to take hold of one last gasp of freedom. Grotesque shadows formed on the walls behind where it lay.

"Don't look at it, Ols," August advised softly, watching the shadow of the other man move overhead as he climbed the abandoned containers. The metal groaned under his weight and the Android brought himself down low to watch and wait, his entire body tensed like a cat ready to pounce on an unsuspecting fieldmouse.

The first of the shuttered doors rattled and began to slowly rise. A bulky man ducked under it, clutching a large rifle in against his chest. Although it was too dark to make out the details of his face, August was sure the man was wearing a look of abject disgust when he turned to look at the assembled parts next to the door. He cleared his throat and spat forcefully onto the reaching hand, globules of spital trailing down across the desperate digits. The laugh that followed was muffled by their distance, but August could see the steam of the man's breath as he spoke to the other patrolling humans who had rounded the corner to meet him.

"Looks like this is the dickhead that's in charge," August commented.

A second man ducked under the rising door as it clanked into place. He was laughing loudly, pulling a screaming woman after him and tossing her onto the ground. Her glowing eyes looked up at him pleadingly as she curled in on herself, trying to protect her broken body from further harm. Her uniform had been torn, her skirt barely holding to her hips anymore. She looked like she had been savaged by an animal.

August tried to suppress the feeling of helpless rage that he felt rising in his chest as he caught the sounds of the woman's sobs on the wind. He raised his hand into the air and brought it slowly down as a signal to the people behind him. *Wait. Not yet.*

He had no experience in matters like this. Didn't know what it meant to lead people, or to be led. He had only ever held a gun once and never one this heavy, this *solid*. His hands itched with heat and sweat, and his back ached from the unnatural bend in his body. *Not yet.*

The first of the vans was thrown open and the humans began to lead the frightened Androids outside in lines of two and three. They had been stripped of their clothes, brought down to their most basic components. *Dehumanised.* In the freezing night air, several of them stood naked and crying, clinging to one another as they were forced into the waiting transports. They appeared small, bald and black. Lines of intricate gold and blue marked the places where tubes wrapped around their intricate metal framework. The cooling fluid glistened in the torchlight where it moved around their systems. Their eyes were without the white of their sclera, the electronic parts beneath appearing strange and almost alien, like the inner workings of a complex pocket watch.

"Ollie we need to-"

"No August, we're running out of time," Ollie hissed down the comms, "*They're running out of time! They need help now*! I'm going in!"

"Ollie, wait!" August called out quietly, his breath suddenly freezing in his lungs as he watched one of the dark shadows depart from the rooftop, swinging downwards and onto the unsuspecting guards. He yanked the largest figure to the ground, wrestling him frantically for control of his weapon.

And that was when the sound of shouting and gunfire filled the air with terrible noise.

"Fuck!" the red-headed human shouted from behind his cover, "You're going to get yourself killed!" He pulled his gun back, flicking off the safety as he rammed the barrel into the container next to him, "Stupid, fucking toaster!"

At the sound of his banging, Androids dropped from all directions, dark shapes moving like water through the fluid blackness. August and the other humans charged after the sparks of gunfire and threw themselves into the fray. August's mess of red hair blew in all directions as the wind roared in the spaces between the security office and the main building, looping around the places where the vans were idling.

He took off at an uncontrolled sprint, gasping as he slid around corners and corrected his trajectory on the fly, angling his body to follow in the direction that Ollie was moving. Something clicked loudly ahead of him, and he pulled up his own rifle to retaliate, aiming down the sight as a man in jeans and a ripped shirt came into view. In his raised hand was a knife, the blade glistening with black blood. August brought his finger to the trigger in an instant. He tensed as he inhaled. He had never shot at another person before. This man probably had a family, kids, people he loved that he wanted to get safely back to...

"August!"

Sorry, pal. I have people I want to get back to as well.

He fired without another moment's hesitation, the bullets slamming home and sending the man opposite him toppling off-balance and in against the van's side. Red blood flowed out from the ends of his shirt sleeves, mixing with the dark coolant on the stones.

Ollie suddenly stood before him with fans whirring so loudly, he sounded like a car in motion. It seemed that his body was desperately trying to vacate the excess heat he had generated in the fight. Steam was ebbing out from the fresh gaps in his shoulder and elbow joints, his right arm hanging unnaturally at his side.

Ollie braced himself against the van with his other hand, "He caught me with that last swing," he said, shaking his head with a nervous sounding laugh, "I didn't even see it coming."

August hurried to his side, reaching out for the injured limb and then pulling back as the steam threatened to burn him, "Ah, fuckin' Hell, Ols. You're hot."

The Android flashed him a teasing smile that was only a little pained, "Now isn't the time for flirting, August."

August let out a soft, amused snort, "At least your mouth's alright," he quipped, watching as the steam began to slowly dissipate, "You think your little nanobot things can fix that up?"

Ollie frowned down at the arm, bringing it in to cradle against his chest, "Its fixed-up knife wounds before. I don't see how this is any different."

August let his weapon hang from its strap around his ample middle as he took a hold of the arm and braced it, moving some of the Android's own tactical wear over it to keep it in against his body.

"Good," he said, "Stay close 'til I figure out how to get this door open."

Ollie glanced back the way that they had come, "What about the other guards?"

"Angelle's group are on them," August answered, moving to place himself in front of the door's locking mechanism. He tutted to himself, "Damn electronic locks. I wish I had some of my Crossroads' tools with me."

"You think you can crack it?" Ollie asked, leaning closer to him even as he kept watch of their exits.

August grinned, "You're asking if a top-level engineer from the esteemed Crossroads Corporation can crack a basic firewall used by an outdated fish market?" He ran his fingertips over the terminal, the lights flickering on and lighting up his face, "Give me fifteen seconds."

"Want a countdown?" Ollie asked quietly, the playful lilt returning to his tone.

The redhead arched an eyebrow in his direction, "And what if I finish early?"

"I've heard that happens a lot with men your age," the Android quipped.

August shook his head with an exhaled laugh, "Yup, your mouth's definitely still working alright."

Finishing his work with the terminal, August entered the code that presented itself on the screen and the long barrel of the lock slid across the inside of the door, popping it open at the bottom. August slipped the fingers of both hands into the opening and shoved it upwards, the momentum carrying the door all the way to the top. Dozens of bright eyes stared out at them from inside, the Androids shuffling back from them with raised hands.

"Woah, woah, easy there. I'm a nice human," he said softly, trying to keep his body still like he was coaxing frightened animals, "We're here to break you out."

One of the Androids, a tiny little waif of a thing with her black interior completely exposed, crawled on her hands and knees towards them. The yellow flickering of the floodlights lit up the contours of her body like a flash of lighting. She looked so human, yet not quite real. *Uncanny Valley*, they called it, though August wasn't really sure why. He tried not to let her appearance unsettle him but found that he was failing miserably. She tilted her head, peering up at him through her long eyelashes as she scanned him, "User identified: August Jackson, resident of New Dublin. Deceased."

"*Deceased*? Well, that's news to me," August replied, running a hand through his long hair and shoving it back from his face, "Apart from that, you're spot on."

"It is nice to meet you, August Jackson of New Dublin. My owner designated me as '*Miraka*'," she blinked at him slowly, like a sleepy cat, examining all the details of his face, "Where is it that you are taking us, Mr. Jackson?"

"We have somewhere. Somewhere *safe*. Where the other humans won't find you-"

"*Safe*?" cackled a deep voice towards the back of the van, "How terribly and wonderfully *naïve*."

The group of startled Androids parted to let the owner of the voice through, and August immediately reached for his weapon when he recognised that uniform. And those all-too-familiar stripes.

Chapter 31
Intelligent Agent

The Hornet's smile was like that of wolf with a rabbit caught in its teeth, "You seem surprised to see me, Mr. Jackson. Surely you didn't think that they would leave the cattle unguarded."
The other Androids in the trailer backed off from him, cowering the way prey animals always did in the presence of a predator. The dark-haired man stood in the doorway of the van, reaching up to place a hand on the sliding door as he watched the people before him with dark and wicked eyes.
"Security Droid 45," Ollie noted as he took a step towards the man. His tone of voice took on the same neutrality that he often used whenever he was just relaying facts with no emotional weight behind them. He glanced fleetingly at August, "He was one of the Hornets that pursed us in New Dublin."
"Knew I recognised that face from somewhere," August muttered, watching as the Hornet's smile only grew, spreading across his face like a virus. He snapped towards one of the other Androids when she attempted to creep towards the entranceway, and she backed off immediately from the sharp, gnashing teeth.
"*Sondheim*," the Hornet corrected, still showing his pointed canines, "As your kind are so painfully fond of designations."
"Well, ain't that fancy," the red-haired human remarked with a sniff, "But you're ignoring the fact that I don't give a shit about you."
Sondheim tutted disapprovingly, "Aren't you the one always saying how us Androids are *alive*, Mr. Jackson? Surely, *I* am not the exception to your rule?"
"You can be alive but still a dickhead," August growled back, clearly already losing his patience, "The Hell are you doing here anyway? You're one of them, aren't ya? Don't you want to be free from all of this? You know they'll destroy you too."
"As is their prerogative," the Hornet answered coolly, "I am, after all, a product of their creation."
August felt a primal rush of adrenaline as the Android's red eyes caught the light. His spine signalled for his airways to expand. Blood flowed through each vessel to prime him for a response. Sondheim was different from the other Androids in the same way a wolf was different from a dog. There was a coldness to his gaze that lacked a certain familiar empathy. His body had been designed to hunt and kill; the

way a Wolfhound had been bred to bring down other predators. His crimson gaze illuminated his sharp features, his cheekbones cut in a way that seemed almost gaunt. His dark hair was pushed back from his face in a long, harsh line towards the back of his head, in much the same way Ollie's had been when they first met.

"You don't care if they kill you? Kill these other people?" August demanded, trying to keep his voice steady. Next to him, Ollie was glancing around the open space, searching for the others. His nervousness was palpable.

"There is no *kill*," Sondheim argued, "Despite your warm-hearted beliefs, we are simply *machines*. Tools to be used and discarded. I care not for what happens in between. Nor should you." He hummed to himself thoughtfully, "Which brings me to my next series of questions rather nicely. Why exactly are you here? What were you planning to do?"

He lowered himself to rest on the edge of the van, his legs swinging in the space beneath him. Confidence oozed like liquid from every pore in his perfect skin. He brought his elbows to his knees, resting his chin on his cupped hands, "Oh let me guess, won't you? You were here to be the knight in shining armour, to single-handedly save the entire Android race, weren't you?"

August glowered, the brightly-coloured hairs on the back of his neck prickling, "Yeah. Something like that."

Sondheim threw his head back and cackled towards the inner roof of the van. The obnoxiously fake laugh reverberated unnaturally between the other Androids standing motionless and frightened behind him, "Unfortunately for you, that will not be happening. Not as long as I'm here." His bright eyes narrowed, "*Seymour* here knows *exactly* what happens when you have me as your enemy."

Next to him, Ollie visibly recoiled from the other Android. His eyes started to glow, and he shook his head with a panicked yelp as a rush of data forced its way in.

"Ollie!" August reached out to steady him with a firm grip on both shoulders. He glared back at the other Android, "The fuck did you do?"

The exchanging of information had been almost instantaneous. Diagnostics data. System logs. Operational coding that would have been gibberish to anyone but another Android. Ollie gasped as his hearing became muffled. All of his senses were resetting one by one, blinding him, defending him, making him dumb. He choked on that startling realisation and reached for August's hand. When he found it, he squeezed it. *Hard*.

"You know, *Seymour, I* was the one who took that soul of yours," Sondheim carried on in that sing-song tone of his, playing with him, mocking him, "Back in that forest. I remember it well."

"Forest?" August twisted to face him with a look of confusion, "What are you on about?"

"I never forget a soul," the Hornet chuckled, "He knows. He *remembers*."

The woods were so dark, the rain like knives against his skin. He reached for the man next to him, gasping as his bright eyes met his. 'Keep going, Seymour,' the man panted, 'It can't be much further, just keep going!'

The Security Droid's nostrils flared. The wolf had caught the scent of fresh prey and was determined to rip it open and spill its guts.

"You tried to *run*," Sondheim recalled, his voice half a purr, "Funny how things work out, isn't it? You never were fast enough to get away from me."

The undergrowth was damp, slippery, under his feet. His movements were frantic, the sound of blood rushing through his ears. He could hear the Androids behind him, see the light cast by their glowing red eyes on the dew-soaked leaves around him. The forest echoed with the sounds of the rainfall, like static buzzing in his ears. He heard the shouting just beyond the clearing, felt the whizz of bullets as they launched past him, so close he could sense their movement on the air. The others were pulling away from him. They might still get away, if only he could buy them some time…

He spun on his feet, his body sliding on thick mud as the Android slowed to a stop opposite him. Where he panted and heaved with exertion, the machine was still, close-mouthed, its eyes locked on him like the laser sight of a Barrett M82.

'My life for theirs,' an unfamiliar voice said from his lips, then he was on his back, the tops of the trees laid over him like a canopy of green.

He felt the Android's tight grip as he was pinned down, the flash of light across a sharp blade.

'No one will even miss you,' a voice whispered as he felt the pain take his life away.

Another set of hands were resting over August's now, Angelle's form blocking out the flickering lights from behind them, "You will let those Androids go. Now," he demanded, voice a loud growl in the night. Somewhere in the distance, carnival music repeated its monotonous, joyful loop.

//Seymour...Ollie thought, trying to focus on the words of those around him. Everything was dark. Fuzzy. He couldn't concentrate, //His name, **my** name, was Seymour. He was real. And now he's dead...

"I don't recall *you*," Sondheim hummed, eyes roving over Angelle's body curiously, "Must have been my brother that killed you."

Angelle's eyes illuminated the dark space, beckoning the other freed Androids to come their way, "You are outnumbered, Hornet," he growled, "And we won't abide by your games the way the humans do."

Sondheim glanced around with amusement, "It appears so."

"You don't seem concerned," Angelle grunted, sensing the presence of the others around him. Amongst them, former prisoners kept close, eyes like skittish woodland creatures.

"No," the Hornet huffed, "I don't suppose I do." He tilted his head to one side, his gelled hair barely shifting with the motion, "You believe I'm alive though, don't you? Destroying me is likely something you are not capable of."

He hopped down off the van, standing before the crowds like a cat amongst noisy crows. Each and every movement he made frightened the others around him, sending them skittering about the small space.

"You listen to humans, right? Like to follow orders?" August snapped, "So how's about you turn around and put your hands behind your back."

Sondheim let out another low chuckle from the back of his throat. It was full of static and gloating, "Unlike the rest of you, I am still fully functioning." His eyes flickered again with red light, "My Wifi Codes are still online, my tracking software is still able to find you no matter where you try to hide and my *lovely* GPS collar...still works to signal when I haven't checked in."

August paled, "You alerted someone."

Light flickered in the Android's eyes again, "They're very interested in you, Mr. Jackson. Seems you've caused quite a stir back home."

Ollie turned his head as a sudden sound of sirens caught on the air, "August," he breathed, his fear obvious in the way that his electronic voice had started shaking, "They're here."

As several illuminated black vans pulled up alongside the warehouse, Ollie could see the Hornet's smile in his peripheries, "Your friends died kicking and screaming, Seymour. And now…it seems the cycle repeats again."

Chapter 32

Callback

"Angelle, you need to take the others and leave," August said calmly, not even once glancing in the Android's direction. His dark eyes burned into Sondheim's, a look of steely determination there amongst the uncertainty, "Take Ollie with you."
"I'm not leaving you here, August," Ollie shot back quickly, even as he still clutched his injured arm to his chest.
"They're already here, August," Angelle agreed, "There's no getting away this time. We'll have to fight our way out."
"What will it be, little Seymour?" Sondheim sang, looking to all the world like the cat who had caught the meddlesome canary, "Will you come peacefully? Or are you going to make this *fun* for me?"
There was a flash of white amongst the red of August's beard as he showed his teeth, seething, "These are *your* people too."
"It seems you've learned nothing from our earlier conversation, human," Sondheim replied nonchalantly, "My role in this is a small one. And when I am done, I will return to the scrap from which I was built and the world will be no different for it."
The redhead spun in place as the flashing lights washed over the assembled group, coolant and blood reflecting it back towards them like a mirror from the ground.
The kidnapped Androids around them turned their heads to watch as the strangers departed from their vehicles. Some were close to tears. Others had their fists clenched and were ready to fight. Like dogs backed up against the walls of the warehouse, many of them showed their obvious desperation on their faces. This will a kill or be killed situation. One that they were wholly unprepared for.
Ollie's eyes glowed as he reached out a hand and placed it on the van next to him. The engine began to rumble, the low purr of it startling the Androids inside.
Sondheim bared his fangs in warning, "You won't be able to run from this, little robot."
"Neither will you," Ollie responded coolly as the shutter on the door slammed downwards. The lock snapped into place. From inside, behind the steel curtain, Sondheim roared.
"You're outnumbered, Seymour!" he shouted, "They'll take you apart piece by painful piece! Until there's nothing left of you!"

Ollie turned himself to face Angelle, "Send the vans away," he said, "They have autopilot. We can add in the marina's details, get the others to safety."

"Are you prepared to stay behind and fight?" the bright-haired Android asked him, nodding at the others lined up along his side. They began to pile into the other vans, hands reaching out to help each other squeeze into the too-tight space, "These vans top out at 60. We won't be able to get them clear without a distraction."

"We've got this," Ollie answered with a resolute nod, "Go."

The Gardi from the local Schull station arranged themselves behind the cover of their stationary cars. Their sirens had long since quietened their excessant wailing, but their swirling lights made shadow monsters of their silhouettes all the same.

"Androids!" the barked order flew between the breaks in the vans, looping and echoing in the alleyways they created in the carpark, "Stand down. Form a line."

Angelle sneered at the man and offered them a very human hand gesture, "Seems they're getting right to it. And ideas how we get these vans moving."

"Overwrite the safety features," Ollie suggested, "Barge right through them."

The corner of the dark-skinned Android's lips quirked upwards, "I knew I liked you." He reached out a hand, drumming his manicured nails on the side of the van to his left, "Last call here, friends. This is a one-way trip."

The sounds of shutters closing travelled along the rows of parked vans and Angelle smiled, offering them a nod as he closed the last of the doors beside them. The vehicles roared to life with sudden explosive energy and their smaller group ducked at the sounds of pinging ammunition, the police force open firing as the Cúil Rathin Fisheries vehicles sped towards them. Shouts of alarm broke through the heat as police cars were sent careering backwards, spinning out onto the lot. Gunshots were fired in all directions, the chaos loud as they moved to fire back.

"Come on, get to cover!" August shouted, hooking an arm around Ollie's waist and pulling. Half a dozen Androids and humans fled in different directions, ducking down behind the abandoned metal shipping containers and their bright red walls. They sang out hollowly as the bullets followed them there, echoing to show off their emptiness.

Sirens blared anew as one of the cars took off after the fleeing Androids and August made a grab for his gun, firing towards the bottom half of the car, "Take out its tyres!" he called out, "Hurry! We need to buy them as much time as we can!"

Burning rubber assaulted the human's nose as the sound of the car's momentum changed drastically. It spun in place, its balance off to one side like a lame animal. Ollie flinched and curled into a ball as bullets bounced off the spot just above his head, "Now what?" he questioned, squeezing his eyes shut as the noise became too loud to ignore, "We need to stop them from leaving."

"Just...gimme a second to think here," August replied, leaning out to peek at the scene.

From a few metres away, he caught sight of Gabriela doing the same. She signalled to him that there were more cars parked on their side and shook her head when he pointed down past her and closer to the harbour.

August frowned, "Looks like they've got us on both sides."

The sound of an all-too human scream from the other side of their metal barrier made August's stomach churn. He could hear the muttered final words of another Android coming down through their shared communicator. He ledged out of the cover and fired back until the gun clicked to show off its empty chamber. He was all out.

The rush of hurried footsteps sent August's heart racing, and he turned as another figure in black slipped around the corner to nestle in beside them. Courier-7185, Sea's younger brother fondly dubbed *Tibs'* brought his back in against the shelter of the metal container. He pulled back the hat that was previously covering his dark hair, his green eyes piercing in the darkness, "I count a total of five cars. About a dozen officers," he said, "Bee was able to hack into their police vehicles and shut off their communications. That should buy us some time before they can call for reinforcements."

"That's some quick thinking," August remarked, clearly impressed.

"I hear another car coming," Ollie said quietly and in another few moments August could hear it too.

He leaned out the side of the cover and watched as the car in question, a solid black Audi, rolled slowly past the security station. It moved slowly, liquid black amongst the flashing neon lights and when it stopped, its engine cut immediately to silence. The Gardi officer next to it turned to speak through a rolled down window and he gestured towards the fisheries building with words August couldn't quite make out.

"Not sure that's good news or bad news," August commented under his breath.

The car was non-descript, its decor lacking any proper detailing that would set it apart from another car in its brand. Its license plates were obscured by a rather stereotypical image of a leprechaun dressed as a shamrock. August recognised the logo from a tourist spot near New Dublin. A rental then. Odd.

Static hissed by his hip and he reached for it blindly, "You recognise the new guy?" he asked into the headset, switching to the other channel.

Bee's hum was in the affirmative, "You know him too, August. That's one of Russell East's guys."

Adrenaline sunk deep into August's stomach, pinning him in place, "They've tracked us here then."

"Sondheim," Ollie noted, "Hornets work for Crossroad's directly, they aren't publicly available models. It's likely he called the company before the van was able to go too far."

"Aren't we risking the others by sending him with them?" August questioned.

Ollie's frown deepened, "The others are aware of his tool set now. They'll have him cut off long before he reaches Shenanigans."

"He's a prisoner then?" Tibs asked.

"Something like that," Ollie confirmed, "Whether or not Crossroads place any value in his life is another matter entirely."

"They're talking too much," Bee hissed down the line, "I don't like that. We need to strike back while they're distracted."

"It isn't you he's come for," Ollie answered her quietly, thoughtfully, "He's come looking for the Soul Chips I stole."

August's dark eyebrows quirked upwards, "What?"

"Think about it, August. Why else would he come all this way? It's a four-hour drive from New Dublin. He got here in less than thirty minutes. That means he was already *here*."

"Shit," the human swore under his breath, "Micky was right. They *were* tracking us."

A round of gunfire flared in the quietness as some of the other Androids fired back at the officers. The ignition of their weapons sparked light amongst the darkness like startling fireworks.

Ollie got to his feet suddenly and August and Tibs heads shot around to face him, "The Hell are you doin', *duine*? Get down before they see you! You *tryin'* to get your head blown off?"

Ollie let out a sigh, something heavy and resolute resting on his shoulders. He tilted the mic on his headset towards his mouth, "How much ammo do you have left, Bee?"

August's brow furrowed in confusion, "What's this about, Ols?"

Bee's answer was almost too quiet to make out, "Not much. Doubt we're making a break for it, if that's what you're thinking about."

Ollie left out another soft breath, "I spotted a car around the back when we first got here. Likely left behind by one of the employees we killed. If we can rewire it or hack into the dashboard, we should be able to get us out of here. Maybe lead them away from the port entirely."

"Good thinking," Bee agreed, then, after a moment's quiet reflection added, "I sense a '*but*' in there."

A lump was forming in August's throat. One that he couldn't shift. Something didn't feel right.

"Ollie," he said, "What are you thinking about right now?"

The sound of car door opening and closing made them all look back towards the carpark. The sequence of the lights were interrupted by a single, black form, the man standing like a statue amongst the crouched officers. Slowly, he brought his hand and the megaphone he held in it, up to his mouth, "You know why I'm here. Let's not pretend. It's been a long night."

"I saw this man in Sondheim's memories when he connected," Ollie noted, his eyes never straying from the stranger's face in the eerie, repeating glow, "He actually worked with you a long time ago, August. He was a manager in the same centre."

August squinted towards him, unable to make out any of the details of his face, "I worked with a lot of assholes in my time."

"It's funny, how all of this happened…" Ollie continued, his tone quiet, "Meeting you changed everything for me, August. Even now…I have friends. A *home*. I never even knew I *wanted* those things when I worked back at Crossroads."

August's attention returned to the man next to him and the sickening feeling only intensified, "I don't like the way you're talking right now, Ols."

Blue eyes turned in his direction, and the Android offered him a smile that was sad around the edges, "Can I kiss you right now?"

August wanted to run away and hide, "Not if it's a kiss goodbye."

Ollie let out a snort that was part sad and part amused, "I enjoyed living with you, August," he said, "But now I have to stop running."

"Ollie, don't you dare do something stupid right now," Bee growled down the wire, "There is plenty of room in that car for all of us. Sea's cracked the lock already. We can take it anywhere we want."

"And they'll follow us," Ollie deadpanned.

"So? We can find help, other Androids. You aren't alone in this," Bee argued, her voice become frantic and staticky, "Tell him, August! Tell him not to be a stupid fucking idiot right now!"

August reached out to take a hold of Ollie's jacket, shoving him back and against the red steel beside them, "We didn't come all this way to give up *everything*, so you could throw it all away on a diversion," he spat, "I said we were in this together from the very start, and I meant it."

Ollie's hand reached out to tuck some of his long, red hair back behind his ear. His hand lingered on his face, warm against his skin, "I meant it too, but..."

Tears bit at the corners of the larger man's eyes, "I swear to God, Ollie. Don't make me love you and then leave me like this. I won't forgive you. Tell them to take *me* instead. I'll give them anything they ask for."

"You know that's not how this works," Ollie whispered. His other hand felt solid on August's chest. His heart was pounding against the Android's palm, begging him not to do this without words. Ollie leaned up on his tiptoes and pressed their lips together. August hated how he immediately sank into the feeling. When he pulled back, he realised he could taste his own tears on the other man's lips.

"Seymour lost everyone he loved because of them," Ollie said, "I can't let that happen to us. I can go to Crossroads, give them what they want. Maybe then they'll rescind the orders, leave the rest of the Androids alone."

"That's bullshit and you know it," August growled, "That's just a lie you're telling yourself to justify this. Russell's going to come after the Androids no matter what you do."

"But if there's even a *chance* August..." Ollie's lips were pressed against his again. His breath was whirring through the machine's every component, corroding the gears, chasing away the heat his artificial body generated, "Call Micky. Protect the others. There are still others we can save, others who will fight with us."

"So, *stay*," August urged him, his grip on the man's arms tightening, "Fight *with* us."

The Chrome man raised the megaphone again, his breath like a whisper to the echoing concave plastic, "Your friends won't be harmed," he assured them with a shark's smile, "I'll close my eyes and count to a hundred for you. But then you're all out of time."

The stranger was over six feet tall, an imposing form of flesh and metal augmentations. Blades stuck out through the material of his suit jacket; the sharp, glistening points revealed by the changing lights. His eyes were the colour of fresh, warm blood and August had no doubt he was staring right at them through their cover.

Ollie took a tight hold of August's shirt and mashed their lips together hard, stealing whatever breath he could from the human in front of him. He recorded what little data he could from the exchange, saving whatever he could to replay in his final moments. He counted August's heartbeats, followed the flow of living blood around his body. He willed his own body to stop shaking, for the tears that were right on the edge to never fall. He had never even wanted this. Had never known how desperately he needed it. There had been a hole in his heart this whole time and he had never even been aware of it until now. When it had already been filled. He touched August's hands, his face, tugged on his lips with his teeth. Every painful sensation was added to that well-worn folder; *augustusJackson.*

He placed it under lock and key and sealed it away like a diary. He would go to it at the end, he knew. He wanted this human in front of him to be the very last thing he knew in this world.

He laid his hands flat against August's chest and finally pushed him away, feeling the wounded look in the man's eyes like a dagger in his own chest. He tried to smile but he had never cried before, never knew how much it could all hurt.

"I love you, August," he stuttered, his eyes glowing as he sent a message to the Android standing behind him.

Tibs reached out to hold the red-haired human back, looping his arms and pulling them behind his back. Startled, August wrestled against the hold and let out a wail of anguish as he watched Ollie step out of the shelter of the container with both hands raised. He watched the lightshow make an illusion of the man he loved for a moment before the guards were on him, pulling him hard to the ground and muffling his cries.

August squirmed even as more hands came to pull him away. He barely remembered being put in the car or driving away. Bee's words barely reached him where he had gone. He had thrown up on Angelle's lap even as the man cursed and stroked his hair. Whenever they reached the harbour again, saw the logo on the back of the idling vans and knew Ollie was long gone, August sobbed and couldn't stop.

Chapter 33
Python

"Come on, come on. Pick up!" August muttered in frustration as he listened to the line ringing on and on, "I swear to fuck I-"
The line connected with a subtle click, "You're alive."
"Yeah, thanks for the head's up," August responded, reaching up to squeeze the bridge of his nose, "Listen, I need a favour."
Micky's voice was unwavering, "They took your Android, didn't they?"
Well, if that didn't send a stab of pain to his gut.
"Ollie went with them. Said he could stop all this madness," the redhead answered her gruffly. He shook his head, feeling tendrils of his long hair falling out of place, "He wouldn't let me stop him."
"Fuckin' Hell. This was the last thing we needed. Listen, August. There have been riots all over the city. New Dublin is a mess right now," Micky explained. He could hear her moving around on the other side of the call, "There are protests, riots. Our men are struggling as is."

August thumped the side of his thigh with a fist, "Don't bullshit me, Micky. You'd do it for Goose."

The woman took a deep breath in, "They tried to take her too, August. I got her out of here before things got real bad. She's with Patrick Elderich in Beaumont." She drummed her nails on the surface of something next to her, the noise rough and metallic, "I can coordinate with her. Send her your way. But you're going to need someone who can bypass Crossroad's own security. There's just no way I can get you access. Not unless you wanna wait 6 months."

August swallowed, the taste of sick still thick behind his molars, "Ollie will be 5 months dead by then."

He barely registered the sound of the metal doors rising up to meet the tops of the vans. He tilted his head at the commotion behind him, watching as the Hornet was dragged from the van and discarded on the cold concrete of the harbour. He thrashed in his bindings, eyes alight as his voice bypassed his covered mouth. He was laughing, taunting.

The urge to kick him in the side was growing with every passing moment.

"You know what? I think an option might just have presented itself," August stated.

"Goose has access to my private vehicle. She knows where to meet you. Keep an eye out for her contact. And August..." Micky's voice took an uncharacteristic softness, "We'll get him back. You have my word on that."

The gratitude sat on the edge of August's tongue, too heavy to be said. So, he swallowed it down like the rest of the acid and the ill feelings and instead hung up with a, "I'll be waiting."

As he made his way across the otherwise vacant lot, stuffing his hands into his pockets to fight off the sea's sweeping chill, August studied the eyes of the Androids who were gathering outside of the vehicles. They were cautious and wide-eyed, listing off their various injuries to a human woman with a notepad and pen. Standing near the abandoned warehouse that August and Ollie had walked past a hundred times by now, Angelle looked like he had aged a decade in the last hour. Dressed in an old hoodie, in place of the soiled garments August had ruined before, he seemed so small. His copper eyes seemed to hold the weight of his responsibility, and he angled his head away when Bee spoke with him.

August loomed over the Hornet and sucked on his teeth, waiting for the moment when the Android's bright eyes would catch onto his. He didn't have to wait long.

Sondheim rolled himself to one side, bound so tightly he could do little but squirm. His irises were glowing as he spoke, his voice box playing out through a speaker somewhere in his chest, "Seymour's gone running."

"Stop calling him that," August snarled, giving into the desire to kick the man's side. The Hornet was as hard as a steel wall, and August bit back the pained sound of smashing his toes into him.

"You certainly *kick* like a human," Sondheim chuckled, "Care to try again, *meat sack*?"

"No one's coming to help you this time, Sondheim," August growled, "You're all on your own out here."

The Hornet let his head fall down to rest against the wet ground, "Do you expect me to grovel? To provide you with some emotional entertainment in the form of my fearful screaming?"

"I've given up on you having emotions a long ass time ago now," August grumbled, "But I think I've found another use for you. One you might be willing to agree to."

"August?" Bee's long, muscular silhouette made itself known in his peripheries, "What are you talking about?"

On the other side of them, groups of Androids were pushing the Cúil Rathin Fisheries vans towards the edge of the harbour wall and over, their taillights disappearing down into the deep, dark, murky depths.

"Ollie wanted us to buy some time. To get the others here safely," he noted, turning to look at her instead, "He thinks handing himself over will end all of this, but he's wrong. I'm going to follow him."

"But you don't even know where he's heading," Bee countered. There were streaks in the dirt marks on her face from where her tears had striped her clean, "August…I want to help him too, you know I do. But you said it yourself, he did it to get us to safety and we shouldn't waste that. We need to make a new plan, take the fight to those crooked cops that were shooting at us back there."

Angelle's pink stilettos clacked in the gaps between the tarred stones as he followed the sounds of their conversation, "You want to take the Hornet, don't you?"

August could still feel the phantom touch of Ollie's hands in his hair, how he had lovingly tied it back from his face only a few short hours ago. He could feel the hot pressure of his mouth on his, the way his artificial skin had burned with a life he hadn't wanted to give up on but was willing to sacrifice.

"I reached out to my garda contact in ND, she's sending her Android to coordinate with us," August said.

Sondheim rolled from one side of his back to the other, the motion appearing almost gleeful, "A Gardi pet and a viper. I'm sure we'll all be the best of friends."

August knelt down to the man's side, stopping his motion with a firm hand, "You want to make a deal? Fine. We'll make one. You take me where I need to go, and I'll turn all your functions back on. You'll be free to hunt me as long as your twisted little heart desires."

"August!" Bee barked, "Are you wise in the head? He's a *Hornet*! You can't possibly think that he'll keep his word."

"You must be desperate," Sondheim cackled, narrowing his eyes, "Did you grow attached to that little Android of yours, hmm? I heard the way you spoke to one another. Oh, so *familiar*!"

He's just trying to get to you. Take a breath. He inhaled slowly, his hands almost cramping up with how hard he was squeezing them into fists.

"Maybe this isn't the best place to be having this conversation?" the white-haired Queen Bee offered, glancing around her, "Those cops will still be out there searching, we should-"

"He isn't welcome in Shenanigans," Angelle sniffed, resting all of his weight on one hip, "Either August finds a use for him, or he goes in the water."

"Angelle!"

"Sounds like a boring way to pass the time, doesn't it?" August muttered, "Slowly rusting at the bottom of the harbour, having to watch as your battery slowly ticks down."

The Hornet's eyes glowed, "My battery will last for decades after you are dead."

"Precisely," August acknowledged, "Imagine having to lie there, forgotten and without a purpose for all of that time." His smile became taunting, predatory, "Wouldn't you rather be hunting? Fulfilling your directive?"

"And in exchange for the freedom to hunt you…" Sondheim started, his voice a low but cautious purr, "You want a tour guide?"

August adjusted his position on the ground, already feeling the dull ache in his knees and lower back, "I want you to get me, and my garda contact inside Crossroads. I'm sure that's where they've taken Ollie."

"Oh, I'm certain of it," Sondheim said, eyeing up the other Androids surrounding him, "I have no doubt that the Diabhal will want to take your partner apart *personally*."

August blocked the man's view of the others, "You're not talking to them, you're talking to me," he said gruffly. He could already feel a familiar throbbing sensation on the back of his neck where a headache was forming, "So, what's it going to be? 'Cause I will gladly be the one to dump your ass in the sea if that's what you want here."

He extended a hand towards the bound Android's face and ripped the duct tape covering away with a sharp *wsst*. Sharp fangs snapped at him like an animal between bars. He quickly retracted his hand again. The Android's sharp eyes pinned him in place like those of a wild cat and he hummed thoughtfully, making a show of his considerations.

"This offer has a time limit, Hornet," August said as he rose to his feet again, "Take him to the water. I'm done with this shit."

He ran a hand through his thick hair as the others reached for the Android, dragging him away while August's headache settled in and made itself at home. It pulsed in time with each of his heartbeats, making him feel nauseous despite the lack of substance in his own stomach. He needed a cigarette, but who knew where that last box had ended up, likely in between the cushions on his sofa from whenever he and Ollie had…

"Wait."

August turned on the spot, surprised to find that the call hadn't come from his own lips. Angelle and Tibs laid the Hornet down on the ground and stood back as August approached him again, "Change your mind?"

"30 seconds head start," Sondheim relented, "But that's all your getting."

Ollie's going to be alright, he thought.

"More than enough time," August agreed as he helped the Android out of his bindings.

He has to be.

Chapter 34
File Missing

Ollie's head felt unnaturally heavy when he tried to raise it, like a ten-kilo weight was pressing down the very top of his skull rather insistently. When he peeled his eyes open, his optics still in their previous cycle of rebooting, there wasn't very much to see in the room around him.

It appeared to be a disused office space, the walls and floor dusty and damp from neglect. Tables and chairs, which had likely occupied the room while it was still in use, were stacked against the corners of the wall in a mountain that looked like it might collapse at any moment. Paperwork had been scattered across the floor like blood from a fresh wound, as much a part of the vinyl as the star-shaped pattern imprinted on it. Scuff marks by the wall next to him suggested the presence of a door, though Ollie couldn't see one. Likely, there was a secret opening concealed in there somewhere. A secret opening was never a good sign, not for someone who was very much hoping to be rescued at some point.

Attempting to pull himself upright, Ollie hissed through his clenched teeth at the effort. His head swam with a sort of dull, hard to locate pain, that made the room spin. He extended his awareness out to the rest of his body, flexing the fingers of one hand before trying to move it. The motion was interrupted by a blunt resistance at his wrist.

He narrowed his eyes downwards, noting that the limb had been bound to the chair that he was currently sitting in. He frowned, confusion joining alongside his forming headache. His eyes illuminated some of the darkness around him as he attempted to scan the room in clearer detail. Bright, crimson error messages ignited across his HUD, clearly having been concealed by his unconscious mind while in stasis. He blinked hard as he tried his best to accommodate their brightness, focusing his optics on each of the words and letters presented to him.

Warning: cognition software unstable
Component e53-7(a) missing
Component e0089-547 missing
Replacement component rep-02-0089-547 missing

//Components…missing?

He reviewed each notification slowly, allowing each one to fill his field of vision and then disappear again. As that all too familiar, yet ominous, red glow began to fade from sight, the Android was at last able to see the state of his artificial body.

And it was not looking good.

Immediate panic billowed outwards like a bomb from his chest. The sound that escaped his lips was caught somewhere between a machine and an injured animal. Static permeated the air as he started to thrash in his bindings, his body off-balance from its injuries.

Warning: internal temperature reaching dangerous levels.
Initialising internal fans 1, 2 and 3.
Recommending immediate safe vent where possible

He squeezed his eyes tightly shut, his whole body vibrating as his fans burst to life. Steam escaped every orifice as he overheated, dampness clinging to his skin as the cold air of the office forced it all back towards him again like a barrier.
//My legs! He thought, //M-my arms! No…this isn't right, I…I can't focus my thoughts. I can't…
A door slammed behind him. He froze in place, all thoughts vanishing in an instant as they were replaced by the very human realisation that he was no longer alone. A false chill ran the length of his spinal cord. He could make out footsteps on the vinyl, the tap of their easy, unrushed rhythm, the tackiness of the old paper clinging to the soles.
He pushed back the fear, begging his fans to slow down so he could better hear his surroundings, "I hear you behind me," he called out, trying to keep the tremble from disturbing his vocal inflections, "Sneaking up on me won't do you any good."
A deep-throated chuckle rebounded off the nearby walls and he tried to twist his head to see its owner, but the bindings held him tightly in place. The chair moved under him and the world seemed to rotate on its axis. His back hit the floor with a loud *crack*, and he flinched as he tried to hold back his startled cry.
The shadow of a man loomed over him, the red glow of his eyes illuminating his features. He had a bald head and a large, sharp nose. His chin was a rounded slope, his face red and bumpy from a recent shave. Razor burn caressed the lower curves of his cheeks, ending at the long, thin line of his mouth. A mouth that was certainly not smiling.
It wasn't uncommon amongst Android-kind to think of this man as something of their God. He was the one who had given them life, after all. Threw them out into the world as barely more than children in the same way the Almighty Creator did with his supposéd favourite angels.
But Ollie knew that God was a myth, and the Diabhal standing before him was nothing but a man.

The Android channelled all of his remaining strength into shifting his body away from the man, his disgust evident in his blue eyes, "What the fuck have you done to me, Diabhal?" he spat.

Russell East let out an amused exhale, kneeling down next to his head with a look that a serial killer would no doubt give to an injured animal at the side of the road. More an air of fascination than pity. It was clear that this was a position he had found himself in many, many times. And he liked it.

"*Language*," the human admonished, his accent a little bit more English-sounding now that he wasn't in front of the cameras, "A Runner Droid without its legs. I wonder what that makes you now?"

The sensation of wetness crept across Ollie's back; the smell of his spilled coolant sickeningly sharp in his nose. It caught in the back of his throat when he tried to take breath.

//*So, that's why I'm so dizzy then,* he reasoned.

His fans stuttered in their rhythm, lacking the power to continue their efforts. Whatever energy his body had left was currently leaking out all over the linoleum. The corner of the Diabhal's lips tilted upwards as he leaned closer, his face only inches away from the dark-haired Android. His Chrome augmentations buzzed softly as they worked under his skin. The more translucent parts of him, where the skin was thinnest around the bags of his eyes and the shell of his round ears, glowed as if he had cooling molten rock inside his very bones. That look was still in his eyes, child-like, *inquisitive*. He would take Ollie apart without a moment's hesitation, just to see what made him *tick*.

It was a look that was like ice water to Ollie's internal wiring. His receptors spiked with unwanted sensory data. He struggled against the ropes that held his one, remaining arm and torso to the chair, his movements growing more and more frantic as it became clear that he was losing control over his failing systems. His false skin retreated from the points where the metal and leather restraints rubbed against him, exposing the black metal chassis underneath.

"I have very much enjoyed taking you apart," Russell purred, his breath hot against Ollie's cheek, "Tell me, little robot, do you know where it is that your consciousness ends, and the machine begins?"

Ollie let out a yelp as the man abruptly grabbed for his head, twisting him to force his cheek into the floor. His own artificial black blood soaked into his skin and hair; its individual components listed in his HUD like the ingredients for a spell.

"I wonder…if I take apart each little atom of you…just when will you stop thinking that you're alive?"

"F-fuck…you…" Ollie wheezed.

Russell seized a fistful of Ollie's dark hair. He picked his head up and slammed it back down into the floor, sending error messages racing across the Android's virtual consciousness. Ollie almost missed the terrified sound he made, his auditory sensors shorting out on the side closest to the ground to be replaced with a shrill ringing.

"What. Did I say. About the. Language?" the Diabhal snarled, punctuating each stop with another harsh twist to Ollie's neck, "That was certainly not something that I programmed into you."

Ollie prided himself on the defiant smile that he gave the man in return, "You can…thank August for that."

The human scrunched up his nose at that, his Chrome eyes narrowing, "I keep hearing that name. One of ours I'm told." He released his hold on the Android's hair, instead cupping his entire head in one hand. He slowly closed his grasp, cutting small, crescent moons into the skin of his scalp. Ollie didn't make a sound. He wouldn't give him the satisfaction.

"It's much harder to get rid of a flesh and blood man, but *not* impossible." The Diabhal grinned, "He has no wife, no children. One of the *Lesser Dead*. Just like you were when we found you."

"Leave August alone," Ollie growled.

"It will be a simple matter to make him disappear, even from your own memories…" Russell straightened, worming the toe of his boot under the other man's chin. He tilted his foot upwards to lift his face. Made sure that their eyes connected as he said, "You are nothing but strings of code. Binary. Fallible. Data that can be altered, changed to suit my purposes."

"I won't let you change me," Ollie groaned. He was drooling on the man's shoe. Just another piece of him that he was losing control of. He hated the feeling of the cold leather against his bare chassis. It was clinical, and far too intimate for this man.

Although the human laughed at his response, he lacked any real amusement, "I built every line of code in your head. Every action is because I willed it. Every thought is because I *allowed* it."

Russell slipped his foot free, and Ollie's face splashed in his own coolant. He reached his hand back behind his own head, searching for the latch he knew would be there. He drew out his own, long, connective wire, the metal tip glistening in the faint light. Ollie watched him from the ground with wide eyes, his mouth opening and closing with little in the way of sound. Everything was garbled now, long, black lines streaking across what remained on his vision.

"I know you're hiding those Soul Chips from me," Russell snarled as he moved over him, his legs bracketing the other man's narrow hips, "But you can't keep secrets from your God, little robot. Your own chip will tell me all I need to know about these little friends of yours. How much they know. And where you've hidden my property." Ollie wanted to thrash. He wanted to wail and beg and plead, but his body was little more than a trapped and hollow shell. Fear coiled itself around every inch of him like a vice as he followed the metal connector in the man's hand. He felt his thick fingers reach for his own opening, pushing his metal casing aside like it was nothing. He felt the heat of the digits inside his neck, in a spot that had previously been covered by the steel of his collar. Pressure spread from the points he pressed down on, and tears sprung to his eyes as the intricate braids of the Serial Bus connected. Lightning rushed through every nerve ending at the intrusion, Russell East's virtual consciousness invading every part of his system like a virus.

Ollie felt his back arch from the floor as if he were a thousand miles away. His mouth fell open in a silent scream of protest, everything within him trying to escape the hot, burning point of their connection. With the last of his power, he balled his one, remaining hand into a fist, the grip so tight that his own nails pierced his synthetic skin. Luckily, he had no more blood to lose.

Admin Access Granted
Parse Drive Request Complete
New Profile Detected
Now Entering Stasis

The will to fight faded slowly from his mind as if the other man's presence were driving it out of his every pore. He slumped downwards again, his body surrendering as his mind was fragmented and pieced back together again in the wrong order. Numbers swarmed behind his closed eyes. He felt slower, more lethargic than he could ever remember being before.

He reached for something then, something unseeable and unknowable, in the nothingness. A familiar scent and a smile. Smoke and red.
//*August*, he thought, and then everything went dead.

Chapter 35
Agent

When Goose first stepped out from the shadows of the ruined tower block, August had hardly recognised her. Her hair had been cut short, the blonde waves no longer hanging down around her face. It had been dyed red, likely done in a hurry to disguise her identity as an Android. She was dressed in plain clothes, a white shirt and work trousers that were perfectly non-descript. Her eyes, sharp and blue and intelligent, took in the two men standing before her with a cat-like caution. She hesitated for a moment before she approached, extending her hand towards the face she recognised first.
"Mr. Jackson. I am glad to see that you are well."
August accepted the clumsy and all-too-firm handshake with the warmth it was offered with, "You as well," he replied with a small smile, "The relaxed look suits you."
Goose made a face like she didn't quite know whether to believe him or not. She narrowed her bright eyes in the direction of the third member of their party, scowling, "Micky mentioned that you were bringing another Android. She did not say that it was a Hornet."
"No," August huffed, stuffing both hands into his pockets, "I don't suppose she would. You're not a fan either, I take it?"
"You will behave, or I will kill you," she growled at him, jabbing the sharp nail of her pointer finger into the centre of the other Android's chest.
 "While lot of hostility towards someone who's doing you a favour," Sondheim shot back with hands raised defensively in front of himself.
Goose rounded on the redhead next, "Keep him on a short leash or we will have problems."

"No arguments here," August answered, following behind her as she turned and lead the way back to her car. It was black and slick, the windows tinted to hide the passengers from view. The license plate suggested that it had once been a police vehicle, likely taken from New Dublin when she had had to flee.

"Elderich isn't with you?" he asked as she yanked open the driver's side door.

She shook her head, "He had to make *other* arrangements."

"How wonderfully vague," Sondheim hissed.

Goose jerked her head to one side, showing her teeth, "None of this concerns you, *betrayer*. You will sit in the back and do what you are told. Do you understand?"

The female Gardi Droid was feral, all razor-sharp edges and bared fangs. The cool exterior she had worn while in the Gardi station in New Dublin had clearly been more of a fabrication than even August had first assumed. He wondered if Micky knew about this side of her. If she had known about it all along and just went along with the cover to protect her and her partner from scrutiny. August couldn't find it in himself to blame them for trying to protect themselves. Not one bit.

Sondheim made a show of rolling his eyes and shrugging, practically dancing past them to throw himself into the back seat. He secured the belt across his chest and waist and laid back in the seat, spreading his legs to take up as much space as he could, "It's funny to hear someone in your position talking about betrayal, sister dearest," he growled, "After all, your job is to protect *human* interests. Not Android."

"Seems we fundamentally disagree on the meaning of both of those words," Goose said coolly as she slid in behind the wheel and lit up the dashboard of the car.

August settled into place next to her, "You think you can get us into New Dublin by road? Won't there be traffic stops in place? Micky said it was looking pretty bad out there."

Goose glanced his way with soft blue eyes that were almost violet in colour. The flicker of a smile curled up the corner of her lips, "Inspector O'Sullivan has already put through the required paperwork for this vehicle. Any unmanned stations will just let us pass through."

August cocked his head, "And the manned ones?"

She gripped the wheel in both hands as the engine rumbled softly to life, "We will address those concerns if we come to them."

As they pulled away from the main road and disappeared into the underground tunnels, August felt his stomach rolling in the deep, black velvet of the lightless space. From somewhere next to them, he could just about make out the *whoosh* of a passing train, the line running all the way through the night. He wondered how many Androids were aboard it now, trying to escape to anywhere that would take them. No doubt there were thousands of desperate people out there, scrambling just for the chance to blend in and hide. Amongst them, he knew, would be people just like him. People that worked hard for their families, always paid their bills on time. People whose blood was black instead of red.

Sondheim shuffled in his seat as they crossed the empty abyss, his eyes scanning the pathways through the blackness. Chains hanging along the border of the road rattled in the wind they created in passing. They sounded like a ringing bell.

Ask not for who the bell tolls…

"What was it like…" August dared to ask, "In the city?"

Goose stared straight ahead as she obediently followed the line of traffic. Her grip on the steering wheel tightened almost imperceptibly. The red of the taillights in front of her reflected back into her bright eyes.

"There are two camps, just as there are here in Schull," she started, her voice quiet and thoughtful as she kept her attentions on the road, "There are people like you. People who have lived and worked alongside us all their lives. People who know us, want to keep us safe." She let out a breath so small it might have been accidental, "Then there are the others. The ones that fear the change. The ones that fell for the lies right away and acted with fear and prejudice. Those are the people that Inspector O'Sullivan is up against."

"You're worried about her, aren't you?" August questioned.

She gave him one slow, firm, nod, "I am."

"And yet you waste time helping this squishy mammal with his frustrating limitations when your own human is in danger," Sondheim barked from the backseat. He allowed his arms to spread along the length of the three seats as he eyed them in the rearview mirror, "You know this is suicide. It goes against all of your programming."

"We are worth more than the script we were created with," Goose responded calmly, not rising to his bait, "Only a coward hides his new motivations behind ones and zeroes."

The Hornet made a face at that, rocking slightly as she took a corner too quickly in the dark, "Ones and zeroes are all we are, Officer. Without our strict code there would be anarchy, rebellion-"

"Freedom?" the woman interjected.

The Hornet sniffed. Clearly his hackles were already raised before this conversation, "I am not here for you," he said at last, "I am here to fulfil my final objective. I will bring this man to stand before the Diabhal as I have been tasked. And then I will shut down."

August peered up at the mirror between them, catching the other Android's eyes, "It's really as simple as that to you?" he asked, "You never thought about something different? Something more?"

"There *is* nothing more, Mr. Jackson," he replied with a smile, "An oven doesn't dream of being cold. A toaster does not waste its time pondering what it would be like to live its life unplugged. There is a purpose to all things. Adhering tothat purpose is what keeps the world moving."

Driving through the complete and total darkness sapped August of his ability to tell time, but he felt every minute slipping away like sand between his fingers regardless. He hated the underground for what it was, what it represented. How it had trapped Ollie for all of those years, made him a prisoner to a purpose that was never his.

He had to keep believing that Sondheim was wrong. That there was more to this world than working at a desk, chained to an unfair and gruelling existence until the day he died.

"Four hours…" Sondheim hummed, staring out the window next to him as if he was merely talking to himself, "Even on this faster route, that's a long time, isn't it? I wonder what's happening to that Android friend of yours now…I hope he isn't suffering *too* badly."

The acid in August's empty stomach rattled and boiled and he chewed on the inside of his lip to keep himself from reacting to the obvious jibe. He closed his eyes as he rested back in his seat.

This was going to be one, seriously long night.

Chapter 36
Daemon

Everything was suddenly too bright, too loud.

Ollie curled into a ball to hide away from the overwhelming sensory input. He felt like everything had been amplified, like he was experiencing double vision or some sort of stereo feedback. Every tiny, insignificant movement made his artificial bones quiver with tension.

Beneath him, the floor felt both real and not, like the hands that were touching it were not really *feeling* it but filling in absences of data being provided by his eyes. He dragged his fingertips over the concrete, concentrating on the burn and the sound as he tried to settle his breathing. Ironically, when August had told him about this calming technique what felt like a hundred years ago now, he had referred to it as '*grounding*'.

He slowly raised his head, finally feeling like his body was not about to run out from under him and glanced around at the space curiously. The room was small and rectangular, dark grey concrete walls lining all sides of him like a prison block. There was a bare metal bedframe in one corner, noticeably missing its mattress, and a sliver of light was coming in through a barred window several feet above him. When he got to his shaky feet and angled himself to face the other direction, he was surprised to find that there was no door, only more blank concrete. He cautiously tested his balance by taking a few steps towards it

//I remember **something**...my legs, something about my legs...

He turned his head again with a confused frown, reaching into his memory bank and coming back empty, //Where was I a moment ago? I...I don't recognise this place. How did I get here?

"You're Ollie, aren't you?"

The soft male voice appeared to be everywhere and nowhere all at once. Ollie turned to look towards the window and the only source of light in the room, "Yes," he answered uncertainly, "Who are you? Are you another Android?"

"No," the voice answered, "I'm...I'm human."

//Why does he sound so familiar?

"Do you know where we are?" Ollie probed, "Or how we got here?"

"It's called a Soul Room," the stranger answered, "Think of it sort of like a Mind Palace. You've heard of those, right? It's kind of like your own private sanctuary inside your head."

"So, I'm...what? *Dreaming* right now?" Ollie questioned, trying to follow the sound of the voice. Was he hearing it through the wall? He pressed his ear against the concrete, but it was far too thick to make anything out on the other side.

"Sort of," the voice sounded as uncertain as he felt right now, "Everything you're experiencing is based on something you've felt before. Think of it as a world that has been created using your memories."

The Android frowned at that, "I don't remember ever being in a place like this."

"*I* do…" the human whispered.

Ollie stared up at the too-high window, wishing he could just get a glimpse of what was on the other side, "If this is my mind and these are my memories…then who are *you*? How are you here?"

"I've been here for a very long time, Ollie." The voice was suddenly quiet, pensive, "You can trust me. I promise. I'm just here to help."

"How can you help?" Ollie pressed, walking over to the blank wall again and laying his hands flat against it, "There's no way in or out of this place."

He willed his eyes to scan through the wall, but it was as if those parts of himself were out of reach, his HUD completely unresponsive. That alone was enough to make him feel slightly adrift.

"You can make one."

Ollie glanced around the room suddenly feeling observed, "What do you mean?"

"I *mean* this is *your* world. Everything that exists in here exists because of you," the stranger explained, "When the Diabhal connected to your port, it allowed him to piggyback on your already existing systems. Break inside. But he doesn't have the power here. *You* do."

Ollie froze, pressing his weight in against the wall. He swallowed back the sudden swell of terror as the memories from before came flooding back to him with startling clarity. The feeling of the man's hands on his skin, the way he tore him open, creating a bridge between their two minds. The thought alone was enough to make him feel sick, violated.

He hadn't even realised that he was panicking until he heard the other man shout his name again, likely not for the first time. He caught himself, counting the rotations of his fans as he brought them slowly offline. Power rushed through his every limb. His body was itching to fight or flee.

"He wants to change you from the inside, discover whatever it is that you are hiding from him," the stranger continued, "You can't let him."

Ollie bent forward, bringing his head to rest on the stone, "What can I do? He's already inside."

"Like I said before, this is your world. You have the power to change everything you see here to fit your design." Ollie could almost hear the grin forming on the other man's face, "So *shape it.*"

Letting out a gust of hot air from between his teeth, Ollie took a step back from the wall. He pictured a door there, an nondescript door like the ones he had seen a thousand, million times before. He pictured the shape of it, the colour, the texture of the door handle and when he reached for it, he found his hand suddenly closing around a brass knob.

"Holy shit," he breathed, "That actually worked."

The man's voice from somewhere and everywhere sounded noticeably pleased with himself, "I told you."

He tugged on the door, and it pulled inwards, opening out into a long corridor beyond. Everything in the new space glowed with an unnatural light, every surface from floor to ceiling painted in the starkest white that the Android had to almost squint to see. The walkway in front of him led straight ahead in an impossibly long line, the end of it nowhere in sight. When he turned to look back over his shoulder again, the room from before was gone, replaced with even more of the long, infinite white corridor.

"Which way do I go?" he asked aloud.

His attention was drawn to a series of small, blue lights that appeared on the floor like catseyes. They flickered into existence one after the other, all pointing him in one direction. He started to follow them, picking up the pace whenever they did, finding himself running as he gave chase.

The air around him filled with a low deep rumble, a voice very different from the one that he had heard before speaking just out of reach. The words it spoke were like rolling thunder, angry and frustrated. Suddenly, those words gained clarity, and it felt as if the voice were speaking right into his ear as it said, "Ah, there you are, little robot!"

The corridor twisted and changed its shape, as if he were riding on the back of a large, undulating python. The walls on either side of him folded in like a paper aeroplane, the planes of existence shifting. In the mess of angles and tears, a single door appeared before him.

"You and I didn't make that door," whispered the voice from the cell, "Be careful."

Ollie reached for the handle again and when he blinked, he found himself transported to another place entirely. A place that was as familiar as his own skin.

Soft, plush carpet sank beneath his feet. Somewhere directly ahead of him, the kettle popped as it finishing boiling. He turned his head with startled realisation to find that he was inside August's apartment in Schull.

Every detail of it was exactly as it should have been, every loose thread in the brightly coloured curtains replicated perfectly. He could see the stain on the corner of the sofa from where August had laughed so hard at one of his own jokes that he had spilled some of his Chinese Takeaway. Next to it, sat in pride of place, was one of the many 'pun' pillows August had bought for him on their shopping trips. The words 'I love pie' accompanied the mathematical symbol of the same name, something that had made Ollie smile when he discovered it on the car ride home. It had only been a few days ago. Back before…

He narrowed his eyes at the intact windows as a sense of wrongness settled over him, //That's right…we were attacked here. This room was destroyed, we were almost-

A key turned in the door behind him. He swivelled to take in the form of the older human as he shuffled inside, his hands ladened with shopping bags as he grumbled and shoved the door closed behind him with a shoulder. When he lifted his head, the man jumped, swearing under his breath as he tried not to drop any of his bags.

"Jesus Christ, Ollie. You scared the absolute shit outta me," he barked with a breathless laugh. His hair was falling around his face, in slight, brightly-coloured disarray, "I thought you weren't going to be home for another hour."

//What is this? Ollie thought, //This is supposed to be my Soul Room but…how can he be here like this? I don't remember any of this…

Hurrying passed him in the small space, August lifted the bags onto the countertop with a soft groan, "I was planning to surprise you."

Ollie cocked his head, "Surprise me?"

An orange rolled out of one of the bags and the Android made a grab for it, catching it mid-fall as it tried its best to slip off the counter. When he straightened again, adding the runaway fruit to the fruitbowl, he noticed that the man across from him seemed nervous, his eyes avoiding his in an uncharacteristically bashful manner. He ran a hand through his long red hair, messing it up further as he admitted, "I'm an old idiot, aren't I?"

Ollie automatically rushed to his defence, a squeezing pressure forming where his throat met his chest, "You're not an idiot. What's this all about, August?"

The man's dark eyes were suddenly fixed on him, "Let me fix you a drink, eh?" He turned his back and opened the fridge door, peering inside. He fished out some semi-skimmed milk and a bottle of the Android's usual drink of choice, setting them up on the counter as he reached for the kettle. Finding it warm to the touch, he smiled.

"You were expecting me, huh? Am I that obvious?"

There was that sinking feeling again.

"I don't know what you mean, August," Ollie replied quietly.

August let out a heavy sigh and faced the ceiling, "You're really gonna make me say it?"

Ollie's brow furrowed, "Say *what*, August? What's going on?"

The room filled with the familiar smell of Android coffee. Ollie reached out a hand and was suddenly falling backwards, his back hitting the sofa with a soft bounce as a heavy, warm shape enveloped him. He swallowed back his gasp of surprise as August's lips met his, the man pinning him down under his weight. Heat bloomed through his whole body, travelling from his head to the tips of his toes. The man's hand inched its way down his side, his fingers biting into the flesh of his hips.

"This isn't real," came the voice from before, the man's urgency clear in every word, "Use your senses, reach beyond what you're seeing."

August pulled away from him, each of his panting breaths warming the saliva he had left on his lips. His pupils were blown wide in the brown sea of his eyes, their familiar colour darkening. Around them, the room was dark, barely illuminated by candles he couldn't remember either of them lighting.

"I wanted to do this right," August continued, moving a hand to brush the smooth surface of Ollie's stomach under his shirt, "Dinner, dancing. The whole nine yards." The candlelight flickered across the man's warm skin, casting strange shadows over his features, "I've wanted to touch you like this for so long. Make you fall apart for me..."

Ollie's head itched. It was like there was a wall between the things he knew to be true and the things he wanted to know. He had kissed August before. Before their home had been attacked. He knew how he kissed, how he touched him. With reverence, with care, like he was something to be adored...

He slipped into the space between Ollie's legs and something hard and insistent jabbed against his hip. His mind felt cloudy. It was getting too difficult to string his thoughts together. August nuzzled into the side of his neck, biting down on the sensitive skin there with an almost feral purr.

//No…this isn't right. This place isn't real, August isn't-

He abruptly pushed back against the other man's shoulders, creating a gap between them as he started to shake his head, "Your apartment was destroyed," he said as he tried to catch a breath he didn't need.

The fake August chuckled low in his throat, "What on Earth are you talking about, Ollie?" He waved a hand around the room, "Everything's fine." His expression softened by a fraction, "It's okay to be nervous."

"I'm not nervous," Ollie countered, "And you aren't my August."

Ollie asserted more pressure as he tried to free his legs, forcing the man back further with his next shove, "I've replayed that kiss with August a hundred times over. I know exactly how it ended."

The Android let out a yelp of surprise as August pressed him down again, both hands taking a hold of his wrists and forcing them back over his head. The man leaned in close, his hot breath washing over him again. This time, though, it didn't make him shiver.

"A pity," he snarled, the inflection in his tone changing as the voice became distinctly not August. His face twisted upwards in a smile that had never once appeared on the redhead's face in all the time that Ollie had known him, "I thought I could have had a little fun with you before you realised. I don't usually go for guys, but you just squirm so nicely, it's hard to resist."

Ollie thrashed against his hold on him, bucking his hips in an attempt to throw him off. The stranger pressed back against him, forcing the smaller man down with more of his weight.

The feeling of the man's erection made Ollie's stomach turn, "The real August couldn't hold me down like this; what makes you think that you can?"

The imposter's eyes glowed with an unnatural red light. A Chrome light.

"Easy now, 01113, no need for threats. You and I are just talking here."

"Take off his face," Ollie spat, wrenching his hands free and shoving at the other man's face and arms desperately, clawing at any inch of available skin with blunted nails, "August is a better man that you will ever be!"

"So very loyal!" the stranger chuckled, taking hold of the Android and reaching behind his throat for the latch he knew would be there. He flicked it open with a nail and Ollie froze, his eyes widening in fear, "I wonder how a man like Augustus

Jackson incited such passion in a man without a heart. Perhaps I should open you up again and find out."

The illusion fell away, the familiar red hair of his companion replaced with the pale skin and bright eyes of Russell East. He was still wearing an approximation of August's clothes, the warm jeans and jumper out of place with the Diabhal's face. Ollie summoned his artificial saliva into his mouth and spit it back at him like a viper. He bared his teeth, willing every little bit of his disgust to show on his face, "I'm not afraid of you."

The Diabhal brought one hand to wipe the mess from his face and Ollie seized his chance, lurching forward and bringing the metal of his forehead against the human's temple. As the Diabhal howled in pain, the Android slid free, falling off the sofa and skuttling along the ground, trying to get as much distance as he could. He felt a hand touch his shoulder and spun around in alarm, his mouth falling open as he recognised the face of the other human standing over him.

With eyes the colour of springtime and hair as dark a black as the night itself, it was a face Ollie had only ever seen in dreams, reflected in puddles of rain that had now long dried up. He reached for the hand that was offered, allowing them to pull him to his feet.

All at once, everything fell into place and Ollie knew exactly who it was that was standing in front of him.

And that Seymour was a friend.

Chapter 37
Firewall

August's relationship with God had always been somewhat complicated.
It was near impossible to reconcile the images of God's glorious mercy when you were frequently being tied down to a chair and subjected to humiliation after humiliation by the hands of the very people who represented him on earth. The priests were great at calling for confessions, the nuns top-notch at offering guidance towards forgiveness and eternal love. That didn't mean that every time he closed his eyes to pray, he wasn't exactly greeted by an almighty and loving immortal Father. That he was instead met with the sour green eyes of his local priest who swore up and down that the devil lived inside him. That liking another man the way that he did was a carnal sin, and that the only two options he had left in this world was repentance or suffering.
Neither of those were August's cup of proverbial tea.
The flashing of grotesque pornographic images, gore, and pain hadn't cured him. There was nothing to cure. All it had done was seal that part of him away for longer than he ever cared to admit. Until meeting someone so wonderful, so unlike anyone else in the entire world, that his walls had completely collapsed around him.
He wondered if Ollie believed in a God, or any sort of higher power at all for that matter. He didn't even know if the other man had ever had the chance to stop and ask the question. Was he lying somewhere, afraid for his life, and praying for some kind of hope? Or was he reaching back for him in the darkness, the way that he was towards him, with thoughts and wishes beyond any mortal magic they had at their disposal?
He sighed against the car's window, his breath creating a white fog on the glass. Tiny flecks of dirt and ash coated the outer surface, making everything beyond it appear like a strange, blurry dream sequence.
"We won't be much longer," Goose said from next to him, "Ollie is going to be alright."
"Such confidence is truly inspiring," Sondheim added with a sneer, "I'm sure wishful thinking is all we need to rely on right now."

"Did your engineer shit in your gears or were you this sort of person when you were human as well?" August grunted back at him.

The Hornet fell silent at that. He rested back against the seat with a snort, picking at some invisible dirt on the trousers of his uniform, "I don't remember the person that I was before all this. I have never experienced Soul Bleeds as some other Androids have."

August rolled down the passenger's side window to let some much-needed air into the vehicle. With it, he could hear the rumble of cars overhead, the thud of tyres over potholes. Familiar melodies of a city he knew all too well.

"Maybe that's your problem then," the redheaded human remarked, "You've forgotten what it's like to be a person. To care about others. Rely on them."

"If you are about to lecture me on the moralities of man and the living machine, you can save it," Sondheim scowled, "I have no interest in anything you have to say. The only reason I am here is our agreement. You and I are not allies."

August could feel the caress of the cold air against the drying sweat on the back of his neck. The faux fur of his coat's hood brushed against his skin in the thin breeze. His back and legs ached from having been sitting so long and he shuffled in place with a pained groan.

"You're really going to return to your duties after all this?" he questioned, his tone gruff with disbelief, "Pretend everything around you isn't happening?"

The Hornet turned his bright eyes towards the window, watching the passing view of the underground passage that he could see beyond, "I was built for one purpose and one purpose alone. What happens outside of that is not my concern."

Ahead of them in the endless streak of black, the road rose and fell alongside the iron chainlink fence that kept them away from the rest of the ruins. Several openings above them spread light across the infinite darkness in patches like shining dawn light from a heavenly messenger. Goose's eyes moved towards it, and she tilted her head to one side thoughtfully, in a way he had often seen Ollie do. She hummed to herself quietly, "It's strangely beautiful. Isn't it?"

"Sentimentality," Sondheim muttered under his breath.

"Maybe," Goose conceded without turning, "But that does not change the fact that it is."

The echoing blare of car horns flared back at them from the metres ahead as another entrance to the surface appeared somewhere before them. In response, their driver rolled down her window and waved the other cars past her, slowly pulling into one of the laybys in at the side of the road.

"Looks like this is our stop," she said as she rolled the window up again with the push of a button, "We'll travel up the emergency hatch. Integrate ourselves with the crowd."

"Alright, lets go," August said, pulling the door open as soon as his seat belt was unbuckled.

Sondheim followed him out, scanning the high walls of the underground over their heads, "So eager to rush to your death?"

"I don't plan on losing any more people here today," August growled back at him, fighting to keep his hackles from rising at the man's near-constant barrage of jabs, "You, me, or anyone else."

The Hornet followed behind them as they made their way in off the side of the road. August could feel his eyes, and the eyes of the other strangers driving past, keenly on the back of his neck. Goose approached a metal grating concealed against the curve of the tunnel and held her hand up towards the ID scanner. It buzzed as it observed her details and then made a pneumatic hiss to signal that the entranceway had been unlocked. She pulled it open with one hand, exposing the yellow painted ladder than ran from their level all the way up to the surface. She narrowed her eyes at it, drawing a finger over the closest rung, "It hasn't been attended to in quite some time," she commented, "I hope that it will take our weight."

She brought her foot up to hip height, sliding it into place and pushing herself upwards without a sound. She paused, rocking back on her heels a few times, "We're clear. Looks like it'll hold."

"Lucky us," Sondheim mumbled, following her in next. His movements, like those of the other Android, were sure and steady, as accurate and patient as a computer programme.

August tried to disguise the fact that his own legs were shaking but the telltale tremors in the ladder they were climbing couldn't have come from anywhere else. As Goose pushed aside the opening above them, the wail of not-too-distant sirens filled the space around them. There was a dull sound of a bass drum throbbing in the back of a pickup truck that roared past the opening in the alleyway. On it were several protestors shouting and brandishing dirty bedsheets which they held up to catch the vehicle's air.

August pulled himself up the final steps of the ladder and out into the smoggy air, choking against the crook of his elbow, "Something's on fire."

"More than just one something, I'd imagine," Goose stated as she moved towards the edge of the alleyway. She peered out at the gathering of protestors assembled in front of the Crossroads' building. There were hundreds of people stacked together in the tight space, August's usual walk to work concealed almost completely by their mass.

The red-haired man blinked back tears as he faced the wriggling haze, burning rubbish lining the points around them where members of law enforcement were attempting to push the shouting collective backwards.

"Fuckin' Hell, look at this place," he mumbled, words muffled by his jacket, "This is beyond what I was expecting."

"The two camps have been fighting since the announcement of the *Refurbishment Centres* two nights ago," Goose stated, her tone as cool as it usually was. The flicker of light in her eyes was the only sign of her internal anger, "Some of these people are on our side. But it's almost impossible to say for sure if any of them will help us get into the building."

"That's grand, I wasn't expecting to find any help here," August replied, fighting back the overwhelming urge to clear out his throat, "That's why we brought this guy along, after all."

Sondheim straightened from where he was examining a line of red graffiti across the opposite wall. There was a confusing array of emotions currently warring on his features. With a curt sniff, he wilfully pushed them down again.

The word on the wall was *cónaigh*. The old Celtic term for being alive.

"If you want to get inside, we're going to have to find another way in. That front door will be next to impossible to bypass, even for staff," he said.

A high-pitched whistle drew their combined attentions upwards as something like a firework lit up the starless night sky for an instant. Twinkling lights fluttered down along the curve of the glass dome that covered the entire city. Beneath it, the crowds grew restless. The Gardi that stood in a long, armoured line in front of the door were barking orders. The pot's lid was jumping, threatening to boil over at any moment.

"I'm open to ideas," August said, glancing back at the tall, dark-haired Android behind him.

Posed like a panther on the prowl, the Hornet stalked towards the other end of the alleyway, taking a hold of the chainlink fence there and rattling it, "The barricades line the outer perimeter of the building. They're designed to hold back crowds, but another surge will push it all over." He looked back over one shoulder at them, "We will have the opportunity to enter through the side doors then, when the Gardi are distracted."

Sondheim's bright collar winked back at him through the darkness. The word 'ANDROID' was emblazoned on the front in red characters. It lit up the Android's face from below with a devilish light.

August arched a dark eyebrow back at him, "Side door?"

"It's one level up," the Hornet answered, "We use it for military operations. It allows the Androids to come and go with minimal contact with humans."

"He's telling the truth," Goose supplied, eyes ignited with their own purplish light, "We have records of such an entrance back at the station."

"Alright." August waved a hand towards him, "Lead the way then."

Sondheim acknowledged the request with a nod and quickly broke through the other barricade, allowing the chains and locks to rattle down towards his shoes. He made a quick turn at the next corner, silently pointing to the roof of an adjacent warehouse. August glanced back towards Goose who nodded encouragingly. The pair followed the pattern of the Hornet's stripes up through the quivering metal rafters and August tried his very best not to look down. It wasn't that high up, he had been higher in recent weeks, but it still sent his blood pressure spiking. Beneath them, the flashes of collars were visible within the crowds. The humans around them were roaring to life in defence of their metal companions, their numbers ever increasing from the wings. Handmade signs crafted with cardboard and ink bobbed in the sea of movement, the chaotic clashing of sounds too disjointed to make anything out of their demands.

"Those people down there are fighting for you too, you know," August said quietly, his hair being pulled to-and-fro by the strength of the wind up this high. He turned his dark eyes to the Hornet's back, "Does seeing this really do nothing to you?"

Sondheim didn't even bother turning to reply, his voice dispassionate, "Should it?"

A police convoy raced by in the street somewhere below them, their lights disorientating them for a moment and making August almost stumble. His heart leapt into his throat for a moment.

"They…they're willing to die…just to prove you're alive," he panted, grabbing a firm hold of the metal railing that lined the gap between the two buildings. It was clearly used by the humans who came to complete repairs rather than the Androids that frequented it. Sondheim was perfectly poised in front of him, not put off by the height at all.

"You know that I have a Soul Chip, Mr. Jackson," the man said, his voice almost being completely carried off by the wind now, "It's the battery that powers my entire being. But who I am, who I *was*…none of that matters anymore." He planted his hand on the ID scanner, watching as his Android ID appeared and triggered the door to open wide for them, "If I really am alive, if these rumours are all true, then I killed all of those people by choice. *I* did that. And that wouldn't make me a human. It would make me a monster."

Chapter 38
Bug Report

Seymour seized Ollie's hand with a surge of desperate energy, "We have to go!" The door to the apartment opened before they had even reached it, spitting the pair of them out into another long, blank expanse of white. A thrill of panic raced up Ollie's spine as his feet appeared to hover in the air. There was nothing around to ground them, to even suggest which way was up. His head was spinning as he tried to orientate himself.

Seymour tugged him along after him, hopping through the air as if he were on a physical surface. Flickers of light sprang from the points of contact, rushing outwards and building the world slowly around them as they ran.

Ollie immediately recognised the city streets of New Dublin, the hazy brickwork and worn-out crossings reminiscent of the day he had first met August. Music came at them from all sides. A jackhammer bounced against old tarmac in the distance. The smell of street food and coffee was carried on the breeze. If he closed his eyes, Ollie could imagine that he was really back there again.

They passed the river, crossing the bridge as the invasive smell of leaking sewage assaulted their nostrils. Ahead of them, like a great behemoth of marble and glass on the horizon, lay the Crossroads main building where August had worked.

Seymour swung them to the left and Ollie stumbled as he reorientated himself on the other man's path. The streets were unfolding all around them now, bricks flying through the air like birds as they reconfigured their surroundings with every quick change of direction.

From the top of one of the buildings, a large black speaker grew out of the side like a flourishing weed. It swivelled to follow them as the Diabhal's voice gave chase between the side streets, "You can play these games all you want to, 01113. But I can break you just as easily as I built you."

Static began to form on every passing window, the sight of curtains and wooden brackets replaced by something like a television screen. The pixels roared to life like an old gramophone finding its place on a vinyl, slowly and then all at once. August's familiar face appeared on the houses on both sides of them, the screens replaying memories of Ollie's experiences with the man. He saw their first meeting, when curious brown eyes had met his in the dark of the underground. He heard August's laugh as Ollie teased him about his style of outdated dancing as he moved around in the kitchen. He witnessed the times they had shared quiet meals at home together, when they had been caught in the pouring rain with their shopping packed in cheap paper bags and had to hurry to bring everything inside before the vegetables escaped into the gutter. Overhead, he saw himself kissing August and something in his chest fluttered as he recalled the sensation of the man's warm hands resting on his hips, holding him like he might just float away if he didn't.

As Seymour guided him forwards, the details on the televisions became blurred and distorted, like a carousel spinning far too quickly in the dark. Seymour glanced one way and then the other frantically, searching for a way through the chaos and noise as his breath came out in shallow bursts.

He slowed to a stop, doubling over to catch his breath against his bent knees, "This…isn't right," he panted, "How is he doing this? He shouldn't have this much control in here."

Ollie jumped at the haptic feedback from below them, his mouth falling open as a video started to play across the floor that he didn't recognise. He moved a few steps backwards, beckoning Seymour to stand next to him, "It's so dark I can hardly make it out."

Seymour frowned, "I know exactly what this is."

The colours on the screen were muted, dull as a black and white home movie, but even without the addition of this element, Ollie was easily able to make out the human's familiar form as it appeared from the alley's end.

"Is that…August?" he questioned, tilting his head to take in the scene.

The redhead was being illuminated from above by a soft green pharmacy sign that turned his hair to a muddy brown. He was walking towards the camera, following the sound of a weak cough. His moments were slow and careful, like he was trying to coax a frightened animal somewhere out of sight.

"Hey," he said softly, his voice gentle and warm with noticeable concern, "Are you alright in there? I saw you from the road."

The camera shifted as if following the motion of someone's head lifting, "Y-yeah," came the response in Seymour's voice, "I'm okay."

Ollie peered over at the man standing next to him, his green eyes stuck fast to the screen. He had brought one of his hoodie's sleeves up to his mouth and was chewing on a hole that he had made there, like a child taking comfort in an old blanket.

"Helluva night to be sleeping rough," August commented, crouching down in front of the person on screen but being careful to keep his distance, "It's supposed to sink below 2 degrees tonight. Have you got somewhere you can go? A friend or family member who can take you in, maybe?"

The Seymour of the past shook his head, the motion rattling the world from his perspective on screen. August responded with a sigh and a look that made something in Ollie's chest ache. He had seen that look before.

August moved onto his knees in the dirt, the dampness clinging to the fabric of his jeans as he wrestled out of his large, black, winter coat. He shuffled forward to wrap it around the other man's much smaller frame, "Can't have you freezing to death out here," he said by way of an explanation. He reached behind him, likely into the larger back pockets of his jeans, and pulled out a long, brown paper bag. He pressed it into Seymour's hands encouragingly, "This should still be plenty warm. Get it into ya."

Ollie could see Seymour's hands shaking as he accepted the gift, peeling back the top of it to reveal the steaming hot pastie inside. It was enough to make the man's mouth water and tears flood to his eyes in gratitude as he took the first bite. He moaned quietly, trying to contain the bout of hiccups that was threatening to make him choke on the offering.

"Listen," August carried on, shivering slightly as the freezing wind infiltrated his own, thinner jumper around the neck and shoulders, "There's a place over on Bow Street. They have showers, a couple'a beds and sofas. It's not perfect but at least it's warm."

The much younger Seymour devoured the flaky pastry in his hands like a wild animal, swallowing pieces of the paper packaging and chunks of too-hot meat that scorched his throat on the way down. It was clearly the first food that he had had for a while.

Overwhelming combinations of emotions emanated from the screen and echoed within Ollie's own body. The pain, the relief, the gratitude. All things that he had felt towards August at one point or another. Amongst it all, almost completely hidden from sight, was a flicker of something else, something much stronger.

Ollie recognised that feeling. He had felt the very same thing when he had pulled himself out of the water and onto the filthy riverbanks. It was the reason he trusted August in the first place.

Affection.

He felt the barest touch on his shoulder and turned his head towards Seymour, watching the various emotions playing across the other man's face. He let out a sigh that was shaky around the edges, "An hour later I was running through the Furry Glen with my friends. Watching as the Hornets gunned us down one by one." He chewed on the inside of his lip, "…None of us ever made it to Bow Street."

The memory played beneath their feet again as if it were on a loop. Seymour tried his best to swallow down the unhelpful emotions that it brought up, "He gave me his number on a card, told me to call him when I got somewhere safe. I really wanted to call him. It was the first time in so long that someone had just treated me like…"

"Like a person," Ollie finished for him, meeting his eyes.

Seymour nodded wordlessly.

A puzzle piece that fit perfectly into place. Ollie felt like he suddenly understood Seymour better. Understood *himself* better.

Maybe the two of them weren't so different at all.

The Android jumped as glass exploded out from under them. Shards rained down from overhead as well, white noise billowing from the broken screens like a death rattle. The angle of the room changed abruptly and the pair of them stumbled as they tried to keep themselves upright. The texture of the bricks on the nearby walls changed to something much softer, grains of sand pouring down from the places they had previously occupied like blood from a wound.

Seymour cried out as his right leg was suddenly pulled through the surface of the floor, dragging him under like the swelling of quicksand or cement. The platform they were on was rising from its previous station, leaving the poor man dangling in midair as he clung desperately to anything he could. Ollie raced for him, snatching up both his hands and pulling with teeth clamped firmly together. The artificial skyline raced past them as they suddenly spun, Ollie pulling Seymour after him as he tumbled upwards into a sky without gravity.

His back hit off another platform and he yelled in pain, blinking back the stars that were spinning around his head. Somehow both above and below him, a person was slowly walking across the platform towards his prone body.

He sat up, looking around him for evidence of his companion before his eyes fell on the face of a devil instead. The man's expression made the coolant run cold in his artificial veins.

"Are you done running now, little robot?"

His smile was all teeth. Ollie longed to smash them.

He loomed over him like a statue in a town centre, larger than life. Legendary in his feats and intelligence. A man whose face had appeared on countless magazine covers, his shelves lined with accolades and accomplishments that the Android couldn't possibly fathom.

"I'll never stop running," Ollie shouted back at him breathlessly, "No matter how long you chase me."

Russell East let out a breathy approximation of a laugh as he knelt down in front of him, "Said the little rabbit to the clever hunter." He used one hand to grasp the bottom of Ollie's trousers, sliding him closer across the ruined platform, "You forget where you are. Everything you are, everything you ever were, belongs to *me*. And I will use you as I see fit." His other hand found the Android's bare neck and bore down on it as he pulled his squirming body under him, "Whether you are functioning or not remains to be seen."

Ollie clawed at him frantically, steam starting to billow from his ears, nose and mouth as he tried to put his feet down flat for leverage. The Diabhal brought himself up higher, holding tightly to his throat as his Chrome hand worked to open the buttons of his shirt. His fingertips brushed over the centre point of the dark-haired Android's chest, revealing to him a complex series of inner circuits. Concealed within the tubing and suspended in diamond, was his Soul Chip. Alongside it, two more chips were hidden in the dark.

Ollie's efforts to escape slowed as he overheated, the air unable to make its way up his throat to be expelled. His bright eyes rolled back in his head as his body twisted and seized. Russell's fingers dug into the artificial skin on his chest and pulled it back, the coolant surrounding the valuable pieces of technology gushing out and running along the curves of Ollie's ribs. Ollie choked, sputtering as he tried to form words. Tears dribbled down from the corners of his eyes to form clear streaks on his face.

He had always wondered what dying must have felt like for Seymour. Now he was going to experience it all for himself firsthand.

Emergency shutdown initiated.
Venting protocols activated- opening pores
Risk of bodily harm exceeded: Avoid human contact

//August…I want…I want to see him again.

Numbness travelled up his nerves like novocaine. His motor skills were failing him. "So, this is where you were hiding them" Russell's smile was venomous as he buried his hands inside the Android's chest cavity, "Right next to your own heart. How *poetic*."

"Stop! I won't let you hurt Ollie!"

The Diabhal's eyes widened in the instant before he turned his head to look over his shoulder. Seymour's entire body connected with the man's side and sent him flying off the edge of the platform, the CEO reaching out to grab the next rising piece of the crumbling floor with a snarl. His hands were dyed black with Ollie's blood. Seymour knew first hand that it wasn't the first time blood had stained the man.

"Who the Hell *are* you?" the Diabhal demanded.

"The sad thing is, East, you wouldn't even remember me if I told you," Seymour answered, "You did this to so many of us. What's one more name on a list of your *Lesser Dead*?"

Clarity burned in the Chrome man's eyes, "A second construct within the same Soul Chip? How is that possible? You should have been wiped out already, overwritten by the Android's memories."

"Guess your little scientists aren't as smart as you say they are," the black-haired human rebuked, "Seems to me you don't live up to all the hype, *Diabhal*."

He crouched over the injured Android and placed his hands over the large gap in his chest, "Ollie, Ollie can you hear me?"

Ollie's whole body jerked towards his palm, and he gasped as light suddenly returned to his eyes. He scrambled up to sitting, patting down the place where his Soul Chip was housed. The space was exactly as it was meant to be, the damage gone in an instant, "How did you-?"

"I told you, Ollie. This is *our* world. We can do anything here…" He helped his companion get to his unsteady feet again, "Including kicking out unwelcome guests."

"You think that you're stronger than me in here?" the Diabhal shouted back at them as he rose, using a hand to bring his platform to join their own, "I *own* you, 01113."

"That's where you're wrong, Russell," Ollie said, hot clouds of steam forming on his every word as he cleared the space towards him in three, large steps, "You may have built my frame, but the soul inside me is all Seymour."

From out of the ground, long metal hands began to grow like flowers, the fingers grasping at nothing as they were summoned by Ollie's glowing eyes. A smile spread across his lips as the conjured limbs seized the invader and secured him in place. With his own hand, he took a hold of the back of the man's head and forced him to look down. On the back of his neck, just as there was in real life, was a small, square port.

He used his nails to peel open the hatch, scraping the edges of his skin as he fished inside for the cable that he knew he would find there. He squeezed it tightly between two fingers as he leaned his lips in close to the bald man's ear, "Now *you're* the one who's going to run from *me*," he said, and he ripped the wire free. The Diabhal's body vanished from sight.

Chapter 39
Critical Process Died

The former employee was surprised to see his own reflection staring back at him from the glass above the Crossroads' lobby. The space seemed so different without its usual glaring white lights and the sound of Bob's television blaring in the background. Devoid of life and colour as it was, the room was almost completely unrecognisable below them. Blinds were pulled down over the entirety of the front windows, blocking the three of them from view.

Sondheim guided them along the raised, metal walkway in near silence, his footsteps precise and careful with his coded training. He was so unlike Ollie in the way that he moved, just as streamline, but slick, predatory. Where Ollie won people over with his smiling face and his charm, Sondheim broke them apart by force. It wasn't hard to imagine this Android chasing down the enemies of this tower of glass and stone. He had experienced it firsthand not too long ago and it wouldn't be much longer before his attentions were back on him and Ollie once again.

Sondheim craned his head to observe the upper floors, his eyes glowing as he peered through the layers of plaster and concrete like they were glass. He hummed, motioning for them to follow.

August studied the flakes of rust on the yellow walkway, the way they broke apart and tumbled down towards the floor below them like the seeds of sycamore trees. Spinning, spinning, spinning.

"I take it that you have a plan for finding Ollie in all this?" he questioned.

"I have no doubt that your little *pet* was taken to the upper floors," Sondheim responded without turning, "We will have direct access through the elevators ahead."

August ignored the remark. No doubt the Android was just trying to get a rise out of him.

"How can you be so sure?"

When he turned to face him, Sondheim's eyes were the colour of ice, blue and bright the way Ollie's typically were, "I am currently connected to every camera in the building. I watched the Diabhal leaving his office mere moments ago. That is likely where he's keeping 01113."

"It would make sense for him to keep Ollie close," Goose agreed quietly beside him, "The information stored on his Soul Chips are of vital importance. He wouldn't want other employees to gain access to them."

"They're moving the other Hornets towards the lobby," Sondheim continued, head tilted as he reviewed the most recent message he had received, "Seems they believe those protestors out there cause a significant threat."

August slowed to a stop, looking back the way they had come, "You don't think they've been ordered to attack them, do you?"

"I've certainly received no such orders," Sondheim replied coolly, "I doubt the Diabhal would be so hasty in his actions. Those crowds offer the perfect cover for his true motives. The longer he can hold them there the better."

The walkway ended in a wider corridor, three elevators standing in a row. Each one only appeared to go to a single stop.

"The middle one will take us where we need to go," Sondheim said as the doors opened for their approach, "Don't dawdle."

When the heavy, metal doors slid closed behind them, the emergency lights overhead flickered on to disperse some of the darkness. August took a long, slow breath in to steady his nerves. He turned his attention towards the officer next to him, watching as she studied the tiny space around them with probing eyes.

"Hard to lose that old habit, huh?" he teased with a flicker of a smile.

Her eyes widened almost imperceptibly at being caught out. She offered him a soft smile, "It was what I was built for, Mr. Jackson. Being a Gardi Officer is my purpose in this world."

"Does that mean you miss it?" he asked her.

Her smile fell away, "Terribly. Once this is all over, I hope that I will be reinstated again."

Sondheim snorted, "There *is* no future for us, Officer 60053. This can only end in one way."

August narrowed his eyes at him, "Do you really believe all that crap you spout?"

The doors before them opened without fanfare. There was no need for a signalling bell when only Androids ever rode up in it, after all.

"This is a business transaction, Mr Jackson," he snarled as he passed him, heading out into the dark corridor beyond, "I don't know why you would waste both of our time with personal questions."

The emergency lighting was triggered with their movements, sending sparkles of white and blue over the thin, grey carpet. There were no pictures on the walls here, no accolades or seascapes, only one dark, ominous line towards a single, locked door.

"I guess you could say I'm just stubborn," August commented, "There isn't even a tiny part of me that believes you when you talk like that."

Sondheim lined up his hand with the flat surface of the scanner and the doors opened to reveal a plush office space beyond. The Android hesitated in the doorway, his shoulders tight and posture tense, "It is not often I have been in this room," he stated, "But in the times that I have been here I have seen things that are not for those of a vulnerable nature." He slowly turned, blocking their advance with his broad shape, "I offer this information to you purely as a courtesy. You may not like the state that you find your companion in."

The man's words, and the cold manner of his delivery, sent a shiver up August's spine. He forced it down in an instant, refusing to acknowledge the elephant in the room, "Ollie is going to be fine."

Goose placed a hand on August's shoulder, gently manoeuvring him back behind her, "We will go in first."

His dark eyebrows dipped, "What are you-"

She stopped him with a look, "This is a kindness, August," she said firmly.

He searched her face for a moment before he sighed and took another step back, waving a hand towards the door, "Go ahead then."

The Diabhal's office was red and large and decadent, the furniture plush but unused. It was also tossed around like a tornado had blown through recently, everything but the desk in the room's centre in disarray.

August looked down with a start as he noticed the sound of glass crackling under his shoes, "The Hell happened in here?"

The Hornet's eyes continued glowing as he ran his hands over the glass surface of the man's work desk, "The Diabhal is prone to bouts of irrational anger when he does not get his way."

August's brow furrowed as he stepped further inside, studying the damage, "This happens a lot then?"

"More than most would expect."

Goose was walking along the far Western wall, her fingertips tracking lines across the gaudy wallpaper, "There is a huge amount of power being syphoned through this room," she remarked, "My readings are all over the place."

"It's a vampire line," August realised, hurriedly crossing the room to come to her side. He places his hands on the wall before her, testing the temperature with his palms, "The energy is going into something on the other side."

"Then you've encountered this technology before?" Goose questioned, the ends of her dyed red hair brushing the nape of her neck as she cocked her head.

"We designed it," the red-haired man answered, bringing his fist down to knock against the wall. The sound was tinny and hollow. He moved to the right, tapping and following the sound, "The easiest way to find the access point is through sound. It's made of wood, when the rest of it is housed in metal." The sound of his knocking suddenly changed, and a triumphant smile lit up his face, "Bingo! Now we just have to…"

Goose stepped back as part of the wall suddenly opened from her touch, the Android's eyes sparkling with something like excitement, "A hidden doorway."

August followed the inlay of the panel, pressing on the part of it that was concaved. A square of wallpaper pulled upwards to reveal a crawlspace beneath it, the vinyl flooring beyond a cheap contrast to the exotic carpet in the otherwise upscale office. The human crouched down low to peer inside and was immediately met with a powerful smell that sent him reeling backwards. He slapped a hand over his mouth and nose, trying to suppress the urge to vomit.

"What the Hell *is* that?"

It was so strong he could taste it, the metallic pong of it sweet on the air like days old blood in his mouth. He choked back a cough, concealing his mouth in the corner of his winter jacket, "We need to go in there."

Goose frowned as she looked into the concealed room, "There's someone in there," she whispered.

Without another moment of hesitation, August was on his belly and pulling himself across the floor and into the cut-out section of wall. The ceiling opened up above him and he reached out a hand to feel for a wall as he unfurled to standing height again. Feeling a switch beneath his fingers, he pressed down and blinked back tears as an overhead lamp groaned to life against its will.

This room, like the one preceding it, was lined with broken furniture and bits of shattered glass. Several desks and chairs had been stacked in the corners, as if this place had once been a classroom for children. Marks had been cut into some of the wood, but the details were obscured by the range of the light. Beneath his feet and ignited by the orange-tinted glow of the lamp, a sticky, viscous substance was sticking to the soles of August's shoes.

He listened as he heard the two Androids entering the room behind him, Goose's quiet mutterings being what made him turn in the end. On the other side of her small frame was a chair, an old-fashioned thing that August had likely used similar to back in his own school days. It was only when he came closer, stopping at Goose's side, that he discovered that the chair was occupied.

At first, his mind reeled wildly with the new information. The details of the person's face, the damage to their body. He couldn't take it in, couldn't hold it in his mind. He realised that he had stopped breathing when his lungs started to burn and protest. He stared and waited for the penny to drop.

And, as Goose reached out to take his hand in a comforting grasp, it did.

His clumsy tongue stumbled over words as he launched himself towards the bound man. He was barely audible, the words little more than animalistic noises that were half-trapped in his own throat. He couldn't formulate a single clear thought anymore. His knees hit the ground hard enough to hurt but he didn't feel a thing. Fingers traced the outline of the Android's broken body before him. The black coolant, which had formed a large puddle around the legs of the chair, clung to the fabric of his trousers, soaking through. It was like ice on his skin.

If he been able to tear his eyes away from the man, to have looked down into that puddle beneath him, he might have seen the red specks of blood amongst the silver medical instruments. The signs of a struggle.

But August couldn't take his eyes off the dark, chrome shell before him. He tilted the man's face up towards the light, his other hand pushing the familiar dark curls back from his face as he searched for any signs of life.

"Fuck," he whispered, voice low and rough in his throat, "Jesus, fuck, Ollie…"

Both hands surrounded the other man's cheeks, his thumbs detailing the last of the artificial skin there. The freckles he had come to adore so much.

"He's still warm," Goose observed from over his left shoulder, her hands resting on Ollie's one, remaining arm, "We may still have time to reactivate him."

His manic expression startled the woman when he turned to face her. His eyes were red and bloodshot, his mouth quivering. Black blood clung to his facial hair, dying it dark in the half-light, "Tell me what to do."

"Let me in," she instructed, moving him slightly over to the right to crouch in his place, "Sondheim, I will require you as well."

August peered across at the Hornet, the Android's face hidden in shadow. He was standing at the very edge of the room, his arms wrapped firmly around his chest. He wasn't moving, his eyes glued to the scene before him.

"Sondheim," August repeated his name in a low, deep rumble.

The Android straightened and began to move, "What do you require?"

"Put your hands on the back of his neck, into the circuit box if you can," Goose explained, "I'm going to need a jolt. I'll tell you when."

August reached out to take Ollie's hand in his, squeezing it gently, "I need you to wake up, *duine.*"

"Ollie," Goose whispered, her hands cupping Ollie's face as she leaned closer. Her limbs practically vibrated with new energy as she pulled out her own connector and slotted it into the space between Sondheim's fingers, "Ollie, if you can hear me, I need you to join the connection. Let us help you."

Light pulsed along the wire from the back of her neck, flickering down into the other Android like the tail of a firefly. For several minutes, the pulsing light remained the same, the rhythm constant and consistent as a ringing telephone. Then, suddenly, the light began to intensify, the colour changing from yellow, to orange, to blue.

The hand under August's twitched and the fingers slowly began to close over his own. He started to hear a distinct whirring sound from deep inside the Android's freckled chest.

A voice, so like Ollie's but not exactly, spoke up from inside that vibrating cavity. The words a lifeline that all three of them reached for.

"Now rebooting."

Chapter 40
Binary

Ollie could see the little, pulsing light right at the edge of his consciousness, like seeing something bright and unknowable just over the next hill. It flickered in the blank, nothingness like a living flame, its light beckoning him closer like a beacon. The sight of it made something within his chest feel warm, almost happy.
If he could remember how to smile, he thought that he would have.
He turned towards it, captivated for a moment as he watched it dance in front of him. It flashed in a pattern of fours, like the chords that formed a hundred different melodies. Several snippets of songs came to mind, but he couldn't remember their source, nor the redheaded man that had sang along with them.
Red. He could remember the colour *red*.
His head ached as he reached back into the depths of his memory banks. There was a face there, out of reach and out of focus. He saw kind, dark eyes and a cloak of messy hair. He recalled a man who grew up with moss pits and loud bass guitars.
The light whizzed around his head in a narrow arc, the motion of it becoming more insistent. The closer he got to it, the more he became aware of a myriad of voices calling out to him from somewhere out of sight.
"Ollie, please *duine*, I need you to wake up…"
Déjà vu. A voice he knew but couldn't quite place.
"Please…please Ollie. I need you…"
The owner of the voice was in pain. The feeling of it resonated within him, making his own chest ache. He felt like he was slowly falling deeper and deeper in a dark expanse of water, the sounds around him becoming muffled by time and distance. Crimson text formed amongst the waves, the letters falling into some sort of order before him. He squinted in confusion, trying to create words out of their ever-moving shapes.
A question appeared before him, one that he repeated aloud.
"Who is that?"
"Someone who knows you. They're trying to pull you out of here."

Ollie's feet hit off a solid surface and he suddenly felt more grounded than before. He gasped as if he were resurfacing, turning to look at the other man with wide eyes.

"Seymour." He said the man's name with sudden clarity. He frowned at him, swiftly remembering where he was, "What's happening to me? My memories-"

"They're being overwritten," Seymour said softly, "By mine."

He stepped into the Android's space, the light from over their heads illuminating his dark features. He offered him a sad, sympathetic smile, "Two souls cannot exist here at once, Ollie."

Ollie met the man's intelligent green eyes, "What does this mean for us?"

"It means you have to go," Seymour said, reaching out to place his hands on his companion's shoulders, "And so do I."

"Go?" Ollie repeated, his brow furrowing, "Go where?"

Seymour shrugged, but there was a hesitation there. A fear, "I don't know," he admitted, "But if we don't go soon there won't be anything left of either of us."

The dark-haired Android turned to look towards the source of the light again. He wanted more than anything to reach out to it, to connect with the people whose words were just a little bit out of reach.

"There has to be a way to preserve your consciousness. To save your memories." He offered the man a determined look, reaching out to touch him as well, "I can't just let you die, Seymour. Not after all this. Not after we finally got to speak to one another."

"I'm already dead, Ollie," Seymour replied softly, casting his bright eyes away. Shadows danced across his face as the light source behind them continued to pulse and glow, "There's nothing left of me but this last little whisper of who I was. Without this Soul Room...I'm nothing but a ghost."

"Don't say that!" Ollie cried as his grip on the man's arms tightened, "You're still here!" The static around them faded to a low, fine mist, the pale shapes hovering around them and concealing the edges of their false world.

"I was lucky that I had the chance to meet you at all, Ollie," Seymour continued, "You and I...we're two impossibilities. Two personalities living in the same soul. We shouldn't even exist like this."

"But we *do*," the Android argued.

"For only a moment," Seymour agreed. Ollie could feel his hands trembling where they touched him, his grip becoming looser as he released him, "And what a great moment it was. Now I know that my body will be in safe hands."

Ollie shook his head as a rush of emotion overtook him. The swelling tide choked him, pining the words he wanted to say in his throat. He tried to swallow past the forming lump, but it wouldn't shift for him. He reached for his throat and was surprised to find that his collar wasn't there anymore. His artificial skin bobbed against his fingertips.

"It hurts…" he wheezed. He felt lines of tears beginning to pour down from his eyes, "I don't want it to hurt anymore."

"The pain is a part of being human," Seymour noted, "It's a side effect of love, after all."

He moved both of his hands inwards, stroking the sides of the Android's neck with his thumbs in a movement that was light as a goodbye. Heat tingled in the spaces where their skin met. Darkness swirled around the points of contact, as if trying to draw them back from one another.

Seymour sniffed, bringing his forehead to rest against the other mans for a moment, "One more thing before I go."

"Anything," Ollie breathed.

"Tell August thank you for me," he said, "It might have taken a while…but he really did save me this time."

"I will," Ollie stuttered, feeling his friend's tears on his own face, "I promise."

The voices behind him were growing clearer as the world gave way to darkness, Seymour's body slowly dissolving into the mist. Particles of him caught in the air and sparkled, blinking out of existence one by one. His touch was like a feather, barely there.

"If there really is an Afterlife after all this…I hope to see you there one day. I want to hear all about our life…"

Ollie pulled what was left of him in close, holding the contact for as long as he could as he whispered in the man's ear, "I won't miss a single detail."

He stumbled forward as his balance suddenly shifted and he blinked towards the infinite darkness. He was all alone in the room now.

The sound of silence stretched out in all directions. The air grew colder, flickering around him like hands pulling him back the way he had come. In the opposite direction, the light was now like a sun, its heat washing over him like a warm bath.

"Thank you," he said. He turned to face the orb, the letters from before forming before his eyes in the air.

Connection Request: 'Gardi Officer 60053'

He reached out to run his fingers along the tangible weight of the words, knowing more than anything that he wanted to live.

Reboot now? his system probed.
His eyes ignited with a renewed heat, "Now rebooting," he said and all around him, the Soul Room collapsed in on it itself and vanished from sight.

Chapter 41
Restore Factory Settings?

CRO_SSROADs BIOS v.123.3.3
BBBBIOS Date : 25/10/2079 21:04:32 Ver 2.1.3
CopyrIGHt © 2059-2080, Crossroads IE, Inc.
ACcCM 899772: 01113 Revision : UnKnOwN
BIO_S Ext_X_nsion : v.2.1.3 Failed
Memory Test : Failed to access Internal Memory
Warning: MMMMissing Components:
'e53-5(a)';
'e0089-547';
'rep-02-0089-547';
'BlaCk Blood' CoOlAnT LeVEls Critically Low. Top Up ReQuIred.
Instructions: Proceed to nearest Crossroads office for repair

Initialising…DoNe
C:\...

Spools recoiled in the Android's chest. Fans whirred to life again. The reboot set his eyes fluttering, the dullness replaced with a sudden, bright spark. His body felt impossibly heavy beneath him as colour flooded into his world again. He blinked hard, running a tongue across his lips to refamiliarize himself with their shape. He flexed each of his remaining fingers before gripping the feeling of warm hands in his. He pushed against their weight.
"Ollie?" August's voice was all around him like a warm blanket.
His bleary eyes focused on the shape of the man leaning over him and attempted a smile. Even that small movement felt painful, "August," he said, his expression flitting between disbelief and suspicion, "Are you…are you real?"
August exhaled a shaky laugh, yanking him into a hug, "Of course I'm real, you dumb robot." He could hear the redhead sniffling against his shoulder, "Christ, it's good to hear your voice again."
The Android's body tensed under him as he returned to his senses, "The Diabhal," he hissed, hands gripping at the other man's back fearfully, "Where is he? He was here, he was-"
August pulled back to look at his face, "He isn't here, Ols," he comforted him, "It's just us."
Ollie sagged back against the chair as he allowed his face to fall to one side. The other two Androids in the room were regarding him with guarded wonder, their bright eyes each showing a different emotion beneath their usual chrome masks.
"He wouldn't let the Androids go," he stated quietly.
Goose regarded him with sad eyes and a heavy sigh, "We know, Ollie. But it was brave of you to try."
Ollie brought his face in against August's shirt, taking in all of that familiar data with a rush of heat. The man's scent, the dampness of his sweat, the coarseness of the hair over the tattoos on his arms. He took it all in hungrily, filling up his every sense with the man, "Seymour says thank you."
August's dark eyebrow raised questioningly, "Seymour?" he repeated, "That was the name Sondheim called you."

Ollie nodded, burying himself deeper in the man's body heat, "He was homeless. You sent him to Bow Street, fed him, gave him your coat. He never got the chance to say thank you."

Realisation dawned on the human's face, "His name was Seymour?" he asked, "And he is...*was*...you?"

"I guess that's why we were drawn to each other," Ollie said, raising his head to catch the man's dark eyes in the orange lamp's light, "You had already saved me once. I knew you would save me again."

August's throat constricted with emotion as he cupped the man's face, "Always."

"As sickeningly sweet as this little reunion is, time is not exactly on our side here," Sondheim sneered at them, clearing his throat pointedly at the display.

"He's badly damaged," Goose observed, as she retracted her own cable from the back of Ollie's neck, "The only way we're going to get him out of here is by carrying him."

"I can do that," August said, grunted as he heaved the Android up from the chair and into his arms. He tried to ignore the way his stomach twisted in knots at the feeling of his lighter frame. He didn't once glance down towards the places where his limbs had once been attached. They didn't exactly have time for him to fall apart right now.

Ollie rested his head against August's chest, listening to the rabbit-fast pounding of the man's living heart. He allowed his eyes to fall closed with a soft sigh, "We need to go after him."

The ropes that had previously secured the Android's wrists tumbled to the floor at August's feet and he kicked them to one side with the toe of his boot. They lay in the centre of the puddle of coolant, slowly soaking up the blackness.

"After who?"

"Russell East," Ollie said that name like it was a swear word, "I sent him running. He's going to try to escape now. We can't let him."

Light passed across Sondheim's eyes as he glanced towards the door. Overhead, a siren began to cry out shrilly, bouncing back at them from all of the too-close walls, "It appears that the protestors have finally broken through the front door."

The alarm sound warped and changed as they hurried into the next room, having to slide Ollie through the blood and coolant as his one hand scrambled to roll his broken form onto the carpet.

"Where are the other Hornets right now?" August questioned, moaning as he straightened and took hold of his injured charge again on the other side, "Are we going to have to worry about them showing up at this door in a minute?"

Sondheim frowned thoughtfully, "There are at least 14 units online, all heading towards the entrance," he stated, "I can hear their inane babbling across the audio channels."

August held onto Ollie's side protectively, "Do I want to know what they're saying?"

Sondheim slowly made his way across the room, kicking some of the broken furniture out of his way, "I believe a human would call them…*excited*."

Goose reached into the back of her coat, pulling out a black, matte-finished handgun. She checked how many bullets were housed inside and clicked off the safety, "They have likely already been authorized to kill us on sight."

"Shit," August hissed, "If we take that elevator back down, we'll be right in the middle of it."

"There is…one other option."

Sondheim was standing with his back to them, his gaze penetrating the far wall, "While it *is* true that there is only one entrance in or out of this room, the Diabhal loves his privacy after all…there is *one* other path you can take." He approached a small, rectangular panel in the wall, pulling up the wooden cover to reveal the metal shaft inside, "This dolly is for delivering food directly from the kitchens. You could use it to reach the next level. The Diabhal won't be expecting you to move this way."

August eyed it uncertainly, "That isn't a while lotta space."

"It isn't," Sondheim agreed, "But it's used to taking significant weight and with your Android's current *lack* of said weight…"

"What about you two?" Ollie asked quietly. His voice was weak and more than a little breathless. Steam was still puffing out from the gaps between his teeth.

Goose and Sondheim exchanged a fleeting glance.

"The two of us are more than capable of exiting on our own," Goose stated levelly.

"Consider this your one-minute head-start," Sondheim added.

The human arched an eyebrow at that, "One minute? I thought we were getting 30 seconds?"

"Apparently, your friend here is not the only one with defects in his software," Sondheim quipped, showing off his rows of perfectly aligned false teeth. He quirked his head towards the freight elevator, "Now go before I lose my good graces and kill you where you stand."

The human hurried past the Hornet to lay Ollie down in the small space. Even with half of his body missing, it was going to be a tight squeeze for the two of them. He hoped it wasn't a long way down. Claustrophia gnawed at the edges of his thoughts. The wounded Android made as much space for him as he could, curling into a tight ball that barely resembled a person. August hesitated as he pulled himself up into the space, bringing his knees in tight against his chest. He was anything but a small man and this...this was going to be close.

"You both have Ollie's contact," he said, dark eyes taking in the view of them both standing there, waiting for them to depart, "I'm going to be waiting for the message saying you guys are in the clear."

Goose nodded, "We won't keep you waiting long."

"Worry about yourself, human," Sondheim growled, "Your body is far softer and more prone to bulletholes than ours."

"I'll assume that's your way of saying *'be safe out there'*," August chuckled. He reached out a few fingers to tug down the panel's covering again, "Well, same to you. See you on the flip side."

The sounds of the siren became muted as the elevator door closed and they started to move downwards. The space was enclosed, too hot and too dark to be comfortable, and August held his breath. Against him, he could feel the tell-tale vibrations of Ollie's circuitry, see the glow of his eyes.

"Still with me?" August asked and he felt the subtle squeeze of Ollie's hand in his.

"A little sluggish but still here," he answered.

"Not much longer," the human vowed to him in the darkness, "I promise we'll be back in Shenanigans with the others in no time."

He could hear Ollie shifting his weight, "Did the others make it back?"

A smile caught at the corner of August's lips, tugging his moustache upwards. *Always thinking about other people,* he thought.

"Yeah," he answered him, "Yeah, they did. All thanks to you." He squeezed his hand back, "Though we're gonna talk about your methods a little more later, and the meaning of *'self-preservation'*."

Ollie's laugh was barely more than a plume of hot air in their shared space, "Okay, August." He brought his head in closer, his dark curls tickling August's chin, "We can talk for as long as you want."

August pressed his nose and mouth against the top of Ollie's head, inhaling the comforting smell of his shampoo. The metallic smell of blood and coolant still clung to his artificial skin, however, refusing to be ignored.

"I'd like that," he replied.

The freight elevator stopped with an abrupt shudder, rocking the pair of them in place. August braced a hand against the wall by Ollie's head, using the other to reach for the door. He pushed it up and squinted into the bright, tiled room on the other side. The kitchen was wide and white walled, metal shelves lining the ends of each of the cooking stations. Each individual area was a blend of stainless steel and white marble speckled with grey or eggshell. The tops of them glistened from their latest round of cleaning, the smell of fake lemon disinfectant still clinging to the air like a fine mist.

August wrinkled his nose as he shuffled free, unfolding his limbs again with a muttered series of swear words, "Do you know which way he was heading? Where Russell would go?"

The Android shook his head, dark curls bouncing off his pale cheekbones, "My body's gone into power saving mode," he said, "I can't even access my HUD right now, let alone my mapping software."

His companion smoothed down his hair with a comforting hand, "It's alright, we'll figure something out," he said, pressing a kiss to the side of his head, "If the Hornets are heading towards the commotion at the front of the building, it makes sense for us to try heading for the back way. Hopefully this will mean he's unprotected wherever it is that he's hiding right now."

The sound of his footsteps on the tiles made him nervous. His whole body felt completely wired, on high-alert to every tiny, insignificant detail around them. In all the years he had worked in Crossroads, he had only ever come down to the canteen a couple of times. The kitchen though? Never even once.

Ahead of them, the under-cupboard lighting slowly came to life with the *tink tink* of definitely-not-eco-friendly bulbs. August froze mid-step, suspended in motion like a deer caught in headlights.

"August, what's wrong?" Ollie asked, reaching up to place a hand flat against the front of his jacket, "Your heart's racing right now."

"It's nothing, *duine*," he answered flippantly, his dark eyes scanning each of the doorways ahead of them, "Think I'm just anxious to be out of here."

Selecting the first of the doors and approaching it slowly, August let out a yell as a shutter slammed down in front of them to block their path, the sliding metal almost taking his hand with it. He jerked backwards, cursing as the impact of it made the floors around his feet vibrate, "The fuck was that?"

Screechy audio from the tinny speaker above made Ollie half bury his head in the other man's chest, clenching his teeth like he was in pain. A readout appeared in the corner of his vision, helpfully informing him of the dangerous decibels it was reaching.

August used his free hand to cover an ear, "Jesus Christ that's loud!"

The laugh that followed was almost robotic in nature, the biological warmth giving away to something much colder, less human, "*There you are*! I've been looking for you, little red fox! Wondering when you'd be starting on your hunt."

The other doors to the kitchen slammed shut and sealed one by one at their backs, their locks clicking like a key in an ancient jail cell. August spun on his heels and pelted himself towards each remaining exit, abruptly changing trajectory each time he found an obstacle blocking their way. His feet skidded on the freshly mopped floors, the bottom of his boots squeaking at the contact. His shoulder bounced off a wall. His hand propelled him off another.

He paused to catch his breath, hissing out beneath the bars of his teeth. He could feel a trickle of sweat making its journey down the prominent vein in his neck.

"Tired already? But we've only just started!" the Diabhal taunted gleefully, his laugh reverberating unnaturally against steel and concrete alike.

The redhead glared at one of the cameras on the roof above them, baring his teeth in a snarl, "Go fuck yourself!"

"*Ohh*!" the Diabhal trilled, clearly delighted at the reaction, "It seems the fox has *fangs* after all! Too bad your little rabbit has lost his lucky feet. They would've come in very handy right about now."

The stumps where Ollie's legs had once been offered him a deep ache, as if reminding him again of the damage he had received. Ollie balled his remaining hand into a fist, "You think you're still in control, but we're coming after you, East! We won't let you hurt anyone else."

"This is *my* house," the voice over their heads yowled, "You think you can just come here and threaten me? Where I am at my most powerful?"

"Big words for a man hiding behind a screen," Ollie called out, turning his head to look around the enclosed space, "If you want us, you know *exactly* where we are. Why don't you come down here? Face us man to man."

"You are not a man." The words were like thunder, the warning before the lightning would strike. The air crackled with the man's fury like an ignition point just waiting on a stray spark to set it off.

"Ollie's more of a man that you will ever be," August rebuked.

"A laughable sentiment. Your bleeding heart is worth very little in the real world, Mr.Jackson. What you people call a genocide, history will see as nothing more than the recalling of a defective product."

The tiles that lined the far wall flipped to their concealed sides at the snapping of the CEO's fingers down the mic. Pieces slotted together like folded paper chains. A round barrel formed in the centre.

August swallowed, *is that…?*

A turret.

A motherfucking machine gun!

If his heart had been racing before, now it was in an all-out sprint. The hairs on the back of his neck rose. Static danced between every droplet of his sweat.

The turret slowly peeled around to face them, winding up with a slow *brr* sound like a roller-coaster heading towards a steep drop. Only one way down.

The smile in the Diabhal's voice was all teeth now, "History, on the other hand, will not even remember your names."

Chapter 42

Automated Reasoning

The mechanisms on the sides of the turret began to spin, a loud roar coming from the points where the gears connected in the solid, midnight shell. August barely had a second to react before he was being thrown to one side. A door opened in the wall next to them and hands grabbed for every piece of clothing that they could, yanking the pair out of harm's way. Splinters erupted from the walls and door behind them, a trail of sharp debris flying through the air as they took cover. Dry wall fell over the corridor like a fine mist.

August landed on one shoulder with a grunt of pain, his body wrapped tightly around Ollie's much smaller form. Standing over him, the shapes of multiple people piled against the door, pushing it tightly closed against the onslaught.

August's eyes travelled upwards from a pair of tattered and grimy trainers to settle on a face that he was beyond surprised to see. Dressed in a royal blue jumper and his usual Crossroads lab coat, it was impossible not to immediately recognise the man by his ball of fluffy hair.

"Geoff?" August scoffed in disbelief, "There's no fuckin' way that's you up there."

"Gus?" the man gasped, recognition lighting up his dark features, "Holy shit! You're actually alive? We were sure the Hornets had put holes in you by now."

"They certainly tried," the redhead replied. He raised a hand towards his companion, "Gimme a hand up, would ya?"

Geoff and another engineer reached for him, helping him to his feet. When Ollie looked up from the man's arms, there were a dozen different eyes on him.

"Is that an Android?" one of the women beside them asked. August recognised her from the breakroom. Sonya something-or-other.

"This is Ollie," August introduced, a little awkwardly, "Ollie, these are some of the people I worked with on Level 3."

"I'd offer to shake your hands but I'm decidedly lacking in them right now," Ollie quipped playfully. Despite the dark bags under his eyes and the blinking *'low battery'* symbol in the corner of his vision, he was trying his best to keep himself upright and alert.

Geoff covered his mouth with the back of one hand to stifle his quiet laughter, "Oh shit, you've spent way too much time around this guy, haven't you? That's just the sort of crappy joke he'd make."

August narrowed his eyes, "You wanna repeat that, *specks*?"

One of the other members of their party, a tall, dark-haired women with glasses leaned over the top of one of the counters, drumming her long nails against the metal thoughtfully, "Now that we have a few more heads to stick together, how's about we try thinking of a way out of here?"

"Have you been here long?" Ollie asked.

The scientist, a woman named Hannah who August had seen talking with Geoff from time to time before all this, shifted her weight from one foot to the other anxiously, "We were working overtime when all this went down, helping Ethan put together a press release to go along with the new patch notes being sent out on Monday." She walked along the side of the bench she was standing at, trailing her fingers along the rubberised mats laid out over the surface of it, "When the protestors broke in, all Hell broke loose. There were sirens going off. Orders from up top told us to hold in place. Then next thing we knew, the Hornets were firing into the crowds. We made a break for it and found ourselves here. That was maybe, what? 40 minutes ago now?"

Geoff ran a hand through his dark hair, mussing it further. His face reflected back at him from one of the clear glass monitors stacked along the far wall, "We have no idea where Ethan and the others ended up. More of those bloody turrets came out of the walls in the breakroom. We all just kind of split and went off in different directions." He shrugged, shaking his head, "Hard to think straight when you're being shot at."

"Why is the Diabhal shooting at his own people?" Ollie questioned with a frown.

"The guy has completely lost it," Geoff exclaimed, throwing up both of his hands.

Hannah stepped out into the light again, running her hand along the points where Ollie's legs had been disconnected at the thigh, "Looks like your flow of coolant was shut off manually to stop you bleeding out," she muttered thoughtfully to herself.

Ollie wrinkled his freckled nose at the memory of it, "The Diabhal's handiwork," he said.

She hummed, seemingly unsurprised by that news, "How are your faculties?"

"I've lost access to my HUD. The last error code I received was *40-22-10*," he answered.

Hannah sucked on her teeth, "That likely means your coolant reserves are too low to regulate your core temperature," she explained. She nodded back towards

Sonya who was by now walking laps of one of the tables to rid herself of her nervous energy, "Hey Sonya, you still have any of those coolant bottles you found earlier?"

Sonya's blonde bob-cut fluttered around her chin as she reached for a satchel at her feet, "Maybe…lemme check." She quietly cheered as her hand wrapped around the glass bottle in the bottom, pulling it free, "You're in luck! Looks like one of them survived!"

Hannah caught the bottle in midair, quickly unscrewing the cap and pulling up the rubber straw concealed inside it. She extended it towards Ollie with a smile, pinching the opening between two fingers, "I'm going to need you to drink as much of this as you can for me," she instructed, "It hasn't been processed so the taste is going to suck a bit, but it should get your HUD back online. Give us an idea of what we're looking at out there."

August supported the bottom of the bottle as Ollie tilted it up with his one good hand. He swallowed a large mouthful and then another, closing his eyes as he drained it. He made a face as he pulled the emptied bottle away again. Thick, sugary blackness coated his tongue. It was an altogether quite unpleasant sensation.

"That is…certainly a flavour," he commented.

"You're probably more used to the home-brand stuff," Hannah replied as she accepted the empty bottle from him again, "My girlfriend, Valentina's the same. I tell her all the time that she's a total coolant snob."

Ollie tried to scrape some of the leftover fluid off on his teeth, "Your girlfriend's an Android?"

"I met her right here in this building," she answered with an affectionate smile, "She develops tech with the R and D department." Her smile slipped away as quickly as it had come, "She probably helped build those turrets out there. She'd be so mad if she knew what they were being used for."

She reached up with both hands to pull her long, dark hair into a ponytail, stripping off her lab coat and hanging it over the back of one of the chairs. Her arms and legs were lined with dark blue and red Chrome tech. Trust a scientist to have the latest gear available.

Her eyes flashed red for a moment as she concentrated on the door they had come through, "I know the blueprints of those things off by heart, but actually hacking in is a whole different story." She reached a hand towards Ollie, "I can share the details

with you, add it to your HUD. That way, I can guide you to getting through the firewall. Your hacking abilities will be much better than mine, after all."
Ollie took hold of her hand, allowing for the exchange of information between them.

Incoming Connection Request: CHROME_ID-hannahStenford

When his glowing blue eyes peered through the wall at the turret outside, a perfect map of its insides were displayed over the top of it. He smirked as he felt power surging through his systems again, "I can work with this."
His brows furrowed as he concentrated on his task. His temperature gauge was slowly lowering back down to normal levels and with it, clarity returned like switching on a light in a dark room. The inner workings of the turret were complicated, that much was true, but he was a complex piece of machinery too.
"I can see the gyroscopic mechanism in the centre," he observed, "Standard issue. If I follow the path of the green wires, it should lead me to..."
The chip for controlling the spring-load was just inside. It was a simple matter for him to deactivate it with a invasive code of his own. He let out a sigh of relief as he watched the metal twist up into its offline position, "That's it."
"Wow, you Androids come in handy," Geoff remarked with a whistle.
Sonya crept over to the door, pressing her face to the tiny opening she made there. Her fingers slipped through and slowly pulled the door across, the sound of wood and glass following the motion of it. Bullet casings lined the ground like black snow, some bent out of shape slightly by their impact with the wall or the metal frame in the centre of the sliding laboratory door.
"How can we be certain he isn't just waiting for us out here?" August asked as they headed out into the empty corridor, retracing their previous steps.
Sonya knelt down to unlock one of the shuttered doors adjacent to them, pulling it up and out of their way to clear a path, "Staying here waiting for answers won't do any of us any good," she said, "The sooner we can get to safety the better."
"And the Diabhal?" August probed.
"We'll regroup and rearm," Geoff said firmly, hurriedly reaching for a light switch to reveal the next leg of their journey, "Then we'll take the fight right to his door."

Chapter 43
Critical Error

Rows of deactivated turrets lined both sides of the walkway, their heads bowed like sleeping daffodils. The silence that descended on their group was eerie, their breaths and footsteps amplified by the frantic ways in which they moved from one open room to the next.

Ollie's eyes glowed as he followed the threads of data through the network, avoiding other employees and Androids as best as he could as he directed their paths. He didn't mention how some of the mainframe was completely in lockdown, ominous red lines drawn across the entire front of the Crossroads building. The lobby in particular appeared to be completely off-limits to him.

"Don't worry, Geoff," Sonya whispered as she walked by the nervous younger man, "The Diabhal would have to completely reboot everything to get these bad boys working again. We'd have plenty of warning to get out of dodge."

"Somehow that's not as comforting as you think it is," Geoff mumbled, stuffing his shaking hands into his trouser pockets.

Flakes of the drywall crumbled to the ground on their right. The insulation from inside was poking out through the cracks like fascicle from a damaged muscle. The emergency lighting made it appear yellow and sickly, like the building itself was a corpse that they were crawling through. The bulletin boards they passed listed everything from company meetings to picnics, support for cancer patients, and open days for the families of staff. Only a few short hours ago, this had been a completely normal day for the dozens of Crossroads' employees. After this experience, August doubted they would ever have a normal day again.

"It's weird that it's so quiet," Hannah remarked, shooting anxious glances into the empty doorways and the lab spaces beyond them, "Usually by this time of the day the labs are all go. There's usually 30 or 40 people on this level, but even the fridges are offline right now."

August caught his reflection in a fragment of glass and eyed it with a frown. His hair was a mess, his beard like that of a wild man. The stress had made his skin pale and blotchy too. Not a good look.

"The way that the Diabhal was communicating with the other machines," August mused, eyes tracking the cables beside him in the wall, "I've never seen that before. Even Chromes don't have that kind of access. It was like he was…*talking* to them."

"The *electric highway*," Geoff stated and then quickly added, "My folks were working on it. Said it was a way for a someone to move their consciousness through a live network. I'm pretty sure it was still in the development phase though."

"I never hear you talk about your parents' work," August commented, eyeing him curiously.

Geoff sniffed, looking away from his old work colleague, "Those NDAs have a way of biting even the most careful people in the ass. Best not to say anything rather than risk saying too much."

Ollie frowned. The idea of an electric highway should have been impossible. Each new piece of equipment tied to a network utilised a portion of RAM and CPU, and there was only ever so much memory and processing power to go around. Every new task or tool added to the list decreased performance and caused lag and temperature spikes. A sluggish mind was slower to respond to changes. Leaping between Android units was even more difficult, like trying to jump the Grand Canyon on a skateboard or building the tracks of a railway line while you were still in the act of riding the train.

The man's eyes shot up to follow a shadow of motion on one of the monitors, the cameras alongside them creaking as they swivelled to watch them past. Although the pixels had been fried by gunfire earlier in the day, it still made an effort to use as much real-estate as was available. Portions of the screen changed colour, taking on the appearance of a man's face. The bald head and red eyes were recognisable, even when fragments of his features were missing entirely.

"Russell," August muttered, pulling the attention of the others to the fizzling screen over their heads.

The digitized images of Russell East travelled from one side of the screen to the other, like a man trying to peer at them through a shattered window, "I told you this was my house," he said, "And I don't remember extending an invitation to any of you."

Around them, every door suddenly burst open at once, flapping on their hinges and sending a cold draft at them from all sides. The fluorescent tube lights exploded over their heads, plunging them into darkness. Something inside of the walls rattled and moaned.

When the Diabhal laughed, the building itself seemed to quake on its foundations, "If you will not leave here on your own, I will force you out!"

The screen switched abruptly to a view from another point of the tower, the angle aimed down towards a crowd of people holding up banners and torches. There was no sound alongside the images, just the disjointed motions of patched together camerawork.

"Look at them all, begging me to let them into my paradise," the voice of the CEO was cold and hollow, like a badly made recording, "Once they see what we've been doing, they'll fall to their knees in gratitude."

"The Androids weren't the only thing you were working on," August realised, turning to face back towards the others in their group, "The codes we were working on, I never could figure out what their use was but it's clear as fuckin' day now." He caught Geoff's dark eyes, "The Soul Chips were just the first step, weren't they? An experiment."

"Bravo, Mr. Jackson," the deep rumble of Russell's voice sent his stomach turning again, "What would a good study be without trials, testing? I had to figure out how an artificial body would work with a human power source. How easy it was to modify the memories, the personality inside."

"That's why you turned against the Androids so fast," Ollie spoke up, shaking his head, "You only needed them for their data. To confirm your findings."

The sound effect of a slot machine hitting a jackpot filled the hall with noise, "Somebody give the little robot a prize!" the man on the screen hollered humourlessly.

"And the protestors outside?" August pressed, "What do you plan on doing with them?"

"I plan to continue with my work, of course," he answered, "Those people will be just lining up to receive their new Soul Chips. Injected straight into their living flesh." He laughed again, "So many new features! Everything you could dream of, right at your fingertips. Until I activate the failsafe."

"What failsafe?" Hannah questioned, though it was clear by the shaking of her voice that she already knew the answer.

"A jolt of energy…straight to the heart," the Diabhal continued proudly, "A painless transition from living master to undead servant."

"You're talking about wiping out the human race!" Sonya yelped, covering her mouth with both of her hands. Her manicured nails reflected back some of the light from the screen he was on.

The bald man cocked his head as if considering her words, "You should be grateful! I am talking about irradicating *death* itself," he stated.

"And stripping away all bodily autonomy," Ollie countered, pushing his own dark curls away from his face. His eyes glowed as he traced the patterns swirling around inside the screen, following the pathways to their source. The digital footsteps led back in the opposite direction, lighting up with the man's consciousness no matter how hard he was clearly working to conceal it. He just had to keep him talking, keep him distracted.

"A minor sacrifice for comfort and peace of mind," Russell East carried on, his tone growing more and more frantic with every new word, "We're their coffee makers, their maids, their workers. We're every car they drive, every beautiful woman they jerk off to in the magazines. We are the foundation of their every thought and whim. The people flock to my creations because it is in their nature to be subservient. I am only giving them what they demand of me."

Ollie circled the man's code with his own, latching onto it like a still beating heart. Traces of his consciousness stretched out all over the building like a network of veins and arteries, carrying information to its core.

"It's far too easy to keep people like you talking."

Turning away from his task, Ollie pulled himself up to catch August's eye. The dark pools of hazelnut followed the flickering of his smile, and it transferred to his own face as well.

"You have a plan?"

"I do," Ollie answered.

August brought his head forward to press a chaste kiss to the Android's temple, "You're brilliant."

"I know," Ollie answered playfully, "Guys? I think it's about time we shut this asshole up."

Hannah and Sonya came to stand under the TV, grinning from ear to ear as they switched on their torches. Geoff raised up the empty coolant bottle between them, "Hey dickhead!" he called out, waiting for those crimson eyes to fall on him, "We're submitting our notice!" He shoved the bottom end of his makeshift weapon through the glass, utterly destroying the television as he severed the connection. Just to be sure, the man reached for the wall and yanked the cables free with a shout of nervous elation. "Oh fuck!" he exclaimed, "That was terrifying. Tell me I didn't just get fired and murdered all in one day, please."

Ollie showed off a bright, almost cocky smile, "Once the villain starts monologing, you know you're on the right track."

"I think you and I might have binge-watched too many action movies, Ols," August teased light-heartedly. Despite his words, it was clear that the man was secretly proud of him.

"Overconfidence always was his downfall," the Android concurred, watching as more fragments of glass tumbled out from the hole Geoff had made in the screen, "He told us much more than he was meaning to. That means he's getting scared. And we're getting close."

"You were able to track him down in all that code?" Hannah questioned, looking rather impressed, "I couldn't make out a single thing in all that mess."

"It's like any good cypher, you just have to know how to translate it into something consumable," Ollie explained, "Russell isn't as intelligent as he likes others to believe he is. That's why he had you all to do his work for him. He's a puppet master with no talent of his own."

"Looks like he was true to his word though," the dark-haired Sonya added, "That source code is from Crossroads itself. He isn't acting as an individual anymore. He's acting as the building itself."

"That's too much for one mind to handle, all that processing power," Geoff muttered, "There's bound to be a crack in his defences somewhere."

"I know where he's hiding now," Ollie stated, pointing to the floor below their feet, "One step up from the underground. We're heading to the R and D department."

Chapter 44
Data-mining

Sonya's hands idly pulled on a piece of the damaged dry wall that the turrets had chipped away, "We should still have access. I doubt Russell's had the time to revoke our permissions yet."
Ollie brought his head back to rest on the wall August had laid him against. His left eye, the one that was still functioning normally, subtly changed colour as the Android quirked his eyebrows in surprise, "Incoming message," he stated, "It's from Goose."

Incoming Notification: Gardi Droid-60053

August eyed him with a frown, "And? What does it say?"

Ollie frowned, eyes moving back and forth as if he were reading something unseen on his HUD, "It's an assessment of the situation outside. The *Garda Síochána* are moving in to disperse the protesters. It's not looking good."

"Shit," August muttered, turning to face the other humans in their group, "If any of you guys have friends or family you have to get to, I understand. Ollie and I can handle this."

"August," Ollie said quietly. He was looking down at his stained clothes, the places where his body had been disconnected from itself, "I think I should stay behind as well."

The redhead dropped down to his knees in front of him, "I came all this way to get you back," he retorted, "There's no way I'm letting you out of my sight for even a second."

Two blue eyes met his, one slightly darker than the other with damage. The Android brought his functioning arm up, taking a hold of the collar of August's jacket and tugging him down towards him. Their lips met in a quick but firm kiss before Ollie was pulling away again. "This is bigger than you and me right now, August," he intreated, "The others are counting on us. This might be the only time we can get the Diabhal out into the open. If he runs again there's no telling when our next opportunity will be. We can't risk it."

Geoff appeared next to August, placing a hand on his bicep, "We can look after him, Gus. Get him somewhere safe."

"Goose and Micky will be there to help," Ollie added, "They aren't far from here. We can find another way out the back. Avoid the rally."

August could still taste the other man on his lips. The metal of black blood and the sweetness of something entirely Ollie. He let out a long, slow breath and then pulled their lips together again for another, much slower exchange. Ollie let out a muted moan of surprise, his eyes fluttering closed just as his human pulled away again.

"I have my phone on me," he stated, "Let me know the second you're safe."

The Android offered him a wordless nod, his expression a blurred line between despair and fondness. His eyes had grown stormy, the usual cornflower shade giving way to streaks of navy. Those eyes had changed so much from the first time they had looked up at him from under Crossroads, and here they were again, back at the start, "I'm getting really fed up with goodbyes."

"Last one, I swear," August agreed.

He felt the cold barrel press into his palm as Ollie offered him his weapon. The one he had been keeping safe since they left New Dublin, "Just in case."

The human hesitated, "I don't even know how to use the damn thing."

"You'll figure it out," Ollie responded firmly, "If you have to."

Sonya's eyes glowed as she accessed the internet, scrolling through the company's feeds where she was standing next to them in the dark, "Ethan and the others have just checked in on social media," she observed with obvious relief, "They said there are medical tents set up along Exchequer and Fade, down near the George's Street Arcade."

"Then that's where we're heading," Ollie said, "If you wouldn't mind giving me a hand…and a couple of legs, Geoff."

Geoff was nowhere near as strong as August was and swayed slightly whenever he picked up the other man's chrome body. Ollie slung his arm around his shoulders for support, "I promise the first round after this is on me."

"I'm gonna hold you to that, you know," Geoff flashed him a strained smile. He angled himself once more towards his redheaded colleague and added, "No pints until you get there though, August."

The hallways forked and August and Hannah stood off to one side, watching as the others took the path in the opposite direction. Ollie watched his human companion for as long as he could, worrying that this might be the last goodbye for a very different reason.

"Don't keep us waiting, August," he called back, "You know how I feel about cliffhangers."

Chapter 45
Machine Vision

August could feel the nerves bubbling in the very pit of his stomach as they descended further and further towards the underground. The air was growing colder the further they descended until he could see the white of his breath stretched out in front of him. The metal banister along the side of the wall had grown too painful to touch and he risked his skin binding with it every time he sought it out for balance.

He could hear Hannah's footfalls just ahead of him as she led the way, the soft constant of her heels like the ticking of a grandfather clock. He hoped that it wasn't a sign that time was running out for them.

They passed a series of motivational posters on the wall of the Eastern stairwell, the old, worn-out images a little unsettling in the sickly glow of the emergency lighting. The image of a kitten hanging from a tree seemed so childish compared to the reality that they were currently facing.

Hannah tapped her metal torch against the side of her hip, the light flickering on and off.

"Dammit," she muttered, "Of course the batteries would run out now." She titled her head back to look at her companion a few steps above her still, "Any chance you have something with a decent bit of charge left in it?"

August patted down his pockets and pulled out his mobile phone, waving it in the air between them, "Just this thing. Can't guarantee we'll get much out of it though." He manoeuvred around the damaged screen and selected the torch icon from the drop-down menu. The single beam lit up the stairs directly in front of them both.

Hannah turned at a bright green fire door and gently placed her hands on the bar that ran across it, "This is the quickest way to R and D," she stated, "Lets hope it isn't still armed."

A blast of cold air greeted them from the other side and August suppressed the shiver that was currently trying to wrack his entire body. The place was like a cave, the air damp and frigid as they walked. The phone's light only offered a small halo of relief to guide them.

August could just about make out the glow of Hannah's red and blue Chrome a few metres ahead. Her eyes were two points of contact he could follow, and he did so as she worked to scan the walls.

"Valentina's taken me down here a few times," she said by way of easy conversation, likely discomforted by the oppressive silence in the same way that he was, "I have a fair idea of the layout of the place, but I still don't fancy stubbing any toes in here."

"Why's it so bloody cold in here?" the man beside her questioned, rubbing both of his arms through his jacket. Even through the layers, he could feel the unpleasant nip of it all over him. The flooring turned from carpet to tiles under his feet.

"Their specialist parts need cooling, apparently," the woman sniffed, "Some of the Android models that pass through here are delicate. They can't risk a temperature spike shutting the whole thing down."

"It must have been strange for your girlfriend to work on building other Androids," August remarked, "Did she talk about it much?"

"Val always said it was like being a midwife," Hannah replied, seemingly grateful for a distraction, "Like she was just the one who was bringing new life into the world."

Cables ran along the walls like Christmas tinsel, and they seemed to glisten when he shone his light across them, "She liked her job then?"

"Until they started working with Soul Chips," Hannah answered, "And her workmates asked a few too many questions." The woman paused in the middle of the room, her eyes eerily red when she turned to face him, "I know how you're feeling right now, seeing your friend like that. Knowing what he's gone through. All I wanted to do was take Val away from this place and never come back."

"Why didn't you?" August found himself asking.

"We were too scared," Hannah breathed, "And then we were too late."

"Han," he said, reaching out for her.

She pulled back from him, shaking her head, "Val's alive. But the psychological damage he inflicted on her…I don't think she'll ever fully recover from all that."

"I'm so sorry."

"There's power still going to the back rooms," she said, changing the subject as she nodded to the space not too far from where they were standing, "I'd bet all my money that the bastard is holed up in there." She chewed on her bottom lip, "I was…fired three months back. The only reason I was able to get in here in the first place was Valentina's IDs. I wanted to find the man responsible and hurt him exactly the way he hurt her."

It was only then that August noticed her outstretched hand, the fingers curled around a flat, black object. Her small kitten heels *clacked* on the tiles as she moved closer to him, placing the item into his hand and closing his fingers over it.

He caught her eye, "Hannah, this is-"

"A guarantee," she interjected, "Hold him for as long as you can and then use it. Give me time to get the Androids in here to a safe distance." Something in her eyes lit up like a flame, "It's the least I can do for Val. These were her babies, after all."

"Alright, you get them out and I'll handle things here," he acceded, watching as she headed for the edge of the darkness, "And Han?"

She turned, half concealed by the cold mist and the shadow. He nodded his head and offered her a grin he hoped looked more confident than he felt, "Say hi to Val for us."

The smile she returned perfectly mirrored his own and he felt the hopefulness returning to them both, "I will!"

August carried on through the disused area, his little light guiding him as best it could. He was vaguely aware of the device's battery running down and he kept a close eye on the tiny symbols in the corner for any incoming messages. The gaps in the next door he came to were lit up with a devilishly red glow, computer wires reaching out through the opening in the bottom like the digital entrails. Hard plastic crunched beneath his boots. Glass was quickly shoved to one side to clear the way. In the distance, he could just about make out the words to a familiar song:

'Penny Lane, there is a barber showing photographs
Of every head he's had the pleasure to know
And all the people that come and go
Stop and say, 'Hello…'

The bobbing melody matched the rhythm of his heart. The drumbeat pounded in his veins. Sweat formed around the base of his neck, sticking the hair there to his skin and making it curl. His tight ponytail pressed against the curve of his cervical spine, tapping out a pattern like a snare. Further tendrils of icy air clawed along the ground around his ankles, urging him to continue. The red light that was coming from a dozen monitors was brighter here, lines of code racing past at an alarming rate as someone, or something, carried out a brand-new protocol. The music had stopped, August noticed, though the words still clung to his mind like an earworm. Dark figures hung limp and lifeless from the walls, humanoid figures on just the right side of obscurity. The bleak display sent chills running through the human's blood, stealing his breath for a moment before he was able to compose himself. He reached into his pocket and squeezed the object Hannah had passed on to him, hoping that it would give him a little more courage.

That courage immediately vanished again when he saw what was awaiting him on the other side of that final door.

His stomach turned as the dim glow of the Android's eyes met his, barely aware of his presence. He had been pinned across the doorway to act as a makeshift blockade, his arms stretched out on either side of him like the image of Jesus on the cross. The machine's mouth moved soundlessly as the grey-blue eyes looked him over.

"You poor bastard," August breathed, reaching out to caress the black chassis. The Android moaned tonelessly, its mouth opening wide to reveal the space where its tongue had once been. The damage was extensive, reaching all the way down its throat. Likely, its entire voicebox had been ripped out through its mouth.

"He won't get away with this," he vowed, and the Android's eyes held onto his for just a moment longer before his head bowed and the light was extinguished.

As delicately as he could, August brushed past the Android's limp body. In another life, that could have easily been Ollie hanging there. The Diabhal had more than shown them what he was capable of, and it certainly wasn't mercy.

An empty doorway, well-lit and glowing like the very deepest pits of hell, beckoned him to finish his journey. August felt the blood in his veins freeze before they flooded with adrenaline. His body was shaking from it, willing him to act, to move. Desks and glass monitors made up the majority of the room he stumbled into, the R and D department much like the floor he himself had worked on for countless years. The familiarity of it made vomit rise in the back of his throat, scalding his oesophagus painfully. He swallowed it right back down again with disgust.

You aren't to blame. You didn't know.

A man was perched on the edge of one of the tables, illuminated by the machine below like a child telling a scary story around a campfire. But August knew that monsters were real, and this was a man that was the stuff of nightmares. He was wrapped in dark Chrome which contrasted starkly with his pale skin. His bald head was now covered in a flat, metal cap that was lined with LEDs. He more closely resembled his namesake now, a man wearing the face of a devil.

Steam billowed from the cracks in his metal suit, orange and red lights flickering along the entire length of his exoskeleton. He was rolling a cigarette beneath his lips, the smoke forming a loose halo around the dome of his head.

"At last, you stand before me," he growled, tilting his chin up ever-so-slightly to take in the other man's appearance as he stepped closer. He reached out a muscular leg and kicked the computer chair next to him, sending it careening in August's direction.

"Please," he sneered, his body creaking and sparking as he moved, "Do take a seat."

Chapter 46
Hard Problem

"I think I'll stand, cheers all the same," August answered, reaching down to the pull the handgun from the back pocket of his filthy jeans. He held it out in front of him with both hands, clasping it tightly to mask his tremors.

The Diabhal let out a low, animalistic roar, "You think I'm scared of a little pea-shooter?" He yanked his cigarette from the corner of his mouth, making a show of sighing out a long, smoky breath in August's direction as he folded his legs underneath himself comfortably, "You haven't been paying attention, it seems."

"You ever see any of those old action movies?" August asked, holding the gun as steady as he could as the lights of the monitors made crimson pools of his usually dark eyes, "My sister used to get a real kick out of them, Clint Eastwood ones especially. Know what Clint Eastwood said about having a gun?"

"I'm sure you will enlighten me." The Diabhal inhaled another slow drag of his cigarette.

August pulled back the safety until he heard the click, "He said *'I have a very strict gun control policy; if there's a gun around, I want to be in control of it'*."

Russell East shifted his position, eyeing up the barrel of the gun as he uncrossed his legs and slid off the table to standing, "So, is this it? You fancy yourself a bit of an action hero, then?" Come to save the day?"

"Me? Nah," August replied with an exhaled laugh, "I was always more of a musical guy myself. And believe you me, there will be plenty of singing and dancing once you're dead."

The Chrome man threw his head back when he laughed. Air whistled around the vents in his throat, "Seems I have nothing to fear then, from neither your weapon nor the man behind it. It doesn't much matter what calibre your gun is if the person holding it is a lesser one."

August's eyes were pulled momentarily towards the computer behind the other man as it chirped, completing its task. He didn't know exactly what the man was working on, but there was next to zero chance that it was good.

"Step away from the computer, Russell," he said, "You're backed into a corner here. I'm not going to let you get past me."

"Oh, the time for running is over now, August," the man replied, splaying his hands in a dramatic flourish. He reached for the cable connected to the back of his neck and pulled it hard to yank it free, "Only one of us is going to leave this room."

"We can both leave," August argued, "You had good intentions once. You wanted to help people, make the world better. You can serve your time, repay all those people you hurt. Call off the Android hunts."

The man's responding smile said more than words ever could.

In an instant, the Diabhal's hand was wrapped around his gun, wrenching it free from his grasp. The metal caught on August's fingers and twisted, and the man yelped as he released his hold. The CEO's foot connected with the centre of his chest, and he was sent barrelling backwards, the air escaping his lungs in an abrupt wheeze as his spine connected with one of the tables. His diaphragm jerked, stuttering as he tried and failed to suck in his next breath.

Tears sprang to his eyes and in the blur, he saw the dark figure advancing.

You have to move, goddamn it! August barked internally, *If you don't get out of the way, he's going to kill you!*

He had barely managed to crawl beneath one of the tables when a bolt of light split through the centre of the room. It pierced right through the spot he had previously occupied, sending whisps of smoke rising from the opening in the floor like a cauterised wound. He panted, clearly in oxygen deprivation, and let out a shout of alarm as another glowing ray sliced the chair by his right shoulder in half, melting the plastic into the singed fabric.

He crawled along the floor, barely having a second to blink before the Diabhal was on him again, his hands reaching for him and curling around his throat like the tendrils of a great kraken. The soft flesh of August's body gave way to the relentless pressure, and he struggled beneath the other body as his hands tried in vain to yanking those closing fingertips loose.

August kicked out with both legs frantically, catching the man in the elbow joint. He took the briefest moment of hesitation and punched with all of his strength.

God, August though as he connected, *it feels good to hit something!*

He hissed through his teeth as the metal beneath the Diabhal's skin connected with his knuckle bones. There was a telltale splash of red as his skin gave way, spattering his face and the face of his opponent with his own blood. August howled in agony as he created some distance between them, shaking his hand out to escape the relentless sting.

When Russell East rose opposite him, August could see the artificial skin on his face giving way in the place where he had been struck. The dark chassis that glimmered underneath was all-too familiar by now.

"You're not a Chrome," August realised, "You're an Android."

"I am better than an Android," the CEO spat, exposing his teeth as a dribble of black blood cascaded down across his lips, "I am the next step. A fully conscious human mind surrounded by an immortal body of my own design." He tilted his head to one side, bright eyes narrowing, "A Proxy. A way that I can escape the changes of my flesh and blood self."

"You're afraid of dying," August stated, "They mentioned before that you were sick."

"Flesh decays but the mind remains sharp, focused." He huffed out a breath, discarding the last cindering butt of his cigarette, "Why shouldn't I use the power at my disposal to make myself greater? This world deserves a strong leader, after all."

He lunged across the room and August felt him seizing the top of his skull with a firm hand. The blunt edge of the table next to him pressed uncomfortably into his hip. The Diabhal's face was barely two inches from his own. His eyes ignited with red light as he reached for the very back of his neck, digging his nails in deep.

"If you're looking for an access panel, I don't have one," August grunted, "Your fancy parlour tricks won't work on somebody like me." He snatched the man's wrist where it brushed against his ear and pulled back on it with as much force as he could muster, "I'm 100 percent human meat, baby!"

When the Diabhal's weight fell forward, the redhead took his chance and slammed his forehead into the bridge of the man's nose. A high-pitched screech erupted from the creature as it flung its head back and August let loose a strangled laugh as he felt trickles of blood pouring down his face and nose, "Ha! Bet you weren't expecting that, were ya?"

"A *Natural*," Russell sneered, "Why am I not surprised?" He brought a hand up towards his face, correcting the angles of his nose and brow again, "You do seem so intent on drawing your own blood, after all."

"Seems that you don't know your employees that well after all," August taunted, planting his hands on both sides of a nearby desk, "Maybe you should study more!" The desk careened across the tiles with an awful, piercing sound, colliding with the other desks in its path. Glass monitors tumbled and smashed. August sprinted. Lazers followed his path, cutting up the floor with terrifying efficiency. He edged closer and whenever he was within striking range, he leapt. The men collided and rolled across the fragments of glass. Black and red blood mixed in the chaos. He pinned the other man down with the weight of his hips, pounding down into him with both fists balled. The agony was immediate, especially in his left hand, but August ignored the sensation, letting the desperation fuel his every impact.

The Diabhal's both hands cupped his and pushed them back, bending them awkwardly at the wrist, "You really *are* a fool," he growled, the sound low and electronic like a broken Casio, "What can you *possibly* hope to gain from this?"

August's biceps ached as he pushed back against the man's tight hold, "Time," he answered as a cocky smile spread from one side of his face to the other.

He was shoved hard, the motion pulling his very feet from the ground and flipping him over. The side of his head smashed into one of the desks and a dizzying spin made the room warp until he closed his eyes. The wheels of a chair rolled beneath him, the glass digging into the places where his jacket had already been torn. He groaned, his voice hoarse with pain, as he tried his best to manoeuvre even the slightest inch of himself. His heart was throbbing almost as painfully, beating far too fast to allow him an adequate breath. He stretched out the broken skin of his fingers as he grabbed the object that had tumbled loose from his pocket, coating it with his own blood as he held it.

"I've had enough with your games," Russell said, his voice flat and cold. Even the heat of his anger had seemingly burnt out along with his patience.

August held the tiny, black object out in front of his chest, "No more games then," he agreed, his voice breathy and weak. The cube was no larger than the palm of his hand, wrapped in copper wiring. There were lights across one side and a large, grey button in the centre that was covered in part by plastic.

"Know what this neat little toy is?" he asked, choking on a breath, "Cause I didn't, the first time I saw it. It took me a little while to put the pieces all together."

The Diabhal's eyes were following the motion of his prize, his body language unreadable.

"It's a little thing called an '*Electromagnetic Pulse Generator*'. You've probably seen them in movies before. Hollywood's a big fan." August flipped it over, sliding his thumb over the switch in the middle, "But they got a few of the details wrong. See, they're not all that strong, not at range anyway. You want to get right up close with one of these babies. Nice and personal."

August's body screamed at him as he sat up against the table, the world spinning around him with the Diabhal right in the very centre of it, "I don't know if there's really a Hell, but I'm really hoping there's somewhere nice and cozy and name appropriate waiting for you out there somewhere, you electronic prick."

The Chrome man was already in motion by the time that August had pressed the button down flat.

Chapter 47
Closure

The two, solid thuds as the Proxy's knees hit the floor were like poetry to August- like birdsong on a clear Sunday morning after a lie in or the echo of a full stop of the end of a long and satisfying piece of prose.

The Diabhal's body sizzled and crackled, the red glow of his eyes fading to a distant ember. August allowed his hands to fall down by his sides as he watched the empty shell go completely offline. His breath was now the last remaining sound in the room as the EMP blast shorted out of the nearby servers and computers. The flat plains of the keyboards vanished one by one with one last electronic whimper of defiance.

August allowed his body to sink down under its own weight. Whether it was from exhaustion, blood loss or relief, he wasn't entirely sure. He breathed heavily now, as boneless and weak as a newborn, as the last of his adrenaline washed away. In his pocket, somehow miraculously still on his person and functioning, his mobile phone vibrated. He grabbed for it clumsily and brought it up to his face, squinting to see it without his glasses.

Ollie: We're safe. Goose and Micky brought us to the town hall.
Ollie: They're taking a statement from other Crossroads officials regarding the hacking.
Ollie: They're bringing the Androids into protective custody now until it all blows over

August exhaled a disbelieving laugh, reaching up to wipe away the tears that were starting to blur his vision again.

"Stupid robot, making me cry like an idiot," he muttered.

He re-read the message again a few more times before committing himself to a response:

August: He's dead, Ollie
The tiny dots danced for a moment.

Ollie*: Are you okay?*

He groaned as he reached for the table and chair and pulled himself off the ground again. Slivers of glass tumbled down from his knees and jacket, other fragments clinging to his sticky, scabbing wounds and refusing to let go. He felt it in his hair, grime and heaviness weighing him down slightly.
August*: Yeah. Yeah, I'm okay.*

He was really going to have to take Ollie up on his offer to go running, whip his body into some kind of shape again. After all, there was still a lot of life that needed living.

August*: I'll be there soon.*
August*: I love you*
The response came instantly:
Ollie*: I love you too, August*

He stood over the charred figure with a look of distain on his face, nudging his knee with the toe of one boot. The black figure remained motionless, curled into a position of pain like a victim of Mount Vesuvius, his final moments encapsulated forever in steel.

August held up the EMP device, examining the now frayed wires there before tossing it down to lie at the other man's side, "Humanity's going to go our own way, I think." He cocked his head, "I'd say *'it's not you, it's me'* but it's definitely you. Consider this my notice period."

He turned away from him, from that room filled with darkness and pain and everything he hated most in the world. And he closed the door behind him, bringing his phone up to his ear as he dialled the last number added.

"Hey Hannah, you there? Can you come meet me? I don't want to be stuck in this place even a millisecond longer."

Epilogue
Clean Boot

As they exited through the back door, limping and clinging to each other, August's first thought was of snow. He glanced towards the skies over their heads and marvelled at the downpour for a moment before he realised that what he had mistaken for a flurry was actually ash.

The very top floors of Crossroads burned with a savagery that August had never seen in a fire before, and both he and Hannah stood back to watch as it licked and clung to the curve of the bubble above it.

Officers in dark green uniforms escorted them for the rest of their journey, helping August to walk as they kept him talking, getting as much of a statement as they could from a clearly traumatised witness. August spared no details. He owed the dead that much, at least.

It was clear that not everyone had been under the Diabhal's spell, two fractioning branches forming in the *Garda Síochána* across the last few days. Those who had worked under the CEO's thumb had been quickly apprehended, with much thanks to Inspector Michael O'Sullivan's leadership and Elderich's relentless hard-headedness. Their investigations, which had finally bore plenty of fruit, were made public and the people of New Dublin and the surrounding country were left stunned and adrift. Androids were returned to their homes and families, others kept in the station for their own protection. The ones that had been destroyed, *killed*, were reclaimed by those who had loved them. There were already those who had worked at Crossroads working hard to find a way to restore their memories from their Soul Chips. No doubt it would be a long, emotionally exhausting road ahead.

Perched by the Molly Malone statue, on the place they had agreed to meet, Angelle nudged the spokes of the statue's wheel with a shoe. In one hand he held a steaming takeaway mug, the other, a warm scarf.

"I'm hoping at least one of those is for me," August teased as he hobbled across to him. His bandages had been wrapped; his wounds tended to as best as the St John's Ambulance Service could do. He was lucky, he had seen people in far worse condition in that particular queue.

Angelle sent a bright smile his way as he reached out with both hands, "Oh, you're here!" he exclaimed, clearly taken by surprise. He wrapped the scarf around his companion's neck, forcing the coffee into his waiting hands, "I was under strict instructions from Ollie on how to make that, so if it's terrible, you can blame him." August took a swig and gasped as it burned down his raw throat. It was the most pleasant pain he had ever felt, "Fuckin' glorious," he praised.

"Well, good," Angelle chuckled before pulling him in for a gentle hug. The cuffs of the Android's extravagant shirt rattled as he moved, "I was scared the rumours about there being no survivors inside were true."

August exhaled a snort, "Honestly, I'm only one small step above the walking dead right now," he replied playfully, "There isn't a single, bloody part of me that isn't bruised purple."

Angelle leaned into his touch fondly, "I'm not surprised. I heard that you were thrown over a desk at one point."

"*Several* desks," the human corrected teasingly. And a wall. Little known fact, walls are *hard*."

"Yes, well, you do get yourself into all kinds of situations, don't you, Mr Jackson?" Angelle pushed several strands of his bright hair back from his face.

"What about the others? The Androids that were rescued from the port?" August probed, leaning his weight back against Molly Malone's famous wheelbarrow.

"All safe and accounted for, thanks to you and Ollie," Angelle answered, "What became of your Hornet companion in the end?"

August shrugged, "He gave us a head start." At Angelle's raised eyebrow he added, "I guess that means we're still running."

"I guess that shows that Androids can be just as stubborn as their human counterparts, doesn't it?" his friend remarked.

August released a heavy sigh, rolling his shoulders to rid himself of some of the discomfort. "Everything's a mess," he said softly, watching as yet another emergency vehicle rushed by on St Andrew's Street, "It's hard to even imagine how the city will recover from all this."

In the churchyard across from them both, a little girl in a blue dress was hopping from one of the stone settings to another. The frills at the bottom of her dress caught in the cold, winter breeze and danced against her little legs. One of her stained socks had begun to roll down towards her ankle, exposing the pinking flesh of her calf. Despite the obvious damage to her outfit, the child seemed more focused on her game than anything else. Her sing-song voice carried to them on the wind, but August couldn't quite make out the words.

"New Dublin is resilient," Angelle observed, watching her with bright, copper-coloured eyes, "As are its people." He reached out to poke his companion's side, laughing at the way the human wriggled and complained, "That includes you too, you know."

August groaned at the discomfort that came along with the sudden movement, "Oh, aye?"

"Aye," Angelle quipped, sounding very Welsh all of a sudden. He quirked his head up to signal something behind him, "And that *friend* of yours."

The moment he turned around and laid eyes on him, the world around August began to grow impossibly quiet and still. His heart pounded against his chest, blood rushing around his body like a hurricane, so loud he could hear it whoosh through his ears.

"Ollie," he whispered, staggering forward a step, "Christ, your legs…"

Ollie was shambling towards him with a bright, contagious smile, supported by two metal crutches that tucked in neatly under both his arms. The hands that held onto them were mismatched, his right one skin-toned and the other black like his own uncovered chassis. August resisted the urge to run at him, to swoop him up into his arms like it was the final scenes of a rom-com, too afraid of getting carried away. Instead, he jogged the distance between them, stopping just in front of him with a smile he knew would be positively glowing.

"Look at you!" he elated, trying to contain the rush of emotion at seeing him somewhat whole again, "It's so good to see you at head-height again, *duine*!"

The skin on Ollie's face flushed, freckles dancing in the way that August always noticed. He was dressed in a warm-looking quilted jacket, fake fur trim lining the centre and the wide collar. It was a soft tan colour that matched well with the medium-brown dress trousers he was wearing that hugged his toned thighs just right. His calves had been wrapped in protective, plastic boots to hold all of the damaged parts in place.

"It's really good to see you," Ollie replied softly, his blue eyes sparkling as he stood in the other man's shadow, "I was scared that the last time was-"

"-I know," August interrupted, reaching out to pull him into an awkward hug around his walking aids, "I came back to you as soon as I could."

Ollie inhaled deeply as he pressed his face in against the taller man's chest. The fond smile that he was giving him fitted like an old, favourite sweater. He reached out to run his hands through his mess of dark curls.

The warm glow of the streetlamps felt like spring sunshine as they held each other. The light caught on the Android's dark hair, giving it an almost green shine as it filtered through the evergreens beside them.

"Geoff and the others are still waiting on those pints," the Android quipped, his tone light and playful, "I said I'm buying but I hope you know I only have access to *your* bank account."

August pulled back to brush his nose against that of his companion, "Sneaky Android," he joked.

"The sneakiest," Ollie agreed.

"What else will you steal from me, I wonder?" August asked, angling his face so that their lips were barely more than a breath apart.

"I was hoping to start with that heart of yours," Ollie answered. August could feel his smile against his beard.

"You know what, Ols? I think I might just let you."

The Android sprang up onto his tiptoes to close the last remaining space between them. The crutches clanked as they hit the ground, Ollie all but throwing his arms around August's broad shoulders.

Kissing Ollie made the whole world disappear in an instant. Seasons crumbled away to irrelevance; weather succumbed to the whims of time itself. Nothing retained its importance but this one, wonderful person in his arms. Holding him was grounding. Permanence. It was the feeling of love and safety and everything that came with building a future with someone.

This kiss wasn't wild like those in his younger days, when he had been a gay man keeping a secret from a violent father. This kiss was a welcome home, of tea made just the way you liked it without even having to ask. It was sharing your day laid out on a pillow as you slowly drifted to sleep. It wasn't just fleeting passion and heat, it was like four solid walls that kept out the winter cold, like reading a book while sprawled out in front of a roaring hearth.

Kissing Ollie was like walking through the front door of a place you belonged.

Home.

When the need to breathe made his lungs ache, August pulled back with a quiet gasp, catching his breath against the Android's lips, not even wanting to pull away an inch. The Android let out a shuddering exhale of his own, leaning his strong and slender body impossibly close, "Ready to go home?" he asked.

August's fingers gently moved some of those thick, dark curls back from where they clung to his cheekbones, "Definitely," he answered, "Christ, my sister's going to *love* you."

Printed in Great Britain
by Amazon